PRAISE FOR CHARLES MARTIN

"*The Last Exchange* is somehow equal parts page-turner, heart-breaker, and hope-dealer. Another brilliantly written novel by Charles Martin."
—ANNIE F. DOWNS, *NEW YORK TIMES* BESTSELLING AUTHOR OF *THAT SOUNDS FUN*

"The adrenaline-pumping third entry in Martin's Murphy Shepherd series (after *The Letter Keeper*) explores human depravity and the healing power of love. Series fans will snap this up."
—PUBLISHERS *WEEKLY* FOR *THE RECORD KEEPER*

"Very few contemporary novelists have found acclaim within mainstream and evangelical markets, but Charles Martin is among them. [*The Letter Keeper*] hinges on the Scriptural message of forsaking the found in order to seek the lost, a theme Martin brings to poetic and brilliant life."
—DAVIS BUNN, WRITING FOR *CHRISTIANITY TODAY*

"Martin follows up *The Water Keeper* with this heartrending, action-packed chapter in the saga of Murphy Shepherd . . . those familiar with the series will appreciate the emotional punch this rip-roaring adventure packs."
—PUBLISHERS *WEEKLY* FOR *THE LETTER KEEPER*

"Martin excels at writing characters who exist in the margins of life. Readers who enjoy flawed yet likable characters created by authors such as John Grisham and Nicholas Sparks will want to start reading Martin's fiction."
—*LIBRARY JOURNAL*, STARRED REVIEW, FOR *THE WATER KEEPER*

"*The Water Keeper* is a wonderfully satisfying book with a plot driven by both action and love, and characters who will stay in readers' heads long after the last page."
—*SOUTHERN LITERARY REVIEW*

"*The Water Keeper* is a multilayered story woven together with grace and redemption, and packed tight with tension and achingly real characters. This one will keep you turning pages to see what else—and who else—Murph will encounter as he travels down the coastline of Florida."
—LAUREN K. DENTON, *USA TODAY* BESTSELLING AUTHOR OF *THE HIDEAWAY*

"In *The Water Keeper* Charles Martin crafts a compelling story with skill and sensitivity. Current fans won't be disappointed; new readers will understand why Charles Martin is on the short list of contemporary authors I recommend above all others."

—Robert Whitlow, bestselling author

"Martin explores themes of grace, mercy, and forgiveness in this sweeping love story . . ."

—Publishers Weekly, starred review, for *Send Down the Rain*

"Charles Martin never fails to ask and answer the questions that linger deep within all of us. In this beautifully told story of a prodigal coming home, readers will find the broken and mended pieces of their own hearts."

—Lisa Wingate, national bestselling author of
Before We Were Yours, for *Long Way Gone*

"Martin weaves all the pieces of this story together with a beautiful musical thread, and as the final pieces fall into place, we close this story feeling as if we have witnessed something surreal, a multisensory narrative for anyone who enjoys a redemptive story."

—Julie Cantrell, *New York Times* and *USA TODAY*
bestselling author of *Perennials*, for *Long Way Gone*

"A beautiful story of redemption and love once lost but found again, *Long Way Gone* proves two things: music washes us from the inside out and Charles Martin's words do the same."

—Billy Coffey, author of *Steal Away Home*

"Martin's story charges headlong into the sentimental territory and best-seller terrain of *The Notebook*, which doubtless will mean major studio screen treatment."

—Kirkus, starred review, for *Unwritten*

"Charles Martin understands the power of story, and he uses it to alter the souls and lives of both his characters and his readers."

—Patti Callahan Henry, *New York Times* bestselling author

"Martin is the new king of the romantic novel . . . *A Life Intercepted* is a book that will swallow you up and keep you spellbound."

—Jackie K. Cooper, book critic, *Huffington Post*

THE LAST EXCHANGE

ALSO BY CHARLES MARTIN

THE MURPHY SHEPHERD NOVELS

The Water Keeper
The Letter Keeper
The Record Keeper

STAND-ALONE NOVELS

Send Down the Rain
Long Way Gone
Water from My Heart
A Life Intercepted
Unwritten
Thunder and Rain
The Mountain Between Us
Where the River Ends
Chasing Fireflies
Maggie
When Crickets Cry
Wrapped in Rain
The Dead Don't Dance

NONFICTION

What If It's True?
They Turned the World Upside Down
Son of Man
It Is Finished

THE LAST EXCHANGE

A NOVEL

CHARLES

MARTIN

Published in Nashville, Tennessee, by Thomas Nelson. Thomas Nelson is a registered trademark of HarperCollins Christian Publishing, Inc.

Published in association with The Christopher Ferebee Agency, www.christopherferebee.com.

Thomas Nelson titles may be purchased in bulk for educational, business, fundraising, or sales promotional use. For information, please email SpecialMarkets@ThomasNelson.com.

Scripture taken from the New King James Version®. Copyright © 1982 by Thomas Nelson. Used by permission. All rights reserved.

Library of Congress Cataloging-in-Publication Data

Names: Martin, Charles, 1942- author.
Title: The last exchange / Charles Martin.
Description: Nashville, Tennessee: Thomas Nelson, [2023] | Summary: "The latest novel from New York Times bestselling author Charles Martin travels from Hollywood to rural Montana as one man answers the question: How far would you go-really-to save someone you love?"-- Provided by publisher.
Identifiers: LCCN 2023013256 (print) | LCCN 2023013257 (ebook) | ISBN 9780785255970 (hardcover) | ISBN 9780785255994 (epub) | ISBN 9780785256007 (audio download)
Subjects: LCGFT: Novels.
Classification: LCC PS3563.A72327 L37 2023 (print) | LCC PS3563.A72327 (ebook) | DDC 811/.54--dc23/eng/20230407
LC record available at https://lccn.loc.gov/2023013256
LC ebook record available at https://lccn.loc.gov/2023013257

Printed in the United States of America

23 24 25 26 27 LBC 5 4 3 2 1

For Annie

PROLOGUE

AFTER

PRESENT DAY
LOS ANGELES

The limo was quiet save the tapping of her finger on the faceplate of her phone. The driver glanced at her in the mirror, but she was lost in her own rearview and missed it. And him. From his vantage point, he had a front-row seat of her. And her iconic legs. While she caught the first glance, she didn't catch the second.

The pill fob was attached to a chain around her neck. Knowing the drive from her seaside home could last more than an hour, she unscrewed the lid, dropped one pill discreetly onto her tongue, and then returned the fob to its hiding place at the base of her neck. Something to take the edge off. The seamless motion reminded the driver of a kid with a Pez dispenser. Or the Marlboro Man with a Zippo lighter. Both actions were practiced and subconscious, requiring little thought.

The tapping slowed but only slightly; there was always an edge.

A minute later, her phone pulsed. Something she'd been expecting but it startled her nonetheless. She'd been awaiting word from her private investigator, Roger, but when she eyed the unknown number, her heart leapt. It was not him. She tapped on the text and read furiously as a wrinkle appeared between her eyes. The text was short. To the point. As was the demand. Their last communiqué had promised information if she satisfied their demand. She had. To the penny. In return, they had assured her of something tangible. Hence, the finger tapping the phone.

She read the text a second time, looking for any clue but found none. She typed quickly. "But you promised a picture."

Their response was equally prompt. "Do you really want to play this game?"

She did not. "30 min."

The response was immediate. "15."

She straightened and sent a cryptic text to her financial advisor.

His response returned just as quickly. "You must be joking."

"Please don't argue. Send the money."

The text disappeared into the stratosphere. Two seconds later, her phone rang. He spoke before she had a chance. "Joe, I'm recording this call. I can't wire a half million dollars to an unknown Swiss account from a text. We have procedures. Safeguards. You know this—"

"George." She took a breath. "It's time sensitive. Please . . . just—"

"I need it in writing. Not to mention the fact that we need to have a conversation about fiduciary responsibility."

The driver watched as she polished off the Grey Goose and poured a second. In truth, she didn't really like vodka, but it amplified the pills and left her breath untainted. "This is time sensitive. I need it done now."

"Joe, it's for your pro—"

"George . . . they have my baby."

A long pause. "Is this you or the silver screen talking?"

It was an honest question. "It's me."

Another pause while he filtered for the truth. "I'm sorry. I didn't know. We'd heard rumors but . . ."

"We've been trying to keep it out of the press."

"What about the authorities?"

"It's tricky. They always seem a step ahead."

"Heard she used to work for you." It was a question posed as a statement.

"Two years."

"You were close?"

"Hair and makeup."

"You never really know someone, do you?" He listened to himself and tried to correct. "I'm sorry. That's not helpful."

She nodded again, conscious that the medicine was lowering her defenses. And her filter. Through the silence, she said, "Send me whatever you need me to sign. You're protected."

She heard fingers tapping keys in the background. Her phone pulsed, and she signed with her finger and tapped Submit.

He continued. "I thought you were renovating Malibu or buying a Swiss chalet."

"I wish."

A pause. More keystrokes. "You want the total?"

"One point two," she said calmly.

A long pause. "Can the authorities recover any of this?"

"The FBI says yes. My investigator doubts that."

"Who do you believe?"

"Neither."

On the drive down, the sun had set over the Pacific where deep blue bled into a crimson sky. Now the night had grown dark, lit only by streetlights. After a final keystroke, he said, "We're dealing with different time zones, so hang on a minute while I get confirmation." George tried to fill the awkward silence and address the elephant in the phone. "Did you get the flowers?"

She had. "Yes. Thank you. They were lovely."

"So how was it this time? Any better? I hear mixed reviews."

"Cured." She turned the pill fob in her fingers, her honesty disarming. "Sixth time's the charm."

A pause. "I didn't know. Thought it was more casual." Something must have happened on the electronic screens in front of him because she heard his chair squeak. "Wire confirmed. Check your phone."

She did. A screen of numbers stared back at her.

"Of all the nights . . ." He trailed off.

She stared at the distant searchlights making figure eights in the night sky. "She's no dummy."

"And how much money you make," he quipped. She heard the chair squeaking again. Then he barked, "Unconscionable," followed by a guttural, half-muted curse and ending with "betrayal."

Another slight nod. "Feels that way."

He redirected. "We're pulling for you."

When she spoke, she was staring out the window. "I'd trade it all."

She ended the call and leaned against the window as the Los Angeles skyline came into view. Wasting no time, she forwarded the confirmation to the unknown number that had demanded the sum. From the first contact, they had used different numbers. Now somewhere over two dozen. Not even her ex-CIA private investigator, Roger, could crack the system because each number was untraceable, single use, and prepaid monthly. Used once and discarded. Cartels and ISIS did the same. She knew as soon as she sent this text, this number and this phone would cease to work.

She typed quickly, hoping to sneak it in. "Amber, please, are you okay? Is the baby well?"

The driver watched her knee bounce as she waited for a response.

A minute later, her screen lit. "Baby is kicking." Then came the gut punch. The thing she'd been wanting but never expecting. For which she'd never let herself hope. Which was exactly why Amber sent it. But that, too, raised a question. Had Amber sent it? Was she okay? The wording gave way to doubt. "Baby is kicking" didn't sound like Amber. But did she really know Amber? Regardless, whoever sent it knew it'd knock the air out of her.

That was not the knockout. It would follow. The next pulse included a close-up of a pregnant stomach, complete with tiny stretch marks and a small protrusion to the right of the belly button. The inexplicable and undeniable imprint of the underside of a baby's foot. Complete with slight toe indentions. The pineapple tattoo alongside was their bona fides. Proof that the stomach was, in fact, Amber's. They'd been in Maui on a film set drinking rum punch when she'd sat for it.

The sting was exponential. She'd put Amber through cosmetology school. Taught her the nuance of makeup for screen. Bought her a car. Introduced her. Paid her twice what she was worth. Brought her on vacation. Made her family.

"Amber." She typed furiously. The window was closing. Using as few words as possible. "Boy? Girl!? PLEASE."

The response was quick. "VEI."

She had no idea what this meant. "Sorry. I don't understand."

Somebody was playing her. "That is very expensive information."

This, too, did not sound like Amber, which once again assumed she knew Amber at all. Joe had received very little information over the last two months. All of it consisted of cryptic messages, so she was never certain if she was talking with Amber or someone else. The word choice here didn't sound like Amber. She wouldn't say "very" or "That is." The entire phrase was too polished. Too put together. Too mysterious. It sounded like someone trying to sound like someone they weren't.

Amber had grown up in rural Alabama and quit high school in the tenth grade to start "doing hair" because she had a knack for it and could make more money standing behind a chair than sitting in it. Her language was much more casual. More along the lines of, "Girlfriend, you can't touch that." As much as the texts made it seem like Amber was running the show, Joe had long suspected she was not. Complicit? Yes. In charge? Probably not.

Amber's boyfriend was a hip-hop wannabe. Tall. Fit. Early twenties. Tattooed bumper to bumper. Frank Carter, aka Busta Line, fancied himself an entrepreneur. Businessman. They'd met at Da Beez Neez—a popular dance club where he stared mysteriously through sunglasses, grabbed his groin, and mumbled expletives into a microphone on open mic night. Frank was a classic pretender who convinced Amber he was an artist to watch. On the move. Being courted by Atlanta, LA, New York. "In talks." Seven-figure record deal. In truth, he was a thug. A punk with an attitude. And the only thing he was moving was prescription drugs through the night club. Frank was an opportunist, a shoplifter, a car thief, a drug dealer, and a pathological liar, and his only claim to fame was having spent time in juvie and now dating someone who once had access to someone famous. Someone with money. Making him important by association.

Adding insult to injury, Amber was a terrible judge of men.

Knowing her time was short, Joe sent the one phrase that might break through. Rattle something loose. The muted memory of friendship. Amber had grown up idolizing Dolly Parton, who was no stranger to hair spray. Because, even on a bad day, hair spray can fix anything.

Joe typed, "Tease it to Jesus." Then hit Send.

Come on, Amber.

Seconds passed.

Then a minute.

She stopped tapping, sure the SIM had already been destroyed.

Buzz.

Her heart leapt again. She tapped, then sucked in a deep breath, which she held for nearly thirty seconds.

The text read, "And spray it like hell."

In the previous months, she often wondered if Frank was doing most of the communicating, leaving Joe to wonder if Amber was okay. Or was she in danger herself? Reading this, she knew Amber was present. She might not be holding the phone, and she might not be in charge, but she was close—because only Amber would know how to fill in that phrase. Yes, Frank could've Googled it, but she doubted he was that smart.

But that wasn't the best part. Unsolicited, a second text followed. This time a picture. Joe sucked in a breath and tapped the icon, revealing an ultrasound. Dated yesterday. 3D. So clear it looked almost alien. The nose. Lips. Ears. Perfect in every detail. The hands. Fingers. One folded. One more open. She counted out loud. "One-two-three-four-five. One-two-three-four-five." She stroked the picture with her index finger. "Perfect," she whispered. But what caught her off guard were the eyes. Which seemed to be looking right at the camera. Almost posing. Was it her imagination or was the baby cracking a smile?

Joe typed furiously, ignoring mistakes, offering more money. "Are you safe? Let me help."

But Amber never received the offer. Verizon returned the text as "Undelivered." The window had closed. Frank might have been a punk, but he wasn't a fool. He had street smarts and he was good at being bad. He'd found his sugar mama and wasn't about to let her off the hook. Roger had warned Joe not to underestimate him. Choking on anger and tears, she unscrewed the cap, dropped two more pills onto her tongue, and chased them with more fire in a bottle.

The driver watched, unaffected, as her eyes glazed just slightly and her neck began to wobble. The edge had been taken off. Pain muted.

The driver left the PCH just north of Santa Monica on San Vicente Boulevard, routing them through Brentwood, the southern end of Bel Air, and finally the Hills. Beverly Hills. 90210. Where little girls' dreams come true. Or at least some of them. Maybe one or two.

In the rising haze, Joe entertained a question she might not have were she sober. Dreams. When was the last time she had let herself dream? She leaned her head back. She knew the answer. And that, too, hurt. The problem wasn't the when but the who—and the bitter taste they left in their wake. The unanswered questions. So much left unsaid. She closed her eyes and whispered aloud, "Pockets."

The driver perked up. "Excuse me?"

She waved him off. "Talking to myself."

He stared into the rearview mirror and said, "You okay, Mrs. Joe?"

She noticed for the first time that in order to speak, the driver had to push a button at the base of his esophagus and that his voice was computerized. No doubt the effect of too many cigarettes. She waved him off, but she was anything but okay.

She stared up through the tinted glass and counted streetlights. One, two . . . seven, eight. Long ago, she discovered the monotonous rhythm calmed her. Her chest rose and fell with each deep breath. She had just started to doze when her phone shook her awake. Her voice was shaky. "Yes?"

"Joe." A pause. Roger's voice sounded pained. "They're gone. No trace."

A second passed as she shook off the haze. She was slow to speak. Almost slurring. "But you said—"

Roger cleared his throat. "We've exhausted every lead."

She was more awake now. "But you told me . . . you'd done this before."

"We have. Many times."

"What about, 'These people establish a pattern'?"

"They do. These didn't. Or haven't."

"But I did what you said. Paid every penny."

"There are no guarantees. That said, they have something you want and you have something they want. It's simple economics. Blackmail 101. They'll be in touch."

"It's not simple to me."

He knew he shouldn't have said that, so he made no response.

"So I just sit here and"—she lifted her phone—"wait for the ding?"

"Unfortunately . . . yes."

"You know how hard that is?"

"I understand. They have you on a string."

Normally one to play her cards close to the vest, Joe seldom revealed what she thought, but then there were the pills and the ache. Her voice rose. "You have no idea." In a rare break, the truth slipped out. "No concept. Do you know what I've gone through?" She didn't wait for an answer. "I'll give them whatever they want. I thought I made that clear. They can have it all."

"And if you do, you'll never see—"

"But you told them. Right?"

"Joe." Seconds passed, which told her all she needed to know. "Part of my job is to protect you from them. Help you make wise decisions when your ability to do so might be . . . compromised."

The words *protect you from them* rattled across her mind. In her mind's eye, she saw Pockets. Standing just a few feet behind her. Always in the shadow. An arm's length. Three feet. Tie. Sport coat. Sunglasses. Hands folded. Haircut high and tight. *If he were here . . .* She shook off the thought. *He's the reason I'm in this mess.* She gathered her composure. "Compromi—"

He corrected. "You know what I mean."

"So you didn't?"

"Joe, if I tell these people you will pay them five million, they will take it, then bleed you for another five. And you'll have nothing. Please . . . trust me. Let me do my job."

She untwisted the cap, palmed a single pill, crushed it with her teeth, and chased it with more liquid courage. For a mere mortal, this would turn out the lights, but she'd built quite a tolerance over the years. "So? What now?"

"We wait."

She spoke to herself as much as him. "Death by a thousand cuts." She considered the people around her. Her team. Those working for her. Helping her. And yet she still felt very much alone. And had. Since the jury's decision. Although seven long years had passed, she remembered watching him stand and how the bailiff led him out of the courtroom. Orange jumpsuit. Chains rattling. He had tried to make eye contact but she wouldn't let him. She'd denied him that.

Staring at the phone, her strength returned. "Roger, I did not ask for this."

"I realize that. But it's here. How you respond will determine much of what happens next."

She ended the call and sat tapping her phone. Within a few blocks, the drugs hit her bloodstream but had little effect.

They passed Beverly Boulevard, Melrose Avenue, and the Sunset Strip, finally exiting onto West Sunset Boulevard. *Appropriate*, she thought. *My sunset on Sunset.* The streetlights played a rhythmic and lonely slideshow through the windows as the driver crossed Hollywood Boulevard. Three blocks down lay her star, encased in black polished-and-speckled concrete. The Walk of Fame. Another laugh. *My headstone. Maybe they'll bury me beneath it.*

When they drove by her star, where a group of giddy girls stood taking a selfie in honor of tonight's festivities, Joe never even glanced. She stared out the opposite window, looking for a shadow that no longer stood alongside her and the warmth and safety of a bubble that had been removed.

A block away a hundred cameras lit the black limo in flashes and ten-frames-per-second shutter clicks. The driver slowed to a stop at the red carpet, then deferred to Joe, who stared at the crowd, questioned both her ability and her desire, and nodded. The driver motioned to security, who opened the door and offered a hand.

Joe had unceremoniously aged out of foster care while flipping burgers at an all-night diner. Now in her late thirties, known worldwide as Joe, and loved by tens upon tens of millions, she eyed the crowd.

Despite paying her dues in shampoo, dog treats, and vinyl siding commercials, she had paid the bills—or most of them—working at a local diner. One night, while working a double, she served a burger to a producer at 2:00 a.m. His film was behind schedule and overbudget, but that wasn't his biggest problem. His star was. She was a trainwreck in the process of coming off the rails. Yard sale in the making.

CHAPTER 1

BEFORE

He was a regular. Liked to rewrite scripts from a corner booth in the early morning hours. He ate slowly, studying her smile, her easy conversation, her enthusiasm at 3:00 a.m., and her legs extending out of the 1950s throwback skirt. He stirred his eggs and eyed her name tag, which read "Maybe Joe."

He pointed his fork at her. "That your real name?"

She topped off his coffee. "Yep. Got a birth certificate to prove it too."

He shook his head. "Did you fight a lot as a kid?"

"Tried to but I wasn't very good at it, so . . ." A shrug. "I learned to roll with the punches."

He admired how comfortable she was in her own skin. "What do people call you?"

"Most folks call me Joe."

For whatever reason, "Maybe Joe" looked enough like his lead actress in form and feature that under the right lighting, she might pass as an extra in nonspeaking scenes.

He watched her wipe a table and blow a single strand of hair out of her face. "Your parents do that on purpose?"

"Don't know. Never met them. But"—she tapped her shirt—"that's not the worst of it."

"Do tell."

"My full name is 'Maybe Joe Sue.' Suggesting that maybe whoever birthed me could not make up their mind and was not the smartest hammer in the knife drawer."

"Maybe Joe Sue?"

She curtsied. "In the flesh."

"Surely they had trouble filling out the birth certificate."

She refilled his coffee. "Hope so 'cause the alternative is cruelty, and I've always believed if you don't know something about somebody, you fill the gap with trust until you do."

He turned sideways in his booth. "That would make you different from a lot of people I work with."

She eyed his yellow legal pad. She'd seen him before. Corner booth. Black coffee. Tipped well. "You ever sleep?"

A shrug. "Not much."

"Stressful job?"

"Can be." He tried not to give too much away. "The people I work with can be . . . high maintenance."

She raised an eyebrow and gave a knowing chuckle. "You should try working at an all-night diner. I could tell you some stories."

"I'll take your word for it. How'd you end up here?"

She waved her hand across the room and raised her voice enough to be heard in the kitchen. "Well, when I'm not fast-tracking my way up the corporate ladder of Greasy-Diners-R-Us, owned by a made member of the Mexican drug cartel . . ."

The Irish guy standing over the dishwasher, who looked anything but Mexican, hollered above the steam, "Heard that."

"I am an"—she made quotation marks with her fingers, which were accented by raised eyebrows—"'up-and-coming' and, if it weren't for this place, starving actress with"—she held up three fingers—"three, count 'em, three career-defining roles to my name."

"Oh, do tell."

The dishwasher hollered from his post. "Don't let her fool you. She's good."

She set the coffeepot on his table, careful not to smudge the legal pad. "Well." She swung her ponytail, mimicking the slow-mo cinematography of most hair commercials. "I starred in a twice-nominated shampoo commercial for oily hair, made from nontoxic, recycled plastic bottles collected by hand in New York City." Another swing. "Given that career launch pad, which totally"—she clapped—"shot me out of a cannon, I soon landed the lead role in a commercial for an organic, non-habit-forming, high-fiber, low-sugar, high-protein tofu derivative, low-glycemic, keto dog treat made from South China Sea seaweed. And given that it caught fire among seventy-two-to-eighty-five-year-old retirees in South Florida . . ." She winked, letting him know she'd hit the big time. "It is now 'episodic' or 'recurring.' Syndicated in multiple national markets, that sweet little number pays me royalties." She paused and nodded for effect. "Every month. *Bam!*" Another clap. "Like clockwork. Seventy-four cents. First Tuesday." She wiped her hands on her apron as if preparing for the big reveal.

He interrupted her, trying to disguise his smile. "Seventy-four."

She turned her hand side to side. "Been as high as seventy-eight. Low as thirty. But there was a hurricane in South Florida, so . . ." She regained her composure. "But the pièce de résistance"—she closed her eyes, breathed in, and held her hands out like a symphony conductor— "the role that placed my name in lights and"—she lowered her voice as if relaying a closely guarded secret—"was recognized by *the* academy, was a BOGO, hurricane-proof-to-Cat-4, child-safe, lead-paint-free, vinyl siding infomercial. They said my portrayal of an exasperated, pregnant homemaker with a baby on my hip staring at a leak in my kitchen was so convincing, so *East of Eden*-ish, they doubled sales in three Midwest markets."

Having finished, she bowed, picked up the coffeepot, and accepted the raucous applause from the empty diner and Nick.

The man laughed out loud. "*The* Academy?"

A knowing nod. She spoke slowly. Enunciating every letter. "The UACSLFVPMOA."

He tried but got tongue-tied. "The UA . . . ?"

"The Unionized Academy of Child-Safe Lead-Free Vinyl Producing Manufacturers of America."

"I had no idea." He shook his head. "Quite a mouthful."

"Try saying it three times really fast in a fifteen-second commercial."

He crossed his arms. "Well, I can see you're on your way. Really going places."

"Yeah. I just work here 'cause I can't leave Nick." She pointed to the sweaty, bad-combover, large-bellied man wearing a stained and yellowed wife-beater shirt who was cleaning the grill while the stub of his cigar dangled from the corner of his lip. "He'd never make it without me. Plus," she gushed, "I can't deny it. We're in love and eloping just as soon as he gets the three-million-dollar life insurance payout from his recently deceased wife, who, incidentally, hasn't been seen since she took the dog for a walk six months ago."

Nick laughed, set a steaming plate on the stainless counter, and spoke around his cigar. "Order up, my love."

Joe retrieved the steak and hash browns and set them down for the man. "May I get you anything else?"

He pointed at the seat opposite him. "Give me five minutes?"

She looked at Nick, who had walked around the counter and pointed a spatula at the man. "Hey, nothing funny, fellow. She's a good girl. She don't do stuff like that." He waved his spatula at the black-and-white TV. "One day we'll all be watching her. She's going places."

The man nodded. "Nothing funny. It's all aboveboard. Just hear me out."

Nick crossed his arms, revealing a faded anchor tattoo.

The man spoke to them both. "I'm a producer, and things are not going well." He explained. When finished, he asked if she might be interested. A stand-in. Something to help take the pressure off his star.

She laughed and wiped the sweat off her forehead. "Just stand there and look like me?"

"Yep."

Nick leaned in. "With her clothes on?"

The man laughed. "Yes, but"—he pointed—"not those."

Nick looked at Joe. "I can close up and go with you? Just to be sure."

She looked at the producer and smiled. "Told you we were lovers."

CHAPTER 2

BEFORE

She left straight from work and, despite Nick's objections, met the producer alone at the set. Still wearing the shirt with her name printed on it. Smelling of burger grease and cigarette smoke. An unknown among the known. The producer brought her on set, put her in front of the camera, turned on the light, and said, "Do what you did with me last night. Just have a conversation."

She put a hand on her hip. "Technically, it was this morning. And if I remember correctly, I did most of the talking, so it wasn't really much of a conversation."

He lifted his eye from the camera. "Perfect." Over the next few minutes, as other crew arrived, she came alive. Before their very eyes, the atmosphere shifted. No, better yet, the stratosphere.

Such was her break. The rest is cinematic history.

After her stand-in, she'd accepted a supporting role. The director was an up-and-comer with little to no financing, so he'd promised her, along with the rest of the cast, a share in profits. If it ever made any. She didn't care. It was a foot in the door. After filming, she returned to her roach-infested apartment and Nick's night shift. By then, he'd promoted her to grill assistant, where she learned the art of smashing burgers, scrambling eggs, and hashing browns, earning her an extra dollar an hour.

Then the inexplicable happened. The thing for which every producer will sell his soul and yet none know the recipe. Lightning struck. Desperate to get noticed, the director entered the movie in a small but notable film festival where it was accepted, shown at 2:00 a.m., and viewed by eleven rather unenthusiastic insomniacs—one of whom happened to be a failed novel writer turned unheard-of movie critic who showered the film with the one thing that has killed more good movies than helped: critical acclaim. But that's the funny thing about unheard-of writers. To his credit, the guy could write; there was power in his pen. So word of mouth spread. And just like that, the film caught wind. Traction. Ten screens became fifty. Fifty became one hundred. Shows were sold out. People stood in line. The film went nationwide. Two thousand screens and her face shone on every marquee.

She was finishing a double shift, bussing a four-top, when she read the news ticker at the bottom of the screen. The movie had received six nominations: best director, best cinematography, best editing, best screenwriting, best film, and, wonder of wonders, she for best supporting actress.

She dropped the plates and laughed out loud.

She gave herself a snowball's chance. Broke and smelling of grease, she clocked out, changed in a bus stop bathroom, and arrived on foot in a thrift store dress where, climbing the steps, she'd spotted a pigeon feather that she, laughing at the ridiculous turn in her life, tucked in her hair. An innocent fashion statement that was about to set the world on fire. In the hours following, she took Hollywood, and the world, by storm. The never-heard-of underdog heard them call her name, "Maybe Joe Sue," and walked away with the golden ticket. Media the world over printed her picture, complete with feather rising out of her ponytail like an American Indian headdress.

The nickname stuck.

"Feathers."

Five years later, she won again. This time wearing a wrap made of feathers. And tonight, nominated yet again, she had returned. A single silver feather pinned to her shoulder strap. Devoted fans were calling for a hat trick. Saying if the Academy had any sense at all, she was a shoo-in. She was more realistic. Given her decade-long, public struggle with addiction, the tabloid exposés, the pictures of her walking in and out of treatment not one but six times, the nasty divorce from the "sexiest man alive," not to mention the trial, she was certain the public had tired of her and her high-maintenance life. Her critics cried foul and, over the last few years, had eviscerated what remained of her soul, resulting in a blood-tinged feeding frenzy that lined their pockets and shredded her heart.

But while they could rake her over the coals and cause her to doubt herself, they could not change one thing. The girl could act. Like nobody's business.

And so she had.

Staring through the tinted windows at the crowd, she longed to go back, to turn the car around. But back to what? Around to where? To whom? She was fighting alone and in several directions—the very thing Pockets had told her she must never do. And he was right. *Sparta proved that. It's why they wore breastplates.*

Since his rapid and unexpected and unexplained departure, she had been stuck on the merry-go-round of absurdity, with an occasional lap around the cul-de-sac of loneliness, and she did not recognize her life or what had become of it. Day had bled into day and month into year, during which time she'd lost most everything she'd ever held dear. Save one thing. Acting. In some sick twist of fate, she could still pretend with the best of them. So she stared at the crowd, flipped her switch, and extended one leg into the limelight under the roaring adoration of the multitudes.

Who went wild.

Then she stood and confirmed the rumors. The speculation was true.

She had worn the dress.

As a broke twenty-one-year-old, flipping burgers to pay rent alongside the roaches, she'd found the dress in a thrift store. The tag had read $25 but she'd talked them down to fifteen due to a tear in the bottom hem. She argued, *"Someone caught it on a heel."* Someone had, and by the end of the night, the tabloids had reprinted the picture of the moment the dress's previous owner—who had won twice here—had torn the hem with her heel climbing the very same steps Maybe Joe Sue was only seconds from climbing. Then and now pictures flooded the Internet.

That night, not caught in the drama, she'd exited the bus a block away and walked barefoot to the steps, donned her heels like Cinderella, stuck a feather in her hair, and enjoyed the festivities. Ate the free food. A dreamer living someone else's dream because she'd never had the courage to dream this one.

Then came the last envelope. When all the world went quiet. They played the clips. Announced each name. Flashes on the screen.

"And the winner is . . ."

She blinked, and everyone was looking at her. In a nanosecond, life changed. She now held Willy Wonka's golden ticket. *My dear, "we are the music makers and we are the dreamers of dreams."*

She had stayed up all night, finishing with breakfast at her own diner—still wearing the dress. Cradling the golden statue in her arms like an infant. And while the paparazzi stood on the sidewalk, gorging on the buttery syrup dripping from her lips, the Internet and the public fell in love. "Maybe Joe's Just One of Us." Within days, she surprised her landlord and brought her rent current, including penalties. Within months, she paid cash for a home on the Malibu coast. One with a view of the Pacific. And gardens.

The roles came pouring in. Pick and choose. An elite luxury. With more money than she could spend, she bought a vineyard and continued to grow what was already growing: Pinot and Chardonnay, bottling it under the labels "Rent Money," "One Black Dress," and a Reserva called "Feathers."

CHAPTER 3

BEFORE

Tonight, she had worn the same dress, not because she didn't think she had a chance. She did. Thought her chances were pretty good. Although, in truth, she was pulling for her competition. They were brilliant and deserving. She had worn the now-famous dress because she knew it would draw the attention of the media, and they would spend much of their time talking up the nostalgia of a dress worn, and having won, four times. Twice by the previous owner and twice by her. Could it win five?

As she stepped from the limo onto the red carpet, the signature slit exposed her now iconic legs. After her first win, her agent convinced her to insure them for $20 million. She said he was crazy but he reasoned that if NFL quarterbacks insured their multimillion-dollar arms for careers that might last five to ten years, she should insure her ability to walk up on that stage. She had, along with other pieces of herself. Including her smile. She'd always thought it goofy and a little out of balance to the rest of her face, but fans saw it differently. Her smile endeared her to them. Tonight, her legs were insured for ten times that. Her face even more. An insurer in London held the paper.

Stepping out of the car, she paused. Well measured. Long enough for the cameras to catch the reveal. While they elbowed each other for the next front cover, she chuckled to herself. *Scaffolding. It's all just scaffolding. Let the wind blow and you'll see.*

Dolby Theatre had been home to the Oscars since 2002. Built at a cost of almost $100 million, it had been engineered for nights like this. To place the otherworldly on a pedestal for all the world to see. Those like her. Now shrouded in an Oxy haze, she focused on the door, made note of two wrinkles in the carpet, and told herself, *Door. Focus on the door, and whatever you do, remember* the *step.* At the base of the steps, she paused, feeding the crowd, and accepted an eager, gloved hand and climbed gracefully. Her blood now swimming with enough narcotic to put large farm animals to sleep. The years since her first win had given her plenty of time to build a resistance.

During those years, having been publicly undressed as a trophy wife and left feeling half the woman she once was following several difficult procedures and one horrendous surgery, Joe did what she knew how to do. She acted. Nonstop. Role after role. Stacked up like cordwood. It didn't matter. They all bled together. Proving wrong the critics who claimed success came too early and that she'd never learned the ethic of a working actor.

When asked how she responded to those critics, Joe had folded her hands and leaned into the camera. As if telling a secret. "Between you and me"—she lowered her voice—"they're right. Which explains my fallback." She inched closer. "I make a mean bacon-double-cheese and have never let a cup fall below half full." She raised a finger, her voice now little more than a whisper. "That's the secret. The coffee cup. Keep it warm, keep it full, and the tips will follow."

An answer for which the public loved her all the more.

Her career had brought fame, but never love. Only heartache. Only longing. So from Broadway to Hollywood, she had numbed her pain and made the world believe.

Which explained tonight. And the pill fob. Now she ate them like Skittles.

She had waited six months after the jury's decision. Driven herself to the prison. Checked in. Even asked to see him. But when they put her in that stall with the glass between them, and she waited while they shackled and retrieved him, she changed her mind. Or chickened out. How do you really know someone? So she motioned to the guard. And left. Without ever laying eyes on him. Besides, what would she have said? What could she? After all he'd done.

Then there was Syd. She didn't know who was worse.

She'd left suddenly. Running out of the sterile, echoing halls where everything was granite. Hard. And cold. She wondered how he adapted. Had he? Had he thought of her? And then the question she could not answer: Was he who he led her to believe he was? Was Pockets the man she'd known, and quietly loved, or the evil man described in court?

When she was halfway down the prison steps, knowing a freedom Pockets would not, the tears exploded in a flood and she collapsed. Which made no sense to her. They were not married. Were not lovers. He wouldn't let her. So why? Why had she cried after so deep a betrayal? Maybe it was because no matter what evidence had been presented, she couldn't believe it. Wouldn't. It had never made sense. None of it. The man they'd portrayed in that courtroom and the man she'd come to know and trust were two different people. One of these things was not like the other.

Her life with Pockets had been a three-act drama where fire had engulfed the theater just prior to the final act. Act 1 presented a conflict that demanded a resolution. Her. She had been the conflict. Act 2 raised the tension. The stakes. And the consequences. So much of their interwoven lives had been spent resolving the conflict surrounding her. And in her. Act 3 was poised to bring closure to the whole. Understanding. Hope realized. But where hope once bubbled up through the cracks of impossibility, she now knew only tragedy. Conflict unresolved. Leaving hopelessness in its wake along with the deafening echo of lines never spoken.

A curtainfall and the painful sound of so much left unsaid.

CHAPTER 4

AFTER

Halfway up the steps, counting quietly to herself amid the clamoring shouts and cheers of the faithful, she stopped at "the step." The same step where the first owner of the dress had stumbled, caught her heel in the hem, and torn it while falling. Joe paused just slightly, flashed her heel, mimicked falling, smiled at the crowd, and then turned to check the hem of the dress. A beautiful tipping-of-the-hat to the dress's first owner. Sitting on the step, she turned up the hem for every camera to see—she'd duct-taped the old tear.

She had them eating out of her hand, which was good. She would need that as the opiates dilated her entire body.

By the time security escorted her to her table where her manager and several studio executives waited, the Internet had already declared her the winner. "Say It Ain't So, Joe."

She sat, expressed gratitude, and said little. Around her sat Hollywood's best. The most promising. Rising stars. When their names were called she rose, hugged, and clapped. Expressing genuine excitement. She had this two-finger whistle thing she did that sprayed spit and could split eardrums. People loved her for it. Said it showed her humanity. Proof that she was just one of us. Tonight she whistled a lot. And they loved her for it.

On set, everyone described her as fun-loving. A jokester. Prankster, even. Silly stuff like releasing chickens in her co-star's cabin, crickets in their car, or sipping helium before a love scene. She did this despite riding a pain train she could not stop. Truth was, Joe was good at acting. Maybe as good as anyone. Ever. She had received her third nomination for good reason. But while the world was awarding what they saw on film, it paled in comparison to the performance she gave in real life.

She wasn't nervous when the evening reached its final award. The one for which everyone had been waiting.

She could hear the slow, rhythmic beat of her heart in her ears. "And the nominees are . . ."

Rightly so, she was the last of the nominees. All eyes on her. They showed clips of this year's film. The role of a lifetime. They'd paid her $30 million, plus a percentage of ticket sales and online streaming revenue, but in truth she couldn't remember much of the filming. The opiates had erased it.

"And the award goes to . . ."

Since her explosion onto the screen, there had been no shortage of mystery surrounding her name. A beautiful woman with a man's name. A public records search yielded her birth certificate, which did, in fact, list her name as Maybe Joe Sue. Why would anyone do that to a child? Could they not read? Did they not know? As best she could piece together, she had been brought into the world by a scared young girl who left her at the hospital soon after giving birth and writing on her identification papers the words "Maybe Joe Sue." As if someone older or wiser would make the decision.

As she was unable to raise her own objection, the name stuck. As she got older, she liked to think her mother loved the classics and had named her after Louisa May Alcott's protagonist in her 1868 masterpiece, *Little Women*, but the fantasy was short-lived. She would never know.

Whatever the case, and despite the reason, she did not walk through life making excuses for a name that made no sense.

"Joe."

She never heard them call her name. Despite the standing ovation, the hugs, the smiles, the adoration, her world had gone silent. Only when she saw her face on the screen did it set in. She'd won. For the third time. Rocketing her to rarified air. A stratosphere known only by immortals.

Wishing she could climb in bed and pull the covers over her head, she rose from her chair and ascended the steps to the stage, pausing again at the fourth step. She stared out across the crowd. What had this life cost her? A husband. Children. Anonymity. Pockets. Everybody wanted to be her—except her.

In two decades of acting, she had learned to control her face. Minute muscle movements. Only show them what she wanted them to see because the camera picks up and amplifies everything. She had mastered that. Tonight would be no different. She would once again feed them out of her hand with what crumbs remained.

Joe had not risen to stardom because she was otherworldly beautiful. She was not. She was average. Normal. Nothing special to look at. At best she was cute, but she was no Audrey Hepburn. No Lauren Bacall. The press posited multiple comparisons to Little Orphan Annie, though unlike Annie, Joe couldn't sing to save her life. She sounded like a dying cat. This inability required her to actually act, which made her all the more beautiful when she did what any of us would do.

Her second nomination had come on the heels of a role in which she played the fun-loving wife of an eccentric and deaf artist. Not a lot of dialogue. One-sided at best. Unable to communicate in words with her husband, she'd learned to speak with him through body language. Facial gestures. One of which was crossing her eyes and sticking out her tongue just slightly in the corner of her mouth. The translation was akin to a shrug with these words implied: *"I know things are a bit messed up right now, and we don't know if we'll make it, but hang in there. I'm here. And we've got each other. Sometimes there's beauty in the mess."* From that touching silver-screen moment, "the shrug" became known around the world. It took on the universal meaning of "beauty in the mess." Through something so simple, the world saw her humanity. Her Joe-ness. For once, they saw someone who wasn't trying to make themselves the center of everyone's universe, but someone who was just trying. The hashtag #beautyinthemess became a pop-culture icon and was tagged in tens of millions of selfies. Many being added in the Museum of Selfies, which, oddly enough, sat just down the street from the Dolby Theatre.

If a rising tide floats all boats, then Joe raised the world. She had given the hurting an expression for their angst. Locked arms with the hopeless and put words to their pain. Without speaking a single syllable, she had done the one thing this world could not and never would—she gave them hope. People looked up and saw the sun.

Placed her on a pedestal made for one.

She climbed the last step, too stoned to speak and too broken to want to, but between the whistles and shouts and cries of undying adoration, she did what only a three-time winner could. She paused, letting the silence blanket the room, her eyes suggesting her mind was considering what to say next. She studied the shadows, but he was not there. Only the figment remained. A fact that once again pierced a heart held together by a string. Sometimes she talked to him in her sleep. In the quiet, dark moments when he would watch over her. An offering without expectation. When she had slept without fear. Back when she slept.

After a measured beat, she shook her head, crossed her eyes, stuck out her tongue, bowed slightly, pressed the statue to her heart, and exited stage left.

Beauty in the mess.

An Oscar-worthy performance. For which they loved her all the more.

CHAPTER 5

BEFORE

Kelly MacThomas Pockets was an average-sized man. Six feet. One-eighty. Early forties. Gray setting into his beard. Emerald-green eyes. He was quiet. Unassuming. Fit. He disappeared into crowds more than stood out, and little was known about him. Born and raised in Scotland, he was educated at St. Andrews and joined the Royal Guard while still too young to serve. Most of his record, if not all, was classified. Save the scars. On the downhill side of a distinguished career, he was returning from Israel and the Middle East. Though no one really knew why. Nor did he say.

The flight left early and flew all day. Arriving at Amsterdam late in the afternoon. On a soldier's salary, Pockets had bought a coach seat, but his flight status received a complimentary upgrade, placing him next to a man in jeans scribbling furiously on a yellow pad. The producer noticed his tattoo and asked about it.

Pockets explained, "Something soldiers do."

Over the eight-hour flight, Pockets drank water, tomato juice, and one tonic water. He was tight-lipped about his career and experience, but the producer suspected Pockets had seen much. With a five-hour layover, the producer asked, "Can I buy you a cup of coffee?" At an airport bar, he said, "I'm assuming you have military experience."

Pockets weighed his head side to side.

"I'll take that as a yes." He then explained his film, the actors, and his problem.

Pockets listened. Curious.

The producer continued, "I'm in a pickle. And I need help." He pointed at his pad. "If this were you, how would you do this?"

Pockets eyed the man, lifted a pen from his shirt pocket, then drew four lines. Something he'd evidently done countless times before. The light bulb turned on. They spent the next four hours discussing and laying out the scene.

Before they boarded, the producer asked, "You headed home to family?"

Pockets shook his head.

"You open to a detour?"

"That would depend."

"I'll pay you five thousand dollars to fly back to set with me and consult. Just give your expertise. Three days is all I need. Four if you're feeling generous." When Pockets didn't respond, the producer said, "Ten. And a weeklong vacation at a beachside resort of your choosing."

"Ten thousand dollars?"

The man nodded. "And a chair on a beach with a little gal delivering drinks with umbrellas."

"You'll pay me ten thousand dollars to give you my opinion."

"Twelve."

"And that's all you want? I don't have to dress up like Little Bo Peep?"

"No." The man laughed. "In fact, I'd prefer you not."

"Mate." Pockets extended his hand. "For twelve thousand dollars, I'll give you all the opinion you want."

Pockets flew to Morocco, where Syd was pretending to be what Pockets had spent his life becoming. Over the next three days, Pockets met the husband-and-wife team and Hollywood power duo: Joe and Syd. When asked, he offered his scene-by-scene input. With real-world know-how changing the narrative of their story for the better, the writers rewrote the script. Production was giddy. When "action" returned in the ensuing days, the producer again asked him to stick around, which he did.

During the first take, Syd pitched a hissy about the requirements placed on him during the new scene, throwing his AR-15 at the producer after another failed take and demanding, "You do it!"

At his most basic, Pockets was a rifleman. Seeing one thrown indiscriminately on the ground did not sit well. Pockets picked up the rifle, cleared the chamber of the dummy round, and set it quietly next to the producer, who sized him up. Compared him to Syd. Twenty minutes later, he walked out of Syd's trailer and asked Pockets, "How would you feel about giving this scene a go? Maybe show Syd how to do it."

Pockets pointed at himself. "Me?"

The producer continued, "No lines, but it requires some physicality and weapons experience—both of which you have."

Pockets looked at the scene. "You mean like a stuntman? In a movie?"

The producer nodded.

"So when people watch this, they'll see me?"

The producer shrugged and then shook his head once. "Yes and no." He waved his hand across the production crew. "We'll all know it's you, and you'll know it's you, but after our really talented editors finish with the footage . . ." He pointed at the trailer. "It'll look like him and he'll get credit for it."

Pockets shrugged. "I'm game."

Pockets ran through the scene once, then nodded at the director. "Ready when you are, mate."

"Action."

It's not fair to say Pockets was a natural, and he was no Syd. He knew nothing of "playing" for the cameras. But when it came to stunts, he didn't need to. He'd been performing them for real most of his adult life, making the scene second nature.

Syd watched the filming from his trailer. While he didn't like being upstaged in the eyes of the crew, he was no dummy. He saw the benefits of his new stunt double, and his tune changed completely. Back on set, he treated Pockets as if he'd just met his bestie. BFF.

In the days that followed, Syd got to look oiled, rugged, and poised—and to leave the hard, possibly injurious work to someone of less monetary value. Someone . . . expendable. Pockets, on the other hand, got to storm the castle, save the girl, and shoot bad guys without someone shooting back. Then he got to ride off into the sunset—on a horse, no less—as the credits rolled. For a farm boy from the cold and rainy Highlands of Scotland who'd grown up on Louis L'Amour, it was a dream come true.

Under a Desert Sun garnered seven nominations and granted Joe her second Best Actress. In her acceptance, she'd thanked Syd, who had exited Africa as a sun-touched media darling. Thanked him for his love. And, she smiled, "For the water." Which brought loud applause. Then she turned to Pockets. Standing in the shadows. "For making sure Syd didn't shoot off his own foot." A smile. "Or mine." More ovation. Then she paused. Another beat. Maybe even a tear. Exposing the blurred line between acting and real life. "And your quiet strength . . . when Syd and I needed it most."

But not even Atlas could prevent the fissures.

As Joe's star shot moonward like Halley's comet and Syd jet-set about the globe as America's *GQ* darling—feeding the troops in war-torn regions of the world and shooting clean-earth infomercials on trash-riddled beaches, or filming his next action blockbuster with the next model-turned-actress—one thing became clear to everyone involved: Joe and Syd spent far more time apart than together.

In the process, Joe lost the one thing all the greats lose. An occupational hazard. Better yet, casualty. Her anonymity. No longer just another face in the crowd, she had become *the* face in the crowd. And while she had countless fans, not all were supportive. Women, jealous of her success, spotted her bagging tomatoes in the produce aisle and spouted hurtful words. Sipping cappuccino at a street-side café, callous men capitalized on her petite stature and forced selfies, shoved pie in her face, groped her, or stole her purse and sold the contents. Including the personal information on her phone. In Syd's absence she had no defender.

Looking to round out his career, Syd found himself starring in a rom-com opposite a former Swedish swimsuit model. Early in production on a beach in the Cayman Islands, he couldn't very well pack up and head home because someone said something unkind in the grocery store.

Joe needed help.

CHAPTER 6

AFTER

The marquee was missing a few letters and now advertised the "orner rocer Sto." Judging by appearances, the condition of the sign mirrored that of the aisles. Whatever prosperity it had once known had left with the industry that, once booming, had dried up, taking with it the demand and leaving an orphaned grocer relegated to selling enough lottery tickets and beer to keep the lights on.

They closed at 9:00 p.m., so I arrived a few minutes before, routed through the produce section, then dry goods, and made my way to the checkout. The cashier was late twenties. Hardworking. Too much eye makeup. Jeans two sizes too small. Couple of tattoos. Maybe a little calloused. But a sweet smile. Working the "10 Items or Less" aisle. Her name tag read "Becky Sue." I set my basket on the conveyor belt and waited my turn. The lady in front of me had a cart. Full to the brim. She was slowly setting each item on the belt.

"I know," Becky Sue said, nodding and scanning. "Saw a report today that said it was the Serbian mafia."

The older woman, purple hair, maybe midforties and shaped like a pear, responded, "I saw that! Said they took her to Russia." She set a bag of cheese puffs on the counter. "Some oligarch or something wanted her for his own private toy." She set a case of MoonPies on the belt and lowered her voice. "One of the major news outlets said they've got an eyewitness who said she saw her being forced onto a jet with wealthy Russians." She used the words "major news outlets" like she had inside knowledge.

Becky Sue nodded as she swiped the MoonPies and held up the box. "These are BOGO."

The purple-haired lady set the second box on the belt.

Becky Sue continued, "Police said this morning there was no sign of a struggle, but given her absence, they suspect foul play." Becky Sue said "foul play" in much the same way the purple-haired lady had said "major news." She nodded knowingly.

Above the two of them, a television played. Muted. The nine o'clock local news. When the words *Breaking News* scrolled across the screen, Becky Sue stopped the belt, mashed the remote, and the two ladies stood staring up, ambivalent to my presence.

The anchorman started with these words: "Breaking news tonight. Three-time Academy Award–winning actress Maybe Joe Sue has been abducted. Following her third Oscar win last night, she returned to her Malibu estate where security footage showed her entering her home alone. Internal video obtained by WPOD News shows her crossing into what would be the living room, lying down on the couch, and turning off the lights. Sometime after 3:00 a.m., a man in dark clothing enters the room, lifts her off the couch, and carries her out the door. The same cameras show him loading her into the back seat of a blacked-out Escalade. This morning, cleaning staff reported her missing and found a rag soaked in what authorities have identified as chloroform. Currently, authorities have no leads, and no demands have been received."

Becky Sue pressed the Mute button, pulled a tissue from her pocket, and wiped her smearing mascara. "Can't believe it. Just cannot believe it."

Mind you, the grocery belt was still not moving. Becky Sue continued, "What kind of miscreant freak-show of a human would take Joe?"

Purple Hair chimed in, pointing an index finger at the TV. "I'll tell you what kind . . ."

I looked for an alternate checkout counter, but Becky Sue was closing the store alone. Finally, Becky Sue told Purple Hair, "That'll be $74.96," at which point Purple Hair began digging through her purse—in which she could have hidden a Volkswagen. After a few minutes, she pulled out a smaller purse, licked her fingers, and began flipping through a rolodex of coupons. Eight minutes later, she laid a stack of coupons on the counter. Becky Sue swiped them one at a time. Purple Hair paid Becky Sue $68.42, and the two said their goodbyes.

When my turn arrived, I laid my items on the counter and watched as Becky Sue swiped each one. She was still shaking her head and spoke without looking at me. "I don't understand what kind of world we're living in."

I shook my head once. "Me neither."

At some point here she noticed my food. "Most of the time guys come through here with Pop-Tarts and soda. A case or two of beer. You got actual green stuff—broccoli, spinach, even some kale." She scanned the bag. "Which I can't stand. I don't mind turnips and collards but I am so over the kale revolution. Makes me gassy." She smiled and paused the belt. The stock boy was mopping the floor one lane over. She leaned forward and whispered, "Lotta greens here. You detoxing?" A knowing nod. "Constipated?"

"No. Just trying to turn the train around."

She eyed me. "I'd say that train is doing just fine." She continued bagging my groceries. "You not from 'round here, are you?"

"What makes you say that?"

She waved a dismissive hand across the grocery store. "Honey, we is some of the most uneducated and ignorant human beings on planet Earth, and you don't sound like none of us." She pointed out the window. "Google 'dumb as a bag of hammers,' and maps will lead you right here."

I wasn't sure how to respond, so I didn't.

The television flashed and caught her eye, so she lifted the remote and unmuted the TV, saying, "Oh, I wanted to see this."

The reporter continued: "In other news, Russex State Prison's most famous inmate escaped three days ago." The screen split in half, the reporter on one side and a prison-inmate picture on the right. "Six months shy of satisfying a seven-year sentence, MacThomas Pockets was assigned to a work-release program when he took the state van on a delivery run and never returned. The warden calls it unfortunate as Mr. Pockets was just a few months from release." The camera switched again. This time the reporter was standing next to the warden. "Warden, can you tell us about Mr. Pockets?"

"He's dangerous." The warden was shaking his head. "Man with that type of training. Doing what he did. Folks need to be on the lookout. And don't be a hero. You dial 911."

"Do you have any leads?"

Another shake of his head. "No. But when we find him, he'll serve the remainder of his sentence and the court will tack back on the additional years that had been adjudicated for good behavior."

"Thank you, Warden." The reporter turned to face the camera. "Mr. Pockets—a former member of the Scottish Special Forces and later a stuntman in Hollywood—worked for more than five years as Mrs. Joe's bodyguard but was arrested and later convicted of excessive physical battery and bodily harm after he and Mrs. Joe's husband, Syd Painter, had an altercation at a fertility clinic that put Mr. Painter in a coma and required months of therapy, including memory recovery and learning to feed himself.

"Mr. Painter later described in his number-one *New York Times* best-selling memoir, *My Road Back*, how jealous Mr. Pockets was of their relationship. 'It was an incredibly tough time for us. We were doing everything we knew to do. To conceive. Literally, had flown around the world, but it was just tough. If you've been there, you know what I mean. And when I walked out of the clinic, where I'm attempting to do my best to help my wife, Mr. Pockets just attacks me. A massive betrayal fueled by unchecked jealousy and rage. The most evil thing I can imagine. I can only guess he wanted the love we shared.'

"No reasons were ever given for why Mr. Pockets flew into a fit of rage. At the time, Mr. Painter was a UNICEF ambassador and one of Hollywood's leading men with a string of box-office hits to his name. Even an action figure and a successful string of hamburger restaurants. Syd Painter's recovery would take more than a year, during which time Hollywood's power couple divorced.

"Syd described the pain of that heartbreak in his book: 'Joe was devastated. So was I. She was having trouble coping. But I just couldn't reach her. I tried, but the pain we'd suffered had cracked her, and us, down the middle. As a result, I failed her as a husband.' That failing became public as pictures populated on social media, detailing relationships with multiple women over several years.

"Syd's road to recovery has been long, but the enduring and beloved actor has since made a career as one of Hollywood's leading men, starring in his own hit TV series—a job that, as he says, allows him to stay close to his Northern California home with his new wife and two young children. A role that the once–poster child for the action film says suits him just fine. Mrs. Joe has never remarried but served six rather public stints in rehab reportedly suffering from an oxycodone addiction. Mrs. Maybe Joe remains, to this day, America's leading lady. At this time, no word is known as to whether Mr. Pockets's escape has anything to do with Mrs. Joe's disappearance, but conspiracies and theories have filled the Internet."

The desk anchor interrupted the reporter. "Beth, during the trial, a rumor circulated that Mr. Pockets had once served with distinction in the Royal Marines. Any truth to that?"

Beth nodded. "The rumor did circulate but was never corroborated, and Mr. Pockets himself never supported it."

"Was any romantic connection ever made between MacThomas Pockets and Maybe Joe Sue?"

Beth nodded knowingly. "During the trial, news agencies and tabloids suggested a deep connection between the two, with dozens of pictures admitted into evidence, plus recorded conversations and text threads. But whether Mr. Pockets acted as bodyguard and if and when the two ever became romantically involved, no one can say. No connection was ever proven. As you just heard the warden say, Mr. Pockets is thought to be extremely dangerous. Stephen, back to you."

The desk correspondent continued. "In other news, nine-year-old James Carlton won first prize for his pig, Bessie, at the fair last night. Bessie was a shoo-in this year as she also won the two previous years. This past weekend, the svelte behemoth topped the scales at seven hundred and twenty-two pounds . . ."

Becky Sue turned back to me. "You married?"

"No."

She raised an eyebrow. "Wanna be?"

"Thanks, but no."

She sized me up. Slowly. "I like you even more now." She held up a bag of kale. "How do you eat this?"

"Bake it. Eat it like chips."

"Any good?"

I shrugged. "Put enough salt on it."

She scanned the barcode. "I feel the same way about tequila." A sly smile followed by a practiced single raised eyebrow. "And you know what they say about tequila."

I was pretty sure I didn't want to know so I tried to dodge it. "Not really."

An inviting smile. "Oh, come on, baby, you don't know the song?"

I did not. I shook my head.

"You been hiding in a hole?"

I feigned a smile.

Becky Sue printed my receipt, wrote her number on it, and winked. "Call me sometime and I'll sing it to you." Another smile. "I like a man who knows his way around the kitchen." As I walked away, she was humming.

I loaded into the Blazer, turned onto the county road, and glanced at myself. Trucker hat, ponytail wig, round metal glasses, and a Grizzly Adams beard with a Magnum P.I. mustache. I looked nothing like my picture on the television. Made me wonder how in the world she found me attractive.

CHAPTER 7

BEFORE

After Morocco, Pockets had returned to Scotland and been two days in the seat of his tractor when the phone rang. Joe's voice surprised him. "MacThomas Pockets?" She cleared her throat. "It's Joe. I'm the actre—"

Pockets laughed. "Yes mum. I know who you are." He said "mum" in the honored Scottish tradition as he would address nobility or someone of higher rank. By saying it, the speaker was bestowing honor upon the hearer and also tipping his hat, revealing himself to be a man who had served others most of his life. The *u* in "mum" sounded more like the *oo* in "took" than the *u* in "sum."

Her voice sounded uneasy. "You busy?"

He cut the engine, wiped his brow with his forearm, and said, "No mum."

"You don't have to do that."

"Mum?"

"That." She chuckled. "Call me mum. Or 'moom.' Or however you say it. I mean, you're older than me."

"Yes mum."

She hesitated, considering her suggestion had no effect on him whatsoever. "I was wondering if . . ." Seconds passed.

"Mrs. Joe? You still there?"

"Please call me Joe."

"Yes mum."

She started again. "I was wondering if I could hire you?"

He straightened. Puzzled. While he had enjoyed his time in North Africa, he wasn't sure how else he could serve. "Another movie?"

"Not exactly."

"Yes mum."

"What do you mean 'yes mum'?"

"I can help you."

"But you haven't even heard the job yet."

"Well, okay. Why don't you tell me about it and I'll wait 'til you're finished to tell you I'm agreeable."

She half laughed. "Syd is filming . . . somewhere. Then somewhere else. Followed by another somewhere else. He won't be home for a few months and . . ." Her voice faded.

"Mrs. Joe?"

She gathered herself. "Mr. Pockets, I'm not very good at being famous. I don't know how to . . ." She trailed off.

"Mum?"

"A man shoved me down in the street today. Took selfies. Touched me in places . . . while people stood around and watched . . ."

"Mrs. Joe, you don't have to call me Mr. Pockets. Pockets is fine."

"And so is Joe."

"Yes mum." In the quiet that followed, he put the pieces together. "You want to hire me as protection?"

"You've done that before, right? In your military service?"

He stared out across the pasture. Toward the North Sea. He never talked about his work.

A pause. She continued, "Are you currently working?"

"Not currently." Another pause. "When would you want me to start?"

"Is tomorrow too soon?"

He considered the pasture. "How long would you need me?"

"Couple of weeks. Maybe a month or two. Just 'til I can find someone more permanent."

A moment passed as he stared across the rolling, scenic, and quiet landscape before him while the breeze dried the sweat on his skin.

She continued, "I'll pay you whatever—"

He cut her off. "Yes mum, I can be there tomorrow."

"Oh, that's great." A sigh. "Thank you, Pockets."

"Um, Mrs. Joe?"

Her voice betrayed her smile. "Yes, Pockets?"

"Where are you?"

She laughed. The relief palpable. "I guess that might be helpful."

Pockets arrived at John Wayne Airport, where she was waiting for him in a rented Mercedes SUV with blacked-out windows. She sat in the driver's seat. He studied the car. "You don't have a driver?"

She shook her head as if the thought had not occurred to her.

He walked around to the driver's side and asked, "May I?"

She climbed into the passenger seat and waited as he navigated the airport traffic. *Proficient* would have been an understatement. She was tapping her front tooth with a fingernail. "Let me guess, you've done some of that training where you drive backward at a hundred miles an hour, then swing it one-eighty and never touch the brake."

He clicked on his turn signal and changed lanes, then waved to the driver behind him. "More like sixty."

She was excited now. Sitting up straight. "Can you show me some stuff?"

He shot a quick glance. Still trying to remember how to drive on the right side of the road. "Right now?"

She shrugged, betraying her boredom. "Why not?"

"Mrs. Joe . . ."

She turned sideways, sat on one heel, and made a time-out sign with her hands. "Hold it."

He stopped in the emergency lane. Surveying his perimeter.

"Much of the civilized world calls me Joe. Just Joe."

He nodded, not quite sure where this was going. "Yes mum."

Another T sign with her hands. And more head shaking. "That's another thing. You're killing me with this mum thing. Or 'moom' thing. How old are you?"

"I don't think you are allowed to ask me that."

She laughed out loud. "This isn't a job interview. You already have the job. We're just getting to know each other."

"I'm thirty-five."

"There. I'm twenty-five. Technically, you're my senior. You don't have to call me mum." She tried to tighten her top lip. "Or 'moom.' I'm not the queen."

He shot another quick glance. "Where I come from, if you're female over the age of about twelve, then you're a mum."

"Where are you from?"

"A farm on the eastern shore of Scotland."

"Well, what if I don't want you to call me mum?"

He considered this. The look on his face suggested this was something he'd never thought of before. He spoke as he drove. "Might be easier if you found another bodyguard."

"You feel that strongly about it?"

"No mum, it's just . . . What I mean is, it's like breathing. I been doing it a long time, and if you ask me to stop, I'm not too sure how that's going to work out. Might turn blue in the face and pass out, at which point I'd cease to be effective at my job."

"Well, okay, let's get back to Joe. What about Joe? Minus the 'Mrs.'?"

Without hesitation, he shook his head once. "No mum."

She let out a chuckle and rested her heels on the dash, pressing her bare toes to the inside of the windshield. "And why not?"

A quick shake of his head. "Too informal."

"So we can't be friends?"

"No mum. I mean, we can, but the reason has to do with optics."

"Optics?"

"What others perceive."

"How so?"

"When other people hear us talk or see us interact, you're safer if I refer to you in a professional manner."

She interrupted him. "So you have done this? I knew it."

He continued, "When they do, they'll be less likely to attempt something if they understand I'm focused on your safety and not our friendship."

She nodded. "I'm picking up what you're putting down." She squinted one eye. "You ever escorted dignitaries? Important people?" She waved her hand across the windshield as if she were painting the scene for a director. "Sunglasses, running alongside the limo. Submachine gun bulging beneath your jacket."

He considered how to respond. "Not alongside a limo."

She was getting excited now. She snapped her fingers. "I knew it. "You're a bad a—" She pressed her palm over her mouth. "Sorry." She looked at him out of the corner of her eye. "I cuss sometimes."

"No problem, mum."

She snapped again. "Did you ever blow up sh—" More mouth covering, which muffled the next words coming out of her mouth. "Stuff up?"

He nodded.

"What's the biggest thing you ever blew up?"

"It's probably better if I don't answer that."

"You kill people?"

"That falls in the same category."

She smiled. "I like the mystery. Adds to your mystique." She poked his arm. "You work out?"

He looked at himself then at her. "You have to ask me that?"

This time she squeezed his arm. "Nice." She turned sideways and sat on her heel again, leaning against the door only to realize he seemed to tighten when she did. "Oh." She pressed her index finger to her lip. "That probably crossed some professional-space barrier thing. Like we have to pretend there's this invisible force field around each other."

He nodded. "A good idea."

She extended her arm across the car, her finger just inches from his shoulder. Slowly, she encroached. "Am I making you nervous?"

He glanced at the location of her finger. "A little."

"Why?" She extended farther, poking him in the arm. "You afraid of me?"

He shook his head. "No mum." He considered. "Well . . . maybe." Another pause. "Yes mum. I am terrified of beautiful women. And . . ."

"What then?"

He didn't answer.

She poked him again. This time at the base of his shoulder.

He fidgeted.

She poked again, and he covered his right rib cage with his left hand.

She smiled. "You're ticklish."

He nodded once in admission. A chink in his armor.

"So." She teased him by hovering her finger just inches from his rib cage.

He spoke slowly. "It would be better if you didn't do that while I was driving."

She paused for almost half a second. "You like ice cream?"

He glanced at her. "Do you always talk this much?"

She laughed. "No, but I've been by myself so much lately, it's nice to have someone to talk with."

He returned his eyes to the road. "I don't eat much sugar."

"What? You on a diet?"

"No. Just don't eat it."

"Then, by definition, you're on a diet."

"If you say so."

She pointed. "Turn there."

He did. For the next eight blocks he followed her finger while she hammered him with questions. Finally arriving oceanside at the Little Dipper ice cream shop.

Ten minutes later, while she licked her cone, sitting cross-legged on the bulkhead overlooking the shimmering Pacific, he stood three feet distant—not in front of her but rather off to one side, hands folded behind his back. Sunglasses. Scanning their perimeter.

She eyed him. Trying to hide the smirk. She squinted one eye and raised the other eyebrow. "You packing?"

He leaned in. "Mum?"

She whispered, "Carrying heat?" She made a secretive move with her finger as if pulling a trigger. "You a nine or forty-five guy?"

While they were talking, two kids and a soccer mom approached and held out a phone. "Can we take a—"

He stepped between them. More cat than man.

She stepped around him and whispered, "Easy, killer." Then she took several photos, chatted up the kids and mom, and talked flavors of ice cream and who won the game. How she liked her van and what on earth did she use to get those stains out of their uniforms. When they left, she looked up at him and raised both eyebrows. "You got to learn to tell the difference between the good guys and the bad."

As they were speaking, a man on Rollerblades—half skating, half dancing, half drawing attention to himself and still drunk and high from the night before—skated between them, scooped her off her feet, and swung her over his shoulder. Fireman's carry–style. In the next half second, Pockets kicked the man in the base of the back, forcing him off-balance and launching him off his skates as if he'd slipped on a banana. While the man flew horizontally through the air, Pockets caught Joe, set her down, and then drove one knee into the man's neck and the other into his rib cage.

Problem solved.

A little later, sitting in the passenger seat, she realized she wasn't afraid. She hadn't had time. She studied the man still lying on the sidewalk and the police standing over him. "Nobody tells you it'll be like this."

"Mum, you should know." He paused.

She prodded him. "Yes?"

"On the outside, there is no difference. So when it comes to you, they're all bad, until they're not."

"What makes you say that?"

"Two decades of trying to tell the difference."

She watched the man crawling away. "That's probably good."

He pointed at her cone melting on the sidewalk. "You want some more ice cream?"

"No, not really hungry."

Driving north, she spoke without invitation. "The ice cream thing is a craving. Kinda comes on all of a sudden."

"You ever thought about maybe drinking some milk or something?"

"Yes, but"—she weighed her head side to side and covered her belly with her palm—"he likes ice cream."

"I apologize. I didn't know."

She straightened her baggy sweatshirt. "I'm not showing. Not much. And don't feel bad. Not even Syd knows."

"Congratulations." He studied her. "You sure it's a he?"

She glanced out the window. "Pretty sure."

He chose his words. "You don't look too happy about it."

A careful shrug. "My body seems to be having a tough time with pregnancy. A few days ago, the doctor used the words *high risk*."

CHAPTER 8

AFTER

Joe woke under the familiar weight of a medicated haze. A hangover years in the making. While Oxy was her go-to, she alternated between Adderall, Ambien, Xanax, Valium, Ativan, and trazodone. Something to wake or stay awake. Then something to sleep or keep sleeping. Up. Down. Up. Down. Wash, rinse, repeat. Fortunately, her dealer majored in chemistry and ran an à la carte business. Given her level of usage and resulting tolerance, taking a Percocet was about as effective as a Tic Tac, requiring him to calculate combinations to achieve the same level of high.

She rubbed her eyes and found the light different. Maybe it was cloudy outside. Maybe she'd not closed the curtains. As the spinning slowed, she sat upright, her toes expecting carpet. But they did not find carpet. Nor did they find the floor. Two things were different. One, the floor was not where she left it. Two, when she stretched, she found slick concrete in its place. This, too, did not register. Nor did the fact that the sheets were cotton. Not silk. Oddly, this sensory experience was not new. Most mornings, she woke to a world not where she left it. Upside down or slightly canted, she'd adopted the motto "better living through chemistry," meaning she could right any ship with just a pill or two. Needing a

53

hot shower, some steam, and a double espresso, she stood, turned right, and headed toward her bathroom, where she immediately ran into a wall.

That's about the time she opened her eyes.

Four concrete walls. One door, no handle. One window some twelve feet off the ground. A sink. A shower. And a toilet with no seat. A sterile efficiency apartment.

She sat on the floor and tried to will the world to settle. As her eyes adjusted, she spotted cameras hanging from the ceiling in the four corners of the room. Each shining a single red light. Certain her sponsor from Seven Pines had made a house call and found her passed out, she stood and looked at the cameras. "I know, I know, I goofed." Her voice was hoarse. "Just bring me an espresso. You know I can't talk 'til I get caffeine." She waved them off. "Then we can have whatever kind of intervention you want." She raised a finger. "Caffeine first. Therapy second." Then she sat on the bed and waited for the door to open.

After several minutes, when it did not open, she noticed the thing. A metal collar locked tight around her neck. Something like a hoop necklace made for a Star Trek stand-in. She stared in the mirror and found a single green light staring back at her from the hoop.

Needing to think straight, she reached for the pill fob hanging on her necklace. Finding it where she left it, she unscrewed the lid, dropped one pill on her tongue, and was about to swallow when she decided, *No, drastic measures. Make it two.* She screwed the lid back on, swallowed, and only then realized there'd been no pill. Admittedly, they were small. *A little dab'll do you,* as she often told herself. Given their size, maybe they were stuck in the fob. Maybe she was still numb and had missed it. Holding the fob up to the light from the window, she eyed the inside. Then turned it upside down. Shaking it.

Empty. No wonder she had a hangover.

She spoke to the camera again while holding up a stop-sign hand. "I get it. You win." She dangled the necklace. "I'm done. Point made." She held up both fingers, making quotation marks in the air. "'Intervention.'" She smiled. "Mission accomplished." A half smile. "But this"—she waved her hand across her surroundings—"is starting to freak me out. So can we get on with whatever this is? I'll behave. Start over. I know I need help, which is step one." She pointed toward the ground and spoke with her eyes closed, as the light was splitting her head in two. "Day zero right here."

The door did not open. What's worse, she did not smell coffee. At all. The only thing she smelled was herself. Body odor. The room must have been eighty degrees. Her pits were sweating. There was also the odd smell of compost mixed with manure and that strange aroma of wet earth after the rain. Gaining her composure, Joe sat on the edge of the bed and tried to make sense of what made no sense. She'd heard rumors of a room at Seven Pines where they'd put repeat offenders, leaving them in there for the better part of a day. Locked in a room with no phone and no contact to the outside world, confronted with the knowledge that their money and power could not save them—also known as "being powerless"—patients in that circumstance began to "wake up." And waking up powerless, when moments before you'd held all the power, is often hell on earth to the powerful.

Still no door opened. And no coffee appeared.

The longer the day stretched, the more it felt like prison—especially to those who had grown accustomed to being the center of the universe. They would walk circles, or squares, around the room, counting steps, making resolutions, swearing. For the addicted, the recidivism rate was dramatically low. The therapy worked.

But Joe also knew that, professionally, they would never do this to someone who had been abandoned. And she had. At birth. Multiple times since. Further, she had aged out of foster care. They also knew this. Knew her story as well as she. So this didn't smell like them. Too industrial. Too primitive. Maybe this was something else. Maybe they'd kept this card hidden close to their chest for repeat offenders like her.

Absent a phone, she tapped her foot. Minutes passed. She was growing irritated. She pointed at the cameras. "I don't pay you for this. And for the record, I am not a willing participant in this experiment. However well intended it may be."

An hour passed. Then two. Then four.

This had ceased to be funny.

The light softened, suggesting morning had been replaced by afternoon. By now, Joe was suffering a migraine and the first sign of tremors. Of withdrawal. In the past, when she'd reached this point, where the cravings were all she could think about and her body was screaming for a hit of narcotic, a nurse would enter and give her a cocktail of oral and injected medications and supplements. Something to take the edge off. A merciful extraction. A tapered weaning off. Nothing drastic.

But here there was no nurse. No injection. And no stepped-down relief.

By dusk, she was sitting on the bed. Tapping. Waiting. Drenched in sweat. By dark, she had turned on her side, curled into a ball, and lay rocking back and forth. By the time the moon rose high, she had but one request: make it stop.

CHAPTER 9

BEFORE

Pockets was following behind Joe in the produce market when the bleeding started. He was pushing the cart, she was picking through the avocados. Calmly, he took off his sports coat and wrapped it around her waist, but by the time he got her to the car, she was a mess. Twenty minutes later, the doctor's examination confirmed what she already knew. Given that she was three months along, the process took a while.

That night, Pockets sat outside her door while her body did what her body did. Before daylight, he overheard the whispered phone call to Syd. "Hey, something happened . . ." He couldn't make out Syd's words, but judging by her face in the window's reflection, they did not soothe her. She told him in hushed whispers, "I feel like I let you down . . ." As if she was somehow responsible. Again.

Syd's tone sounded sympathetic. Flowers were waiting at the house the next morning, as was a professional masseuse. But it was weeks before he returned to comfort her, and although Pockets could hear only one side, subsequent conversations suggested Syd was a little too understanding. Pockets often wondered if the trauma of being tackled by the skater had caused the damage. Was it the last straw?

When Syd did come home, he whisked Joe away to a private

Bahamian island complete with a private beach, chef, butler, and fishing guide. Syd called it the "Let's make a baby getaway." During the day, Pockets spearfished; at night, he read a Louis L'Amour paperback in a hut just down the beach.

After three days, Syd departed via seaplane for his next bona fide blockbuster. This one involving aliens. His costar was a newcomer to the acting world. A former *Sports Illustrated* model. Joe stood under a big hat and sunglasses as the sound of the plane faded. When it was gone, she turned to Pockets.

"You okay?"

"Yes mum."

She pulled off her sunglasses. "Is this difficult for you?"

"Mum?"

She waved her hand across the island. The beach. The huts. The firepit. Finally resting her palm flat across her tummy. "This."

"No mum."

"You sure? Certainly it's uncomfortable. You know why we're here."

"Yes mum. I mean, I'm sure. But may I ask you something?"

She nodded.

"When I first started, you said Syd would be returning home more often. That was three months ago."

She had been avoiding this conversation. "Yes, I did say that."

"Said my employ was temporary. Two months at most."

She put her sunglasses back on. Her tone was almost cold. "Want more money? I can pay."

He shook his head. "That's not why I'm asking. I just thought maybe Mr. Syd was going to be around more."

"Yes?"

"He's not."

She studied him. "Do you ever lie? Maybe sugarcoat stuff a little?"

He squinted. "I think that's a trick question. Because if I say no, I'm a liar. Every man has lied. But if I say yes, that's not really true either. 'Cause I make it a practice to tell the truth on things that matter."

"So if I ask you something, you'll tell me the truth?"

"Yes."

"You ever been to London?"

He nodded.

"You mind going back?"

He shook his head once, and his shoulders relaxed because he realized he was about to lose another argument.

She stepped closer. "Question number two."

He waited.

"Do you find me attractive?"

"That's one of those questions that's better left unanswered."

"I know, but do you?"

"Mum, I wouldn't want to answer that without Mr. Syd here."

"Okay, let's suppose for one second that Syd was here. What would you say?"

"I'd say, 'Mr. Syd, you married well, sir.'"

She half smiled. "So, Pockets . . . do you have a girlfriend?"

"No mum."

"What? Occupational hazard?"

"Can be, but my line of work is not really conducive to . . ."

"But you have. I mean, you've dated girls?"

"Yes mum."

"And you like girls?"

He nodded.

"Better than men?"

He saw what she was getting at. "You seriously have to ask me that?"

"You sure?"

"I'm sure."

"So when Syd grabbed me by the hand last night and rushed me out of our hut to go skinny-dipping, that doesn't cause you trouble?"

"It causes me trouble from the standpoint that you two are more difficult to defend in such a vulnerable state, especially one that does not include me, one that puts me at an indefensible distance, and one in which I don't need to intrude."

"But"—she waved her hand across her own body—"when we do, how do you respond to this?"

"I'm paid not to."

She stepped closer. "But you do?"

He looked down at her. "Honestly, mum, if you have to know, no, I don't."

She stepped back. "Why not?"

"Because I work for you." He looked like he had more to say but chose not to.

She prompted him. "And?"

He didn't speak.

"It's okay. Say it."

He cleared his throat. "Mrs. Joe, I work for you."

"So you're just here 'cause I'm writing you a check." A question posed as a statement.

"Well, yes mum. But I'd hope I don't come across as quite so indifferent."

She pressed him. "Does it bother you that I'm Syd's?"

A pause. "Mum?"

She repeated herself. "Does it bother you that I'm Syd's?"

"No mum."

"You were slow to answer on that one. You sure?"

"Trying to figure out if that's a trick question."

"Did you?"

"No. But I do better when I keep my mouth shut and do what I'm paid to do."

She stepped back and smirked. "Were you a Boy Scout?"

He shook his head once. "They didn't have that where I grew up."

"What'd they have?"

He considered this. "Hard work."

Another chuckle, and she hooked her arm in his and said, "Come on. Lunch is on me."

A month later, when she'd called Syd, he was so excited he caught a red-eye and flew in. They'd celebrated. She was sure this time. It would take. It had to. But in the days that followed, while filming a late-Victorian biopic in London, she suffered her third miscarriage. Quietly. Alone. In her trailer.

That evening, Pockets knocked quietly. She spoke through the door. "Yes."

"You need anything, mum?"

A pause. She leaned her head against the door. "No."

"You want me to call Mr. Syd?"

She spoke from behind the door. "Why would you do that?"

"Just thought maybe it'd be easier on you if I told him."

She cracked open the door. She was pale. Eyes puffy. She shook her head. "I'll tell him."

He was holding a brown bag. He looked conflicted and turned to go.

"Pockets?"

"Yes mum."

She pointed. "That gift for me?"

He looked as if he wanted to take it back. "It was."

"Is it a baby gift?"

He nodded.

She held out a hand.

"Mum, I'm not sure it's appropriate—"

She opened the door, took the bag, opened the top, and pulled out a baby blanket.

Pockets tried to explain. "It's my family tartan."

She bowed her head slightly. "It's beautiful. Thank you." She held it to her chest. "I'll save it." The tears returned. "Until next time."

Over the next eighteen months, she stopped counting at five.

Feeling that her inability to make a baby contributed to Syd's perpetual absence, she met with the best doctors and poured herself into painful "corrective" surgery. To help her body do what it wasn't. Something to do with cysts and tubes. Months of slow recovery followed by physical therapy.

Yes, there was also an adoring public. And while they were kind and respectful, and small children asked for a picture through the practiced voice of their favorite animated character, they were also relentless. And they were everywhere. Which meant she couldn't go anywhere. She paid the price of fame by hiding behind hoodies, sunglasses, wigs, and blacked-out windows. A terrible way to live for anyone but possibly the worst way to live for someone struggling to give her husband a baby.

By now, the power couple was surrounded by a "team." Managers, publicity, agents, trainers, cooks. During their transition into A-list stars, where even their assistants had assistants, the only constant was a bodyguard.

CHAPTER 10

AFTER

She woke in a puddle. Clothes soaked. Thanks to the eighty-five-plus-degree heat in the room, a long line of toxins were working their way out of her system. The taste of salt on her lips told her she was woefully dehydrated. She needed water and electrolytes. Pronto.

She sat up. Slowly. The earth spinning. On the counter, she saw a basket of granola and protein bars, along with several liquid IV packets. She bit the top off one packet, poured it into a water bottle, and downed it. Followed by a second. Made it halfway through a third before she made sense of the questions. There were two.

First, if this was in fact treatment, it was unlike any program she'd experienced. She'd never heard of a professionally administered cold-turkey method, and she questioned whether it was medically viable. Who would do this to her? Why? And who would willingly pay to undergo this?

Second, and possibly more terrifying, if this wasn't treatment, what was it? And who was in charge? And what did they intend for her? Why would they be doing this, this way?

She didn't let her mind go there. Not yet.

Late in the afternoon, she sat up but not for very long. Between the freight train and the nausea, she was on the verge. Finally, she yielded to the inevitable, crawled to the toilet, and, for the next hour, clung to the bowl while dry heaves wracked what remained of her. She woke on the floor in the middle of the night, sipped another liquid IV, and managed to pull herself up and into the bed, where the sweating continued. Which she took as a good sign.

Sometime on Day 3, she stood and placed one hand on the wall, whispering to herself, "Weebles wobble but they . . ." Steadying herself with both hands, she shuffled around the room. Her eyes little more than slits. Glancing at the door, she realized it had no handle. No way to pull it open. She pushed it but it didn't budge. She pounded. Still no movement. She stepped back and kicked it, but the sudden motion sent her back across the room to the toilet—retching.

Lying on the bed, catching her breath, she eyed the door again. Which stood slightly open. She lifted her head, her eyes focused, and her brain registered daylight. Pulling herself up, she once again used both hands to navigate the room back to the door, then stared through the crack. She pulled, and the door swung open. Without resistance. Evidently the door had no lock at all and had only been pulled closed.

She laughed out loud, pointing to the cameras. "Really fricking funny. I get it. Fight for my freedom. You've got to want out in order to get out." She waved. "You win. Point made. Only took me three days. I'm outta here."

She stepped into the hallway and wondered about the metal hoop. If they had made their point, what purpose did it serve? At the end of the hallway, she saw an exit. The sign above read, "Whatever you do, do not walk through this door."

Seeing freedom just beyond the threshold, she ran barefoot to the door, pushed, and watched it swing open. Revealing tall evergreens, spiraling up like Jack's beanstalk, and a dense forest. Which looked oddly familiar. Without hesitation, she jumped through the doorway— and made it three feet beyond the threshold only to be hit in the head by something she'd not seen. The blow was akin to a bike wreck. She left her feet and perceived the sensation of falling, followed by someone turning out the lights.

When she woke, she sat up and counted with her fingers, talking to herself. "One, two, three, four. I think." She was losing track but Day 4 seemed about right. The room was dark save what seemed like moonlight leaking in. Letting her eyes adjust, she counted four red lights occasionally flashing back at her from each corner of the room. Sitting up, she found the hoop still locked tight about her neck and, after looking in the mirror, the green light.

Across the room, the door stood half open, hallway exposed. But a new wrinkle had appeared. A pair of cotton sweats, a T-shirt, and underwear lay on the bed next to her. That meant two things: one, someone had put her back in this bed; and two, someone had put those clothes on the bed.

It also meant they had not changed her clothes, which she wasn't quite sure how to read. She stared down at the wrinkled dress that only a few nights before had won its fifth Academy Award. A stark contrast to the room in which she found herself. If she was in rehab for what would be the seventh time, she could understand the clothes being laid out. But something was telling her this wasn't rehab—at least not in the typical sense. She stared at the cameras, and the thought occurred that she might have been kidnapped by some creepy savant.

The shower stood in the corner of the room. In full view of three of the cameras but surrounded on three sides by opaque glass. This meant when she was inside the shower, the cameras might record the top of her head but that was about it, unless some pervert had placed a camera in the shadow. She checked. They had not. Hoping to prompt a reaction, she grabbed the clothes and a towel, walked to the shower, and turned it on. Once the steam began to rise, she stepped into the shower, fully dressed. She then undressed under cover of the opaque glass and showered. Taking her time. All the while keeping an eye on the door. If it opened, if it so much as moved, she was going to rip the towel rod off the wall and beat whoever walked through that door. At least that was her plan.

But the door did not open and no pervert barged in. That didn't mean one wasn't watching her every move at some computer terminal, but for the moment, she showered in peace. And the water felt fantastic. At one point, she sat in the shower and let it drench her. Having spent twenty minutes under glorious water pressure, she cut it off and dressed once again behind the glass. Once clothed and smelling more human, she reappeared and continued sipping her electrolytes while she tried to think through her options.

She didn't have many.

Having cheated whomever was staring at her through the wall-mounted cameras out of a peek at her naked self, she defiantly folded her dress and stood tapping her foot. Waiting. She spoke, but there was little strength in it.

"I can do this all day."

Still no one appeared. Walking slowly toward the door, she spied the hallway. Which was clear. Without hesitation, she launched herself out the door, down the hallway, through the exit door, and out into the moonlight and the cool night air where—just as the possibility of freedom impressed its frail self upon her cranium—someone once again hit her. A two-by-four to the temple. She left her feet, perceived herself falling, and there in that slow-motion descent, someone once again turned out the lights.

She woke to high-noon daylight with the worst headache in the history of headaches. Against it she counted, ". . . three, four, five. Day 5." The reality struck her. "I've been in this place almost a week?" Surveying her room, she saw the bed had not changed. And the floor was still too far from her feet. Concrete warm. Room uncomfortable. Dress folded. Pits sweating. And she had to go to the bathroom. Things were dire. She really needed to go. She didn't care. Whoever was watching was about to get a show. She stood, walked to the toilet, and did what most every human on the planet does first thing in the morning. Given that she had not done that at all yesterday, this took a while. When finished, she stood, flushed, and returned to her bed, waiting for either her therapist to enter or the pervert who was holding her captive. But neither appeared.

The only thing different about the room was that next to her on the bed lay a stick of natural deodorant, a toothbrush, and a tube of toothpaste. *Weird* didn't begin to explain this. Above her came the sound of birds chirping. She couldn't see out the window—it was too high above her—but it sat open. Cracked. Letting outside sound and air in.

The sound of birds singing was a strange comfort, and she almost smiled. She stood, walked down the hall to the exit door, and swung it open, revealing the forest. But rather than bolting through, she stood, staring out into the trees. Next to her on the wall hung a mirror at neck height, which reflected her distraught face and the metal hoop. With one difference. The green light was now red.

She turned toward the door and once again read the sign above it: "Whatever you do, do not walk through this door." She leaned slightly through the imaginary line of the threshold, and the hoop light began to flash. Another inch and the hoop beeped. Something she'd never heard before. Two more inches and the hoop pulsed slightly. Like a phone receiving an incoming text. Another few inches and the pulsing was accompanied by the slightest of electronic shocks. Almost imperceptible. A few more inches and the shock grew in intensity, as did the beeping. Sort of like a TENS unit physical therapists use for muscle rehab. Another step and both increased again. None of which she'd remembered from the last two times it had knocked her out.

Any drug addiction is difficult to break. Opiate addiction maybe more so. Detaching from its hooks brings with it a substantial amount of mental haze, disorientation, and no small amount of fight. All of which she'd suffered before, and all of which were now affecting her ability to make sense of the door and the hoop. Not to mention this sterile place, which, while strange, also felt oddly familiar. Something about the trees and the smell suggested she'd been here before.

She whispered to herself, "We are not in Kansas anymore, Toto."

With about six inches to go before the electronic shock issued another brachial stun, turning out her lights and rendering her unconscious for the better part of three to five minutes, she heard a voice over the intercom. The voice was computerized to disguise the speaker's identity but had been programmed to sound like a man.

He cleared his throat. "Mrs. Joe Sue . . ."

The voice startled her, and she jumped, slipping closer to the edge.

His voice again. "Wouldn't do that if I was you."

The echo of his voice brought her attention to the multiple speakers mounted in most every corner and hallway. And while there were umpteen speakers, there were twice as many cameras, which, while she was no technology guru, looked to be cutting edge. How new? She had no idea, but they were small, sleek, and similar to the almost invisible 5K versions installed in her home along the Pacific.

She stiffened. Analyzing the voice. And the fact that it suggested someone was watching her in real time. A minute passed while she considered the safety of her room or a conversation with him. Or her. Or whoever it was. Then she remembered the cameras in her room. The voice didn't sound threatening, but what did that mean? She'd taken a few self-defense classes on three different set locations. Not to mention that in one role she'd played a rogue government agent and spent three months training with former operatives.

"What is this place?" she asked.

The voice crackled over the speakers, which echoed around her. "Home." A pause. "At least for a little while."

She froze. "How do I get out?"

The voice again. "Do you mean out of this predicament or out of this building?"

"I'll settle for the building."

"Press that button. Or turn right and walk up the stairs."

She turned to her left and read "PRESS FOR EXIT" above a bright silver button about the size of a dinner plate. Similar to those used in hospitals.

When she pressed it, the hoop light turned green, a low, pleasant bell sounded, and the door automatically opened. Feet from freedom, she took one step, then another, and finally a third. Waiting for the knockout blow that did not arrive. Now, well beyond the reach of the door's invisible fence, she studied the world into which she'd walked.

She needed about half a second to determine this was not the arid desert of Seven Pines. This was an ancient forest surrounded by trees a hundred and twenty feet tall and three to five feet in diameter. Beneath her feet was a carpet of evergreen needles that muted most sound.

She took a deep breath and turned, studying her prison. This was not Malibu, though possibly Northern California. The air held very little humidity and smelled clean. It was also completely quiet. Without thinking, she reached for the pill fob with one hand while raising the other and pointing with her index finger. "Excuse me, sir?"

"Yes."

"You mind telling me where I am?"

"Montana."

The word rattled around her brain. "Montana?"

"Correct."

"Why Montana?"

"Because logistically this worked and you'll be safe here."

She shook her head, trying to make sense of her present unreal reality. "Safe from who?"

"Yourself."

She pointed at herself. "Look, I know me and I'm not a danger to me."

"Yes, you are, which is why I'm holding you here."

"So, just to be clear, you are holding me."

"Yes."

"Against my will."

"For the time being."

The fact that she was having a conversation with an unknown voice did strike her as strange, but she wanted to keep him—if he was in fact a him—talking as long as possible. Both because it was an odd comfort to her and because she might learn something. "What is this facility?"

"Why don't you walk upstairs?"

"What's up there?"

"Your answer."

Her eyes narrowed. "Are you being smart with me? My head is splitting and I'm not in the mood."

A light clicked on in the hallway behind her, revealing a beautiful wooden spiral staircase that looked like something she'd seen in a picture before. "If I climb that thing, I'll puke. Too many turns."

"Then walk slowly."

One hand on the wall to guide her, she shuffled toward the stairs, climbed three, felt the spin, and sat down, leaning her head against the center post and closing her eyes while clinging to the post with both hands. She cleared her throat, trying to sound as unthreatening as possible. "Can you please tell me why I'm here?"

"Opiate addiction."

She nodded. "Very true. May I ask another question?"

"Yes."

"Many people find themselves addicted to Oxy. Why am I the only one here?"

The voice was quick in responding. "Great question. Probably best answered at the top of the stairs."

"You mean I have to get up there for this to make any sense?"

"Yes."

"So I'm free up there?"

"Not exactly."

"What do you mean?"

"You're free-er, not necessarily free."

"And whose idea was this?"

"Mine."

"Well, who are you?"

"I'm the person who brought you here."

"You admit that?"

"Of course."

"Why did you do that?"

"Wouldn't do me much good to lie about it."

"No, I appreciate your honesty, but I mean, why did you kidnap me?"

"You need help."

She nodded. "I don't disagree, but with all due respect, I'm not convinced this is exactly what I need either."

"Always a possibility. Regardless, this is where you are. Better make the most of it."

"Do I get any say-so in my own help?"

"After six trips to rehab at three grand a day, do you really think you're qualified to provide the solution to your problem?"

"I can tell you what didn't work."

"Let's be honest—nothing has worked."

"I can't really argue with you there." She climbed two more steps. "How long will I be here?"

"How long does it take to get un-addicted to Oxy?"

"Un-addicted?"

"What would you call it?"

She was having difficulty adjusting to the computerized voice. "That's just not very professional language."

"What makes you think I'm a professional?"

She pointed around her. "This place."

"Hate to break it to you, but I'm not an addiction professional."

"What are you?"

"Do you want to talk about me or your length of stay here?"

She considered this. "Both."

"Your length of stay is up to you but a month at a minimum. Probably more like three."

She opened both eyes and raised her voice. "Three months! Alone? Have you lost your ever-loving mind?"

A pause. "You're talking to a voice who's holding you captive against your will. Chances are good that something is wrong with me."

She did not argue this point. "What's going to happen to me?"

"That's up to you."

"Can I go home now?"

"You are home."

She didn't press it. "Okay, tell me about you."

"Probably a bit too soon for that."

"Are you the person who's been sending me texts and demanding money?"

"Probably a bit too soon for that one too."

"Are you going to hurt me?"

"No."

"How can I trust you?"

"You can't."

"Why should I believe you?"

"You shouldn't."

"So you *are* going to hurt me?"

"No."

"Wait. I'm confused. Are you or are you not going to hurt me?"

"I'm not going to hurt you."

"But I can't trust you or believe you, so I probably shouldn't believe that either."

"I get where you're coming from, but I'm not going to hurt you."

"Are you a man or woman?"

"Man."

"Have you ever done this with anyone else?"

"That falls into that same 'too early' category."

"What's your success and recidivism rate?"

"Same category."

"Why won't you show your face?"

"Because I don't want you to see it."

She wanted to ask him if he was a sick, perverted coward but didn't. Instead, he offered it. "And no, I'm not some sick pervert who intends to take advantage of you."

"That's comforting. I don't believe you."

"Suit yourself. Here's the deal. Some days we'll talk. Some days we won't. Food is and will be available at the top of the stairs. Along with most everything else. After the first week or ten days, I'll turn on the A/C controller in your room and you can adjust the temperature. Until then I control it, so get ready to sweat."

"Why are you doing that?"

"To rid your body of toxins."

"Why do you care about what toxins are in my body?"

"Same category."

"Do you work for my manager or therapist?"

"No."

"Is someone paying you to do this?"

"I know you have questions. One day I will answer them. This is not that day."

"So someone is paying you to do this? How much? Chances are good I can pay more."

"No one is paying me."

"Okay, let's just skip all this. How much?"

"I don't want money."

"Everybody has a price."

"I tend to agree with you, but I do not."

She let it go, knowing she needed to keep him talking. She climbed three more steps and continued resting her head on the post. "What am I supposed to do?"

"Get clean."

"Can I ask one more?"

"Sure."

"Do you have my phone?"

"Sort of."

"What do you mean 'sort of'?"

"Too many people are looking for that phone, so I've forwarded your communication to another number and destroyed yours."

"Are you reading my texts?"

"Yes."

"Do you understand what's going on?"

"Yes."

"Then you realize how important it is that I respond to them?"

"I realize how important you believe it to be."

She raised her voice. "I don't think you understand." She shook her head. "They have my baby."

"I'm well aware of that."

"Then you're cold and heartless."

"I've been called worse, but you're going to have to trust me on this one."

"Trust you?"

"Yes."

"This coming from a man who kidnapped me, is currently holding me captive, and won't show his face?"

"Correct."

"What do I call you?"

"You don't."

"Can I come up with my own name?"

"If you must."

She was starting to get edgy. "How about Prison?" She chuckled. "To remind you where you're going when I get out of here."

"Great."

"You know, people are looking for me right now. Talented people. And they'll find me."

His tone was matter-of-fact. "I know."

"You know they'll find me?"

"I know they're talented."

"And you think you're more talented?"

"I think they'll find you when I want them to."

"How'd you get me here?"

"I drove you."

"You drove me from California to Montana?"

"Sort of."

"Define 'sort of.'"

"There was a plane wedged in between two cars."

"You flew me on a plane?"

"Yes."

"You own a plane?"

"Didn't say that."

"You stole a plane?"

"Borrowed."

"And it never crossed your mind to sexually assault me?"

"It crossed my mind frequently, minus the assault part."

"Why didn't you?"

A pause. "I have my reasons."

"Care to share?"

"In time."

"Look, you seem like a nice enough fellow. Why don't you just open the gate, and I'll go one way and you go the other? Give you a forty-eight-hour head start. You can get away. No one is the wiser."

"And how long would it take you to start the pills again?"

"What if I promised?"

"How many times have you made that same promise?"

She nodded. "A lot."

"See what I mean?"

"Why do you care?"

"I have my reasons."

"Which you're not going to share."

"In time."

Despite the weirdness of this whole thing, the sound of his voice was a strange comfort. She pressed him to keep him talking. "Have we ever met?"

A pause. "Do you honestly think I'd kidnap you, drag you out in the middle of nowhere, and hold you prisoner if we had not?"

"I'm not sure I follow that logic. So you're saying we have met?"

"I'm saying I have reason to be doing what I'm doing."

"Which is?"

"In time."

"You're really not going to tell me, are you?"

"In time."

"You keep saying that."

"That's because it's the best answer."

"Do the cameras in my room work?"

"Yes."

"So you can see me shower, dress, undress, etc."

"Not exactly. The cameras are blocked by the opaque glass. Anytime you want privacy, stand in the shower."

"But you'd like to see me naked?"

"Of course. So would most of the civilized world."

"Why haven't you?"

"Same category."

"You gay?"

Laughter. "No. Not gay."

"You sure?"

"Yes, I'm sure."

"Okay, at least throw me a bone. Why are you doing this?"

A pause. "Does it need to be done?"

She laughed. "What, the getting-clean part or the kidnapped-and-taken-captive?"

"Let's just stick with the getting-clean part."

"Of course."

"Then you have your answer."

"Well, begging your pardon, but who died and made you God?"

"There it is, and it only took you fifteen minutes to ask me." A laugh. "One day I will answer that, but—"

"I know, 'This is not that day.' So are you always watching me?"

"I do have a life outside of this one."

"What do you do?"

"I'm an architect."

"Seriously?"

"'Course I'm not serious. You really think I'm going to tell you?"

"It was worth a shot." She raised her finger again. "You know, you sound like a reasonable, likable guy. Are you sure we can't work out some sort of deal? I do have a lot of money."

"I don't want your money."

"A million dollars."

"Nope."

"Five million."

"You're not a very good negotiator."

"What do you mean?" she asked.

"You don't jump from one to five so quickly."

"What does it matter? It's all the same to me."

"No. Not five million."

"Ten?"

"No."

"You don't sound quite so resolved."

"No to ten."

"Twenty?"

"No."

"Is there a number?"

"Thirty."

"Thirty million?"

"Thirty days."

"What?"

"Thirty days clean."

"That's all? Thirty days in this place, no drugs, and you're going to let me walk out the front door having not been molested by you?"

"You're still stuck on the molested part."

"Wouldn't you be?"

A pause. "I get your point."

"Well?"

"Correct."

"'Correct' what?"

"Correct. Thirty days. Ninety on the outside. And you walk out of here."

"You're not a very good negotiator either."

"Possibly. But you're five down, eighty-five to go."

"I thought you said thirty."

"Okay. Twenty-five to go."

"You do realize I've done the whole thirty-day clean thing six times now. Chances are good I got this."

"According to the tabloids, there was a seventh."

She smiled. He was sneaky. "They actually got that right. But"—she shrugged again—"how many times does it take?"

"Evidently more than seven." A pause. "And let's be honest, you don't got this."

Her hand unconsciously felt for the fob. She nodded. "This is true." She tried to throw him off guard. "You ever killed anybody?"

"Same category."

She pressed him. "But it's possible?"

He turned it on her. "Have you?"

"Have I what?"

"Ever killed anyone?"

"Of course not."

He answered her question. "But is it possible?"

She saw the logic. "Okay, let me ask it this way. Have you ever caused physical harm to another human being that they did not invite or deserve?"

"Do car wrecks count?"

She hadn't thought about that. "You know what I mean."

A pause. "We're in a gray area there."

"How so?"

"'Deserve' is difficult to measure."

"Okay, let me ask it this way. Do I deserve to be harmed by you?"

"You're still stuck on this 'being harmed by me' thing."

"Wouldn't you be?"

"Not really. I'm not as attractive as you."

"Funny. Now answer my question."

"No, you do not deserve to be harmed by me. Not by a long shot."

That last phrase was the first opening he'd given her. "What makes you say that?"

"Dinner will be in an hour."

"That's it? But we were just starting to get to know one another."

"There will be plenty of time for that."

"What's for dinner?"

"What would you prefer?"

"Are you serious?"

"Yes."

"You're really going to let me make a dinner request?"

"You can request it. Doesn't mean you'll get it. But I'll try."

"Are you sure you don't work for my manager? This sounds exactly like something she'd set up."

"Positive."

"How are you at fettuccine Alfredo?"

"Fine, so long as it looks like noodles with olive oil."

"Sautéed spinach?"

"Don't press your luck."

"That's not difficult. Throw it in a pan with a little water. Put a lid on it."

"I'll see what I can do."

"That's all I get?"

"Would you like something else, Your Highness?"

"Look, you're the one who kidnapped me. I didn't do this. I was minding my own business."

"I'm waiting."

"Asparagus?"

"I can do that."

"Salad?"

"Not tonight."

"Why not?"

"Because I'm already cooking the entire produce aisle."

"By the way, have you seen my award? Little golden statue dude."

"Yes."

"Where is it?"

"Safekeeping."

"Could I have a newspaper?"

"No."

"Book?"

"Sure. Go to the library."

She tried to sound impressed. "This place has a library?"

"You're stalling."

"Yes, I am. But who else am I going to talk to?" A pause. "Where's the library?"

"You'll figure it out soon enough."

"What if I get hurt?"

"Don't."

"But what if?"

He could see where she was going. "Suck it up."

"But let's say—"

He cut her off. "Let's don't."

"So you don't really have a plan for that."

"Nope."

"And you admit that?"

"Doesn't change your situation."

"Did you know I'm allergic to bee stings?"

He knew she was not. "Don't get stung."

She paused, finally asking her big question. "Have they attempted to contact me?"

There was no need to beat around the bush. "Yes."

"What'd you say?"

"Same category."

Her voice cracked. "I don't think you understand."

He didn't respond.

"What? No snappy comeback?"

Still no response. Her head was splitting. And the nausea was growing worse. She shook her head. Between the ache, the cravings, the withdrawals, and the rising frustration, she wasn't sure if she'd awakened in Alice's wonderland or a bad dream.

She studied her surroundings, looking for an exit, and whispered to herself, "I am a prisoner in a nuthouse with a complete nutjob."

He laughed but made no other audible response.

She'd heard enough. She climbed the remaining five steps, stretched out on the floor, closed her eyes, and placed her palm flat on the wall to force the world to quit spinning. When it did not, her body revolted and she rolled on her side to empty what little remained in her stomach, followed by several dry heaves, which only served to increase the pressure in her head.

Wiping her chin, she pointed. "You're cleaning that up."

CHAPTER 11

BEFORE

After months working his fingers to the bone, Syd returned. Again. This time he jetted Joe off to a cabin in Beaver Creek, Colorado. Said he thought a week on the slopes might do them good. In truth, they seldom saw the snow.

Syd, who'd been training in jiu-jitsu, told Pockets he could handle the "protection," so Pockets watched from a distance. Checking in when needed. Late in the week, a late-night knock occurred. Pockets opened the door to find Syd standing with two beers. He gave one to Pockets and let himself in. "Pockets, my man, how's things?"

He looked around Syd for Joe. Not seeing her, he said, "Who's watching Joe?"

Syd waved him off. "She's napping." Syd swigged his beer. "You happy with your job?"

Pockets was Syd's senior by a decade. With a slightly different build. Where Syd was taller, Pockets was thicker. He was also quicker, but that wouldn't matter for some time. "I am."

Syd shut the door behind him. "Pockets, how long have I employed you?"

Syd's tone of voice emphasized "I" over "you." "Ten months."

"Given your trustworthiness . . ." Syd nodded. "I need to add to your duties."

Pockets set the beer down.

"I'm going to be working in Hawaii for a couple months, and I need you to keep a little more diligent eye on Joe for me. Send me frequent updates."

"You mean about doctors' appointments et cetera?"

Syd shook his head. "Sort of. Not really. More like movement. Who she's hanging with. Friends. Where she goes." His voice changed in intonation, suggesting he was asking Pockets to do something without asking him. Read between the lines. He attempted a fist bump. "Know what I mean, bro?"

Pockets quit beating around the bush. "You want me to spy for you?"

Syd swigged, surprised he'd so quickly been called on the carpet. "I wouldn't call it that."

"What would you call it?"

"Heightened surveillance." He paused. "Joe can be naive, and I don't want her putting herself in danger. Since I won't be around, I need you to be my eyes and ears."

"You want my answer now?"

Syd looked further surprised. "I didn't realize the request was up for discussion. I pay you to do a job."

Pockets held the door open. "The answer is no. Find someone else."

Syd finished his beer, then returned to the door. "Leave the keys on your way out."

Syd returned to his condo, where things were quiet for about fifteen minutes. Pockets was loading his car when he heard angry voices and glass breaking. Letting himself in, he found Joe hunkered in a corner, knees pulled into her chest, and Syd, who had now moved to whiskey, standing across the room. One hand on the fireplace. Teetering.

On the floor between them lay shattered pieces of what was once a lamp. From the looks of it, Joe had thrown it. Syd spotted Pockets. His words were slightly slurred. "Thought I fired you."

Pockets never took his eyes off Joe. "You did."

Syd lifted his glass. "There's the door."

"Yes, sir. Just thought maybe I'd let one of you sleep at my condo tonight. Sometimes it helps to cool down."

Syd stepped briskly up to Pockets, set his glass down, and swung in one motion. Despite being drunk, his movements were fast and measured. Pockets sidestepped and dodged the haymaker while not swinging in return. "Mr. Syd, I think maybe—"

Syd, who'd studied boxing and martial arts for several roles and worked out with a trainer five days a week, was having none of it. He swung again with the same result. Swing and a miss. On the third attempt, Pockets caught his fist and held it midair.

"Mr. Syd. I'm just—"

Realizing his punches were not making contact and that he was now caught in a vise grip, Syd lunged, attempting to take Pockets to the ground. Whereas Syd was more bull in a china shop, Pockets was more cat, so he stepped backward, pressed Syd's head and shoulders to the carpet, and then, straddling his helpless body, pinned one arm behind Syd's back, levering it up in an unnatural direction like a chicken wing. The pain got Syd's attention. As did the carpet burn across his nose and forehead.

Pockets spoke softly. "Mr. Syd, sometimes we say and do things we later regret. Might be good if I helped you down the hall. Sober up a bit."

Syd was cussing and kicking with little effect. Every third word an expletive. "Get off me, old man."

Pockets didn't move. "Yes, sir. I will."

"Get off me now, you arthritic, Geritol—"

Pockets stood, as did Syd, but Pockets didn't let go of his arm. He maintained upward pressure and sent Syd tumbling toward the door. Syd stumbled, grabbed his phone and jacket, and was making a call as he closed the door. Moments later, a black Range Rover stopped outside. Syd stepped in and the SUV sped into the night.

Joe half smiled. "What'd you do to make him so mad?"

"He asked me to spy on you."

"Thought so." A pause.

"I told him no."

"I gathered that." She laughed. "He doesn't do well with people who don't do what he tells them."

Pockets surveyed the room. "Yeah, I gathered that." He began picking up the broken pieces. "Maybe I better hang here a while. Just in case . . ."

She pulled on a jean jacket. "I got a better idea."

Pockets waited.

"I'm starving and you just beat up my dinner date, so why don't we grab some pizza and give him some time to cool off."

A while later, sitting cross-legged in the booth, she pressed him. Her tone of voice suggested she was impressed with Pockets's evasion tactics. "Syd doesn't like losing." She raised an eyebrow.

Pockets took a bite of his pizza and spoke with his mouth full. "Permission to speak freely?"

"Granted."

"No offense, mum, but your husband is an idiot."

She chuckled. "He can make life difficult for you. He's very well connected."

"I'm sure he is."

"No kidding. All he has to do is make a phone call."

"I'll be all right."

"You sure?"

He continued eating.

She leaned her elbows on the table and rested her chin on her palms. She was concerned he wasn't taking her seriously. "You need to listen to me. He's made political friends. Had dinner at the White House."

Pockets studied his pizza, considering what to reveal and to what extent. "Mum . . . your husband's influence does not bother me. Nor does he."

"He studies jiu-jitsu. Has for years. It's how he got into acting."

Still no response.

She had brought him to a local honky-tonk complete with country music, peanut shells on the floor, worn dance floor, and frozen pizza prepared to order. She raised an eyebrow. "You would not be the first guy to underestimate him."

"Yes mum."

"He brags about bar arms and dislocating elbows and breaking knees."

"It's called an arm bar." He tapped the table with a finger. "May I ask a question?"

She sat up. "By all means."

"Why Syd?"

She stared at the spinning disco ball. "I am admittedly not a good judge of men." A moment passed while she studied Pockets. "We met on set. He was somebody. I was not. He's also good at pretending. It's what makes him good at his job. He swept me off my feet, convinced me I was special. Punched all the right buttons. Spoke into all my"—she raised her hands, making quotations marks with her fingers—"'daddy issues.' I thought he was someone else."

He sipped his soda water.

She tried to crack a joke. "Gotta be careful around those actors. Never quite sure who you're going to get."

Pockets made no response.

"Pockets, you're like a sphinx. I can't read you." She laughed, admitting what many had already suspected. "I have become what I did not want to be."

"What's that?"

"A trophy wife."

"I'm sorry. I didn't mean to suggest . . ."

She waved him off. "The tabloids have been writing about it for months." She pointed to his soda water. "How do you drink that? Just makes me want to burp."

He lifted his glass. "Because I like it."

"Isn't it better with something in it?"

"Depends on your definition of 'better.'"

When they returned home, Pockets unlocked her door to find the condo empty. She spoke over her shoulder. "You mind hanging around? He's a belligerent drunk with a terrible memory, and when he sobers up, he has a tendency to return to the scene of the crime and grovel because he needs to remind himself what he should apologize for."

"No problem." He paused. And then he did not say what he wanted to say.

She raised a hand. "I know. But can we hold off on that conversation?"

He nodded.

She continued, "Syd is two people. One I love. And one . . ." She shook her head. "He does not like it when people get the better of him. And you did."

"I realize that."

"Probably won't be the last time he comes at you."

"I realize that too."

She walked to her bedroom and leaned against the door. "Despite what you see on the screen, Syd number two is not kind to those who don't do what he expects."

When he spoke, his voice was calm and he was staring out the window and into a memory. "I quit being afraid a long time ago."

She paused. Standing several seconds at the door. "Teach me sometime?"

He considered this. "It's not something you teach."

"What then?"

"You face it. Run headlong into it."

She studied him. He was different. Unlike anyone she'd met or known. Honest. Without pretension. Hundreds, maybe thousands of guys would give their left arms to be in his position, here with her. Within an arm's reach of otherworldly fame. Famous by association. And he could take it or leave it. Proximity to her did not define him. But proximity from her did. "Might need help with that."

"Yes mum."

CHAPTER 12

AFTER

Day 6 cast an amber hue across her sweaty body, suggesting afternoon had come and gone. She watched the shadows descend the wall only to be replaced by darkness and then more iridescent shadows as the moon rose bright. She was too tired to get up and walk around, and too sure she'd vomit more if she did. So she lay still with her eyes closed, promising herself she would sue this person when she got out of here. There was a reason cold turkey was not recommended. She also knew not to roll to her right as she'd tumble down the spiral staircase— the thought of which reminded her of that teacup ride at Disney.

It had been a while since she sat still enough to watch the time pass. She was tired and her eyelids heavy, and incredibly thirsty. Without moving, she asked, "May I have some water?"

The voice was quick in responding. "To your left."

Her fingers found the bottle and broke the seal, and she sipped. Sparkling. Her favorite.

She was both terrified and annoyed, but she would not let herself fall asleep. Through the early morning hours of Day 7 she fought it, but somewhere in the second watch, she lost the battle, curled up, and drifted off. She had made it through the first week. *Come what may.*

Midmorning daylight startled her and brought her back. She rubbed her eyes and wished for a painkiller to numb her need for a painkiller. Something to medicate her need to medicate. During her other stints in rehab, at about this point in the process they gave her something to lessen the withdrawal timeline. Usually either methadone or buprenorphine. She rubbed her eyes but did not open them.

"Could I get a Tylenol or something?"

No response.

She spoke again. "You're bordering on cruel. My whole body aches. I didn't sleep well. I sweated through my clothes. It's Africa-hot in here, and I'm pretty sure I'm running a fever. Not to mention the fact that"— she touched her carotid and counted—"my pulse is elevated, my nose is running, and my stomach is a wreck." She waved her hands at the cameras. "Hello? Anybody home? These are classic signs. Things don't get better from here. I'm in full withdrawal, and you're starting to piss me off!" She threw the empty bottle at the nearest camera. "And how about some breakfast!" She was shouting now. "With coffee!"

No sooner had she finished speaking than his voice sounded. "Sit up."

She was not in the mood for his monotonal and one-sided games. "What?"

"Take a look around."

She pulled onto her side, slid to an upright position, and braced herself for the piercing light that was soon to split her cranium the second she opened her eyes. When she did, she was pleasantly surprised.

A beautiful wooden table, large enough for a dozen people, sat across the room. Beyond that was a large glass wall. And on the table, a plate. Poached eggs. Spinach. Avocado. Fresh-cut fruit including blueberries, strawberries, and mango. Fresh English muffin. Butter and raspberry jam. She stared at the steam rising off the plate. But the thing that caught her eye was the pour-over. Still dripping. The smell of coffee permeated the room.

She crawled across the floor, pulled herself up on the counter, poured herself a cup, and leaned against the counter, sipping. As the caffeine hit her bloodstream, the first drug she'd ingested in seven days, life returned to her head, partially clearing her vision. Staring at the room, she realized she'd not slept on the floor next to the stairwell. She'd slept on a couch. A nice leather couch. Which meant someone had carried her from the top of the stairwell to said couch. Which also meant whoever was keeping her captive was strong enough to do that. Not that she was heavy by any means, but carrying a hundred-and-thirty-pound person across a room and setting them on a couch without disturbing their sleep was not something she could do without much difficulty. She also noticed a blanket and a pillow. With the world starting to spin again, giving rise to that unsettled feeling in her stomach, she shuffled back to the couch and lay down, wrapping herself in the blanket, which was new, fleece, and quite cozy.

She spoke with her eyes closed. "I think I will call you Houdini."

Laughter over the intercom.

She slowly sat up and sipped her coffee, but her head was splitting and the muscle aches were a real thing. She had been down this road before and didn't like it the first, second, third, or seventh time. As the sweats returned, she said, "I don't suppose you have any Probuphine, lofexidine, or clonidine?" She mimicked her last therapist. "'They're marginally effective but they do seem to limit symptomatic response.'" She tapped the neck collar with her finger. "And is this really necessary? I've seen documentaries where they do this to monkeys." She shook her head. "Never works out well for the primate. Plus"—she pointed at her head—"repeated head trauma has been proven detrimental to one's health."

His voice cracked through the static. "The size of the retention device is uncomfortable for a reason. It's a reminder. I don't want you tempted."

"So you are paying attention?"

He seemed amused. "Vaguely."

She scratched her head. "Retention device. That's what you call it?"

"Yes."

"How about medieval torture device." She pointed to the food. "How'd you get in here?"

"It's not difficult."

She studied her surroundings, held the mug with both hands, and sipped. "So how's your day going?"

"I brought you some medicine."

"Where?"

A box of Alka-Seltzer Hangover Relief sat on the kitchen counter.

She studied the box. "You're kidding." But she also noticed the granite countertops, which reminded her of her own.

He made no response.

"This is not medicine."

"Take it or leave it."

She crawled across the floor, dropped four tabs in a glass of water, let them dissolve, and chugged the milky, effervescent contents.

He spoke as she drank. "You need to know that there will be times I'll be gone for a few days, but I will be back."

"What?"

He spoke slowly, enunciating every word. "I. May. Be. Gone. A. Few. Days."

"Why? Where are you going?"

"Not here."

"How long will you be gone?"

"Few days."

"What if I have a seizure?"

"Don't have one."

"In the past, cold-turkey withdrawals have sent me into seizures. Jaw lock. Foam at the mouth. Bite my tongue. It's not pretty." She raised her voice. "Which is why professionals administer medication to people like me."

He knew this, too, was not true. "I'm terribly sorry."

"You're enjoying this, aren't you?"

"Not in the least."

She heard rustling in the background. "What are you doing?"

"Clipping coupons. Kidnapping someone is expensive."

Looking around, she began to question her surroundings, which looked vaguely familiar. "Where am I?"

"You don't remember?"

She stood and rubbed her eyes. That's when it hit her. "I'm in my home?" Another two seconds and it became clear. "I'm in my home."

"Correct."

Clarity was returning. "You kidnapped me and are holding me in my own Montana cabin?"

"Yes."

"Why?"

"No footprint. It runs on solar and generators. Sits on ample acreage. And given that you kept it a secret from everyone, no one knows to look here. Seemed logical to me."

"Evidently it wasn't a total secret."

"What makes you say that?"

"Um . . . you brought me here."

"Public record. Just had to know where to look and under what name."

"How'd you know to look there?"

"Did my homework."

She waved her hand around the room. "Do I get to leave this room?"

"Yes."

"So I can wander the house and this thing"—she fingered the collar—"isn't going to knock me out?"

"Correct. Just don't wander more than fifty feet from the perimeter of the structure or it will."

"That's my boundary? Fifty feet?"

"Correct."

"Why don't you just say yes like normal humans?"

"Yes."

"Funny." The Alka-Seltzer was doing little to take the edge off. "Houdini, I really don't like you right now."

"Look on the bright side."

"I can't wait to hear this."

"I could have taken you anywhere, yet you're a prisoner in your own home. That should give you some comfort."

"And just what do you want me to do with that information?"

"Take comfort."

"Oh yeah. Right. I feel so much better. This just keeps getting creepier and freaking me out more by the second." The knowledge that he was holding her in her own cabin explained a lot. He could work and sleep in the annexed building that served as an art studio and security monitoring station. From there, her captor could cook and prepare meals that he or she, but probably he, then served to her via the lazy Susan, which had been installed by the former owner to pass food back and forth between the indoor and outdoor kitchens.

Six hours later, at 2:00 a.m. on Day 8, she did in fact have a seizure. Her body locked up, and she began choking on her tongue. Thirty seconds later, she began foaming at the mouth. The foam spilled out between her locked lips and trickled down both cheeks. This continued for two minutes and included eye flutter, banging her head on the mattress, and a violent leg kick accompanied by a low gurgle that suggested her airway had been shut off. At the three-minute mark, her body fell limp, her head rolled to one side, and her lips appeared blue.

No rescue came and no one barged in the door.

At the ten-minute mark, she raised her head and threw up her arms. "Have you no heart? What is this sick place? You're really not going to help me, are you?"

"No, but you should get an award for that. I was almost convinced."

"So you just sat there and watched the whole thing like some voyeur?"

He said nothing.

"Well?"

"Yes."

She had grown testy. "Why? What pleasure do you derive from watching me suffer?"

"You weren't suffering."

"But you didn't know that."

"Yes. I did."

"I cannot believe you sat there and didn't offer to help me."

He paused. "I've seen seizures. That wasn't one."

She wiped the Alka-Seltzer foam off her cheeks. "How'd you know?"

"I've seen your movies."

During one role, she'd played a strung-out prostitute who suffered a seizure at the movie's climax. To produce foam, the director had used part of an Alka-Seltzer. "Oh. Do you have a favorite?"

"Yes. Now please go to sleep. I'd like to do the same."

This was his second admission. Which did not slip by her. "You sleep only when I do?"

"Yes."

"So if I stay awake forty-eight hours, you will too?"

"No."

"But you just said—"

"I'll shoot you in the neck with a dart gun long before that."

"You wouldn't dare."

"Good night."

She climbed back into bed. "Still don't like you, Houdini."

"Probably a good idea."

She straightened. Tried to sound tough. "People are looking for me."

"No." He paused. "The whole world is looking for you."

This comforted her but not as much as knowing he knew this. "That doesn't bother you?"

"Not really."

"So you've done this before? You're a pro?"

"We've already covered that."

"How many times?"

He ignored her. "Good night."

She pointed at the camera. "I'm not saying good night to some sick miscreant Houdini holding me against my will."

He laughed. "I don't blame you."

Minutes passed while she sat in darkness and silence. The heat in her room was intolerable. It had to be close to ninety degrees. "It's hot as hell in here."

He made no response.

She lay on the bed, sticking to the sheets. "Could I please have some air-conditioning?"

Still no response.

"How about a fan?"

Crickets.

Her head was splitting. Body aching. And while she'd made it eight days, the cravings and her need for narcotics were not lessening. She felt as though someone had plugged her into an electrical outlet. Having had enough, she stood, turned on a light, and pointed at the camera. "We'll see how tough you are."

With that, she stripped to her birthday suit. Totally naked. Spinning in a circle, she put herself on display for the cameras. What the world had been clamoring for, begging for, offering her large sums of money for, she gave him—out of spite. For several minutes, she stared into the four cameras staring down at her. Finally, she lay down on the bed, put a T-shirt over her eyes to block out the light, and attempted to sleep. Having covered nothing.

A minute later, cold air blew into the room, washed over her body, dried the sweat on her skin, and raised goose bumps. She spoke without lifting her head. "Thank you."

Still no response. And still she did not cover herself.

She chuckled, sat up, and looked into the cameras. "Oh come on, you know you're enjoying this." She threw a flip-flop at the camera. Followed by tears. Proving how unstable she had become. "It's why guys like you do things like this. Your own private peep show. Admit it! It's what you've been wanting the entire time. Meantime, really bad people walk free and get away with stealing someone's child."

A pause. "You would do well to eat a cheeseburger."

"Now just what do you mean by that?"

"You're skinny."

She waved him off. "Occupational hazard. Cameras add weight. Make you look bigger on-screen than you are in life."

The voice did not sound convinced. "Mm-hmm."

"Okay, maybe I am, but if you must know, I've been a bit stressed lately, and every time I eat something, my stomach rejects it."

"That's TMI."

"You asked."

"No. I didn't."

"Well, you intimated."

"Nope. Didn't do that either. I just offered you an opinion."

"Only after staring at me."

A pause. "True."

"So you did stare?" His nonresponse suggested that, possibly for the first time, she had him on the ropes in their mental jousting. "Just admit it."

Seconds later, the light clicked off while cold air continued to fill the room.

CHAPTER 13

BEFORE

Work had brought her to New York City. A break in filming offered a few hours off. Hence, the drive. Pockets parked the car and waited for further instruction. Joe tapped him on the arm. She was giddy. "Come on. You might need to do this one day."

The jewelry district in New York City is home to some of the finest diamond cutters in the world. Not to mention some of the rarest and most beautiful jewelry ever crafted. They rode the elevator down, and when they reached the metal detectors and the security desk, Pockets presented his State of New York and New York City carry permits—both of which were rare. Fort Knox wasn't this well guarded.

The guard looked at him and shook his head. "Those don't work in here."

Pockets knew better than to argue. Doing so would get him nowhere. Plus, the kind of people who posed a threat to Joe weren't making it through this checkpoint and all three of the locked doors coming up. He deposited his Glock in a safe and kept the key, at which point the guard entered a few keystrokes and the first magnetic door opened. Only after he and Joe had walked through and the door had closed and locked behind them did the guard enter more keystrokes, unlocking the second door that emptied onto the first of the jewelers' floors. The building was ten or twelve stories of nothing but jewelers. Most owned mines in Africa, or partnered with them, which removed all middlemen and provided vertical integration from source to finger. Or chest. Or ear. Or . . . you get the point.

Joe wound through the building but her internal GPS wasn't very good. In fact, her sense of direction was terrible. Finally, she turned to Pockets and held up the business card. "I'm trying to get us here."

Pockets pointed up.

She looked at the elevators, then back at the card. "Oh."

When they exited the elevator, a smallish woman in her midsixties met them. Pockets didn't know much about jewelry, but he had a feeling that whatever she was wearing was worth more than he made in a year. Maybe five years. She extended her hand to Joe. "So glad to see you again." She gestured to another glass door behind her. "Please."

When they approached, someone unseen pressed a button that unlocked a third magnetic lock, opening to a small glass room. When that door locked behind them, the last door was manually unlocked and opened by a man wearing white gloves, speaking in a sophisticated foreign accent, and welcoming Joe into a showroom where everything sparkled.

Accompanied by the lady, Joe wandered the room, trying on piece after piece. Bracelet, earrings, necklace—it was Cinderella's dream. Finally, she zeroed in on a simple necklace. Five diamonds. A carat each. Stacked vertically on top of each other. She clasped it about her neck and admired it in the mirror. Turning this way, then that. The lady approved.

Joe turned to Pockets. "You like?"

"Yes mum."

She smiled. "But would you buy it?"

"That depends."

"On?"

"Two things. First, the cost."

She laughed. Then she told him.

"Mum, I can't afford the sales tax on that."

"And the second thing?"

"The reason."

She touched each stone with her fingertips. And when she spoke, tears appeared. "One for each."

That's when he understood. "Then yes mum. I would. And I'd mortgage the house if need be."

She turned to the lady. "Can I wear it out?"

CHAPTER 14

BEFORE

She was filming a cop drama in and around Austin. Pockets had worked out and eaten breakfast but the sun wouldn't rise for another hour when his phone rang. He could tell she was on speakerphone. "You busy?"

"No mum."

"Top floor." A chuckle. "You're needed."

The elevator doors opened into her suite, which consumed the entire floor. He navigated the foyer, stepping around people scurrying to and fro, carrying clothing, props, bagels, espresso, and a tarp, which spiked his curiosity. Based on their facial expressions and the speed with which they moved, everybody was behind schedule. Given the hour and the fact that the sun had yet to rise, he wondered why these people weren't asleep. While he'd been around the filming of movies for several years now, he still didn't understand the rationale.

He turned a corner and found her sitting in what looked like a barber chair. Leaned back. Facing the ceiling. Mirror on the wall in front of her. Foam separators sticking up through the space between her toes caused them to look like the fingers on an inflated doctor's glove. Evidently, the pedicurist who had just finished her toes was now working on her hands.

Joe saw him out of the corner of her eye. "Oh, thank goodness. Can you grab that little bottle right there?"

The countertop was littered with five hundred little bottles. He pointed.

"No. Three left." He lifted it, and she said, "Yep. Now put that on my eyelashes."

He looked around, his head on a swivel. "Mum?"

A nod, then a glance at the clock. "I have to be downstairs in . . . twenty-seven minutes looking like a cross between Margaret Thatcher and Cruella de Vil."

He lifted the bottle. "I don't know anything about . . ."

"Then consider this on-the-job training." When he didn't move, she said, "Pockets, our makeup artist failed to show. I've been filming all night. I'm crazy tired, and you are my last hope." A fake smile. "Step closer. I'll walk you through it."

He looked to the lady painting her nails. "What about her?"

"She's busy."

He stood over her, holding the mascara bottle, unscrewed the top, and stood holding the small black brush.

"Great." She closed one eye. "Now just feather that on— Wait. See that little box next to those other bottles?"

He lifted a clear, thin container that looked like it could hold fishing lures.

"That's it. Okay, open it."

He did.

"See those lashes in number seven?"

The small case held fake eyelashes. Labeled one through eight. He nodded, trying to figure out where this ended up.

"Add a thin layer of glue and stick it on my eyelid."

"You've got to be kidding."

"Nope. And . . ." She eyed the wall. "Clock's ticking."

"You're serious."

"As a heart attack." She waited.

He lifted the lash with the tweezers, applied the thinnest line of glue he could, and then stood over her, trying to size up how they would best adhere to her eyelid.

She closed an eye and then spoke without moving her facial muscles. "Apply it straight across. Can't be crooked."

He studied the people moving in circles around him. "You sure you wouldn't rather—"

She opened both eyes. "Pockets. Shh. Just set it on my eyelid."

He did.

She blinked. Then again. "Now the other."

He repeated the process. She blinked, then lifted her head and studied herself in the mirror. "Perfect. Okay, while that's drying I need you to take that black liner and run a line across the top lid."

He grabbed the liner, pulled up a chair to help steady his hand, and spoke as he did what he'd seen makeup artists do to her a hundred times over. "When I woke this morning, this wasn't how I saw my day panning out."

She smiled. "Trust me. Me either."

He lined both eyes, and she said, "Lip liner."

He searched the counter, found it, and she did that thing women do with their lips when they're applying either lipstick or liner. He found this more challenging than the eyeliner.

When finished, she smacked her lips. "Great. Now, brush the lashes. They should be dry by now."

He pulled the brush out of the tube, then reinserted it several times to fill the brushes with the black stuff, then slowly and gently painted her enormous fake eyelashes. When he sat back, he said, "You look ridiculous."

She nodded. "Great. That's what we're shooting for. Now the other."

He complied.

She studied herself in the mirror and nodded. Surprised. "Pockets, you're a natural. Thanks, doll."

He tried to find an exit and whispered to himself, "Doll."

She extricated herself from the chair, waddled to her room, waved and called out "Toodles" over her shoulder, and disappeared.

Riding the elevator down, he found himself talking to himself. "I wonder if what happens in the makeup chair stays in the makeup chair."

Fortunately for her and yet unfortunately for him, it did not. Word spread. The crew began referring to him as "Doll" and asked if he was taking appointments.

The next morning, when his phone rang, he was summoned yet again for round two. To which he replied, "Not a chance."

"Please, Pockets! It's an emergency."

"Mum, a man's got to have his limitations."

"I promise I won't ask again."

"Given my experience with you, I highly doubt that."

"Okay, I'll try not to." She paused. "Pockets . . ."

He exited the elevator and found her in the same chair. This time, no pedicurist. Leaving her hands free. He waited for instructions. She sipped coffee and nodded at the same bottles he'd used yesterday morning. He objected quietly. "Mum, no offense, but can't you do it?"

She nodded. "Yes, I can, but . . ." She lifted her right hand, demonstrating the shake. There was no possible way she could apply eyeliner. Much less lip liner. The shake was a clear indication that she'd been using drugs to stay awake.

"How long have you been awake?"

Her eyes moved up and to the left. "I last slept Tuesday."

"It's Friday."

She nodded.

He pulled the cap and began slowly applying the liner to her eyes. "In my former life, we did that to people."

Her eyes were jittery. Like someone had plugged her into an electrical socket. "What?"

"Kept them awake."

"Why?"

He paused and spoke slowly. "To drive them crazy."

She spoke matter-of-factly, proving she was buzzing on something. "I can see how that would work." When he was finished with her face, she stood and raced off to her dressing room for costume change.

He stayed close during filming, knowing her battery would run out sooner rather than later. Which it did. She was in midsentence when he saw her knee buckle. He stepped in, steadied her, and said, "Mum, you're needed inside." He knew if he could get her moving, he maybe could get her upstairs.

She followed him but her eyes were glazed over. She was asleep and didn't know it. When the elevator doors opened, she stepped in but collapsed soon after. He caught and held her while the car rode to the suite. The doors opened and he carried her to her room, set her gently on her bed, and, given that it was 4:00 p.m., closed the blinds and covered her eyes with the blackout mask they give you on airplanes. Making her look a bit like Catwoman. Then he closed the door behind him, set a chair in front of it, and began his vigil.

Twenty minutes later, crew assistants came calling. He simply shook his head. Ten minutes after that, the director arrived, expressing a bit of attitude. Pockets politely declined. When the director tried to push past him, Pockets lifted him off his feet, pressed him against the wall, and told him, "Mrs. Joe does not want to be disturbed. You can resume tomorrow."

Ten minutes after the director left, two producers walked in, threatening to call the police and charging that Pockets was holding her hostage. Pockets stood, took off his jacket, loosened his tie, and began rolling up his sleeves. "Gentlemen, I understand you have a deadline. I can appreciate that. But your film is not my concern." He thumbed over his shoulder. "She is. And she has instructed me that no one is to enter that room. Period. You may resume filming tomorrow morning when she's rested, which she is not currently."

One of the producers tried to elbow his way past Pockets, which was a mistake. He found himself on his back with the wind knocked out of him.

Pockets spoke kindly and reiterated his timeline. "Tomorrow."

The producer nodded. From then on, everyone left him alone. At 10:00 p.m., he checked on her and found she'd not moved, so he combed through her bathroom, found her stash of drugs, kept looking and found a second, only to keep looking and find a third. He bagged them up and placed them in a small duffel, which he hid in a TV cabinet next to his chair. Throughout the night, he did not sleep but checked on her every hour.

At 7:00 a.m., her door cracked open and he found her staring down at him. Hair matted. Eyes puffy. Barely more than slits.

She whispered, "Coffee?"

CHAPTER 15

AFTER

By late afternoon on Day 9, the headache had subsided enough to allow her to move without nausea and the very real possibility of throwing up. She climbed off the couch and peered out the floor-to-ceiling window. It was the reason she'd bought the cabin in the first place, although "cabin" is a bit misleading.

She'd been on location. Filming. A western epic. Between the bison and the mountains and the cool air and the quiet and the cathedral of evergreens, she'd fallen in love. Asked Pockets to take her for a drive and stumbled upon a cabin. Introduced herself to an elderly widow working in the garden and accepted an invite to share a cup of tea. She signed the paperwork a few weeks later. Not even Syd knew about it.

The cabin was a couple thousand square feet. One story with a basement and a separate art studio. After purchasing, she'd made little alteration. Not feeling the need to update it, she chose to leave it as she found it. One small change, at Pockets's suggestion, had been security and surround sound—with which she was now being held captive.

The view off the porch spanned miles to the horizon. Nothing but mountains in the distance and buffalo sprinkled in the pasture below. Her isolation reminded her of that old Dustin Hoffman film *Papillon*, where they put all the prisoners on the island—and then leave them there. Forever. To fend for themselves. It also reminded her of walking in New York City. Nothing but concrete and asphalt with skyscrapers rising on either side. Minus the people of course. She'd been here only a few times. Alone.

She had tried, unsuccessfully, to rid herself of the need for medication. She'd come out here after the trial, after the divorce, to try to make sense of what made no sense. How had it all gone so poorly? She'd stay a few days or a week or two, then return. Driving herself. Feeling clean and free. But what pain she'd escaped waited for her upon her return, and her only answer was a pile of small pills chased by a few sips of liquid courage. A recurring thought never far from her mind. But every time she stared at the pile in her hand, *What if?* bubbled up. What if her baby was born, healthy and reaching for her? What then? Would her child grow up motherless as she had? Would she cheat her only child of a mother in the same way life had cheated her? This thought alone kept her up nights and caused her to eat the pills one by one rather than all at once. Death by a thousand cuts.

She had spent much of the night considering Houdini, and when morning broke, she had decided she was not afraid of him. Trust him? No. Not really. But if he was going to hurt her, she doubted he'd wait this long or do it like this. If he was going to do something horrible, she was pretty sure he'd have done it by now. She'd be the first to admit she possessed horrible judgment in men—just look at her track record, total yard sale—but she didn't think Houdini had it in him. What made her think that? When she looked inside, she found curiosity, not fear. And as strange as she knew it sounded, she liked talking with him. She found him honest in a sick and twisted sort of way. It reminded her of conversations she used to have. She'd heard somewhere about some syndrome where captives fall in love with their captors. Stockholm something or other. She guessed that, too, was a possibility. But after nine days with no chemicals, she was either thinking clearly or in the latter stages of losing her mind. Either was possible.

She climbed off the couch, wrapped the fleece blanket around her shoulders, and noticed someone had made coffee. In a coffeepot. Realizing her captor must have been close, she walked to the door leading to the porch. Leaning close to the door, she watched her neck-hoop light flash red and beep. Not wanting a repeat of the freight train that had taken her out on two previous occasions, she stepped back, only to notice that someone had recently mounted a large steel "Press Here" button. When she did, the door swung open, the light on her neck collar turned green, and she stepped out into the sun for the first time in more than a week.

Given the coffee, she assumed he was watching. Thanks to Pockets, this place had more cameras than Disney. Stretching her legs, she studied the world around her. Nothing but Montana forest. Outside of her thousand acres, she was surrounded by a million acres of national forest. She might as well be on the moon. The cabin had no power line, no phone line, no satellite subscription, no connection to the outside world. Even if she found a way to set fire to this entire place, she doubted anyone would rescue her before he whisked her away. Despite deciding she wasn't afraid of him, she reminded herself that he was her captor, and she had not asked for this. Nor had she agreed to it—although it could be worse. The mental gymnastics of her situation caused her to shake her head and return inside, where she scoured the kitchen for anything sharp. Heavy. Anything that could be used as a weapon.

Opening the first drawer, she found it full of kitchen knives, any one of which she could use to defend herself. Not wanting to overreact, she leaned against the counter and poured herself a second cup. Holding the mug with both hands, she felt confused. He had to see these, and only an idiot would leave them there. She considered sliding one out and hiding it inside the blanket, which gave rise to another thought. Something more exciting.

She set down her mug, stretched, and—not wanting to give rise to suspicion—circled and ambled about the room, opening drawers and staring out the window. Trying to look natural. When she reached the closet, she opened the door and leaned against the left side, hiding the adjacent wall from the camera. Then she pushed gently, causing it to click open.

When she'd bought the home, the previous owner was moving into an assisted living facility, so she'd sold it "as is." The widow showed her this pocket door at closing and explained, "There are things out here that will hurt you. And you're a long way from help. It's best if you can defend yourself." Swinging open the hidden door, she found a shotgun, two rifles, and a revolver. And thanks to Pockets, she knew how to use them.

She stared into the closet, remembering her training, and chewed on next steps. If Houdini did not know about the pocket door or the guns inside, she'd do well to keep the secret until such time as she could use them. Lifting a weapon out now, in plain view of the cameras, was not a smart move. She couldn't shoot a voice. She needed a face. A person. And he had yet to reveal himself. But what if he did? What if he walked through the door unannounced? A bad man with bad intentions? On the other hand, if he did know about the guns, and he left them there anyway, then she wasn't quite sure what to think.

She decided discretion was the better part of valor. Without being too obvious, she studied the position of the cameras and thought it possible that they might not have a view of the pocket door or what lay inside. Acting casual, she lifted the revolver off the hook, then wrapped her hand inside the fleece blanket, closing the closet door with an elbow. Returning to the sofa, she pretended to make herself comfortable on the cushions while sliding the revolver into the crack between her hip and the armrest. Once it was hidden, she picked up her coffee and considered her options.

She had leverage, she could defend herself, and the tables were turning in her favor. Things were looking up. Save one thing.

He consumed her thinking. She couldn't get him out of her mind. She tried to imagine him, and every time she did, he still didn't scare her. No matter what rabbit trail she wandered, she still found his voice was rather soothing. And he hadn't done anything to her. Not even when she stripped. Which confused her. For years, producers had been offering her ridiculous money to take her clothes off for the camera, and she'd refused. Flatly. Not a chance. But then she did so for him, and it elicited no response other than telling her she needed to fatten up.

She tried to think of something or someone else, but that only made it worse.

She woke toward dusk, her stomach growling. The end of Day 9. She did not know how long she'd been asleep but guessed several hours. She'd been doing that a lot these last few days. Drifting off and sleeping long and deep, suggesting her body was remembering how to live without chemical intervention. She walked to the kitchen in search of food and found dinner already prepared. Steak kabob, salad, and sautéed vegetables. Steam rose off the plate. Not to mention someone had set the table. Silverware, a paper napkin, and a pitcher filled with water, limes, and slices of cucumber.

The sight of the food reminded her that while she felt alone, she wasn't. He'd been in this room. Just feet away. Trying once again to act casual, she lifted dinner off the table, circled back to the sofa, and sat in the same corner, trying to feel the revolver with her hip. When she couldn't, she searched with her hand. Still nothing. Growing slightly worried, she sat up and looked, but that only confirmed it was gone. Turning back to her seat, she propped her feet on the coffee table, almost setting them on top of the revolver, which rested there, cylinder open and unloaded, six shells standing upright next to it.

She looked at the camera. "Very funny."

He responded quickly. "Didn't want you to shoot yourself in the hip."

She glanced at the closet. "You saw that?"

"Yes."

She spoke as much to herself as him. "And to think I made a living acting."

He corrected her. "*Make*. Not *made*. You're still very much alive."

She lifted the revolver and began inserting the shells one by one back into the cylinder, eventually pointing the loaded weapon at the camera. "I'm not afraid to use this."

"I believe you."

She pointed it at the door. "You come through that door, and I'll shoot you in the face."

"I'll try to remember that."

She laid the revolver on the coffee table. "You're not very smart."

"What makes you say that?"

She hefted the gun. "Duh."

"I keep trying to tell you I'm not going to hurt you."

"But you're keeping me here and keeping me from the people who are keeping my child from me."

"Sounds like a lot of keeping going on."

She set the gun in her lap and tapped her fingers on the wooden grip. "Did you know about the closet?"

"Yes."

"How?"

"Wasn't difficult."

"You've got to do better than that."

"Markings on the floor where it scratched the wood when opened."

She walked to the closet. He was right. How had she missed that? "Oh."

While considering her next move, his voice sounded. "Do you even know you're doing that?"

She took an inventory and found her fingers at the base of her neck, looking for the pill fob. Maybe she wasn't as far from her addiction as she thought. She shook her head. "No." Frustrated with herself and him, she picked up her dinner, returned to the porch door, pressed the large metal button, and leaned on the railing. She stared out over the mountains while speaking to him. "You ever married?"

He poked fun at her. "You always have to be in control of a conversation?"

"Humor me."

"No."

She looked at both the speaker and the camera. "You're rude."

He laughed. "No, never been married."

"Oh." His honesty again caught her off guard. "Come on, Houdini, throw me a bone here. Tell me something about yourself."

He threw it back at her. "Tell me about the pills."

She shrugged. "Better living through chemistry."

"Is it really?"

"Really what?"

"Better."

She shook her head. "No, it just sounds quippy."

"Then why does a woman who has everything need so many to get through a single day?"

"Because swallowing that little pill is easier than swallowing my life."

"What makes it hard to swallow?"

"That's a long story."

"What's the short version?"

"I'm sure you know my story."

"Assume I don't."

"You really don't know my story?"

"I don't keep up with people like you."

"What do you mean, 'like you'?"

"Movie stars."

"But you read the tabloids. You knew about my seventh stint in rehab."

"That was in more than just the tabloids."

"True."

"Despite what you might think of me, the details of your personal life are not my entertainment."

She considered this. "That would make you different than many."

"Look around you. We've established that."

"Again, true." What did she have to lose? "I had aged out of the foster system with more than a few daddy issues that left me deficient in my judgment of men. Truth is, I'm horrible. And given my limited experience with you, I'd wager to say it hasn't improved. Given that fracture in my makeup, I married the first one who came along and showed any real interest in me. I thought, *Gee, here's what I've always been looking for. Plus, he's good-looking. Treats me well. Winner, winner, chicken dinner.* About three months pass and I learn he's not who he said he was. So I, in my infinite wisdom, thought having children might mend things. Make life better. Give us a reason to rally around each other. But, as you have no doubt guessed, I was not able to have children. So he left me for about six other women."

"I'm sorry."

She shot a glance at the camera over her shoulder and pushed her food around her plate with her fork. "I'm having a difficult time finding the sincerity in that while you hold me captive against my will."

"I don't blame you." A pregnant pause. "For what it's worth, I'm still sorry."

She nodded. "Me too."

He continued, "You still want kids?"

"Have you or have you not been reading my texts?"

"I have."

"Then are you that stupid?"

"Just checking."

She paused. "More than anything." She stared at the camera, closed her eyes, and shook her head. "And in case you don't believe me, I have put my money where my mouth is, paying that stupid surrogate 1.2 million dollars."

"You scared to go it alone?"

His question poked at something she'd tried to ignore. She took a bite of her kabob and shrugged. "Maybe."

"According to the tabloids, you filed for divorce after social media populated with pictures of Syd and his harem. So, since then, is there a man in your life? Somebody to walk with you through this whole children thing?"

Pointing her fork at her plate, she said, "This is good." Then shook her head once. "I find this whole line of questioning just creepy."

"Humor me."

She crossed her arms. "What do I get?"

"What do you want?"

She smirked. "Skittles."

"You really think that will help anything?"

"No. But it'd make me feel better."

"Wanting to feel better is what got you in this mess."

"No." She raised a finger. "You got me in this mess when you kidnapped me, took away my phone, and locked this ugly hoop around my neck."

He paused. "True. But I'm talking about the mess that existed before this mess."

She'd made her point. "Once Syd left, I found I was in love with another man only to discover that his betrayal was worse than Syd's. Despite his recurring claims to the contrary, he also was not who he'd led me to believe. He was anything but. So I spent a few years being angry." She continued pushing her food around her plate. "Then sad. Giving rise to my growing dependency on chemistry to get me out of bed. Since then, I have questioned whether I'd make a very good mom. So, no. I don't 'have' a man."

He prodded her. "You are one of the more sought-after women on the planet, yet you've loved two idiots who ran off with other women?"

"The first, yes. The second . . ."

He waited.

"He didn't run off with another woman." She weighed her head side to side. "We never really had any closure."

"Why?"

"He went to prison."

"Is he still there?"

"Yes."

"You could go see him."

"I did once."

"What happened?"

"Chickened out. Got to the glass. Couldn't do it."

"Why?"

"Just hurt too much." She gestured with her hands. An uncomfortable chuckle. "Proving once again I am the world's worst judge of men."

"What convinced you?"

"The courtroom." She paused. "Why are you asking me this as though you're some normal person?" She shook her head. "You're weird, freaking me out, and, if I have anything to say about it, also headed to a courtroom."

He hesitated. "You look lonely."

A wrinkle appeared between her eyes as if the solution were obvious. "Then let me go."

"Eighty days."

"Whoa! Whatever happened to thirty?"

"Okay. Twenty days."

"You're really going to open the gates and take this thing off me and let me walk?"

"Yes."

"You'll understand if I don't believe you?"

"I will."

"What if I promise?"

"Promise what?"

"To stay clean."

"How many times have you made and broken that promise?"

She nodded. "Did you know that even the best major league baseball players do not get on base seven out of every ten attempts at bat?"

"I did. But what does that have to do with you and your broken promise?"

"There's always the chance that I might keep it. Just this once."

"Unlikely."

"Yes, but 'unlikely' doesn't justify you keeping me here."

"Agreed."

She raised her voice. "Then why are you?"

"That answer is a bit more complicated."

"I'm all ears."

He didn't respond.

"For the record, I'll never make twenty more days in this cabin. I'll lose my ever-loving mind. You need to come up with a plan B before I start losing my sh—" She shook her head. "My ability to reason."

He chuckled. "It's eighty. Not twenty."

"But you just agreed to twenty."

"I'm allowed to change my mind based on your condition."

She let it go. After a few minutes, she turned the tables. "You?"

He responded quickly. "Me, what?"

"Ever been in love?"

A pause. "Yes."

She goaded him. "Oh, my invisible, heartless, cowardly captor who hides behind the anonymity of a speaker has feelings after all."

"I am not heartless."

"Um . . . I beg to differ." She pointed at herself. "When I get out of here and someone more powerful than me locks you away for what you are currently doing to me, I'll come see you in prison and remind you of this little interaction."

"I look forward to the visit."

She continued, "So what happened?"

"Your ability to switch from one topic to the next without warning astounds me."

"Life as an actor."

"Evidently."

"Well . . . ?"

"Long story."

She didn't let it go. "Painful?"

Another pause. "Yes."

"Good. I was hoping you'd say that." She smiled. "Guess we share that in common." She stared into the camera. "Anybody ever hold you captive against your will?"

"You mean like I'm doing right now with you?"

She nodded. "Exactly."

"Yes."

"Did you deserve it?"

"I didn't think so."

"What's the truth?"

For several seconds he said nothing. When he did, even the computer could not disguise his change in tone. "Long time ago, John Milton wrote a pamphlet called *Areopagitica*. America's Founding Fathers used it to argue first amendment rights. Milton said, 'And though all the winds of doctrine were let loose to play upon the earth, so Truth be in the field, we do injuriously, by licensing and prohibiting, to misdoubt her strength. Let her and Falsehood grapple; who ever knew Truth put to the worse, in a free and open encounter?'"

"Meaning?"

"A lie can never stand toe-to-toe with truth."

"So?"

"Defend truth. No matter the cost."

She nodded slowly. "So you're an educated man?"

"Quoting Milton makes me educated?"

"It makes you different."

"I thought we'd already established that."

She raised a finger. "I'm not sure 'we' have done anything. That said, most folks don't go around quoting Milton."

"If you're going to kidnap someone, you better have a good reason."

"Do you?"

"I'd like to think so."

"Care to share it with me?"

"In time."

"You keep saying that."

He was quiet a minute. "I'll be gone a few days."

"How long?"

"A week. Maybe longer."

"So I'm stuck in this place alone?"

"Yes. But look on the bright side. It's your home. And you have a gun. And coffee."

The prospect of being alone out here and not being able to contact anyone frightened her a bit more than she liked to let on. "How will I reach you?"

"You won't."

"But what if I need help?"

"Too bad."

"What if I get hurt?"

"Rub some dirt on it."

"You're cruel, you know that?"

"Cruelty depends on perspective."

She studied her surroundings. "My perspective is the only one that really matters to me right now, and looking through it, you're cruel."

"I know."

She glanced from camera to camera. "And that doesn't bother you?" No response.

"Houdini . . ." Having played tough as long as she could, she dropped her head in her hands. "Someone out there has my child, and you have me stuck here." She sat shaking her head. Tears trailing both cheeks. "I am powerless to do anything for the one thing that matters most to me."

"Not true."

"How so?"

"You can keep your promise."

"That doesn't help me find my child."

He didn't respond.

She continued, "You ever been completely powerless?"

"Yes."

Her voice dropped to a whisper. "Then please let me out of here."

He redirected. "Can I ask you one more question?"

"And what if I say no?"

"I won't."

She knew if she could keep him talking, he might grow attached to her. And she needed him attached for what she was planning. "Yes. You may."

"After everything. All the betrayal. The heartache. Why the surrogate?"

She shook her head, searching for her own answer. "I was done. Finished. Wanted to close off my heart. Put it behind me. Then the clinic called and said I had one frozen embryo remaining. And all I could hear was him whispering in my mind, *What if?* and—"

"Him?"

She thumbed over her shoulder toward her past. "Prison boy." She continued, "I don't even understand how you take a frozen embryo, thaw it out, and then place it inside a womb and it returns to life. How does that even work? But if it could, if it was possible, what might my son or daughter look like? Would he have my nose? Would she have my chin? Tall? Short? What color eyes? Would they sound like me? Next thing I knew I was standing in a room holding Amber's hand as they inserted that one remaining possibility. I remember sitting up that night, just wondering what was going on inside her. What wonder. What mystery.

Did it take?" She ran her fingers through her hair, fell silent, returned to the couch, lay down, curled her knees into her chest, and stared well beyond the walls of her captivity. "After everything, I lie awake at night asking, *What if?*"

"And prison boy did that?"

She had buried this years ago. Unearthing it was painful. "Yes." A pause. "I used to think about him staring at a dark cell, at cold bars, and wonder if he thought of me. Then I'd wonder why I even cared after everything he did. And when I couldn't make sense of how someone I loved so much could betray me so deeply, when I was about to lose my mind, I started swallowing pills again. And I kept swallowing until the pain stopped."

"Did it?"

She shook her head. "After the verdict, they cuffed his hands and feet and began leading him out of the courtroom. Staring at fifteen years. The whole world, inside and out of the courtroom, wanted his head on a platter because of what he did to me. To us. I watched him shuffle out, and . . ." She closed her eyes. "He was looking at me. Trying to make eye contact. Telling me I'd be okay. And I just began shouting. Telling him how much I hated him. How I hoped he burned in hell. How I . . ." She shook her head. "I said the most terrible things. That's when it sank in. I had trusted him with my next breath, and then the door closed and I couldn't breathe." She opened her eyes and sat up, staring out across the mountains. "Either he was and is the most evil person I'd ever met, or . . ." She trailed off again.

"Sounds like he deserved it."

A pause. "I used to think so."

"Used to?"

"I have never been able to reconcile who he was to me, and with me, and who they said he was in court."

"I'm sorry."

She glanced at the camera. "Why are you apologizing to me?"

"The look on your face."

She nodded. "You asked me about the pills." She motioned with both hands. "There you have it."

"How much longer does he have?"

"Six months. Three days."

"Sounds like you're keeping track."

She nodded. "My therapist tells me I'm holding on."

"To?"

She chose her words carefully. "When I was a girl, through twenty-seven foster homes, I heard a lot of late-night husband-and-wife conversations through the wall, air vent, or open window. Some good. Many not. And from the first night, I knew the truth of them. I could tell if they loved one another not by what they said but how they said it. How he spoke to her. She to him. I could tell the effect of him on her by the sound of her response. Fear. Frustration. Anger. Disappointment. Did she feel safe? Was her heart at peace? It was as if every home had a heartbeat, and I could curl up in that closet, place my palm to the wall, and feel the pulse."

She crossed her arms as if to brace herself against the wind. "When I married Syd, I thought I heard that tone in his voice." A single shake of her head. "Syd was spray-on tan and a weekly pedicure. He would"—she made quotation marks with her fingers—"pencil me in. But . . . Pockets stood in a cold rain during filming. Holding a hot cup of Earl Grey. Having added milk and honey. Syd didn't even know I liked tea, and yet he always called the barista by her first name."

A pause. "Years passed and the world put me on a pedestal. Showered me with awards. Shined a spotlight. Pretty soon Syd was playing catch-up. Clinging to my coattails. Chasing the next big thing." She had closed her eyes again. A slight smile cracking her lips as the memory returned. "Most nights, as my career took me from one hotel suite to the next, I would lie down in the closet, press my ear to the wall, and listen to Pockets prepping for the next day. Preparing for every contingency. Every night, as he left no stone unturned, he put me to sleep by the sound of his voice."

She was quiet several minutes. "When my world crumbled, Syd played the victim and abandoned me. Straight into the arms of other women." Another long pause. "News pundits said I locked arms with the hopeless and put words to their pain. That I gave them hope." She shook her head. "When I looked down from my pedestal, nothing but shards of glass all around, I found Pockets's shoulders beneath my feet. The pedestal upon which I stood." She crinkled her nose, made her trademark facial expression, and shrugged. "If there was beauty in my mess, Pockets sifted it from the rubble and placed it in my hands."

Night had fallen. Ten trillion stars but no moon. And the voice made no response.

She pointed to the bedroom but tapped her neck hoop. "Can I sleep up here or is this thing going to knock me out?"

"The bed has fresh sheets."

"I know we've just had our little heart-to-heart, but . . ." She grabbed the revolver and waved it at the camera. "I know how to use this thing. I had a good teacher."

When she walked into the room, a bag of Skittles lay on the pillow.

CHAPTER 16

BEFORE

He knew production was tapping their fingers, wanting her back on set, but he also knew they could wait. She needed a minute. He poured her a cup and found her running a hot bath, rummaging through her luggage. He handed her the coffee and then opened the duffel, exposing the contents. "Looking for this?"

She sipped and nodded.

"When does filming end?"

Her voice was barely more than a whisper. "Supposed to end yesterday."

"And when are you going back to Seven Pines?"

"Can we talk about that?"

"No."

Wearing the clothes she'd been wearing since yesterday, she stepped into the tub, leaned back, closed her eyes, and sipped. He stood over the toilet and began flushing drugs. When finished, he stood next to the tub. "Mrs. Joe?"

She whispered but didn't open her eyes. "Yes."

"Seven Pines or find another bodyguard. You pick."

She cracked open one eyelid, considering him. "You serious?"

A nod.

She turned off the water with her foot. After a minute of silence she said, "You drive me?"

Another nod.

She dunked her head, careful to keep her coffee dry. When she re-appeared, she said, "We finish filming tomorrow. Or . . . maybe today because I think today is tomorrow, but whatever." An honest nod. "I'll go."

He returned to his room and napped throughout the day. That evening, after the team had commenced filming, she called. "You got a second?"

"Yes mum."

"You mind coming up here?"

He exited the elevator into her suite to find it empty save her. Either she'd sent everyone home or they were all at the postproduction party. The TV was on. She picked up a remote and pressed a button, and a rather high-res video of her suite began playing. She explained, "Whenever I travel, they put cameras in the public areas of my suites." She shrugged. "To keep people honest. Few know they're there."

"Seems like as your head of security, I'd know this."

She paused before she spoke. "I kept you out of the loop . . . to pro-tect you."

"From?"

She looked at him. "Syd. But that's another conversation." She pressed Play, and the video showed Pockets entering the suite carrying a passed-out Joe. Through the open door to her room, he could be seen settling her in bed, gathering her pills, and then assuming his post outside her closed door. She fast-forwarded through the downtime, stopping at the interactions with the assistants, the director, and the producers.

When the video finished, he pointed. "Mum, those people don't—"

She held up her hand. "I want to thank you." She turned off the TV. "You didn't have to do that, and I know it." She pulled her shoulders back and held her hands behind her the way a child does when they're called to the principal's office and they know they're guilty. "I don't pay you to protect me from me, and yet you did. Thank you."

He nodded.

"You look like you have something you want to say."

Pockets paused. "You ever heard the story about the fifth column?"

She shook her head.

"Spanish Civil War. Four columns were approaching Madrid from all sides. The attacking general commented that while the four columns were strong, and Madrid could not repel them, it was the fifth column he expected to win the battle."

She waited.

"The fifth column was a group of sympathizers on the inside. Subversives. Attacking from the inside. Bent on undermining the solidarity of the nation at any cost."

"Meaning?"

"The pain in you is undermining you."

She stared out the window, down on the city. "We'll leave first thing." She checked her watch. "I need help with something."

"Yes mum."

"In about thirty seconds, my dealer is going to ring that bell." She rubbed her face with both hands. "I need him to go away and never come back, no matter how much I plead or beg in the future. Understood?"

Pockets walked to the door and was about to open it when she stopped him. "Are you going to hurt him?"

"Not permanently."

Pockets peered through the peephole and then flung open the door, grabbed a smug, skinny kid around the neck, squeezed off his air supply, and carried him to the bathroom where he bound his hands and lay him, head down and feet up, in the tub. Joe watched from the door, biting a fingernail, as Pockets waterboarded the unsuspecting pharmacist turned dealer. Between soakings, Pockets asked him, "You ever coming back here again?"

The kid spat, sputtered, and cussed. "I don't know what you're talking about."

More water.

Same question.

More cussing.

More water.

Same question.

By now the kid was starting to get the picture. Pockets unzipped the kid's fanny pack and littered the tub with dozens of prescription bottles of pills of various color. Evidently, tonight's stop was one of many. One by one, Pockets unscrewed the safety caps and emptied the pills into the toilet.

The kid screamed at Pockets. "Dude, I run a legit pharmacy! People depend on those. You're literally killing people right now!"

At this, Pockets lifted the kid, shoved his head into the toilet, and flushed it. Then returned him to the tub and continued waterboarding, refilling the trash can with water from the spigot every time he emptied it.

Realizing this was not going to end well for him, the kid changed his tune. "I'm never coming back. Never coming back."

"Not ever?"

"Never."

More water.

More choking.

"Even if she begs and pleads?"

The kid was losing strength and scared. "Never. Never."

"Are you ever going to sell drugs to anyone again?"

"No."

"Ever?"

"No. Never."

Pockets sifted through the kids' pants and pulled out his phone. He realized what he was about to do was not a permanent solution, but it would be an inconvenience. He unlocked the phone, deleted not only Joe's contact information but all contacts, then opened Settings and tapped "Sync with cloud." When the phone responded with, "Are you sure you want to delete 874 contacts?" Pockets pressed Yes. At which point the phone requested a PIN. Pockets looked at the kid and said, "PIN."

The kid closed his eyes and said, "Man, come on . . ."

Pockets didn't say it a second time. He filled the trash can and began pouring water over the kid's face, which brought a garbled number out of the kid's mouth. Pockets entered the number into the phone and permanently deleted the information from the cloud. He knew most kids like this usually had two or three phones, so restoring access to his livelihood would be more a time-requiring formality—but a nuisance nonetheless.

When finished, Pockets led the kid to the door, handed him his phone, and pointed to Joe. "We clear?"

The kid nodded.

"Say it."

"We're clear."

Pockets closed the door and found Joe sitting on the couch, shell-shocked, knees pulled up to her chest. "I thought you were just going to talk to him or something."

"Would it have done any good?"

"Probably not. I just didn't expect that." Her face betrayed her surprise at the efficiency of his persuasion tactics. "You've done that before?"

Pockets nodded.

"Will he be okay?"

"No permanent damage."

"Why does it work?"

"We are born with two fears: falling and drowning." He thumbed over his shoulder at the bathroom. "That triggers the second while not actually filling the lungs with fluid, provided you allow the person to breathe at some point."

"You ever had it done to you?"

He nodded matter-of-factly.

"Was it part of your training or . . . bad guys?"

His expression was sympathetic. "Knowing that answer won't help you make sense of today."

She stared out the window. Then glanced at the bathroom. "If you were smart, you'd do that to me." She wiped her face with her palm. "He's *a* problem but he's not *the* problem. No one has broken more promises to me than me." A pause, then she turned to him. "Promise me something. Please."

"Yes mum."

"Don't ever leave me . . . to me."

He nodded. "Yes mum."

Seeking to capitalize on her addiction, Syd made the talk show rounds and talked openly of her willing self-admission. Her bravery. Of the courage required to confront her own demons. He talked of his visits with her, of their dreams of children, and of her sobriety. How she'd put on some much-needed weight. And most importantly, the soul-work she was doing to get healthy.

Six weeks later, she emerged clean.

For a time.

On the drive home, she climbed up in the front seat, opposite Pockets, and said, "I need a cheeseburger. Turn here."

"Yes mum."

Pockets followed her finger to In-N-Out where she ate two cheeseburgers, fries, and a milkshake, then crawled into the back seat and slept the three-hour drive home.

CHAPTER 17

BEFORE

Work took her to Australia and New Zealand to film a war epic in which she learned to fly a single engine and expressed interest in getting her pilot's license upon returning to the States. When filming wrapped, she and her growing entourage boarded a jet and returned to LA, landing at the private airport at 2:00 a.m. Having spent three months halfway around the world, her body clock was set seventeen hours ahead. Which meant that while most of California was asleep, she was already living 7:00 p.m. the following day. Dinnertime.

Her entire crew was starving. But where to feed them in the middle of the night? Like New York City, Los Angeles seldom sleeps, so options were many. But rather than try to find some back room where they could enjoy dinner unmolested, she had a better idea. "Follow me."

Pockets drove the team to Nick's All-Nite Diner, where Nick stood sweat-stained and greasy behind the griddle while a half dozen patrons fought for the attention of the single disinterested and overworked waitress. Not much had changed. Hidden beneath a hood, Joe walked in, leaned on the counter, lowered her glasses, and whispered, "Mind if I take a turn?"

Squinting through one eye, Nick glanced over the cigar dangling from his lips, smiled, and untied his apron. "Hey, pretty girl!"

Joe hugged Nick, wrapped herself in the apron, hefted the spatula, and starting breaking eggs with one hand and flipping hash browns with the other. Within minutes, she was barking, "Order up!" and carrying plates to wide-eyed patrons and refilling coffee cups in her sweetest southern drawl. "More coffee, honey?"

Wasn't long before a news truck appeared outside. The restaurant filled and gawkers pressed their faces to the glass. Meanwhile, Joe gave the spatula back to Nick and then began taking orders from folks standing in line, serving coffee and eggs on the sidewalk. An hour in to her shift, she turned to Pockets.

"Relax. You think somebody's gonna hurt me at an all-night diner?"

He looked at her as if the answer were obvious.

She pointed at the counter. "Have a seat. I'm cooking."

Pockets sat on the corner, his back to the side wall where he could both eat and watch everyone entering or leaving. A few minutes later, Joe set a bacon double cheeseburger in front of him. "Two mostly all-beef patties. Four slices of something that's almost cheese. Extra bacon. Extra pickles. And my secret sauce."

"I don't like pickles."

She leaned on the counter. "Pockets. Pockets. Pockets."

"But—"

"For once in your life, do what I tell you. Please."

"But what if—"

"Nope. No questions. Sit there and eat and act like you enjoy my cooking. Besides, Nick keeps a double-barreled shotgun under the counter and he's not afraid to use it. He can handle anything that comes through that door."

Nick winked at Pockets, who then eyed the ginormous burger. "I'm partial to fish and chips."

"Shut up and eat the thing before I drop it on your head."

He lifted the top bun. "What's the sauce?"

"Can't tell you."

"Why?"

"'Cause it would cease to be secret." Joe sat alongside, loosened his tie, and patted his arm with an "I'm waiting" look on her face.

Pockets relented, said, "Yes mum," and took his first bite. Which was quickly followed by a second and a third. The smile told Joe everything she needed to know.

By now, Nick had called in his nephew—a bouncer at a local pub just getting off work—to man the door before they were overrun by the crowd.

The following day, apron-clad and spatula-wielding, Joe was on the front page of the *LA Times* and viral on social media. The hashtag was #oneofus, making her once again the talk of every local news outlet in town.

Driving her home, Pockets said, "Thank you, mum."

"You like?"

"Best burger I've ever had."

Joe sat staring out the window, spinning her wedding ring around her ring finger. "I've been told it's wrong of me to blame my addiction on another's absence." A pause. "But there is a certain level of shame that comes from constant rejection."

Pockets listened but said nothing.

Joe weighed her head side to side and her voice fell to a whisper. "The nights are hardest."

Pockets watched her in the rearview. "Yes mum."

CHAPTER 18

AFTER

The texts had been arriving with increasing regularity over the last few days. Much like sonar pings. On the surface, Frank sounded tough. Demanding. In control. Beneath the surface, and reading between the lines, Frank sounded desperate. Joe had been kidnapped and, as a result, his sugar mama had gone quiet. To make matters worse, he didn't know who he was dealing with. His house of cards was teetering. Never good for someone in his position.

I had not answered his texts as I wanted to provoke a reaction. I wanted to see what he'd do when I said nothing at all. How desperate might he become when he realized whoever now had Joe's phone was not the pushover Joe had become? How would his tactics change? He was dealing with someone else, and what did that someone else know? He had no idea. Not knowing the identity of that someone else, he'd want to flush him or her or them out of hiding. To see who he was dealing with. Assess the other side. Determine what I knew.

So I told them nothing at all.

I had two assumptions. Of neither could I be certain, but given the amount of money at stake, I felt confident. First, Frank was no dummy; he wasn't about to burn his lottery ticket. Joe's kidnapping had certainly altered his plan, but he still held Willy Wonka's golden ticket. My guess was that he'd go into hiding. Then stretch it out. But if he wasn't negotiating with Joe—just some random, unidentified stranger—he could never be sure how much leverage he held because he didn't know to what extent I valued what he valued. Or if I valued it at all. Maybe I couldn't care less. Maybe I didn't even know what he had. Maybe I just wanted Joe. Frank had no way of knowing what I knew or didn't know, what I wanted or didn't want. Which explained the frequency of the incoming texts. I also changed Joe's phone setting to let him know not only that the text had been delivered but that it had been read and at what time it had been read. So he knew someone was receiving his communication. My silence told him I was refusing to respond, which, I suspected, was only hacking him off. Which was good. I wanted Frank angry. Angry people tend to make rash decisions.

Second, life in Camelot was soon to sour, and tension between the lovebirds was about to crack the thin facade. Frank would get desperate and angry because, once in control, easy street within reach, he was no longer. It had slipped through his fingers like water. And given his braggadocious behavior and the claims he'd made—not to mention his plans for the future, which centered on him doing a whole lot of nothing—he needed to save face. A man like him couldn't afford to not be in control. His image depended on it. Further, other people's perspective of him depended on his control of the pieces on his chessboard. That is, Amber and the baby. And while Frank had professed undying love to Amber, that was before Joe's abduction. Amber would soon learn the truth. She was a commodity, and Frank loved Amber for what she offered him. Life on the beach collecting the interest. But she was only of value if the person now holding Joe's phone valued her.

Also, Frank was young and he was an idiot. He failed to understand one thing about Amber: she was female. A woman. And not only was she a woman—she was a pregnant woman who could not button her jeans and could no longer slide them over her full hips. For nine months, Amber had been growing a baby in her tummy. A baby that kicked. Woke her up. Sat on her bladder. Stuck its foot into her stomach so that the imprint was visible from the outside. Since month three, Amber had exited the shower only to stare in the mirror, marvel at the change, and whisper with a kind smile, "I got fat for you."

First, she'd held her rounded tummy in one hand. Then two. Now she cradled the basketball in her arms. She felt the pressure. Swollen feet. Raging hormones. And while Frank could feign indifference, Amber would not. The baby had toes. She'd seen the indentions next to her belly button. Amber was not about to let Frank hurt the baby. This did not mean she'd turned soft. She hadn't. Amber still wanted the money. And lots of it. She just wanted it on her own terms and not at the expense of the baby. She could still have her cake and eat it too.

While I couldn't be sure, I guessed Amber had a well-thought-out exit plan if Frank turned physical. Or threatened her. Or changed his tune. At all. And while Frank played the part of the tough gangster with a posse, he was little more than a two-bit punk playing a high-stakes game with real and long-lasting consequences. Amber, on the other hand, while possessing poor taste in men, was actually quite smart. She was also conniving and deceptive and evil, given that she'd stolen a tormented woman's baby—but nonetheless, highly intelligent. Frank couldn't hold a candle to that.

My guess was that once she learned he'd lost control, Amber would disappear and lay low until more details surfaced about Joe's disappearance and who had taken her. And if running were on the table, I also wondered if Amber had a second lover dangling in the wind some-where. Some unsuspecting stand-up guy, working nine-to-five with his name on his shirt, whom she'd been dragging along for just this possibility—someone who had no knowledge of any of this. A pawn in her sick game who'd make a good father in the event she had to keep this baby longer than five minutes. She'd appear on his doorstep with a sad story and bat her fake eyelashes.

But these were just assumptions. In truth, I was as blind to their intentions as they were to mine. The only place I could see clearly was this: Amber was a month away from giving birth, and there was nothing anyone could do about that. The clock was ticking.

CHAPTER 19

BEFORE

Joe was working on a film in Canada in which two strangers are caught in a storm in a three-seater plane. The pilot has a mid-flight heart attack with a storm approaching, dies midair, and the plane crashes in the middle of nowhere. Sixty miles from the nearest light bulb. After a few days the search is called off, everyone thinks they're dead—"No one could have survived that"—and the two of them walk out a month later. The role won her another Oscar nomination but no win.

During filming, much of which was shot in cold and snow, Joe busied herself in her downtime taking flying lessons and beginning the process of earning her pilot's license. In the months prior, Joe had received multiple personal and credible threats, including items being left in her bedroom and certain items of clothing being stolen. To counter, Pockets increased security, never venturing more than five feet from her person. This meant wherever Joe went, Pockets went, and she was never the first to enter a room or automobile.

Syd called this paranoia and eventually told Pockets, "Take a hike. I got it." Syd soon learned he didn't have it when he woke to find

Pockets wrestling a man to the ground. Next to the bed in which he and Joe slept.

Given heightened measures, Pockets sat in the back of the plane during all her lessons, including her "solo" flight. While the instructor argued, Pockets maintained if Joe had to make an emergency landing, she would not do so alone and he'd be the first off the plane. It wasn't until she began studying for her written exam that she learned he'd earned his license nearly fifteen years earlier as a function of his job.

She read the question out loud. "This makes no sense to me. Listen to this: 'Determine the approximate ground roll distance required for takeoff. Outside air temperature (OAT) equals 38 degrees Celsius. Pressure altitude equals 2,000 feet. Takeoff weight equals 2,750 pounds. Headwind component equals Calm.' It's multiple choice. '(a) 1,150 feet, (b) 1,300 feet, (c) 1,800 feet.'"

Pockets thought. "Draw a vertical line from 38 degrees Celsius until it intersects the 2,000-foot pressure altitude curve. Draw a horizontal line to the first reference line. Then draw a line that parallels the closest guideline, until it reaches 2,750 pounds. Finally, draw a horizontal line to move to the second reference line. You've got calm wind and you're only looking for ground roll and not distance to clear an obstacle, like trees or a building, so move the line horizontally to the right margin of your chart, and read the distance figure off the side. Should be something close to 1,150 feet."

Joe pursed her lips. "You're a pilot?"

"Yes mum."

"How long?"

"Fifteen years."

"And you're just now telling me?"

"You didn't ask."

"But you've been sitting there letting me suffer through all this when you've known all these answers all along?"

Pockets weighed his head side to side and then shrugged.

Joe shook her head. "Unbelievable."

CHAPTER 20

BEFORE

Following Canada, Joe and her team moved to the mountains above Albuquerque. A crime thriller centered on a single mom defending her family and farm. Near the end of the film, she confronts the bad men. With a gun.

That afternoon, Joe tugged on Pockets's arm. She was shaking. "You ever shoot anybody?"

"Yes mum."

She looked around and spoke quietly. "You teach me?"

They drove into the mountains and squared off to a hillside. Pockets opened the back of the Escalade and a black, hard plastic case, revealing two handguns and a shotgun. Throughout the afternoon, Pockets put on his instructor's hat and educated Joe.

"This is a Glock 17. This is the trigger. This end breathes fire . . ."

He schooled her on the four laws and had her repeat them back to him several times. "Treat all guns as if they're always loaded. Never point it at anything you don't want to destroy. Keep your finger straight and off the trigger until you are on target and ready to fire. Make sure of your target and backstop."

Then he started with the basics: grip, movement from the holster, sight picture, trigger pull, and trigger reset. Once she was comfortable with dryfire, he transitioned her to live rounds, which naturally led to reloads. With every exercise, they worked on marksmanship.

"The front sight is your last visual control over the round. The trigger is your last physical control."

Once they'd put a few hundred rounds downrange, he worked through malfunctions: stovepipes, failure to feed, and double feeds. In the afternoons that followed, he walked her through movement, multiple targets, and cover and concealment and the difference between the two.

With filming wrapping and production moving to another set the following day, Pockets sat her down. She'd become comfortable, proficient, accurate, and, maybe most important, confident. Gone was the fear.

During a break late in the afternoon, he squared up to her. "If somebody is threatening you, intending you harm"—he tapped the pistol in his holster—"this is not your only weapon. You have another."

She considered this. "Where is it?"

He tapped his voice box. "Right here. So use it. If somebody is charging down on you, you put on your big-girl pants and holler as loud and angry as you can. Tell them what's going to happen if they come through that door. Make them think twice." He turned her to the target. "On the up command, draw to target and give me your best attempt at verbal compliance."

She nodded.

"Up."

Joe acquired a firm firing grip, drew the weapon up and close to her body with the muzzle pointed toward the target, pressed the meat of her left thumb alongside her right, laid the fingers of her left hand over her right, acquired a good sight picture, and said rather calmly, "Halt!"

Pockets tried not to laugh. "A good start. Now let's throw something else at them. Just anything. And remember, big-girl pants."

Joe adjusted her feet, swallowed, and spoke again. The level of her voice was on par with answering her phone. "Stop!"

At this point, Pockets could not conceal his smile.

Keeping the muzzle pointed downrange, Joe shot a glance at Pockets. "What's so funny?"

"Mum, I need you to imagine me as a bad guy. Coming through your bedroom door and I'm going to do things to you that you'd never want anyone to do to you. If that were the case, how would you respond?"

Joe's eyes narrowed and she pursed her lips as she returned her focus to the paper target in the shape of a man.

"You ready?"

A nod.

"Up!"

Summoning some primal sound from her toes, Joe screamed at the top of her lungs, "*Come through that door and*"—as she spoke, she began pressing the trigger—"*I'll shoot you in the face!*" When she finished screaming, she had emptied all seventeen rounds, plus the one in the chamber, into the target. When the slide locked back, indicating she was empty, she dropped the magazine, inserted a second from her back left pocket, and cycled the slide. Having reloaded, she reacquired her firing grip and continued pressing the trigger and screaming. This time louder. "*I called the cops. Get out of my house. I'll shoot you in the face!*" When the slide locked back once more and she realized she did not have a third magazine, she dropped the slide on an empty chamber and stood at the ready, breathing heavily and sweating. While smoke trailed up and out of the muzzle.

Joe glanced over her shoulder at Pockets.

Pockets studied the swiss-cheese target, then her, the target again, and finally her. With a nod, he said, "That'll do." Nodding a second time, he said with a smile, "That'll do just fine."

Standing at the back of the Escalade, unloading, she looked up at him. "You ever shot anybody?"

He nodded.

"More than once?"

Another nod.

"Were you afraid?"

"No mum."

"Were you guarding someone?"

Pockets closed the slide on an empty chamber and set the Glock in the case. "Yes mum."

"Were they hurt?"

"No."

"Were you?"

He laughed. "Which time?"

She turned and sat just inside the back of the SUV. "Do you think I could?"

"Could what?"

"Really shoot somebody in the face?"

Pockets closed the case. "In my experience, that's the wrong question."

"What is the right question?"

"Do you love?"

"What do you mean?"

"Do you love someone enough to fight for them?"

She considered this. "I would hope so."

He waved his hand across the black box. "These things are just tools. In a fight, you use the tools at hand. If you have car keys, use the car keys. Broom handle? Broom handle. Have one of these? Use it. The question is, why are you fighting? What drives you? Love or something else?"

She nodded.

He continued. "If you're driven by love for another, then in my experience, there's nothing you wouldn't do for them."

"What if a bad man walks in my hotel room and I'm just fighting for me?"

He chuckled. "Well, if I do my job, that won't happen. But assuming for a second it did, then you do whatever is required to stop them from hurting you."

She looked like she was having trouble with this.

He sat alongside her. "If someone intends you harm, then they're saying by their actions, 'I value me more than you.' Or 'I want what you have and I intend to take it.' For whatever reason, they've come to the selfish conclusion that they matter more. That in their sick and twisted mind, they have more right to be here. To take something from you, whether your body or your possessions, simply because they want it." He shook his head. "But they don't. You're a human being. You have as much right to stand on planet Earth as anyone else. I'm not telling you to become a bully. But stand your ground. You fight for you." He nodded and motioned for her to stand, then shut the back of the SUV.

She looked hesitant. "How are you certain?"

"Because . . . you're worth fighting for. And don't ever let anyone tell you different."

"What if I lose?"

He chuckled again. "Then lose fighting."

She sat in the front seat as he put the Cadillac in Drive and began winding down out of the mountains. Halfway down, she turned and put a hand on his forearm. "Thanks, Pockets."

He glanced at her hand, then back at the road. "Yes mum."

CHAPTER 21

AFTER

Da Beez Neez had been born in the late nineties during the explosion of West Coast hip-hop. In an attempt to attract and emulate Death Row headliners like Dr. Dre, Snoop, and 2Pac, no expense was spared—which seemed to work. Curious fans filled it to capacity. Line out the door. Paid the cover charge. Something about a mermaid pool. Their presence, not to mention their unpaid bar tabs and growing posse, led to constant infighting among the greedy partners, along with a fair amount of cooking the books. When enough bills weren't paid over a long enough period of time, the only way to satisfy creditors was to cash out and acquire new owners who, in turn, had a bit more street smarts and knew the only way to right the ship was better living through chemistry. So they sold drugs. And lots of them.

Today Da Neez, as it's commonly known, sits on the outskirts of LA in a once prosperous landscape, now almost forgotten. Covered in brown bags, broken bottles, empty cans, and twice-used syringes. The only attraction it can boast is its roots. Music critics describe it as "Birthed in the heyday. When the beat was real." Despite the disrepair, the stage is still revered among the next generation and the wannabes. Riding the trade winds of the pseudo-renaissance occurring in most floundering big-city downtowns across the country, the DJ and dance scene has grown. Tickets have actually sold. Crowds have returned. Parking is a problem. As is security, but that's nothing new. What is new are the metal detectors at the front door and the near strip search required to gain access.

I sat in the parking lot in a borrowed '80s Ford Bronco with tinted windows. The Bronco was old school, had a six-inch lift, thirty-five-inch BFGoodrich tires, a normally aspirated 350 ci engine, and no computers or satellite connections, which made it difficult to track. From my vantage point in a dirt lot across the street, I could see the front door and side doors but not the rear. Two out of three. Busta Line had gained some notoriety as a sought-after DJ with tolerable copycat rap instincts. Tattooed neck to thigh, he had made much about his short stint in juvie, which he called "the joint," and liked to travel with a bit of a posse.

The three-car caravan of blacked-out Escalades arrived just shy of midnight, when Busta was slated to take the "historic" stage. A dozen or so scantily clad, champagne-sipping ladies exited the vehicles and waited as earpiece-wearing security parted the waters, creating an entrance for Frank to walk across the sea on dry ground. At which point, security would utter into their mics, "Moses has entered the building."

Frank exited the SUV to shouts and far more limited applause than his entrance would dictate, but Frank was not deterred. He had plans. He had paid attention in school—that is, juvie—and knew that in order to run a successful drug business, you needed other people to be your hands. Frank was the voice, the mouthpiece, the front man. And so, in his kindness, he let others do the legwork, let them get caught with their fingers in the cookie jar. Frank was an idiot, yes; he just wasn't stupid. So as his entourage grew, so did his drug sales. But like most successful entrepreneurs, Frank had plans, and in order to accomplish those plans, he needed an influx of cash. Lots of cash. He also needed medical insurance, but that was a separate issue.

With the crowd in a booze-infused frenzy, Frank entered the building where he would "work" until 5:00 a.m. Truth was, Frank was good for business, so the owners tolerated most of his demands and growing need for attention and general sucking-up. While the line outside filtered its way through the metal detectors and the growing, eardrum-splitting *boom-boom-boom* echoed through the walls, I exited the Bronco holding a brown bag and wearing clothes I'd bought at a thrift store and a dreadlock wig I'd ordered. Walking these streets at this time of night was not wise, but between the store-bought beard and dreads, I was unrecognizable even to myself.

I stumbled my way across the street and then down the sidewalk where the five Escalades were prominently parked out front. Announcing Frank's presence. Two of the drivers stood talking over a shared joint while the third snoozed in his seat, listening to Mississippi blues. I sipped water out of my emptied gin bottle and stumbled a serpentine and mumbling path toward the cars.

Reaching the rear of the first, I slipped, fell, and pulled myself up by the bumper. Leaving magnet number one. I then routed around the second, saying something about "The president must be in da house t'night." One of the two dope-smoking drivers told me to get my expletive hands off his expletive-expletive car before he broke my expletive-expletiving neck. But it was too late. The magnet held. When the third driver spotted me in his rearview, I shoved two peanut crackers and a few peanuts in my mouth, swigged some water, and tried to chew quickly. Then, as he stepped toward the rear of his vehicle, I bent at the waist and blew chunks across the asphalt, which were indistinguishable from real vomit, careful not to splatter his immaculate vehicle. This caused him to look like he'd just sucked on a lemon, so he pointed, said something about me "getting the expletive out of there," and climbed back in his car. I pulled myself up by his bumper and returned to my car in the lot across the street, where I cranked the engine and drove to my motel.

My computer showed all three AirTags were registering nicely and lined up in a neat row right where I'd left them, so I set an alarm and slept for a few hours. At 5:00 a.m., I grabbed a coffee and watched the Find My app while the tags sat dormant. Then at 5:27 a.m., the first tag began to move, followed by the second and third. All three cars exited the parking lot, made their way to the interstate, and drove north to a recently rented home on the coast, where the party exited their vehicles and stumbled inside. To be continued.

A few of the less inebriated members of the entourage made brave efforts to find a second wind, but after discovering that the pool water was too cold for naked nighttime swimming, most found beds, couches, or vacant spots on the carpet. At ten thirty, a single man wearing a hoodie exited the side door, hopped the fence, and walked discreetly three blocks down the street, where he climbed into the driver's side of a parked Chevrolet Caprice Classic. With spinners.

As a driver, Frank was a model citizen and not difficult to follow. He drove less than three miles per hour over the limit at all times and obeyed all traffic laws. Twenty-seven minutes later, he pulled into a strip mall on the outskirts of town, parked in the rear, and knocked on the back door of Mail-Time, where he promptly rolled up his sleeves and sorted mail for the next eight hours. According to their website, Mail-Time offered full benefits including health, dental, and paid maternity leave—and because they had locations in over eight states, their medical coverage was rather extensive. Interestingly, Mail-Time also rented PO boxes and sold prepaid cellular phones.

At 7:07 p.m., Frank exited the same door, wearing the same hoodie, bought a sub at the sandwich shop next door, and climbed into his

Chevy. Where he ate the sandwich, drank two beers, smoked a joint, and slept until 11:00 p.m. At which time he returned the Chevy to its parking spot on the street and went to the now bustling party at his ocean-side home, which he was renting with Joe's extortion money. Twenty minutes later, the Escalade caravan rolled up, the drivers opened the doors, and the half-dressed entourage exited the house like mice returning to cheese. All while Frank grabbed his groin, postured, and strutted like a peacock.

Watching him conduct this orchestra, I almost admired him. Over the weekend, the AirTags continued to send clear signals, showing their location within just a few feet. But while they were active and accurate, they did not answer my biggest question—because while Frank was visible, Amber was not. In fact, she was nowhere to be found.

Until Monday morning, when both she and Frank exited the lavish rental house and climbed into the blacked-out Denali parked in the drive. She, too, was hooded, but while the sweatshirt covered her face, it was stretched rather tightly around her stomach. Now nine months pregnant, she had started to waddle. And judging by the location of her right hand on the back of her right hip, she was suffering back pain.

The AirTag allowed me to follow at a distance, which I did until the car pulled into the St. Vincent Medical Center north of LA where the loving couple parked and walked, midargument, through the parking lot. I couldn't hear what they were saying, but judging by their body language, Amber was not happy with something Frank had done. And given his response, that something might have had to do with another female. Tough to say from a distance, but Frank was groveling and Amber was finger-pointing and occasionally screaming. Judging from appearances, things were not well in Camelot.

Two hours later, the now hand-holding couple returned, bearing a folder of paperwork and two ear-to-ear smiles. They drove slowly south, stopping at an In-N-Out and choosing to walk in rather than drive through. Which was fortunate for me. Also fortunate was the fact that Frank, ever occupied on two cell phones, left the Denali unlocked, allowing me to photograph the contents of the folder. Which gave specific details, including date, time, and location, for the planned C-section in four weeks. Lastly, I found printed screen captures of a high-res 3D ultrasound, which provided uncanny realism.

After leaving In-N-Out, Frank pulled into a gas station, so I took a gamble. I donned a second wig, making me look like an LA punk rock wannabe. Long trench coat, mirrored shades. While he started the pump, I entered the convenience store and stared at the tabloids. A minute later, Frank opened the door and approached the soda fountain where he prepared two thirty-two-ounce Dr Pepper Zeroes. Then, as he made his way to the counter, I stepped in line—in front of him—and asked for two lottery tickets, paying with crumpled bills.

As the cashier rang up Frank, I began scratching at the ticket on the counter just off to one side. Paying for both gas and sodas, Frank pulled out a wad of hundreds and fifties that looked to be valued in the thousands. With practiced flair, he laid a fifty on the counter, accepted his change, and eyed my progress. When I cussed beneath my breath, expressing my disgust by tearing my tickets in two and throwing them in the trash, Frank spoke up. "That ain't no way to get rich."

I glanced at him briefly, wanting to engage, not antagonize. "Yeah." I forced my voice to sound weak. "What is?"

He pulled down his sunglasses, sipped, and stared at the passenger seat of the Denali. And kept walking.

I tried to act both dumb and inviting, making my voice sound like the class nerd who had traded his pocket protector for spiked blue hair. When I spoke to him, I stepped off the curb, forcing me to look up at him. "You mean like Apple with a new iPhone every year?"

Frank chuckled, finally pointing his straw at me. His tone of voice held disregard, disdain, and supreme arrogance. He looked down. "Not exactly." It was only when he turned his head, and the sun shone through the space between his glasses and skin, that I saw the resident evil there.

Frank headed toward his car and I feigned more ignorance. "What, you mean like the lottery?"

Frank was finished with me. He'd sized me up, and I'd been found wanting. Comfortable with his progress and the execution of his plan, he stepped off the curb and walked to his vehicle. When he spoke, he did so more to himself than me. Little more than a mumble. Frank had a habit of grabbing his groin with every third or fourth syllable and this interaction was no different. "I'm 'bout to punch my ticket and be done with all 'dis."

When he said that, he was looking at Amber.

I followed at a measured distance. "What about the thing they love?"

He shrugged and threw his receipt on the ground, where the wind caught it and brushed it across the parking lot.

CHAPTER 22

BEFORE

Pockets signed off at midnight but Joe didn't answer. Pockets's established security protocol required her to respond, "AC," or "All clear." Letting him know she was safe. When her text didn't return, he began knocking on doors, but everyone had gone to sleep. All quiet. He would not let himself in her room without invitation or emergency, but he couldn't sign off until she released him.

He swiped his keycard, called out, "Mrs. Joe?" When she did not respond, he stepped inside. She had rented the entire top floor. New York City stretching like a carpet of lights and spires out every window. "Mum?" He checked the living rooms, game room, theater, kitchen, laundry room, balcony, and finally, her bedroom. Knocking, he received no response. Stepping into the dark room, he walked across the carpet to the bathroom, where he heard a whimper, followed by choking.

He hopped the bed, bounded into the bathroom, ripped the closet door open, tearing one hinge loose from the wall, and found her lying in a pile, her soaked and matted hair falling down over her face. Her words were slurred. The treatment at Seven Pines had not taken and her relapse didn't take long. She held up a shaky stop-sign hand. "Don't look."

He knelt.

She dropped both her head and hand on the floor. "Don't want you to see me this way."

He carried her to the toilet and stood behind her, holding her hair out of her face while she emptied what remained. After thirty minutes, she sat against the wall. Facing him. Afraid to look at him. "You disappointed?"

He shook his head. "No mum."

"Mad?"

He shook his head and handed her another washcloth.

"Does anything rattle you?"

He shrugged.

She mimicked him. "You're always so put together. Straight. Proper. It's like you've always got your sh—I mean, stuff together."

He rinsed the washcloth and placed it back over her forehead. "I have my moments."

She pulled an empty pill bottle from her pocket and rolled it across the floor. "Here's the truth of me."

He dropped it in the trash can.

She tilted her head sideways. "You know?"

A single nod.

"How long?"

He shrugged. "Since you started back up."

She laid her head back against the wall and closed her eyes. "Why didn't you try to stop me?"

He waited until she opened her eyes again. "The Band-Aid does not cause the cancer."

"Meaning?"

"Correcting the behavior does little to make the bad man stop."

She raised one eyebrow. "Did you study psychology or something?"

"No."

"What then?"

"Life."

"Well, you're a good student. And I'm failing."

She turned and heaved again. This time dry. By now, only the heaves remained. Sitting back, she wiped her face again. "Well, don't ever start. This stuff'll kill you. And once it gets ahold of you . . ." She sat staring at the closet out of which he'd pulled her. Still messy. "I should probably clean that up." She tried crawling across the floor, but that only made the world spin faster. She stopped and placed one hand on the wall, the other on the floor, trying to slow it down. Her breathing was rapid and shallow. He grabbed a pillow, rolled her gently, and propped her up.

She closed her eyes. "I feel horrible."

"Yes mum."

"Why do I do this to myself?"

He sat quietly, dimming the lights. An hour passed while she napped, snoring slightly. Then two.

Somewhere in the middle of the night she woke to find him sitting a few feet away. Leaning against the wall. Sleeves rolled up. Tie loose. "You still here?"

A nod in the darkness.

The air smelled of Pine-Sol.

She glanced at the closet. "Why'd you do that?"

He didn't answer.

"I should've done that."

A shrug.

Her voice was weak. She closed her eyes. "I'm sorry."

He whispered, "No problem."

"Trust me." She chuckled with her eyes closed. "If I had to clean up your puke, I'd have a problem. I'm a sympathetic vomiter."

He smiled.

After a minute she rolled toward him, slowly, lest the world start up again. Facing the closet, she reached out and touched the door. Reaching into memory. "When I was a girl, I was passed around so much and woke in so many different rooms that nothing felt like home. I found if I could shrink the room, I felt safe. The world wasn't so big. So scary. So I slept in a lot of closets." A pause while she extended both arms. "Walls I could touch comforted me." She turned toward him. "You think I'm nuts?"

"I used to climb out my window. Lie on the roof. Stare at the heavens. Watch shooting stars. Made me feel a part of something bigger. Then I'd try to wrap my head around the wonder of it all."

"Did you?"

He shook his head once.

Her voice was a little too loud. "And look at you now." A sheepish grin. "Mopping up after me."

"Not how I see it."

"How do you see it?"

He leaned his head back. Chose his words. "In my line of work, I've met people. All kinds. All walks. Some up. Some down. One thing is true of all of us: nobody has their stuff together. Not presidents. Not paupers. Not soldiers. Not actors." He glanced at her. "We are all a mess. And no amount of money, and no amount of drugs, changes that. When you're broken, life is about finding the beauty in the mess. And then holding on for dear life. And there's no shame in that. Provided we're honest about it."

She nodded once. "But there's the rub." She tried to straighten and could not. "You know, it's the da—" She covered her mouth. "I mean, it's the truth that hurts." She poked herself in the chest. "The truth of me. That's all I'm trying to drown or swallow." She closed her eyes and spoke. "But if I'm being honest"—she looked to the closet—"it's not working out too well."

He made no reply.

After several minutes, she turned toward him. "What changes it?"

"Not *what*." A pause. "*Who*."

"Who then?"

"The one who walks with you down into your closet. Down where you hide the bodies. Who isn't afraid of the stuff you're taking to the grave. The stuff you don't share with anyone."

She closed her eyes and was still several minutes. Finally, she lay her arm flat across the floor, opening her hand. "Walk with me?"

He pressed her. "You want to get clean?"

She turned her eyes to him and nodded.

"Go back. I'll go with you."

"You'd do that?"

He nodded.

"Shut the front door." She laughed. "Syd wouldn't."

He made no response.

Hours later, as the sun broke the tops of the skyscrapers to the east, she rolled over and looked up at him. "You been sitting there all night?"

"Yes mum."

"Why?"

"Making sure you didn't choke again."

She squinted one eye. "I did that?"

"Yes mum."

She covered her eyes with her hands. "That's a bright light."

"Yes, it is."

She split two fingers wide enough to see through. "Were you serious?"

"I am."

She pulled her knees up and closed her eyes. "You drive me?"

This time she stayed six weeks. Seven Pines was a desert oasis hidden in the mountains outside Big Bear. Pockets rented a cabin off-site. For people in his line of work. Seven Pines was used to celebrities. They also had to be sure he was not a source of her problem, so they had no contact. No communication. He could only observe from a distance. After four weeks, when they were more certain of her sources and triggers, they gave her permission to receive certain guests.

Syd appeared first with flowers. A trinket of jewelry he bought in Qatar. They ate lunch, and he talked about her getting out, where he'd take her. She listened. And breathed. Then he asked to see her cabin. When Syd left a few hours later, Joe found Pockets on the hill behind his cabin. The fitness course. Pull-up bar. She'd never seen him with his shirt off. Never seen the scars.

When he saw her, he wiped his face with a towel and pulled on his T-shirt. "Hey." He smiled. "Was wondering if you were still in there."

She nodded. "I am."

"You look good."

She did. She'd gained a few pounds, which she'd needed. "For the first time in a long time, I am." They small-talked. She sounded peaceful. Rested. The calm after the battle. She pointed at the exercise loop. "Walk with me?"

They walked the three-mile loop. Breathing the thin air at ten thousand feet. "I get to go home soon."

"Pity. I was just starting to like it here." They were standing on a mountaintop.

She turned and studied the vista. "Me too, but that's the thing about mountaintops. While we might prefer those 'high' moments, most of life"—she pointed at a town in the valley—"happens down there. Along the way." She tilted her head side to side. "It's where the water is."

He glanced at the buildings and grounds where she'd been seques-tered. "They teach you that inside?"

She shook her head. "No." Her eyes found his. And for the first time he saw something he'd never seen. "You did." She put her hand on his arm. "Pockets?"

"Yes mum."

"Thank you for being here. For being everywhere but especially the bathroom. These last few weeks, it's been a . . . a strength knowing you were just beyond the wall."

He nodded once.

She turned and they began walking back. She tapped his back. "You tell me about those scars?"

"No." He paused. "Scars are just the body's response to things that shouldn't be there. A reminder of the pain."

Three days later, he drove her home. Where she stayed clean a week.

CHAPTER 23

BEFORE

It was August. Filming had wrapped and to thank the crew, she'd rented eight villas owned by the Ritz-Carlton on Lake Oconee, south of Atlanta. Forty cast and crew spent the week frolicking on the lake on rented pontoon boats, paddleboards, kayaks, and sailboats, playing golf on one of three courses, shooting skeet, water-skiing, or floating in the infinity pool or hot tub. Meals were prepared by the Ritz's Michelin star culinary team and ferried over in golf carts. Massage and spa treatments were available twenty-four seven, and comedians and musicians provided nightly entertainment.

Finding a break in his work and travel schedule, a bronzed and muscled Syd appeared fresh from a project in Cuba, entertaining everyone with harrowing stories of how an action-figure actor tore a pectoral muscle while learning to make cigars in his now beloved Havana. Having become an aficionado, he spent hours holding forth on the nuances of the various leaves, sizes, types of roll, and whatever else he could make up. Joe watched with amusement because the crew seemed to like it.

One evening, she rented a small paddleboat—a miniature version of what once floated the Mississippi—and took everyone on a "three-hour tour," in which the Gilligan reference was only lost on the younger members. The boat motored south, stopped an hour later at a granite outcropping affectionately called "jump rock," and anchored while everyone floated and scored jumpers on a 1 to 10 scale with added points for flare or incompetency. Belly flops were given an automatic 12. Cigar-puffing Syd spearheaded the scoring while standing on a paddleboard like Aquaman and pointing his paddle like a trident.

Joe had informed Pockets she had hired a security detail who would sit invisible on their perimeter and that he was to take this week off. That was an order. Period. Under no circumstance was he to guard anyone—least of all her.

"Do you understand me?"

"Yes mum."

When she found him on the paddleboat dressed in sport coat and tie, she had gently patted his right hip, where she found his concealed Sig P320X. Hands on hips, she said, "Pockets, what'd I tell you?"

"You said to enjoy myself."

"Correct." She waved a hand across him. "But you can't do it dressed like that."

"I'm having a good time, mum."

She pointed to the water. "No, they're having a good time. You're standing up here on overwatch while I hired six other guys to do that this week."

"Yes mum."

She pointed again. "Get in the water."

Pockets studied the chaos. "No mum."

"Pockets, do you work for me?"

"Yes mum."

"Don't make me give you an order."

"Yes mum."

A third point.

Pockets shook his head.

Joe considered the reason for his insubordination. Then it hit her and she covered her mouth. "Oh, I'm so sorry. You can't swim, can you?"

Pockets shook his head. "No mum. I can swim."

Joe's face grew red. "Then get in the da— I mean, get in the water before I fire you."

"No mum."

"Pockets!"

"Mum, the water looks nice and I'm sure everyone is having a good time, and I thank you for wanting to include me, I do. But I cannot do that." She was about to object when he said, "Whether you fire me is up to you, but I was hired to do a job. And I'm doing that. Even when you can't see it. I understand your intention, mum, but I cannot do what you're asking me."

Joe studied Pockets. "You really can't, can you?"

"No mum."

Joe turned and leaned on the railing, and the two watched the circus in the water. After several minutes, she said, "Is there anything I can do for you?"

Pockets nodded with a smirk. "Don't fire me."

Joe smiled and rejoined the party.

That evening, after the boat had docked at the villas and the party had resumed at the infinity pool, Joe found Pockets mopping up a spill on the second floor of the paddleboat. "Pockets, you coming?"

"Yes mum, just . . ."

That's when she smelled it. "Pockets, what're you doing?" She covered her nose. "I have other people who can do that."

He nodded and kept mopping.

Joe investigated, realizing the extent to which someone had gotten sick. That's also about the time she saw Syd passed out and covered in his own mess. "Oh, Pockets, here, let me—"

Pockets put out a hand. "No mum. You tend to your guests. I've got this."

"Pockets, he's my husband."

"Yes mum."

Hands on hips again. "But . . ."

Pockets was spraying something that smelled of Pine-Sol. "It's not a problem. Only be a minute."

Joe stepped alongside him. Surveying the totality. "Pockets, why?"

He paused but didn't look at her. "Because this reflects badly on you. Now"—he pointed to the guests—"I'll get Mr. Syd to his room, and you can . . ."

She put a hand on his shoulder, then grabbed a paper towel roll, knelt, and began mopping up her husband's face. Moments later, Pockets discreetly carried Syd to his room where the two put him in bed and closed the door.

An hour later, Joe found Pockets sitting in the shadows of the pool deck, eating a BLT. She flipped over a five-gallon bucket and sat alongside him. "You get some dinner?"

Pockets offered the sandwich. "Yes mum. I don't know where they get this bacon, but it's about the best I've ever had."

She sat quietly a moment. "Thank you for that."

Pockets nodded and said nothing.

"Can I do anything for you?"

Pockets pointed at the pool. "No mum. I've got all I need."

Joe leaned closer, putting a hand on his shoulder. Invading the personal three-foot bubble he spent such energy maintaining. Pockets quit chewing, swallowed, and waited.

After an uncomfortable moment, he said, "Yes, Mrs. Joe?"

"Pockets?"

"Mum?"

"You're sweating."

"Yes mum."

"Do you want to take that sport coat off?"

"No mum."

"How 'bout that tie?"

"I'm good, mum."

She leaned in. Her breath on his face. Her lips inches from his. "Would you let me kiss you?"

Pockets stared uncomfortably out of the corner of his eye. "I'd rather not, mum."

"I'd like to thank you."

"You've already done that."

She leaned closer. "What if I told you I needed to see you in your room. Right away."

"Mum?"

She stood up and put her hands on her hips. "I'm trying to thank you."

"For?"

"Being you."

"You do that every other Friday."

She shook her head. "Sometimes I swear you're dumb as a bag of hammers."

He lifted his half-eaten sandwich. "I'm good as new, mum."

Joe tapped her teeth. "Pockets, you thick-skulled Highlander, I'm making a pass at you! Please tell me you see that and I'm not so out of practice that it's not working."

Pockets set his sandwich down. "Mum, I'm a man, and I'm not immune to what you're saying or offering." He pulled a handkerchief from his back pocket and wiped his brow.

"You realize my husband is passed out."

"Yes mum."

"He's passed out most nights or just takes what he wants."

"Yes mum."

"Which means"—she straightened his jacket—"it's been a while." She shook her head, voice rising. "A long while."

Pockets swallowed. "Sorry mum."

"But you knew this."

Pockets hesitated. "I suspected, but . . ."

She was wearing a robe, which she loosened. "Sure I can't change your mind?"

The reveal was not lost on Pockets. "With all due respect . . ." Another nod.

"You do find me attractive, don't you, Pockets?"

He glanced with his eyes but his head never moved. "Yes mum."

She chuckled. "And you're not secretly infatuated with men, or boys, or sheep?"

"No mum."

"Just checking."

"Mum . . ." Pockets straightened. "If I did what you're asking, and what, honestly, a part of me would very much like to do, I'd have to fire me."

She laid her hand flat across his heart. "What if I gave you an order?"

Pockets swallowed. "I can't obey that one, mum."

She smirked. "Are all you Brits like this?"

"I'm Scottish, mum."

She tested him. "Same thing."

He shook his head. "No mum. Not by a long shot."

She leaned forward, kissed his cheek, then kissed it again, and began folding his handkerchief. "I think the world would be a better place if more of us were like you."

He smiled. "And all of Scotland would agree with you." While some of Pockets's Scottish accent had worn thin over the years, he continued to trill his *r*'s. And "agree" was one word that showcased his true origin.

She closed one eye, framing him with the other, her robe opening wider as her body moved beneath it. "Pockets, I want to tell you something. You listening?"

The sight of her skin was not lost on him. He swallowed. "Yes mum."

"You keep trilling your *r*'s at me and you're not going to have much choice. I'm going to tackle you and rip your clothes off your body. Consider yourself warned." Then she stood, not closing her robe.

Pockets smirked, wiped the sweat off his brow, and closed her robe, tying the belt in a bow. "I pray for the grace to remain armed with righteous restraint and not regress into retrograde reciprocity, or responsive revulsion rising out of an unrighteous rescue."

CHAPTER 24

AFTER

Mike's Pawn Shop offered "fast cash for anything," so I tested that theory, carried in some power tools, and spread them across the counter. "Are these of any value?"

He surveyed the used tools and looked at me. Then he shook his head. "Not really." He glanced down again, embarrassed for me. "I mean . . ." He rubbed his hands together. "I can give you a hundred bucks if it helps."

It did. And it would. And it was about what I expected. "I'll take it." Then I dug in my pocket and pulled out a purple Crown Royal bag. "How about these?"

The sight of the bag piqued his interest, so he lifted it and dumped the contents in his hand. Over his shoulder, a soap opera played on a small television. He pressed a button and switched to the local news affiliate. "Can't stand that stuff. My wife's been watching that thing for thirty years and every day the story is the same." He laughed. "Nothing changes."

The midday news affiliate was interviewing people on the street regarding Joe's abduction. Evidently it was a slow news day, and with no leads, the up-and-coming reporter decided to spice up the afternoon broadcast with baseless opinions on "Who kidnapped Joe?"

The answers ranged from ISIS to the Russians to a serial killer to a mother of triplets pushing a stroller. "Maybe she doesn't want to be found. You ever considered that? Maybe the weight of fame is just more than she can bear."

The news outlet had requested anyone with a personal history with Joe to come forward and tell what they knew. Yes, this brought every Tom, Dick, and Harry out of the woodwork, but the producer culled the list and came up with a few credibles. The last was a man in his late thirties. Fit. Graying around the edges.

"Tell me, sir, how do you know Joe?"

He hesitated. "We had a professional relationship."

"You worked with her?"

Another pause. "I was her broker."

The reporter continued, "Do you have a theory regarding her abduction?"

He shook his head. "No, not really."

His answer did not dampen the reporter's enthusiasm. She pulled the microphone back. "What about MacThomas Pockets? The escaped convict responsible for the savage beating of Syd Painter."

The man wiped his forehead. "I don't know if it was savage or not. Maybe Syd deserved it. What I do know is that man saved my life."

"Who? Syd Painter?"

"No. MacThomas Pockets."

The reporter chuckled in disbelief. "He saved your life?"

The man looked around and nodded. "That's right."

"How so?"

He chose his words carefully. "I was doing some things I should not have been. Caught up in a game, making quick money on the side." The man paused, and for the first time I looked at him. He'd matured. Aged. A wedding band. The decade had been kind to him. He continued, "Let's just say he got my attention. Opened my eyes. That's when I met my wife. Now we've got kids. I own a business. None of that would have happened had Mr. Pockets not done what he did."

She smiled. "Just what did he do?"

"Probably better if I keep that to myself."

"Are you saying he saved you from making some bad choices?"

"I'm saying he saved my life."

"Interesting. And tell me, what do you do now, sir?"

"I'm a pharmacist. Own four locations here in town. We also fund an addiction counseling and treatment center."

The reporter looked sympathetic. "You're doing some good work, sir. You mind telling me why?"

More uncertainty. His hands were fidgety all of a sudden. Like he wanted to be anywhere but in front of that camera. "Because . . . I'm trying to make amends."

I smiled as the reporter moved on to the next unsuspecting parkgoer. At the table, Mike eyed the silver belt buckle and the old Rolex. "You sure you want to sell this? It's worth more than I'm going to give you. You could probably post it on some forum and make a few bucks more."

I'd bought it early in my career. On assignment in the Mideast. A silver Rolex Submariner. Bought it with my "danger pay." We all did. Wore them with the idea that if we ever needed to buy our way out of a bad place, we could barter with it. Which is what I was doing right now. "What's it worth to you?"

"The buckle, maybe one-fifty. The watch . . . I'm going to sell it for somewhere between thirty-five hundred and four. I'll give you twenty-five hundred for it."

"How about three for the tools, the buckle, and the watch?"

He nodded. "I'll do that."

CHAPTER 25

BEFORE

Life after treatment changed. Slightly. Trading one drug for another. What she once medicated with drugs she now appeased with money. And what was once clear and rational turned twisted. Or foggy.

Pockets watched her closely. One morning she couldn't find her car keys. Which was strange in itself because she never drove anywhere. She hated to drive. Especially in California traffic. But for some reason she got a bee in her bonnet about driving herself to a spin class. Turned the house upside down looking for a key fob. When she couldn't find it, she called the dealership. And bought a new car. Twice. Pockets eyed the three blacked-out Cadillac SUVs sitting in the driveway, two of which had less than a hundred miles, and wondered what they said about Joe. One plus one was not equaling two.

One afternoon Pockets sat in the basement downstairs while Joe and two other actors rehearsed lines upstairs. One of the actors had just returned from New York City, where he'd starred in an off-Broadway production. He spoke fondly of his time there and the food cart parked at the back door of the theater. Some guy out of Boston named Billy brought in fresh crab daily and served crab legs on a bun, crab cakes, and fried lobster tail. Twenty-four seven. He never slept. The actor relayed how he'd leave the theater any hour of the morning and yet that guy was sitting there, steam rolling out beneath his umbrella; whether it was dinner or breakfast, he didn't care.

A few minutes later, Pockets heard Joe on the phone. He could only hear her side of the conversation, but what he heard did not encourage him. She was talking with her pilot.

The next morning, Joe served "Boston Billy" to the two actors. Crab cakes. Crab legs. Lobster. They were elated. Couldn't believe she'd sent the plane. Pockets did the math. Her plane could cross the country without refueling at a cost of eight thousand an hour. The flight, with a tailwind, took three and a half hours. Four coming back. Not to mention pilot overtime. All for a sixty-thousand-dollar breakfast.

Joe didn't spend money on herself. Always other people. Even the car purchases were for the comfort of others. When her housekeeper mentioned how she had missed a rent payment, Joe bought her a house. When her yard man asked for new yard equipment to upkeep her yard, she bought five of each item, including a new trailer. And when a piece of fan mail appeared asking for tuition help for acting school, she endowed a scholarship—for ten kids.

Her kindness was never in question, but her process was. And the more Pockets watched, the more irrational it became. She also slept less. As in, she slept almost never. She would go two or three days without ever closing her eyes. She didn't party and she cared nothing for the social elite or their ladder, but she did teach herself to cross-stitch and she would work three one-thousand-piece jigsaw puzzles at once, or finish an entire Sudoku puzzle book in three days. The effect was weight loss, eyes that never focused, and conversations that were never complete. She would respond to a question, fade off, return, then fade again, with little to no resolution.

Pockets knew she was not clicking on all cylinders, but he also felt the cause of the misfire might be deeper than detox. While no psychologist, he felt the cause was closer to grief. Though she put on a happy face, he knew her well enough to know she was held together by a string. One more pick at her soul and the whole thing might unravel. She was trying to hold it together, but what she failed to see was that most everything else was falling apart. Save her career. Which was all up and to the right. But personally, when the cameras weren't filming, she'd dug herself into a hole and lacked the reason to climb out. Which was the problem. She didn't have a reason, and Syd wasn't much help.

Later that year, Joe accepted a role in a period piece in which she played a young eighteenth-century British monarch. Turned out the present-day Queen was a fan of Joe's work and asked for a meeting at Balmoral, the Scottish home and hunting estate of the royal family.

Two weeks into filming, Joe found Pockets in the laundry, ironing his shirts. She was bouncing when she spoke. "Got a second?"

"Yes mum."

Joe continued dancing around the laundry room. "I just got invited to have tea with the Queen." She bounced nervously. "I thought maybe you'd like to accompany me, seeing as how you're from here and she's your queen and all."

Pockets nodded. "Yes mum."

Joe paused and studied him. His reaction didn't quite meet her expectation. "Pockets, I'm going to meet the bloody Queen. Tea! It's a thing. You should be excited. This is a once-in-a-lifetime opportunity."

Another nod. "Yes mum. I am. Thank you."

She pointed at the hot iron. "I'm happy to send that out for you so you don't have to spend time—"

He nodded. "I don't mind."

She rolled her eyes. "Just be ready at 2:00 p.m. It's 'high tea.'" She snapped her fingers. "That's 2:00 p.m. sharp. Got it?"

"Got it, mum."

Pockets pulled the car around at two and drove through the Cairngorms National Park, arriving at the castle at a quarter to three. Joe was giddy. She leaned forward between the seats, pointing to a map on her phone. "They said come to this gate."

Pockets nodded but didn't look at the map. "Yes mum."

Not surprisingly, Syd jetted in from parts unknown to attend the tea. For years, Syd had been politicking to become the next James Bond. So in an attempt to impress the Queen, and the tabloids covering the event, he wore a custom Savile Row blue suit, an Omega Seamaster, and in what he thought a generous nod to Scotland, a tartan scarf to which he had no connection whatsoever but rather thought it matched his suit.

Pockets drove the scenic route. Sheep. Stag. Hairy cows. At one point, Syd commented, "We should buy a home up here. The scenery would do us good and maybe get us invited to dinner."

Pockets parked and opened the doors, and Joe, staring at the castle, whispered to Pockets, "I can't promise they'll let you into the room, but I'll do my best."

Pockets nodded. "Yes mum."

Syd punched Pockets on the shoulder. Pal to pal. Donned his Bond sunglasses. "Stick with me, buddy. I'll get you in there. We can snap a pic with the old gal."

"Thank you, sir."

Ordinarily a junior staff member or even the chief of staff would greet someone for afternoon tea and lead them into another room, but as it turned out, the Queen was quite a fan and just as eager to meet Joe as Joe her. In a beautiful breach of protocol, she met them at the door. Syd bowed. Joe curtsied. "How do you do" was exchanged, and the Queen walked alongside, leading them into a wing of the castle.

Pockets followed, entered the room, and assumed his quiet post in the corner.

When Syd wasn't interrupting, selling his latest charity work or the success of his latest blockbuster, Joe and the Queen shared an intimate and laughter-filled visit involving two cups of tea, with the Queen asking multiple questions about Joe's work, her personal life, and the roles she'd played—most all of which the Queen had viewed in her private theater.

As they said their goodbyes, Syd shook the Queen's hand, then placed the same hand around her waist, snapped a selfie—which amused the Queen—and thanked her for a "spot of tea" in his best and most practiced Bond impression.

With one arm locked inside Joe's, the Queen walked Joe to the car, thanking her for taking time out of "what I know must be a very busy schedule to stop by and visit with an old lady. You must come back."

Joe curtsied and responded with, "I'd like that very much."

At the car, the Queen turned to Pockets, who stood holding the door. With one arm locked inside Joe's, the Queen squared up to Pockets and hesitated. Looking up. Then she stepped forward, inside his three-foot bubble. When she did, Pockets never flinched. After several seconds, the Queen nodded, touched his arm, and leaned in, further crossing the line.

"Pockets, you take care of this one. You hear me?"

Pockets nodded slightly. "Yes mum."

After a slight change in tone, the Queen straightened and asked, "How's the shoulder?"

"Good as new, mum."

For several seconds the Queen stared up at Pockets. Studying him. Or was it something else? Satisfied, she patted Pockets's cheek, letting her hand come to rest on his salt-and-pepper beard and saying with a chuckle, "Showing your age, young man."

Pockets glanced at Joe, then back at the Queen, and bowed slightly. "Yes mum."

Satisfied, she straightened his lapel, letting her hand come to rest just slightly above his heart. Patting his chest, she turned, whispered to herself, and headed back inside.

The three were not out of the gate when Joe squealed and launched herself into the front seat, pounding on Pockets's arm. "You know the Queen? You know the Queen! How do you know the Queen? I cannot believe you didn't tell me you knew the Queen! Aaaahhhh!" Joe squealed like a teenage girl at a Justin Bieber concert. "How? How did you keep that a secret?" Another punch. "You liar! Tell me, tell me, tell me!"

Syd sat in the back seat posting his selfie to his social media account. Hashtag bondjamesbond. Not lifting his eyes off his phone. "Dude, what's the story with you and the old Betty?"

Pockets didn't take his eyes off the road. "No story."

When Pockets's answer didn't satisfy her, Joe pressed him. She leaned across the center console. "Pockets." Joe tapped his chest. "She called you by your name."

"Just protocol, mum."

"And she straightened your lapel"—Joe mimicked the Queen's movements—"and patted your chest. Above your heart. She brushed your beard. What gives?"

Syd waved him off. "Her security detail knew about us long before we arrived. She's a good politician. She read his name in a report."

Joe was not convinced. She sat with lifted eyebrows, tapping a finger on the console. Pockets glanced in the rearview at Syd, who was lost in his screen, and then back at Joe before returning his focus to his driving. "Just protocol, mum. Just protocol."

Filming continued another month. Long hours and little sleep took their toll. Joe needed some time alone but didn't want to spend it in a hotel. She bumped into Pockets in the fitness center before daylight. He was finishing up. She was just getting started. She lingered one beat too long. He picked up on it.

"You all right, mum?"

"Just need a break." The black circles crowding her eyes told a different story.

He stared out the window at a waning moon. "Filming today?"

She shook her head. "Schedule conflicts."

He knew the answer but asked anyway. "And Syd?"

She looked away. "Dubai."

Her voice was hollow, echoing inside herself. He wiped the sweat off his face. "Feel like going for a ride?"

She stepped off the treadmill. "You show me your Scotland?"

"Something like that."

"Does it include fish and chips?"

"It can."

"And a beer?"

"If you wish."

"Then yes."

Thirty minutes later, he drove a black Range Rover out of the hotel parking garage and turned north as a light rain misted the windshield. She sat in the back seat, her hand wrapped around an espresso, taking shallow breaths. They stopped at the grocery store, where Pockets left the car running, returning a few minutes later with two bags of groceries. Excited at the mystery, she asked, "Where to?"

"I can tell you or you can just let it happen. Your choice."

She smiled, leaned her seat back, and closed her eyes, amazed at how Pockets could seamlessly transition to driving from the right side of the car on the left side of the road. Ten minutes and they were winding north along Scottish country roads. She spoke with one eye closed. "Pockets?"

"Yes mum."

"You can take that tie off."

He cleared his throat. "You took the day off. Not me."

She closed both eyes. "Do you work for me?"

"Yes mum."

"Then take off the bloody tie." A smile. "You're making me uncomfortable."

The road wound along the coast, where patches of sunshine glistened on a calm North Sea. She sat up when they pulled onto a dirt road. Unable to contain her curiosity, she climbed across the console and sat in the front seat. Leaning forward. He slowed, rolled down the windows, and began pointing.

"That was old man McDougal's farm. Had two really beautiful daughters who wanted nothing to do with me." Another curve. Another mile. Another point. "Hamish MacGregor. Best footballer in all of Scotland. Played on a few World Cup teams." Two more miles rolled by. "The widow Smythe lived up there. Husband owned a distillery. She used to give us samples."

Joe laughed, relishing the fact that Pockets was driving her through his childhood. Dirt road changed to hard top and an old courthouse and town square came into view. "That's the garage where I built my first car, which, in fact, was a tractor. Got my first haircut in that barbershop. Kissed a girl in that field. Got in my first fistfight in that same field. Same night."

"Sounds like a story there."

"Didn't know she had a boyfriend." A chuckle. "I lost." Followed by a shrug. "Which is what happens in most fights." They wound through old brick streets and ancient stone buildings dotted with fat, cooing pigeons. "I pulled eggs at that chicken house, worked that farm cutting hay and wheat, and mowed these lawns to buy diesel for the tractor." The road turned to dirt again and wound through rolling fields and long stone fences. In the distance, castle ruins stood silhouetted against the coastline. Pockets pointed. "Tenth century."

Finally, he slowed and turned down a smaller dirt path. More lane than road. After a half mile, an old farmhouse came into view. Then a church and cemetery. Followed by a barn. Off to one side stood the remains of a giant windmill. Beyond that, a dilapidated chicken coop and small fenced pasture. A spring-fed pond spread out below them. "Learned to swim down there. Albeit cold." He pointed to a scar above his eye, then to a big walnut tree next to the water. "Used to be a rope swing on that limb. Back when I thought I wanted to be an astronaut."

Pockets parked the car, and they got out to walk. The breeze blew in from the sea and smelled of salt. Before them, the pasture disappeared into a rocky and rolling coastline. Standing on a cliff overlooking the sea, he pointed to the pools of rocks that filled and emptied with every rising and falling tide. "Caught cod down there. Shot rabbits with my bow up there." A shrug. "Trying to be Robin Hood." The gravel crunched beneath their feet. "Worked my mum's garden over there. Fell out of that tree. Broke this arm when I got thrown from a mule over there. Raised a stag in that pen. Grew a county-fair-winning sheep down there. Kissed a girl in that barn. Twice."

Joe smiled but didn't interrupt him.

"Drank my first beer over there. Got my first whupping in that barn. Distilled spirits in that shed."

"You owned a still?"

"With my dad." A chuckle. "Bought my tractor with spirit money."

Joe smiled at the sound of Pockets's pronunciation of the *r* in "tractor" and "spirit." She raised an eyebrow. "You're trilling your *r*'s again."

He shook his head once. "Tough habit to break."

She closed her eyes. "I swear, the Brits are just smarter than the rest of us. Even the way you talk sounds more intelligent."

He glanced at her out of the corner of his eye. "Scots, mum. Scots."

She laughed and punched him gently in the bicep. "Just testing you."

The breeze filtered through the barley in waves. Staring into the misting rain, he spoke softly. "I became me here."

Realizing he had driven her down memory lane, she let him talk. Not interrupting. An hour later, she would realize the gift. Her mind was not racing. Her thoughts were here. And she was here. She was present. He spread a picnic in an abandoned barn sitting high on a cliff. To their left sat the sea. Disappearing into the deep blue horizon. To their right stood the smooth stone church and cemetery.

He handed her a baguette prepared with brie, tomato, arugula, basil, smoked salmon, and a thin layer of butter.

She accepted it. "Okay, this is better than fish and chips."

Not feeling the need to fill the air with noise, they ate in silence. Comfortable in their own skin and each other's presence. He poured her a cup of coffee from a thermos and handed it to her. Black.

She accepted, shaking her lead. "Syd thinks I like my coffee with cream. And it's not even good cream. It's the powdered kind. How is it that you know I take it black and after several years of marriage, he has no clue?"

They ate and drank in silence for several minutes. Pockets spoke first. "I wasn't entirely honest when I said there was no story."

"What are you talking about?"

"When we met the Queen."

"I was wondering when you were going to come clean on that little omission."

He spoke, staring at the church. "My dad was the parson here."

"You're a preacher's kid?"

A nod. "He had what you might call a small theological problem with the Church of Scotland, so they relegated him to a dead church"— a point—"and forgot about him."

"What was the disagreement?"

"My dad believed. They didn't."

"Yeah, I can see how that might upset them."

"For years my dad held Sunday service for one or two people. Sometimes none. Didn't matter to him. He'd stand up there and preach to me and my mom. Or an empty room. Got so cold sometimes in that church, we'd huddle around the fireplace." A pause. "The church paid Dad by allowing him to live in the parsonage, so Dad supplemented his income with farming. We grew barley and rye for the local distilleries. Including our own. We also raised sheep for the wool and had a small herd of Scottish hairy cows. I loved farm life. I was up early, working before school, and spent a lot of afternoons on a tractor. I also learned to tend our still. Along about the age of twelve, we had a Sunday morning visitor. Dad met her at the door, about my size but maybe a year older than me, and he led her to the front row and sat her between me and Mom. Then he returned to the altar. 'Shall we begin?' That's when I noticed the two men in dark suits standing in the rear and two more standing outside. Turns out the daughter of the Queen was a believer too."

"The princess?"

Pockets nodded. "She would have been fourteen at the time. Her family—"

"By 'family' you mean the royal family?"

"Yes mum."

"You are killing me, Pockets."

Pockets continued, "Her family owned a coastal home on property contiguous to ours. Real hush-hush, and she came here often, enjoying the solitude and quiet of country life. No hustle and bustle. No pretension. Every now and then the Queen would accompany. They'd walk through their field, cross that fence, and walk up that road and into the chapel. I remember sitting there on a bench. Me, Mom, the Queen, and her daughter, Catherine." A chuckle. "And about a half dozen men, armed to the hilt, scattered around us."

"The Queen of England came to your dad's church?"

"Dad never told a soul. None of us did." Pockets continued eating, letting the memory bubble up slowly. "Maybe a year later, I was working one evening when a storm rolled in, so I sought shelter in this barn to wait out the rain. Turns out Catherine had too. She'd been walking the coastline when the lightning scared her. I built a fire, and we huddled up close to the heat. Just two kids drying out. I kept looking for the Royal Guard, but none appeared. I told her, 'We better get you home. They'll be looking for you.' She nodded, and that's about the time three men entered the barn."

Pockets paused. "Drunks from the pub. No good. Beset with bad intention. I was not as big as I am now, but farm life had toughened me up maybe more than some. And given my taste for rabbit, I was pretty good with a longbow at short distance, so I nocked an arrow and sent it into the groin of the first man. The second came at me pretty fast, so I knocked out several of his teeth with a shovel handle. I was turning my attention to the third one when I felt the lightning bolt shoot through my shoulder. The bullet ripped through me, knocked me to the ground, and he was dragging Catherine kicking and screaming out the barn when I got to my feet and broke his arm with the poker and put a pretty good gash in his face. The second man stood, spitting teeth, and lunged for me, so I swung the poker and shattered his jaw. The two of them crawled out the barn into the mud while the first idiot screamed for his momma.

"I was bleeding out when the Royal Guard appeared. They found me lying on the ground and Catherine applying pressure to the holes. Next thing I knew, I heard the sound of a helicopter and then felt the sensation of being lifted. Weird. When I woke, the Queen was sitting on one side of my bed, holding my hand, while my mom and dad sat on the other. She had called in her surgeon and told him not to leave that operating room until he'd saved my life. In the coming months, she deeded this land to my folks and paid to put me through school just up the road at St. Andrews. Same school where she sent her own children. I was a fish out of water, and given that we were not wealthy, I got picked on a good bit. But I was tough, word spread, and the opportunities were many. At graduation, she—"

"And by 'she,' you still mean the Queen of England?"

Pockets laughed. "She asked me what I wanted to do, and I told her I'd like to join the Royal Guard."

Joe shook her head. "You're a member of the Royal-freaking-Guard?"

Pockets laughed. "I spent a few tours on foreign soil. Partnered up with American and British special forces. Then came home and, given some events that happened while serving in the foreign theater, I was decorated. When the Queen hung that medal around my neck, she said, 'Well, Pockets, what'll it be this time?' I'd suffered some injuries and needed some extended time to heal up, so she put me on family detail."

Joe's jaw opened slightly. "You guarded the royal family?"

A nod. Followed by a pause. "Finished up my twenty years working a detail in Israel. Was flying back here, wondering what was next, when

I met your producer on the plane. He asked me to give him my opinion, and with no one expecting me here, I agreed. Couple months later, you called." He shrugged. "Here we are."

"I can't believe you didn't tell me any of this before."

"You never asked." He laughed. "Truth is, I wouldn't have known who you are, were it not for Catherine. She's a huge fan. So is her mum. They used to make me watch your movies. I've seen most of them several times."

Joe shook her head. "I cannot believe we are having this conversation."

Pockets stood. "Can I show you something?"

"You have more surprises? I don't know if I can handle any more. Do you have a keycard to Area 51? King Tut's tomb?"

Pockets led her to a small door, unlocked it, and turned on a light, which shone on two flights of stone stairs leading down. Landing on a stone floor and surrounded by stone walls. They headed down and Pockets explained, "Built long before refrigeration." He motioned to the stone. "This room is eight hundred to a thousand years old. Was once part of a larger castle of which the chapel is the only remaining structure." The air was cool and smelled of earth. "Stays constant in the midfifties year-round, no matter what's going on upstairs."

Joe turned in a circle, surrounded by large wooden whiskey barrels stacked in neat rows. Each barrel was date-stamped. "Dad and I turned it into a distillery in my teens. The money we made got us through the winters. That barrel over there will be thirty years old this year. These are in their twenties. That's last year."

"Last year?"

Pockets nodded. "Most years I spend my vacation time down here. Distill a few barrels. Then put them up." He chuckled. "My retirement plan."

"May I?"

He lifted a bottle from a shelf, removed a cork, and handed her a small glass. "A wee dram."

The trilling of the *r* was not lost on her. Joe sipped and nodded.

"You got time for one more story?"

"Are you telling it?" she asked with a smile.

Pockets led her outside, where the sky had turned dark and a storm threatened. The path had been worn at one time, but now the brush and grass had grown waist-high. It led toward the coastline and a stone wall, maybe eight feet high. Pockets pushed open the iron gate, revealing an ancient cemetery. Many of the names were worn smooth by the constant coastal winds. Pockets peeled off his coat and offered it to Joe, who draped it over her shoulders. He pointed. "*Le Morte d'Arthur* was one of Dad's favorites. He found a two-book edition and used to read it to me at night, then walk me through here and tell me how several of the Knights of the Round Table were buried here. Lancelot. Gawain. Percival. Did wonders for my imagination."

He stopped at a newer headstone. Plain. Modest. Recently swept. Two names. "Dad died a few months after the mess in the barn. He made a house call to a sick widow and contracted something. Got in his lungs. My ma would come down here at night, a blanket, two wee drams, sit right there, and talk to him. Some nights I'd come with her. She followed him four years later. Doctors said it was broken heart syndrome. I didn't know it at the time because it was all I knew, but my folks lived a beautiful love affair. Kind of stuff they write stories about. We knew laughter, dancing. They were tender even when we didn't have two coins to rub together. Which was most of the time."

Joe sat, pulled her knees up into her chest, and wrapped herself in Pockets's jacket.

"Mum"—he pointed over his shoulder toward the adjacent royal compound—"watched over me. Made sure I had opportunity. Chance for advancement. As a result, I've seen much of this world. Met kings and important people few ever will." He stared at the stone. "The life I've lived is not suitable for marriage. Not fair. Too much travel. Too little time at the dinner table when your knees are touching." He chose his words. "Mom told me Dad's love for her was like moonlight on stone. No matter what—cold, heat, drought, or a storm raging offshore—he was there, shining down." He brushed the stone with his hand. "Guarded by all these ancient knights and their stones."

Joe wiped her eyes. Her voice a whisper. "It's beautiful."

Both were staring across the North Sea when Pockets broke the silence. "I've been places. Seen things. Things that trouble me when I try to sleep. But"—he pointed at the gate—"they don't get in here."

Moments passed. When she spoke, her voice was little more than a whisper. "I used to dream that something like this existed. But somewhere in my childhood, that dream died. I swore I would never let myself dream about that place again. And I swore I'd never have kids, just to protect them from the possibility of the pain I'd known. Then I got married and . . ." A shake of her head. "It's difficult." A pause. "Syd wants kids one day. Not the next. He's a moving target. So I decided maybe if I could give him a child, give love, maybe . . ." She trailed off. "Maybe it'd fill this big, giant hole in the center of my chest."

"What does Syd say when you say all this?"

"I haven't told him." She looked at him. The admission either painful or purging, he wasn't sure. A single shake of her head. "Syd doesn't understand"—she shot him a sideways glance—"me."

"Tried couples therapy?"

"Tried? No. Asked for? Yes."

"Why do you stay married?"

The storm had moved in and brought with it sheets of salty mist. They stared into it while it misted their faces. "Grow up like me and you discover there are two kinds of kids. Those who quit and give up hope, and those who hold on for dear life. Clinging till your knuckles bleed. I've never quit on anything and I don't plan to start with Syd."

"What if he quits on you?"

"I don't know." A pause. She pointed to the royal family's property. "Whatever happened with you and . . . ?"

"The reason they trusted me then, and trust me now, is because I never used what happened as leverage to become something I'm not. Never acted as though they owed me something. I stayed in my place. I maintained the line."

She raised an eyebrow. "The line?"

He nodded. "That invisible barrier that exists between them and us. It's an acknowledgment that while I stand on the perimeter of their lives, even defending their lives, they are entitled to live their lives without me stepping into their circle. It's an unspoken understanding that I have no right to insert myself into that. Not even if they invite me. And it's up to me to never cross it. Be seen but not heard. Because the moment I do cross the line, the moment I take a casual seat at the table and act as though I exist on a level equal to them, they lose all faith in my ability to protect them." He shook his head. "And in this line of work, that's unacceptable."

"Sounds harsh."

"It's the job."

"But back at the castle, when the Queen walked me to the car, she stepped inside your line. Touched your face."

"That's her prerogative. Not mine. She may cross it at will. I may not."

"Seems unfair."

"We don't do this job because it's fair. It's not a question of fair."

"What then?"

"It's deeper than fairness. You know it when you do it."

"Do what?"

He shrugged. "Is there anything you wouldn't do to get pregnant?"

"I don't think so."

"Why?"

She considered this. "I don't know that I can answer that."

He nodded. "It's something like that."

"When do you ever think about you?"

He chuckled. "Not very often."

"Seems like an un-fun way to live."

"I don't know if this will make sense to you, but a life laid down is better than one picked up."

She studied him. "It only makes sense because I know you."

He glanced at his watch. "We've got a bit of a drive."

He held the door while she climbed in, and she touched his arm, slipping inside his circle. "Pockets?"

"Yes mum."

"This was"—she glanced around the world he called home—"an extravagant gift."

He nodded.

She looked up at him and smirked. "Tell the truth—good-looking guy like you, how many girls have you serenaded at the property with these fairy tales about knights and queens and castles?"

He never took his eyes off the land. "None, mum."

On the way back to the hotel, she made a few calls and then spent an hour memorizing lines for the following day's work. Pulling into the valet line, she asked, "Do you own a dark suit?"

"Yes mum."

"I've got to go to this thing and was wondering if you would mind going with me. With us?"

He was well aware of the event and had spent considerable time prepping for it. "Yes mum."

In the few weeks leading up to the awards ceremony, Pockets began noticing the changes. Time with Joe became split between moments of real lucidity, of presence, and lapses of confusion and absence. Of an inability to differentiate this reality from the painful one in her heart.

Following the trip to his family home, Pockets returned her to her room at the hotel, then walked down the hall to his room. As he stood in front of the closet untying his tie, someone knocked on the door. He opened it to find Joe. Ten minutes had passed since he saw her last. She held the phone to her ear and appeared to be repeating what was just spoken to her.

"Five bedrooms, six baths, a pool house . . ." She paused. Nodding. "The fitness center will be great. He works out more than Thor." Another pause. "What's in the garage?" A smile. "Does that come with the purchase price?" A final pause. "I'll take it."

She hung up, smiling, and stood there staring at Pockets.

"Yes mum."

"I bought you a house."

"Mum?"

"Well, I know you have a home here, but you're in the States more than not and I just figured you'd like to have a place to call home. So when the place next to ours came up for sale, I called." She opened her phone and began scrolling through pictures. "It's on the ocean."

"Yes mum, I know the house, but—"

"It comes with six Harley-Davidsons, a huge truck, and a trailer. I thought you might like a Harley. Also, the fitness center has an infrared sauna and the pool is one of those infinity kind with a waterfall." She clutched her hands to her chest. "Now we're neighbors. Do you own a helmet?"

He nodded. "Yes mum."

The following week she handed him the keys and gave him a tour of his new seven-million-dollar ocean-side home—for which she paid cash. He followed her through the home as reality set in. She was going crazy. In the weeks that followed, when she asked him how he was enjoying the home, he smiled. "Very much." But he never moved out of his closet-sized room in her basement—the one that left him thirty-seven feet from her door at any moment. If anything, declining conditions demanded he be closer. Not farther away.

Two weeks later, George, her financial advisor, appeared with paperwork placing the home in his name. That night, he walked upstairs. "Mum? Was wondering if I could talk to you about this paperwork?"

He found her asleep on the couch. A rare sight given that she slept little these days. Laying the papers aside, he covered her with a blanket and pulled the blinds, hoping she'd sleep past sunup.

Three weeks later, with sun-god Syd in attendance and bronzed by the Venezuelan sun, Joe won her second Academy Award. And when she did, Pockets watched from the shadows.

CHAPTER 26

AFTER

The party continued into the early hours of the morning. Most slept where they fell or found a couch within reach. The house was littered with medicated bodies. Frank was up early and out of the house but I let him go, choosing instead to sit tight. I cracked the windows, allowing the sea breeze to dry the sweat on my skin. I thought about cranking the car but needed to save my gas in the event Amber made a run for it.

My suspicion was that cracks had surfaced in the life of the happy couple. Amber had signed up to carry a child and then profit off having done so. She had not signed up to be one insignificant member of a multi-person posse. And given the party that occurred here last night, I'd wager Amber was feeling a bit overlooked and underappreciated. She had retreated to the master bedroom just after 9:00 p.m. while Frank played video games in the basement until almost midnight, which was when the pool party started hopping. At which point he'd entertained the crowd, eventually disappearing discreetly with three girls into the pool house. Amber emerged from her room around 2:00 a.m., scoured the pool deck trying to find him, could not, and returned to her room only to reemerge five minutes later, load into the blacked-out Escalade, and drive herself to the hospital.

I followed the Cadillac to the emergency room where Amber stayed until early morning, during which time I secured a second AirTag. Just to be sure. Unless their relationship was entirely business, I sensed trouble in paradise. At 8:17 a.m., she exited the hospital, got into her car, and spent the next hour talking on the phone and driving aimlessly through the streets of LA and Hollywood, eventually returning home. Twenty minutes later, an argument commenced. From what I could tell, Amber woke Frank, who did not want to be awakened on his day off, and relayed the night's events. Frank, not interested, told her to go away, although he used one or two more colorful words.

So Amber did what he said. She went away. Far away.

The range in my rented Lincoln might top four hundred miles, while the range in Amber's Cadillac was probably five to six hundred, which I doubted would get used given that it was being driven by a woman with a baby sitting on her bladder.

I was right. We stopped every hour to ninety minutes. Each time for the bathroom and then potato chips, M&M's, ice cream, and a cheese-burger. In that order. Followed by a two-hour nap in the shade in a Walmart parking lot. My thermal showed that with the engine running, she crawled in the back, stretched out, and lay very still for a little over two hours. Well rested, she entered the Walmart and routed through the bathroom and then the grocery aisles, emerging with several plastic bags. Loading into the Cadillac, she pulled her SIM card from her existing phone, opened the packaging on a prepaid, and made the swap. She then pitched the old phone, backed out of the Walmart lot, and headed toward Vegas.

Amber was running, and she was serious about it.

As the afternoon moved into evening, I kept an eye on my phone and the remaining four AirTags sitting still in Frank's driveway back in Los Angeles. In unison, at 5:00 p.m., all four departed the driveway in single file and merged onto the highway. Headed for Vegas. At what I calculated as a hundred miles an hour.

Evidently, I was not the only one tracking the Escalade.

An hour later, Amber pulled into the parking lot of a motel on the outskirts of Las Vegas, where she was met by a tall, handsome Native American wearing a cowboy hat, boots, and a badge, carrying a gun, and driving a car marked "Navajo Nation Tribal Police."

This just got interesting.

She exited the car, they hugged, she cried, she kissed him passionately, and he led her into the motel room before reemerging thirty minutes later, during which time I hedged my bets and moved the AirTag to his car. He had changed out of his uniform and into plain clothes. He helped her into his car and let her sit with the engine running while he crawled under the Escalade and scanned the underside of her car, eventually pulling Frank's GPS tracker. He was about to smash it with a hammer when an RV pulled in across the street for gas. When the driver went inside during his fill-up, Amber's new boyfriend switched the tracker. Five minutes later, the new lovebirds were heading northeast toward Mesquite and Provo while her tracker moved south.

Amber had made her choice, and she'd not chosen Frank. She'd also begun using the new prepaid to send texts to Joe's cell demanding six-figure money along with new routing and account numbers. She wasn't messing around. Her wording was terse and no-nonsense. Along the lines of, "If you ever want to see this baby alive, wire the money." Which caused me to wonder what had happened in the hospital. Was the baby coming early? Was he or she not doing well? Was Amber okay? Had they moved up the C-section? I had no way of knowing, but since her hospital visit, she'd shifted into a different gear with a sense of urgency.

Following the new boyfriend, I watched my phone as the RV left the gas station. Shortly thereafter, two of the vehicles in Frank's posse peeled off in an attempt to intersect the snowbirds, while two continued toward the motel. Within an hour of Amber's Escalade, one car continued toward the motel while the second, probably driven by Frank, chose a northern highway that would eventually bring him in behind us—which suggested the new boyfriend had not found all the trackers and should have scanned her bag. Three hours later, one of Frank's cars had pulled into the motel parking lot where they no doubt found her car empty and cold, while Amber and her boyfriend had parked at the sprawling New Beginnings Casino one hundred miles inside tribal boundaries, which brought all sorts of jurisdiction issues into play. Also of interest was the brand-new hospital a mile down the road.

Amber and her boyfriend parked and he led her inside, having shouldered her bag. They walked by the check-in counter and didn't so much check in as the attendant handed the boyfriend a key. More of a baton pass. The happy couple then spent an hour in their suite, which gave me time to check in and nose around.

The boyfriend's name was Ricardo Broadwater. Known locally as Sheriff Broadwater and known throughout the Navajo Nation as Chief Broadwater. Judging from others' body language when around him, he was something of a Navajo godfather. Part of me actually wanted to warn Frank because, if he had not already, he was about to meet his match. A quick online search showed that Ricardo had acted in a few films, where he undoubtedly met Amber.

The two ate dinner at one of the casino's five restaurants, complete with live music and a magic show. At 10:00 p.m., they laughed and played slots as Frank pulled into the drive. I had to hand it to Frank—he was either the smartest and most entrepreneurial mailroom employee in history, or the dumbest. Ricardo was huge and could crush Frank. His hands were paws. Not to mention tribal authorities possessed expanded and near absolute authority in tribal land. They could do what they wanted, when they wanted, with whomever they wanted, and they didn't have to ask anyone's permission. They were a sovereign nation and Ricardo was their chief with a Hollywood pedigree. People loved this guy.

CHAPTER 27

BEFORE

Having finished a rigorous filming schedule, and at the behest of her doctors, Joe turned her attention inward. Focusing on how to help her body do what it was meant to do. She continued to think that if she could just stay pregnant, Syd might stick around for longer than the weekend required to get her pregnant. With the financial means to do so, she traveled to France, Spain, and Switzerland, working with medical professionals to convince her body to produce viable eggs.

For the next several months, Joe underwent painful and expensive procedures and even a clinical trial, all with little effect. One night after a delicate and painful procedure, Pockets was seated in a chair in his hotel room alongside Joe's suite when his phone dinged. The text was short. "Help."

He used his keycard to open the door and called out, "Mrs. Joe?"

Her voice echoed from the bedroom. "Pockets." She sounded out of breath.

Pockets knocked but when she didn't answer, he poked his head in and found Joe crumpled on the floor. Sweating. Half dressed. A towel covering her waist. Gritting her teeth. The pain apparent. "I need to get to the bathroom."

The floor was red.

He lifted her and carried her to the bathroom where he set her on a bench, only to discover the bleeding was more significant than she'd let on. Flirting with consciousness, she leaned her head against the wall and spoke with her eyes closed. "If you could set me in the shower . . ."

He adjusted the water and then tried to help her stand, but she doubled over in pain. So he carried her, setting her gently on the floor. She was ghostly white. He didn't hesitate. He dialed 911 about the time her head bobbed to one side.

The surgery had not taken.

He grabbed a blanket, wrapped her in it, and tried to keep her awake as the elevator descended. When he reached the hotel lobby, the paramedics were entering. "We'll take her from here, sir."

Pockets strode through the doors, into the back of the waiting ambulance, and gently laid her on the stretcher. The driver looked at the blood, then at Pockets. "You're not allowed—"

Pockets pointed through the windshield, his arms covered in blood. "Drive."

Sheet white, lips blue, her blood pressure measured 55 over 17 and dropping, and her pulse was erratic and weak. They started IVs en route but blood was pouring out faster than they could pump fluids in.

Pockets watched but knew they were losing her. She was going to die in this ambulance on the way to the hospital. He'd waited too long. When she stopped breathing, Pockets started chest compressions while the paramedic charged the defibrillator. When she didn't respond, they shocked her a second time. "Come on, lady."

As sweat dripped off his forehead, Pockets counted out loud: "One, two, three, four . . ." He knew from experience that every compression forced more blood out through the hemorrhage, exacerbating the problem, but it also forced it up and into the brain. What might kill her might also help her live. And if she was to live, her brain needed blood.

While Pockets administered CPR, the medic mashed the IV bag between his hands, force-feeding fluid into her collapsing system. A mile from the hospital, they shocked her a third time, and she registered a weak response and a momentary pulse. Then flatline.

Pressing his finger to her carotid, the medic was frantic. "Talk to her, man. We're losing her." Pockets lifted her limp body, cradled her head, pressed his lips to her ear—his breath on her face—and said the only thing he knew to say. The only thing that might call her back. And the one thing he could never tell her.

And somewhere in the dark, the whisper echoed and her shattered soul and battered body heard him. The darkness retreated.

Her eyes flickered, the light returned, and she sucked in a breath. Then another.

When the doors shut, leaving him alone in the emergency room while a team of medical personnel crowded around her, Pockets confronted the unavoidable impossibility of his life. Now more than ever, she needed him—to protect her from both herself and the world in which she found herself. But staring at the blood, Pockets also knew she could never know the truth. No matter the cost. No matter the ache. To protect her, guard her, keep her safe, he could never again allow himself to cross the line. Pockets now lived in a world where he would wake every morning only to die every day. Then do it again tomorrow. And the day after that. He would give her all of himself while taking nothing from her. Because the second he let his guard down, she would slip between his fingers and be gone.

CHAPTER 28

BEFORE

During emergency surgery, Joe required seven units of plasma. Three of which they drew from Pockets. They took two and he said, "Nope. Keep going."

Syd, meanwhile, was caught in an ice storm and couldn't return for nearly a week. He posted a snow-swept, tear-filled plea for prayers on TikTok and Insta. His fans swooned at his emotional authenticity and the post went viral, garnering tens of thousands of likes and thousands of emotional videos from fans worldwide, including several dozen Hollywood elites, pop stars, and professional athletes.

Joe slept three days only to wake to a room overrun with flowers and balloons. The doctor told a weak and ghostlike Joe that she had arrived minutes from death and that it could take weeks, months even, to regain her strength. Four days later, amid doubling social media numbers, heartbroken Syd fought valiantly to de-ice his plane with little effect. He was forced to spend a second week inside the arctic circle.

From her room, Joe texted Pockets. "Can you come in here, please?"

Pockets, sport coat and tie, stood from his perch and cracked open the door. "Yes mum?"

She spotted his appearance and chuckled. "You're really not going to let it go, are you?"

Pockets buttoned his coat. "No mum."

Joe tapped her chest. "They tell me I have you to thank for this."

"What's that?"

"The air in my lungs."

"People are like cars. Once you jump-start them, the engine takes over."

"You just compared me to a car engine."

"My pleasure, mum."

"You're killing me, Pockets."

"Yes mum."

She tapped her chest. "Here's the deal. You breathed into me. Pressed your lips to mine"—she gave him a knowing look, as if he enjoyed it—"for an extended period of time." She waved him off. "So we're past the 'mum' thing. You and me are like lovers without the sex."

"I don't know about—"

She nodded. "Oh, I do." She tried to stand but teetered and fell forward, where he steadied and held her until she gained her footing. She shook her head, trying to shake off the dizziness. Joe eyed the ironed creases in his pants. "Do you starch your pants?"

Pockets looked down as if the answer was obvious. "Yes mum."

She laughed. "Those things could stand on their own." She pointed to the flowers and asked, "Feel like stretching your legs?"

"Yes mum, but . . ."

"But what?"

"We should get you another gown."

She turned in a circle. "What's wrong with this one?"

"Nothing. Provided you don't mind flashing everyone behind you."

Over the next hour, he wheeled her in and out of most every room on the floor as they gave away flowers, tied balloons to bed frames, took pictures, FaceTimed relatives, and generally asked, "How are you feeling?" None of which Joe posted on social media. By the time Syd made it back, Joe had been home a week, mourning yet another failed attempt without him.

CHAPTER 29

AFTER

Frank exited his vehicle with three other men. All bigger than Frank, which caused me to think he might have known about Ricardo prior to his arrival. One watched the entrance, which also happened to mean watching Ricardo's car; the second entered the hotel and disappeared toward the suite and undoubtedly Amber's handbag; and Frank and another young guy skirted the edges of the casino doing their best not to get noticed. Interestingly, every time Ricardo left or spoke to someone, Amber excused herself to use the bathroom. This happened often. She'd turn the corner, type furiously, then wait for a response, but Joe's phone received no texts. Neither did Frank's. She was communicating with someone else.

My gut told me Amber was coordinating a cat-and-mouse game to pit street-savvy Frank against muscled Ricardo, who wielded great authority within tribal boundaries. Watching her communicate with someone not them caused me to think her real savior might soon reveal himself.

When I asked myself why she'd go through all the trouble, all roads led to one answer. Through her friendship with Joe, Amber had tasted the limelight and liked it. Who wouldn't? Through the gift of proximity, Amber had been brought into a world and a life that few experience. Because her fans adored her, and some worshipped her, the world had laid out a silver platter for Joe, and Joe—because her heart was bigger than her petite body and she simply desired to share what she had with others—had offered Amber that same platter. What's mine is yours. Amber had taken a seat at the table and developed a taste for it.

Now, several years down the road, having carried a baby to full term, watched her body change in the process, and come to understand what this pregnancy had cost her, Amber had a change in perspective. What had been an honest offering, a desire to help someone hurting, had morphed into something owed to her. Something she deserved. A right.

Sitting at a slot machine two rows away, hidden beneath a wig, baggy clothes, and sunglasses, I had a feeling Amber wasn't too keen on sharing the winnings with anyone. Including Frank, Ricardo, and whomever else she was talking to.

One of Joe's greatest gifts was her tendency to be self-effacing. So encouraging of others. To make others feel as though they were truly her equal. Sisters all. Truth was, they weren't, but Joe was so personable everyone thought they were her best friend. It's one of the reasons everyone loved her. Because she was reachable. She brought the star to earth and didn't burn anyone with its heat.

Amber was different. She'd been warmed by that star so many times she'd come to believe it was her own. She'd watched how effortlessly Joe did her job and thought she could do what Joe did. *It's not that hard.* Once that thought entered her cranium, she began to think she deserved Joe's life, because when it came right down to it, and let's just be honest, Joe didn't deserve it. Joe was little more than right girl, right place. Everyone knew that. Amber had seen behind the curtain and knew Oz's secret. How the small man lifted all the levers. As a result, she wanted Joe's life and, not only that, she had convinced herself she deserved it. Which was why she stole Joe's baby. The next step in this parade was to get that baby outside her body and then sell him or her to the highest bidder. That is, Joe.

Amber might have stolen Joe's baby and she might well get away with it, but she made one mistake, one fatal flaw, and at a time of its choosing, it would surface. She was no Joe. If she started right now and practiced her whole life, she could never do what Joe did. Never become Joe. What came effortlessly to Joe would never come to Amber. You can train a pig to run with horses, but at the end of the day, all you have is a fast pig. Joe had a gift. She made unbelievers believe. In the selfless offering of her soul, Joe took from the broken the despair of normality and insignificance and gave them something immeasurable. A priceless exchange. She gave them "What if?"

To Frank's credit, he did not storm the castle and make a scene. He waited. Patiently. Ricardo, who was a bit of a drinker, was growing louder and more unsteady with each minute. He was also losing at black-jack, which I thought might buy me a few minutes.

During this stalemate, I made a game-time decision, left the casino, pulled the AirTag from Ricardo's unmarked car, then routed through housekeeping and stole an access key, which I used to let myself into Ricardo's suite, where I found Amber's bag, which turned out to be a treasure chest of information. Without bothering to read each, I took a picture of every sheet of paper in her thick "baby" file save one. The printed 3D ultrasound. I kept that. She might discover it missing, but I had a feeling I'd need it more in the days ahead. I also read enough to know her due date was two weeks away but the scheduled C-section back in LA was only a week away, due to the baby's size and the fact that Amber had no previous children. Finally, I dug through the bag, which revealed clothes and, as I suspected, a GPS tracker sewn into the seam. Hidden from view but recognizable to the touch. No doubt Frank's. Which proved my suspicion—Frank had not trusted Amber from the beginning. She was a means to an end. In like manner, Amber had not trusted Frank, which explained why all of us were currently running around New Beginnings Casino playing a game of cat and mouse.

I wiggled the tracker out and inserted my AirTag in its place. If she flew anywhere, I'd lose it when they climbed above the towers, but it would register again, given cell coverage, once they landed. I also found one other item, which I was certain would be of great interest to Frank. A bag of phones. Prepaids. Eight in all.

This was a gold mine, but the next move was risky. I had already been in this room too long, but these phones might be my lifeline to Amber if she got away. I turned on the phones and began downloading an app called mSpy that allowed me to track the phone without the user knowing it. When loaded, it granted access to my prepaid. Then I turned each phone off. It would only work when the phone was turned on, but sooner or later, Amber would find the AirTag and either destroy it or hang it on a plane for Brazil, and I'd be blind. Thus far I'd been lucky, but Amber was growing desperate.

Hustling to the door, I was met by the sound of a keycard fumbling on the other side.

I opened the coat closet opposite the door, stepped in, and pulled the two doors closed. If someone opened either door, I was toast.

The suite door opened and Ricardo stumbled in, laughing and pulling Amber along with him. Being this close convinced me he was a big man. Even his voice was big. He stumbled past the closet door and down the hall to the bedroom when Amber said, "Be right there, honey. Just need to pee."

Ricardo responded with something like, "Haven't you done that . . ." But the rest was garbled and he trailed off.

Ricardo fell onto the bed and Amber tiptoed to the bathroom, crossing in front of the closet door. Peeking toward the bedroom, she darted to the living room and began packing her toiletries. Then she dialed her phone. After a few seconds, she whispered, "Hey, baby. Yeah, five minutes. He's . . ." She paused, listening to the sound of his breathing. "Out." As she said this, Ricardo began to snore. Emboldened by the growing sound, her voice rose. "I'll meet you at the runway." Another pause. "Love you too. Can't wait to see you, baby. Yeah, and when we get all this behind us . . ." She grabbed her bag and began repacking so I lost a few of her words, but I heard enough to know that Amber was going to duck out of here and leave Frank and Ricardo to shoot it out with one another while she slipped away into the clouds. She had a third lover literally waiting in the wind.

About this time I noticed Ricardo's duffel. Sitting on the ground. Beneath me.

If she cared this little about him, I had a sinking suspicion she was about to grab his bag and pilfer whatever she wanted. I took two steps backward and tried to melt into the wall. About that time, Amber pulled open the right louvered door, grabbed the bag, and dumped it in the hallway. All the while keeping one eye on the bed and the other on the door. Which meant she never looked in the closet.

She rifled through his bag, grabbed a holstered Glock 19, a loaded magazine, an envelope of cash, and another phone. She then threw the bag back into the closet, shut the door, and tiptoed to the bedroom, where she lifted the cash from the wallet chained to his belt. Having robbed Ricardo blind, she shouldered her bag, walked to the door, paused, took two calming breaths, then slowly opened the door and closed it quietly behind her.

After the longest sixty seconds of my life, I followed. My phone showed Amber was winding her way through the maze of the hotel to a rear exit, while Frank's tracker showed Amber in bed with Ricardo. I guessed Frank would let Ricardo get good and asleep before they made any attempt to retake Amber. Also, given the volume and depth of the snore coming out of Ricardo, I was certain someone had dropped something in his drink. Whether Amber or Frank's guys, I had no way of knowing, as both had reason to take him out of the fight. Which, judging by the sound of things, they had.

I climbed into my rental about the same time Amber's AirTag began moving through the rear parking lot. Ten seconds later revealed an Uber. I guessed we were headed to a private airport and I was about to lose Amber to lover number three, but the tail letters of the plane would tell me a lot, so I followed at a safe distance. Ten minutes later, the Uber turned off the hard top into the Mesquite Private Airport. Amber stepped out and rushed into the waiting arms of a medium-sized man wearing glasses, a button-down oxford, high-water khakis, and tube socks with boat shoes. Look up the word *dork* in a dictionary, and this guy's picture would appear. They kissed awkwardly, which she faked enjoying. He took her bag and repositioned his combover, which the cool breeze had lifted like a rooster tail, and the two hurried toward a small single engine sitting on the tarmac. They climbed in, I snapped a picture of the tail, the engine cranked, they turned and taxied, and in less than ninety seconds even the sound had disappeared. The last time the AirTag registered, they were headed east.

I was tired, had been gone five days, had not slept in two, and was uncertain if my decision-making was good or hampered. Sleep deprivation can mess with your head. I had gambled and had no idea if the gamble would pay off or bite me. Only time would tell, which was also my problem. I didn't have much. Straws at best. When I looked at my watch it was almost 1:00 a.m. and I had a long ride ahead of me, followed by a plane ride—all of which might be good as I had far more questions than answers.

CHAPTER 30

BEFORE

Her recovery was painful. Muscles had been cut. Too much blood lost. And CPR and chest compressions, while they helped save her life, stretched ligaments and tendons. She was sore and slow to move, and healing took time. Both in body and in heart. Thinking a change of scenery might help, her medical team suggested she get out of the city. Reduce the stimuli. Find some quiet. And some sun. But she needed solace. No crowds. No fanfare. She also needed space. Clean air.

When asked what she wanted to do, she said, "The one thing that, until now, I've been unable to do. Make something grow."

Her team suggested she rent a farm in Northern California. An expansive place with vineyards, pastures, a barn, animals, a garden, even a truffle farm. Set in the country, far from Peeping Toms, and nestled among rolling rows of pinot noir. The pictures suggested Eden.

She had a better idea.

Joe paused the meeting and called Pockets. "You mind coming in here?"

Pockets knocked, then let himself into a room full of managers, agents, consultants. All jobs above his pay grade. He was normally excluded from these high-level conversations. They were strategic.

Forty-five thousand feet. His job was boots on the ground. Receive the plan and execute. Not insert himself into the planning. The room quieted.

Joe spoke softly. "I'd like to ask you something."

"Mum?"

Joe waved across the room. "I want to return to a place out of my childhood. Maybe the one place where I remember kindness. But also a place where I eventually suffered . . ." She chose her words carefully. "Rejection." A shake of her head. "Some of the memories are good. Some not." She folded her hands. "Would you?"

Pockets studied the faces studying him. Then her. "Why?"

She looked down at her hands and then back at him. "To find something I lost there."

Pockets nodded. "Yes mum."

Another wave across the room. For the first time, Pockets noticed the addition of her doctor, his team, and her therapist. "They say it could be detrimental to my recovery. Set me back."

Pockets paused. Looked across the room. Then back to her. "What does your heart need?"

She nodded slightly. "To go back."

He studied the room again. "Then we go back."

When the bus caravan crossed the Kentucky line, most of the team started humming the dueling banjos theme from *Deliverance*. An hour later, they pulled down the dirt drive where Joe had spent her twelfth birthday and much of the year following. To house "Team Joe" and also give her as much space as possible, trailers were brought in, making it look more movie set than retreat. Pockets slept in the efficiency in the barn, complete with outdoor shower and window A/C unit, which carried with it the smell of leather, hay, and manure. The porch with a single chair gave him a strategic, while not intrusive, view of the house.

The theory behind the "retreat" was to reinvigorate Joe with new surroundings and activities. In addition, everyone came to her. Trainer, masseuse, doctors, nutritionist, chef, even a language coach who helped prep her for her next role. Daily life became a cycle of treatment, work, rest, and play. Treatment, work, rest, and play.

Wash. Rinse. Repeat.

In the days that followed, she let out the breath she'd been holding for the last decade and heard herself laugh. A strange sound. One she'd not heard in a while. On the advice of her doctor, she even learned to cook. Which was a mess but fun.

She found Pockets in the barn. Carving an apple with a yellow-handled Case pocketknife. Over time, the blade had been sharpened to half its original size. "You busy?"

He stood. "No mum."

"Feel like a walk?"

She led him down a country lane. "Lucy was a widow from California who returned to her husband's family farm after he was killed in some type of accident. The California court system isn't too crazy about folks taking kids out of the state, but they granted her special permission when they saw I'd been shuffled through twenty-three prior homes. I guess they were trying to give me a shot anywhere."

She waved her hand across the ground around her. "I lived here a year. And I think I remember being happy for a time. I gravitated toward the country pace. Lucy was kind but fragile and distant. She had her husband's body returned here and buried him down there beneath that pine where he could look out over that pasture. After dinner, she'd sit at the foot of his headstone and talk to him. I used to sneak down and listen. They were tender words." A pause. "After a year, she put me on a train. I never knew what happened to her until she died last year and left me this."

Pockets listened but said nothing.

She shook her head. "Like most of my life, it makes no sense. Rejection is a painful thing." A chuckle. "Took me ten years and tens of thousands of dollars in therapy to be able to say those words. Truth is, it's the most painful." She wandered to the middle of what was once a garden. Now overgrown. "I planted a garden here. Not much. A few vegetables. Had no idea what I was doing. Most of it cooked in the sun. Even then I was trying to make something grow. Given that you know farming, I want to ask a favor."

"Yes mum."

"I want you to teach me to garden."

"Yes mum."

She put a hand on her hip. "For once in your life, will you please just say yes when I ask you a question?"

"Yes . . . mum."

She shook her head. "It's no use." She returned to her original train of thought. "I'd like to make stuff grow." She pushed the dirt around with the toe of her shoe. "Can you help me do that?"

"We can start this morning, if you like."

A nod. "I'd like."

Twenty minutes later, they drove to the nursery in town where they bought, among other things, tomatoes, peppers, manure, and fertilizer. As he loaded fifty-pound bags of fertilizer onto the flatbed cart, she read the label.

"Is this really poop?"

Holding a bag midair, he nodded.

"What do you do with it?"

"Spread it."

"How?"

"Your hands."

She spoke more to herself than him. "I'm gonna need some gloves."

Checking out, the cashier blushed and asked Joe if she could take a picture. Joe obliged and then asked her, "When are you due?"

The girl placed her hand across her rounded tummy. "Three months. But the way he's kicking, it could be tomorrow." She smiled sheepishly. "He wants out."

"Your first?"

"Second. Junior's sleeping in the office." She eyed her watch. "But he'll be screaming his head off in a few minutes."

As she spoke, a young man with "Assistant Manager" printed on his shirt appeared behind her, whispering, "Hey, baby, I got this." He shot a glance at the office. "He's stirring."

Pulling out of the parking lot, Pockets noticed Joe had grown quiet, so he pointed back toward the store. "I didn't know about the . . . I'm sorry."

She waved him off. "Sweet girl." After a minute, she asked, "You think it's like that for some folks?"

"Like what?"

She considered how to phrase it. "Two people working as a team."

"I think it can be."

Another pause. "So it's okay to hope for that?"

Somewhere in here he realized she experienced that exchange on one level, while he experienced it on another. "Yes mum. I think so."

"So I'm not crazy?"

"You're never crazy to hope."

She leaned her head back and forced a laugh. "Good, 'cause for a minute there . . ."

He was about to turn toward home when he changed his mind. "Mum, are you in a hurry?"

She sat cross-legged and shook her head. "Nope."

He studied the contortion her limber legs allowed and realized his stiff hips would break before they let him do that, but he kept any comment to himself. He pulled into a thrift store and parked, and then she followed him as he briskly walked through the aisles, finally handing her a long-sleeved flannel shirt and some denim overalls.

She accepted them. "You want me to wear these?"

"Might be a good idea."

She leaned in and whispered, "So I look the part?"

"No mum, it'll just help with bugs and keep you from itching. Tomato plants can be unkind."

She realized he was being serious. "Oh. Yeah. Can I try them on?"

He had not thought of this. Nor did the thrift store have a dressing room.

She studied the three other people currently shopping. All of whom were trying clothes on where they stood. She mumbled to herself something about getting over herself, pulled both items over her existing clothes, and spun. Admiring herself in the mirror. Both items of clothing were five sizes too large.

Pockets shrugged, realizing he might have chosen poorly. "Never been too good with sizes." He began rifling through the stacks. "I didn't realize—"

"No. They're perfect. To begin with, no one will ever recognize me. And two"—she ran her arms down the waist and legs, accenting the ample room—"when I get pregnant, these will fit perfectly."

At a hardware store he bought her a straw hat, some leather gloves, and rubber boots. Donning all three, she was giddy. "I've never owned any of this."

At the checkout counter, a young man asked if he needed any help. Pockets pointed at the display case. "Two-bladed trapper."

The boy unlocked the case. "CV or stainless?"

"CV."

The boy handed him a yellow-handled Case two-bladed trapper, which he in turn handed to Joe. "You can't very well farm without a farmer's knife."

She held it like a robin's egg, then whispered, "What's CV?"

"Chrome vanadium."

"And that is . . . ?"

"The steel of the blade."

"And that's better than stainless?"

"Yes mum."

"Why?"

"It's softer and can get feather-sharp."

"Does it dull quickly?"

"It can."

"Will it rust?"

"It can."

"Will mine look like yours?"

A nod. "In time."

"You show me how to sharpen it?"

He chuckled. "I will."

The total came to just over a hundred and fifty dollars. She offered him her Amex Black. "Pockets, please. I know how much you make."

He paid the man in cash and began carrying the items to the truck, where she wouldn't let it go. "Pockets, really!"

He helped her into the truck. "Mum, I'd pay you for what I get to do today."

CHAPTER 31

AFTER

"You there?"

No answer.

"Hello?"

Silence.

"Anybody?"

Nothing.

She lay on her back, one leg crossed over the other and bent at the knee. "Bueller?"

Silence.

She raised her voice. "Five days and counting."

Still nothing.

"Which makes this Day 15. Look, I don't need some drawn-out conversation where we talk about our feelings, but if you could just check in. Send a sonar ping. Anything." She'd been talking to and bouncing off the walls for two days with no answer. "Okay. I gave you a chance."

Hearing no answer, she stood, bounced on the bed like a trampoline, and reached for the sheet she'd tied over the single rafter. One end secure, the other tied in a self-tightening loop. Once she slid it over her head and her body's weight pulled on it, the loop would tighten until it closed off her airway. This, along with the fact that she'd fastened the secure end over the single beam not directly over the bed, meant when she stepped off the bed, she would swing out into the middle of the room with nothing but air beneath her feet. A one-way trip. No do-over. The angle of the camera made this abundantly clear.

Joe offered the sheet to the camera, displaying her intention. "Don't say I didn't warn you." She stood on her tiptoes and placed the noose just over her forehead. The verge of commitment. But when no voice rang out through the speaker and no one came barging through the door, she bounced, returned the sheet to its hiding place above the rafter, and lay back down.

Deflected but not defeated.

Later that afternoon, the lazy Susan spun and dinner appeared. A cheeseburger from In-N-Out. A California staple and her favorite, and the object of more than one midnight run. She'd filmed their commercials for years. She eyed it while her mouth watered, but didn't move.

"If you think you can buy my kindness with In-N-Out after you've been AWOL almost six days, you can forget it."

The lazy Susan spun, then spun back. Where the cheeseburger once sat, now only a bologna sandwich rested. She eyed the white bread. "Are you serious right now?"

The lazy Susan spun a second time to the closed position. She stared at the camera. "That's just rude." Knowing she had his attention and that he was close enough to respond to her, she bounced on the bed, grabbed the sheet, offered it to the camera just like she'd practiced, then slid it around her head, tightening the slack around her neck. Her voice thick with sarcasm. "Good luck explaining this."

Waving to the camera, she launched herself off the side of the bed like

Peter Pan. The sheet tightened around her neck and—given gravity—pulled taut on the beam, which immediately broke in two and sent her falling two feet to the floor. She landed on her feet, the sheet draping over one shoulder like a loose toga. She stood in disbelief. Staring at the sheet, trying to make sense of why her plan failed.

His voice echoed. Calmly. "This is not my first rodeo."

This had not gone as she'd planned. "What?" She threw down the sheet. "How?"

"Look up."

She did. The beam had been sawn in two and held in place only by pressure. When pulled upon, it gave way, letting her drop harmlessly to the floor. Seconds passed as she put the pieces together.

She pointed to the clean saw cut. "Did you do that?"

"Told you I'd seen your movies."

Hands on her hips. "You saw that one too?"

"You mean the one where you taunt your forlorn love interest to risk life and limb by jumping across the balcony eight stories up, climbing the railing hanging by a single bolt, then crashing through the door and lifting your dangling, twitching body—which was some great acting by the way—saving you from pretending to kill yourself only to learn that, prior to jumping, you'd torn the sheet nearly in two so that it couldn't hold you for long enough to hang you and that you were only a second from dropping to the floor unharmed? Yes, I saw that one."

She held up the sheet, revealing the nearly complete tear that never had a chance to materialize given his handiwork on the beam. "Am I that predictable?"

"You're not about to off yourself."

"How do you know?"

"I can give you 1.2 million reasons."

"Well, there's that."

He continued, "I also know you want to get me in that room."

She dropped onto the bed, deflated. Quiet for several minutes. Studying her surroundings, she spoke without looking up. "I need one thing more."

"What's that?"

This time she could not control her emotions, which bubbled up before she could smother them. "A reason."

"To?"

"Stick this out." She pointed at the speaker. "Trust the voice."

The lazy Susan spun but she didn't look. She shook her head. "Not hungry."

He waited.

When he didn't respond, she eyed the spinning food delivery service but no food appeared. This time, something else sat on the circular shelf. She walked to the counter and stood studying the single piece of paper. Two seconds later, the image registered in her mind, her jaw opened, and she sucked in a breath. Lifting the paper, holding it as if it would break, she ran her fingers across the 3D image. The face, fingers, toes. A tear broke loose. Then another.

She turned to the cameras, afraid to ask but needing the answer. "Is this . . . ?" Then the thought occurred to her that it might not be. A cruel twist. What if her deranged captor was playing her? Her voice changed. "Because if it isn't, I swear to—"

"It is."

"How'd you . . . ?"

"I found them."

She jumped two feet off the floor. "You found them! But . . . how?" She sat, cradling the picture. "Come on, man! You've got to give me more than just snippets. I'm dying in here."

"It's complicated."

She slapped her thigh. "Welcome to my life. What can you tell me? Is Amber healthy? The baby?"

He hesitated. "It would appear so."

"Where are they?"

"The less you know, the better."

She stood. "How do you figure? That's my baby!"

"If I tell you any more, I make you an accessory. It's better if you only know what I tell you."

"Accessory? How am I an accessory? I am stuck in hell with Houdini."

"I don't think it'll be long."

She studied the picture, only to close her eyes and kiss the image. "Do you know?"

He did. "Know what?"

"Boy or girl?"

"Yes."

"Will you tell me?"

"You sure you want to know?"

She sat staring at the picture. Then she shook her head, closed her eyes, and clutched the ultrasound. "No." A pause. "No." Several minutes passed. "Is Amber okay?"

"Amber is living the good life but she's playing three men against each other. She's already run twice, and I would bet she's about to run again. Soon as she gets this baby on the outside."

Joe lit up. "So you've done this sort of thing before?"

"What? You mean search for a surrogate on the run?"

"Yes."

"No."

Her shoulders dropped. "Oh. How do you know she's okay?"

"I followed them to the doctor. Then I followed her on her road trip. It's how I got the picture."

"Did they see you?"

"No."

She eyed the camera, then traced the image of the face with her fingertips. "So . . . you really do know?"

"Yes."

A pause. "Are you going to let me out of here?"

"Yes."

"Soon?"

"Relatively."

"Can I trust you?"

"Can you really trust a man who would keep you captive against your will?"

She studied the speaker. "Are you going to get my baby for me?"

A pause. "I'm going to try."

As she considered this, another what-if occurred. "When you do, are you going to blackmail me like they are?"

"No."

"So you don't want money?"

"No."

"If you do, just tell me what you want. I'll give you—"

"I don't want your money."

"What do you want?"

"I have my reasons."

"So let me get this straight. You're holding me captive against my will to detox me while you search the country for the surrogate carrying my baby?"

"Pretty much."

"And when Amber delivers, you're going to snatch the kid, drop him or her in my lap, and let me out of here so I can live happily ever after with my child?"

"More or less."

A wrinkle appeared between her eyes. "What do you mean, 'more or less'? It's a yes or no question."

"You make it sound simple. It's not. But yes, that is my intention."

"Why?"

"I have my reasons."

"You just said that, but really, why?"

"In time."

"And you don't want money?"

"No."

"What about a sex slave?"

He laughed. "No."

She sat cross-legged on the bed. "Do we know each other?"

"I'm going to be gone again for a few more—"

"You didn't answer my question."

"It doesn't matter."

"Doesn't matter? It does to me. Did I offend you at some point in life?"

"No."

"So we do know each other?"

No response.

"Where? Did we work on a movie together?"

"I'll be gone. You can't reach me."

She stood, walked to the lazy Susan, and pressed her palms and face to the wall. "Do you really know?"

"Yes."

"And if I ask, will you tell me?"

"Of course."

"You sure I never offended you? Never hurt you?"

"I'm sure."

"If I did, would you tell me?"

"No. But regardless, you haven't."

"And I can trust you?"

"Never trust a man who holds you captive against your will."

"But I want to."

"I know. But don't." The lazy Susan spun, returning the cheeseburger. She pressed her forehead to the wall and closed her eyes. "Okay."

Hours passed. The moon rose and cast a shadow through the single window. She clutched the ultrasound and whispered, "You really know?"

His response was quick. "I do."

"Tell me."

"You sure?"

She smiled. "No. I can wait." She lay on her back and stared at the ceiling. "Are you watching me sleep?"

A pause. "No."

She chuckled. "Liar."

"You're right, I'm lying."

"Are you lying about anything else?"

"No."

"Is that a lie?"

"No."

She shook her head once. "The psychological hoops you're putting me through are worse than the withdrawal."

"I'm sorry. That's not my intention."

"Look on the bright side—you're taking my mind off the pills." She reached for the fob. "I haven't thought about them in . . . almost half a day."

"I need you to promise me something."

"My, how the tables have turned." She smiled. "I'm listening."

"I don't have a plan B, and I can't keep babysitting you because I need to leave again. So . . . no more jumping off the bed."

"I know."

"No more sheets around the neck."

"I hear you."

"I need you to do more than hear me."

"I promise."

"Say it."

"I promise you, mystery kidnapper, aka Houdini, aka the voice, that I will not hang myself with a sheet or attempt to off myself in any way."

"Thank you."

"Does this mean I can get out of here now?"

"No."

"Why?"

He laughed. "Because I don't trust you with you."

She sat quietly for several minutes. "So that's what this comes down to. You don't trust me with me."

"Pretty much."

She let out a deep breath. "I'm powerless over me."

"Yes."

She turned to the camera. "You realize that's like the worst thing you can do to another human being?"

"I realize it's risky."

"So you get your jollies by taking away any power I have over my own life?"

"No."

She pointed at the camera. "But you're still there." Then she pointed at herself. "And I'm still here." She folded her hands. "And you're still doing it?"

"Yes."

She sat up. "And I'm supposed to trust you with me?"

"Admittedly, you don't have much of a choice."

"Ironic, don't you think?"

"Not really. I'm doing a much better job managing you than you."

"How do you figure?"

"Look in the mirror. When was the last time you were two weeks clean?"

"I'm picking up what you're putting down." A pause. "So when do I get to start making decisions about me?"

"We're back to the power thing."

"You didn't answer my question."

"When you can handle it."

She shot a glance at the camera. "You're playing God again."

"Yes."

"You don't deny that?"

"No. Just look around."

"Is there a time when you plan to stop playing God?"

"Yes."

"Can you give me a date?"

"No."

"So you're just going to play God a little while, and then when you, in your omniscient wisdom, think I can handle being me again, you're going to hand me the keys to me and let me walk out of here."

"Yes."

She laughed. "A peaceful transfer of power."

"Something like that."

She lay back down. "This still sucks. And I would imagine that after two weeks, a lot of people are in a frenzy looking for me."

"They are. The networks are just now coming off twenty-four-seven coverage. And social media is a mess."

"What do you mean, 'mess'?"

"You broke Facebook and Instagram."

"I did what?"

"Broke it. Shut it down. The servers couldn't handle the traffic."

She laughed. "I'll bet that really pissed Syd off."

"I wouldn't know."

"Is all that noise making things difficult for you?"

"Things were already difficult."

"What if we made a video and I assured them I was okay?"

"Wouldn't help."

"We could try."

"Only make matters worse. It would confirm you're being held against your will."

"What if I told them I wasn't?"

"You'd be lying."

"Yeah, but they don't know that."

"I would."

She considered this. And for the first time in her captivity, she didn't say a word.

CHAPTER 32

BEFORE

Life on the farm fell into a rhythm—centering around the garden. Daylight often found them huddled around the coffeepot, then riding across the pasture on the tractor en route to their small plot. Pockets repaired the irrigation system, which involved a new pump, a hundred feet of pipe, and a dozen heads. He also taught her how to drive the tractor. Wasn't long and they had plowed, planted, and watered.

Her team called it "vegetative therapy." Soon they were eating from their own garden. Dinners were as farm-to-table as you can get, and her chef thought she'd died and gone to heaven.

Midmornings included treatments, strategy meetings, Zoom calls, reading scripts, memorizing lines, interviews, and photo ops. Postlunch included naps, massage, and reading in the swing. Late afternoons found most everyone sitting on the porch, sipping something cold, listening to doves and cicadas.

One night after dinner, Joe stepped off the porch and found Pockets in the barn. "Can I show you something?"

She led him between a row of pines to a small clearing. Wild grape vines engulfed wire fencing once erected to support them. Years had passed since their last pruning, but by some chance of daylight, shade, and rain, they had thrived. Their gnarly root stock was thicker than a man's thigh, and each produced multiple vines trained by rusty guide wires spreading fifty feet in either direction. All of which were sagging with fruit.

Joe picked a grape and turned it in her hand. "You know anything about making wine?"

Pockets shook his head. "No mum."

"Want to learn?"

"Yes mum."

Wielding small pruning shears and carrying five-gallon buckets held by straps around their necks, she taught him to snip the dark purple grapes the size of pecans, while leaving the smaller, bronzish grapes still on the vine.

She spoke as she dug through the vines. "They're called muscadines. Wild grapes. They like the humidity and the fact that it doesn't freeze too often." Joe bit into a grape. "Lucy used to make jelly for me and wine for her." She took another bite. "One of the few happy memories of my childhood." They were quiet a minute. "Lucy used to tell me that the grape keeps the score. Smoke, drought, heat, all of that is held inside the skin. Only way to get it out is to crush it. And if the grape could talk, it would probably tell you it doesn't like being crushed, but without the crushing, there's no wine."

While the light faded and the cicadas sang their nightly song, the two worked quietly, one on either side of the vine. Filling their buckets. When it was too dark to see, Pockets shouldered both buckets and they walked out of the clearing, returning to the barn. Beneath a rising moon, Joe stared down the road. At the graveside where Lucy held her nightly vigil. Moonlight on stone.

"What kind of love would cause you to wait on someone who's never coming back?"

Pockets offered no answer.

Joe continued, "Whenever she worked the garden, she wore his shirts and overalls but never washed them. Didn't want to wash out the Old Spice." Joe studied Pockets. Standing at attention. Three feet away. Never more. Never less. She had tried before to cross the line and wanted to now. To hang her hand on his arm. To steady herself. Help hold herself up. In truth, to stand with. She had grown tired of standing alone.

She shook her head. "I don't know what my husband smells like."

CHAPTER 33

BEFORE

When August rolled into September, Pockets walked into the barn to find an assembly line. Thawed grapes, a large stainless bin about three feet in diameter and eighteen inches tall, and then several smaller buckets, some cheesecloth, and a couple of machines. In the center stood Joe, barefoot and dumping grapes into the bin. Her team stood in a circle around her. All staring at him. Evidently, they'd been waiting on him.

"We have a tradition," she said, smiling as a man wielding a camera stepped out of a stall and began filming his reaction to what she was about to say. "Or"—she laughed—"we're starting one. We are going to make wine the old-fashioned way."

Pockets smiled for the camera but said nothing as Joe dumped two more bags of grapes into the bin. "Just like the Romans."

Having filled the bin with a foot of grapes, Joe led Pockets by the hand, then knelt down and began slipping off his shoes, leaving him barefoot. "We crush the grapes with our feet. Or . . ." Her team laughed all around her. "Your feet."

Pockets eyed the bin. "You want me to step into that?"

"Yes mum," Joe said in her best Scottish accent.

"Just step right in and let all that stuff squish up between my toes."

"Yep."

The cameraman was laughing.

"And you don't care if my feet are dirty?"

"Nope. Adds to the flavor."

He lifted one foot but then set it back down. "What if I have some strange toe fungus and it gets everyone sick?"

"Then we'll all die due to your poor hygiene, and when this video gets posted on YouTube the whole world will know there was a fungus-among-us."

He eyed her. "You're not going to let me get out of this, are you?"

She shook her head. More accent. "No mum."

Pockets lifted one foot, raised it over the lip of the bin, and began lowering it, only to lift it quickly back out. "But . . . I read about this thing in Africa, that these worms can . . ."

Joe shook her head. "Think of it like Scotch. Alcohol kills worms."

Just before he stepped into the bin, Joe raised a finger. "The trick is to crush slowly. Too fast and you release too much of the skin, making the juice bitter. Too slow or not enough pressure and you don't get all the juice."

"Meaning?"

"The best wine is made with the right amount of pressure over the right amount of time."

Pockets looked at his feet. "How will I know?"

She smiled. "That's why you have me. There's a balance to the crushing."

No one expected him to do it. They had placed bets. "He'll never loosen his tie long enough to step in that bin." But with the camera rolling and all eyes on him, Pockets loosened his tie, rolled up his pant legs, lifted one foot over the edge, and slowly lowered it into the grapes, his face making expressions that matched the squishing sound.

The cameraman knelt and zoomed in, then out, taking in the room, filming through a wide angle.

Having that foot squarely on the bottom of the bin, Pockets brought the second to rest alongside the first while the juice oozed out along his toes. Then, to the amazement of the team, Pockets began squishing the grapes. Raising one foot, then another, setting each down in such a way that doing so accentuated the sounds, the ooze, and everyone's matching facial expressions.

After several minutes of squishing and stepping, Pockets offered his hand to Joe. "Dance?"

Joe laughed. "I think not."

He pulled gently. "I'll teach you."

"But I already know how to dance."

Pockets shook his head once and smiled. "Not like this."

Suspicious but smiling, Joe held both his hands and stepped in as Pockets did what no one expected. Least of all Joe. With one hand held high above his head, the other tapping his thigh in drum-beat rhythm, he rose up on his tiptoes, bounced once, then extended his right leg, tapping in rhythm. Then he pulled his right heel up along his left shin and bounced twice, only to alternate feet and do the same with his left foot. "It's called the four-step Highland fling."

The team howled in delight. They circled, clapped in time, and someone pulled out a phone and began playing the theme song to Riverdance. In five minutes, Joe was bouncing, sweating, twirling, and the two were flinging juice and puree around the barn.

To the delight of the Internet crowd, the cameraman recorded every laughter-filled second. When they finally stopped and Joe caught her breath, she spoke to the camera. "My legs are on fire. I never knew making wine was such a workout." She wiped her forehead on her sleeve. "This could be the next workout craze. We'll call it 'the crush.'"

Both feet and shins were stained purple halfway to her knees. Which the camera captured from every angle, making Joe all the more human to the several million people who watched the video over the next forty-eight hours. The film included her scrubbing with soap, dancing in the bin, splashing juice around the barn, and realizing the soap had little to no effect on the stain. "This isn't funny," she said as she doubled over laughing at the sight of herself. "I'll never film another bathing suit scene again." She looked at the camera, then at her feet, and lifted her skirt. "I look like I'm wearing socks. Permanently."

Finally, Joe stood shin-deep in grape pieces while juice dripped off her chin, hair, and fingertips. She asked Pockets the rather innocent and wide-eyed question, "Are we finished?" The camera then turned to Pockets, who raised a hand and stood on his toes while the team clapped in time. The video showed a slow-motion progression of Joe standing with a devilish grin and hefting grape pieces like a baseball. The film ended as crushed grapes flew through the air. Aimed at Pockets.

To say the short video was organic and magical was a bit of an understatement. The number of views grew to over ten million after a week and was picked up by several news outlets and late-night talk shows. The most celebrated actress of a generation making the common man's wine in a large bin only served to fuel public opinion. They loved her all the more. Syd could only dream his media presence was this viral.

The team filmed successive steps over the next several weeks as they made the wine. Adding yeast and sugar and just enough temperature to stimulate the yeast but not cook the juice. A delicate balance. Unlike fine wine, or what the critics call "real wine," muscadine wine doesn't age in a barrel. The country folk who make it say it robs it of its natural flavor— what connoisseurs call "fruit forward." In truth, they like the sweetness and there will always be more grapes next year.

In a few short days, Joe poured the sweet wine into a jar and handed it to Pockets. He raised an eyebrow. "A mason jar?"

A nod. "It's how we drink wine down here."

Pockets toasted the camera and turned to Joe. "I couldn't possibly. Not before you. The winemaker should have the honor."

The follow-up video surpassed the first in total number of views due primarily to the joke Pockets and the team played on her, which was forever immortalized in the expression on her face as she tasted the wine.

Which was horrible.

The cameraman, knowing full well what was about to happen, zoomed in on her face, catching every nuance—which she tried to control but simply could not. Unable to stop the oncoming wave, Joe coughed, hacked, gagged, and spewed wine across the room and onto the lens of the camera. The lip-puckered, head-shaking, squinty-eyed, tear-filled gag was captured in 4K perfection. She looked as though she'd bit into a hundred lemons. No words could recover this reaction. Her face did not lie. Whatever was in that glass was undrinkable.

But that was just it. While her face had not lied, they had. Which took her about three seconds to figure out. While she struggled to get the taste out of her mouth, the team erupted in raucous laughter.

Not catching the joke, she said, "I'm so sorry. Lucy always made it look so easy. I was really hoping to like it." She looked at Pockets, then at the camera, then back at Pockets, who was struggling to keep a straight face. "I guess it is just an acquired taste."

As the team doubled over and Joe attempted to backpedal, Pockets pulled out a bottle of the real wine they'd made.

Joe pointed at the bottle. "What's that?"

"The wine we made."

She looked at the liquid in her jar. "What's this?"

Pockets masked his smile. "That's one part grape juice and about seven parts apple cider vinegar."

About here it registered. "Vinegar."

"Yes mum."

"So . . . that's not our wine?"

Pockets shook his head.

She wiped her mouth on a towel, then shoe-shined her tongue. When the laughter quieted once again, she placed her hand on the table, tapped her fingers, playing to the camera, and then asked, "May I please taste *our* wine?" With emphasis on "our."

As he poured some of the good wine into her mason jar, her facial expressions began telling everyone, including those watching on video, that she was putting the pieces together. She'd bought the ruse. Smiling between pursed lips, she leaned in and whispered but allowed the camera to pick it up. "You did that on purpose." A question posed as a statement.

Pockets nodded. "Yes mum."

The cameraman shifted his point of focus from Pockets to Joe to the wine, then back to Pockets, then back to Joe, and so on.

Joe could not conceal her smile, so she looked into the camera, shook her head, and then looked back at Pockets. "You're fired."

He nodded. "Yes mum." Which brought more laughter out of the team.

Pockets handed the mason jar to her. She held it much like someone holds a spring-loaded rat trap. Carefully. When her sniff test didn't repel her, she brought it to her lips, gently, allowing the liquid to just touch her skin. And when she didn't involuntarily gag, she licked her lips. Then sipped the wine, followed by a facial expression 180 degrees different from the first take. Ending with a surprised smile.

"It's good!" She looked into the camera. "No, I mean it. It's really good. Well . . ." She sipped again. "I mean, it's no Deerfield Ranch. No Chimney Rock. But it's actually quite good. Like, I would drink this."

Pockets laughed. "Good, 'cause we've got twenty gallons of it."

In classic Joe fashion, she glanced at the camera, leaned in, and whispered for the viewer, another just-between-us secret, "I know what I'm giving everyone for Christmas."

The sunshine did her good. As did the laughter, the grapes, the stain on her shins, and the dirt packed beneath her nails. And somewhere in here, she healed. Months passed, she gained a little much-needed weight; they ate her tomatoes, squash, cucumbers; and she even snapped peas on the porch. She learned to drive a tractor and shoot cans with a .22. And then, wonder of wonders, the treatments took effect. Her body began making eggs. Good eggs. She had made things grow.

Only one thing was missing.

During a break in filming, Syd returned for what were undoubtedly the best three nights of his natural born life. Several weeks later, Pockets sat at the table and watched Syd make coffee for Joe. He filled the mug and then added some of the powdered keto-collagen-creamer stuff, which he pulled from his pack. "Joe says it's good for hair, nails, and . . ." Syd smiled. "Babies."

He flew out the next day. Back to some set somewhere. Wishing he didn't have to go. Two days later, Joe mourned quietly and alone in the bathroom. Through a closed door, she asked Pockets to call Syd as she couldn't bear to hear his voice after she'd let him down. Again. Pockets dialed, Syd answered, and Pockets heard music, waves breaking on the shore, and a female voice in the background.

"Mr. Syd?"

"Pockets, my man." His words were slow in the making and he was a little too happy. "How's things?"

Syd took the news well. Promising to call.

CHAPTER 34

AFTER

Ten days passed. During which Amber sent no texts, which I found interesting given the fact that she could be no more than a week or two from giving birth. The girl was about ready to bust. She could go at any time, and I wasn't sure if it was her scheming or her naivete that kept her quiet. Or was it the dorky guy who flew her off in what I assumed was his plane? I had no way of knowing.

I often thought about Frank and Ricardo. I won't say I felt sorry for them—I didn't—but talk about two guys whose fortunes changed overnight. Ricardo surfaced two days later on the nightly news as a local sheriff forced to resign after tearing up a casino in a drunken rage. And while Frank's picture did not appear on the news, he certainly appeared in Joe's phone. Frank was texting every day. Often two and three times a day. While he had lost both Amber and the baby, he was still trying to act as though he hadn't.

In an odd way, I admired his gumption. Frank was desperate, and while not admitting to losing his golden ticket, he was negotiating for far less than he had previously. Rather than asking for five or ten million, he was only asking for one. To go with the one he already had. Frank didn't know I'd seen him lose Amber to Ricardo, and then seen both he and Ricardo lose her to the pilot with a pocket protector. Frank said that as the baby had grown in Amber's tummy, they'd had a change of heart, and they would exchange the baby for much less. That it seemed only right. He was a talented con artist, and I was sure he'd land on his feet. But when all this was said and done, and the FBI turned Joe's phone inside out, Frank would be able to start his new life in prison.

Until then, I said nothing. Which only served to increase both his anger and his texting.

Frank and Ricardo had lost. Amber had beaten them both. Not to mention Joe. Everyone had underestimated her. And unless this third guy was more evil and conniving than she, he didn't stand a chance.

Which left me with Amber. She knew the stakes. It was why she deceived and ran from Frank and Ricardo. She wanted it all for herself. She also knew she was down to her last card and time was short. Like it or not, her body was going to give birth, and there wasn't a thing she could do about it. I was almost certain she didn't want the baby. If she did, why didn't she just have her own? Would have saved her a lot of trouble. The fact that she'd gone through with all of this but was now out of options meant she would be motivated to make a deal. And I guessed she'd do it before the baby was born. Of course, she'd threaten all manner of horrible things, but at the end of the day, that baby equaled money, and she wasn't about to harm either the baby or her chances. She wanted seven figures in a Swiss account and a beach with some guy in a Speedo delivering little drinks with umbrellas every hour on the hour.

Basically, I had one ace in the hole: the clock. And with every passing second, the odds shifted in my favor.

My uneducated guess was that this third guy was some sort of local doc who could deliver a baby in a pinch. Preferably at home so she could avoid a hospital altogether. That would give rise to too many questions. I also guessed Amber would lay low and sing him some song about the baby and his or her origins, and how she just wanted to "do the right thing" and give him or her up for adoption. And how the trauma she'd experienced made her fearful of hospitals and how she would need him to use his medical skills to prepare their new home for the baby's arrival. Then, after the baby was born and she'd put her painful past behind her, they'd ride off into a sunset of marital bliss. I was also pretty certain that guy number three had no idea about the surrogacy, the texts, the demands, the money paid, and the money at stake. Why would Amber share any of that with him? Unless she could milk him of a few hundred grand, she'd ditch him as soon as she was healthy enough to travel. She'd send him to the store with a list and when he returned, not even the smell of her perfume would remain.

Of course, all of this was just a guess.

The text came in just as one of Amber's phones came online and shared its location with me. Central Georgia.

I didn't respond to the first text, which read, "Want to talk?" I didn't want to appear too eager. Besides, time was on my side. Not hers. A few hours later, she texted again, which made me wonder if she was having Braxton-Hicks contractions. This time she said, "I know you do, so let me make it simple. 50/50. While I don't know who you are, I'm certain you have Joe and you don't care about the baby any more than I do, so let's just split it. I want five million. I know she has that and a lot more. I also know she will pay any number we request. You tell her you want any number above that. I don't care. Five. Ten. Whatever you can get out of her. My number is five. Secure that and you can secure me. When I see the money in my account, I'll lead you to the baby. You can arrange pickup from there. Deal?"

I gave her a few hours. While I didn't believe her or trust her, I wanted her to think I did. So I responded, "Deal," in an attempt to act interested and committed while not needy. I also needed time to follow her phone's location before she convinced some local tech guy to make sure the phone was clean and he stumbled upon the mSpy app open in the background. I didn't know if she was that savvy, but I had to assume she was.

As I zeroed in on the exact location of the phone, it turned out to be Lake Oconee. Interesting.

The road wound around the lake and came to a new development in a cul-de-sac. "The Willows" was a gated community of twelve homes built to look like Augusta National. Or Monticello. Sort of old-world-meets-new. But the developer lacked either vision or training or both, and The Willows came across as a bad blend of new money trying to look like old and failing in most every respect. If you have to spend money to show you have money, then you don't. Not to people who have money.

The homes were red brick with large wraparound porches, outdoor kitchens, infinity pools, four-car garages, and custom golf carts. The American dream in five to eight thousand square feet. The sign on the mailbox read "Don Weathers, MD."

Told you he was a doctor.

I parked a mile down the road at a boat ramp and made my way through the woods. Taking my time. Staying out of sight. A hundred yards from the house, I leaned against a tree and looked through binoculars onto the pool deck, where I found Amber tanning topless in all her pregnant glory alongside the infinity pool while being tended hand and foot by a doting Don.

I immediately felt sorry for the guy.

Aside from her tummy, I almost didn't recognize Amber. Long

brunette hair had been replaced by short and blonde. To her credit, her body was spectacular. She looked like a Pilates instructor with a basketball tucked under her skin. Given her current condition, it would not take her long to recover to pre-baby body following delivery.

Staring at her soaking up the good life, I found myself angry and considered marching through the gate, snatching her up by the hair, and parading her out the front door while she wrestled with her ridiculous thong. My problem was Don. He was a question mark, and while he looked harmless enough, I really had no idea. Maybe he was the mastermind behind all this. Stranger things have happened. He may have been drunk in love, but he was also a doctor and a pilot. No dummy. His home, while secluded behind a security gate, was more accessible from the lake. It was also more visible, which I think he enjoyed. I had the feeling Don liked to show off his toys, as suggested by his waxed and polished golf cart parked out front next to his Corvette, which was parked next to his Escalade, which partially hid his Harley—all of which were being manicured by Derek's Mobile Detailing.

Amber had chosen wisely. Her future looked secure.

Don's house sat perched on a small rise across the lake from the Ritz-Carlton, giving Don and Amber a beautiful view off their pool deck. The meticulously manicured lawns, the subtle accent lighting, the cathedral of trees, the rolling fairways and Augusta-like greens, everything in view elevated their perspective. Whether the reverse was true was questionable. The location of the house gave everyone frolicking in the Ritz pool or lounging in one of the bars an unobstructed view of Don's achievement. Both his massive, Ritz-wannabe home and his trophy, almost-dressed girlfriend who seemed to be counting the days until she could exorcise this thing from her body, cash in her winning ticket, hide the money, and milk Don for everything he was worth—all while sipping martinis, soaking up the sun, and banking the interest.

This eventuality was not lost on Amber, who seemed to float when she walked, having finally been welcomed back into the world to which she'd grown accustomed. Thanks to Joe. Who had given selflessly and without thought of return.

Late in the afternoon, they loaded into Don's new Malibu boat and took a ride around the lake, which gave him a chance to show her off and me a chance to investigate his house. A short-lived walk as the guy had more than twenty cameras pointing every direction. I couldn't get within a hundred feet. So I returned to my hiding place in the woods and waited along with the mosquitoes. He was either really good at pretending, possibly better than Amber, or one of the more paranoid people on the planet. Or, option three, he was a little man with a Napoleon complex who spent his life's energy trying to convince the world he had been passed over and they should take notice. A man on the move. I had no idea which was true, but unless he was a better actor than Joe, I was starting to wonder if he wasn't just a wee little man.

They returned after dark, where he served her dinner at the kitchen table and then the two watched a rom-com on his ginormous TV. I had to hand it to Amber. She had connived and deceived Joe, Frank, Ricardo, and now Don. I stared through the woods and wondered who was next. I couldn't get close enough to the house to hang any type of tracking device on any vehicle or I'd be caught by the motion-detection cameras, so I found the closest motel, paid forty-nine dollars cash for a room, and sat considering Don. I didn't want to raise suspicion and I didn't need to risk a public appearance, but I needed information. So I drove to St. Mary's Good Samaritan Hospital and poked around. It didn't take long.

Weathers Plastic Surgery, PA, sat catty-corner to the hospital in a newly constructed building just as gaudy and overdone as his home. Don's website listed an impressive medical pedigree with residencies and specialties from Harvard to Mayo to time spent in Austria with some renowned, groundbreaking, highly awarded surgeon. He then went on to open a practice in Los Angeles and another in Hollywood with a third in Aspen, but soon grew "tired of the pace" and moved to Georgia where he could "breathe." I wondered what he did to get kicked out of plastic surgery mecca.

Having resettled in Georgia, it would appear he established a boutique business that catered to members of the Ritz crowd who, while patients in his facility, were granted discounted, all-inclusive rates at the Ritz. His site touted several "packages"—my favorite being the Tummy Takeover—with the most popular being a three-week stay during which he lifted and tucked and Botoxed and reduced and enhanced everything known to man, all while the patient recovered in the privacy of a nearby lakeside Ritz retreat with daily "recuperation sessions" at the spa and twenty-four-seven concierge and cabana-boy service.

After ten minutes on his website, I decided this guy was a genius. His business was a cash cow, and the only person smarter than him was Amber.

It didn't take a genius to surmise Amber was going to use Don's connections to give birth quietly and privately, promising him who knows what in return, and then stay long enough to let him "enhance" her appearance. My guess was that within a month of delivery, she'd be independently wealthy, unrecognizable even to herself, and free to move about however she wished.

As crazy as it sounds, she'd not broken any laws related to surrogacy. I did not know the details of her agreement with Joe, had no idea if it was written or verbal, but a quick Internet search proved that the state of Georgia had no law governing surrogacy, and the courts were generally favorable to all different types of parents. Translation? I was no legal scholar, but that sounded to me like Amber had just found a sanctuary. She was getting smarter every day, and the expanding tentacles of this entire situation got me wondering just how long Amber had been planning this charade. Ethically, she'd violated her agreement with Joe, but an ethics violation would never send her to jail. Only make her unpopular, and her millions in cash wouldn't care about her popularity. What about the blackmail and payments from Joe? A good lawyer could argue that all of those requests came through boyfriends, that Amber was in fear for her life the entire time, which is why she escaped to Georgia, where she tried her best to protect herself and the baby until the baby arrived, at which time she had every intent of returning him or her to Joe. And because the baby had yet to be born, who could argue otherwise? A good prosecuting attorney might, at best, make Amber an accessory, while an average defense lawyer could make Amber out to be the victim.

Amber was playing her hand quite well.

When I woke, the sun was high and I'd slept nine hours straight. Not something I do regularly. I returned to the boat ramp where I "borrowed" a kayak from an adjacent dock and paddled toward the Weathers compound, convinced that when it came to conniving, deceitful people, Amber cleared the top of the list. Hiding in plain sight.

I parked the kayak two docks away and swam the last hundred yards under cover of neighboring docks. A quick study of the driveway suggested Don had driven the Escalade to work, which sparked the obvious question—had he left Amber home alone? Fifteen minutes later, Lady Amber appeared in a new bikini, carrying a book and wearing a ridiculously large hat that flopped about and rose and fell with each subtle breeze. It was the kind of hat you'd wear if you wanted to garner attention. Something Amber no doubt craved.

Amber spent the morning on the phone. Talking, texting. Judging from her body language, the calls were business. Not personal. That arm's length posture did not extend to the yard guy, presenting a new wrinkle. Now I had to contend with four eyes, not two. In a surprising move, she convinced Julio of Julio's Perfect Cut Yard Service to apply sunscreen to her back and shoulders and bring her a glass of water, both of which he did with a smile and speed. By the time he left, the guy was foaming at the mouth, promising to return tomorrow to trim the hedges.

At noon she returned to the house, only to pull out of the drive thirty minutes later in a convertible Carrera. Top down. Sunglasses. Ball cap. Semi-see-through sundress. She carried a tote over one shoulder and a little yapping dog under the other. For someone who should be flying under the radar, she was drawing a lot of attention. First stop was Doc Weathers's office where she used a keycard to open the back door to what looked like Don's office. He greeted her with a hug and kiss and the two disappeared inside. Twenty minutes later, she exited and then drove across town to the wealth-management office of Bank of America, where she spent half an hour while people fussed over her paperwork and somebody brought her hot tea and sparkling water and treats for the dog. On a positive note, the butt-kissing bank folks kept her busy and distracted long enough for me to tag her car. With so many vehicles available, I had no guarantee she'd drive this one anytime soon, but I tagged it nonetheless.

Having continued her quest to snow everyone in her stratosphere, Amber returned to her hundred-thousand-dollar Porsche in which she and furball returned home, but only after a quick stop at the local market. It looked like Amber intended to make dinner. Watching her work was a masterpiece in progress. The one thing I could not make sense of was the timing. Amber was very pregnant, was in full pregnant woman waddle, and could go at any time. This baby was coming. By my clock she was two weeks out from her due date, which meant we were running out of time. Fast. But Amber acted as though she had all the time in the world, which caused me to wonder if she'd already scheduled things here and was putting her affairs in order with an imminent arrival maybe days away.

A text that night confirmed my suspicion. "Five days. Either transfer $5M to my account or I drop this kid in a dumpster."

So much for sweet homemaker Amber. I responded, "Done." I wanted to inquire about making the exchange but knew I'd better be delicate. I also wanted to respond with strength. And I wanted to throw her a bit of a curveball. "Will not complete transaction until I have eyes on the child AND personally verify that it comes out of you. That is, I attend delivery."

She responded quickly. "You've got to be joking."

"For $5M, either I am present during delivery, or no deal."

"You're a pervert."

"Calling me names won't get you any closer to the money."

I knew I'd thrown her for a loop and her wheels were spinning. Which was what I wanted. My response was not what she expected. She thought she was in the driver's seat; I had let her know she wasn't. I also knew she knew she couldn't argue with me. I had every right to guarantee product, and for five million dollars, she'd get over it. But I also knew my request presented her with a bigger problem. If she was delivering via C-section, she'd have some type of nerve block and wouldn't be able to walk for a while after delivery. Not to mention stitches. She'd be in no condition to play tough girl. No matter how this child entered the world, she'd be in a compromised position at least for a couple of hours following delivery. How was she going to stop me from marching in and taking the baby? She couldn't. The only way she could control the transaction was to bring in help. Help she trusted. And while Don might be a good plastic surgeon, I questioned his ability to play tough guy. Amber was with him because she could work him like she worked everyone. Not because he offered her strength and protection. Matter of fact, his lack of muscle made him appealing.

Amber was going to need outside help. The question was who.

After several minutes, she texted, "Details to follow." A response without a commitment. A fact not lost on me.

If Amber had the sequence of events planned out in her mind, she now had a problem. While she controlled the baby, I controlled the money—or at least she thought I did. This meant a physical transaction would occur. Baby for money. She'd hold the baby, I'd transfer the money, she'd verify the transfer, and I'd take the baby. All parties happy. The question she had to be asking herself now was this: How was she going to physically trade a baby when she knew full well she'd be unable to carry or hold anything? Or, at a minimum, severely hindered in her ability to do so. She'd certainly be no match for an average-sized man. If I was right and she'd scheduled a C-section, her ability to carry a baby, to drive a car, to do anything, would be compromised. She might pull it off, but at what danger to her own body? Five million was a lot of money, and she wanted to be around to spend it. If she was induced and gave birth naturally, she might be better able to pull it off. Many women have given birth and been up and walking around in no time. I don't understand how they do that, but some people are just tougher than me. The problem with natural delivery was that there were no guarantees. What if delivery was difficult? What if there were complications? What if the baby needed the ICU or an extended stay in the hospital? To me, natural delivery presented too many variables, which left her with a C-section as her best option. Of course, all this depended on her intent to give birth to a live baby. A thought I didn't want to entertain. Since she'd made it this far, I'd wager she wanted the money and could tolerate a few more days. Unless she was motivated by something other than money. In which case, all bets were off.

The more I studied her, the more I wondered what motivated someone to be so evil. To ingratiate herself to someone and promise undying friendship only to steal that person's child. Someone who'd had a tough time getting pregnant, whose whole world was wrapped up in one remaining possibility. Who had hoped and hoped only to be betrayed, abandoned, and blackmailed. Rotten treachery for money. The only answer I could posit was that Amber had tasted life with Joe and decided she would have that life. At any cost. She was finished with makeup artistry. She intended to sit in the chair rather than stand behind it and make others beautiful.

Whatever the case, Amber was scrambling. She had a sizable problem to be solved in a short amount of time. Who could she trust when she'd burned so many bridges? I doubted she'd involve either Frank or Ricardo; they were too strong, and Don was too weak. She needed a fourth man watching over both her and me during delivery. But who could she trust with five million dollars?

Amber was not the only one scrambling. I, too, had a problem. Several actually, and mine might have been more troubling than Amber's. Problem one: if the child was born here, and let's just say for argument's sake that I could kidnap him or her while boyfriend number four and Amber watched over him or her like a hawk, then how was I going to travel back across the country? How was I going to feed and care for a one-day-old baby? While driving or flying a plane? All while every law enforcement agency in Georgia tried to find me? I supposed I could kidnap Amber and force her to give birth in a hotel bathroom, which seemed risky, not to mention how I would keep her quiet. But even if I pulled that off, how would I force Amber to feed the baby while I flew us back to Montana? What would stop her from choking him or her—a child she didn't want in the first place—while I watched? Nothing.

Since problem one seemed insurmountable, problem two involved returning to Montana and bringing Joe to Georgia prior to delivery. That is, right now. But just exactly how would I bring one of the most recognizable actresses in the world anywhere without being noticed, especially when I'd been holding her against her will for a month? Why would she agree to do anything with me, and if she did, what was to stop her from doing that and then screaming her head off the first chance she got in a public setting?

Problem three was taking Amber to Joe. This late in the trimester, air travel risked inducing labor and possible injury to the baby given the change in altitude. With Joe's plane, we could fly lower, but at what risk? What would I do if she went into labor somewhere over Kansas? Land? Probably not. And while I cared little if Amber suffered childbirth sans meds, I did care what happened to the child. What if she had complications midair? Would I set the autopilot, hop in the back, and help calm-and-not-kicking-and-screaming Amber deliver Joe's baby?

Not likely.

Problem four was taking Amber back to Joe while driving back across the country. Something that would take days and risk a greater chance of being seen or giving her a chance to scream and tell everyone within earshot that I'd kidnapped her. Not to mention my need to sleep at some point. So driving was out.

Problem five was to kidnap Amber, tie her hands and feet, shove a sock in her mouth, and lock her in a room for thirty-six to forty-eight hours while I retrieved Joe, which risked harming both Amber and the baby. Not good. That amount of distress could induce labor, which would leave Amber tied up and muted with a newborn uncared for on the bed. I had no desire to wander down that rabbit hole.

No option was good. Not to mention having to pull any of these off while not being arrested or being shot by Frank or Ricardo or Don or whoever Amber was soon to invite to the party. I'd say my chances were about one in ten. Having studied the options, I chose the last door. The best worst option.

CHAPTER 35

BEFORE

Her doctors changed course. "This is not uncommon." On to plan B. In vitro. Harvest viable eggs, fertilize them with help from Syd, let them mature and grow in a petri dish, then reinsert them medically into Joe's body where they'd have the best chance of survival. The medical community made their case. Everyone was helpful. And hopeful. Sadly, the regimen required they return to California.

The daily routine of shots, bed rest, medications, supplements, essential oils, and a dozen other things was exhausting, as were the well-intended questions she tired of answering. Yes, she felt fine. Just weary from the process. Once again, her body responded well to treatment and spiked her bloodstream with more than one hundred times the normal levels of hormones. She could cry without reason, laugh, threaten to rip someone's head off, show deep empathy, vomit, and down a quart of ice cream all within sixty seconds. Only to wipe her chin and poke fun at herself.

"I feel like one of those poor creatures inside a Whac-A-Mole."

The timeline was simple but came with some time constraints. One in particular. For two to four weeks, doctors would suppress the ovaries, then stimulate them for eight to twelve days, monitoring her cycle starting at day five, hoping for ovulation induction between days eight and twelve. Then retrieve the eggs thirty-six hours after an injection of HCG, which triggers ovulation. Both sperm collection and fertilization occur on the day of egg retrieval.

Simple but not really.

And time sensitive.

When it came time to retrieve, they were hoping for at least one good egg. Two would have been amazing. Three too much to hope for.

From behind closed doors, both tearful and ecstatic, Joe texted Pockets. "Three. They got three! Can you believe it?!"

Moments later, she called him. Groggy but coherent. "Help."

"Be right there."

"No, find Syd. We need him."

While the doctors prepared the eggs, Pockets searched for Syd. Who wasn't hard to find. After three attempts, he finally answered his phone. "Yeah . . ."

"Mr. Syd?"

Syd mumbled and something crashed in the background.

"Sir, it's retrieval day. You're needed here at the clinic."

More mumbling.

Pockets continued, "Sir, they've retrieved the eggs and the clock is ticking and—"

The phone sounded with a *thud* as if it'd been dropped. In the muffled background, he could hear Syd snoring.

Fortunately, Syd and Joe had bought a townhome in LA where they'd stay when filming and it was too late or they were too tired to drive the hour home. Twenty minutes later, Pockets knocked on the door, which was not answered. Using his key, he let himself in, where he did not like what he found. Lifting an inebriated Syd out of bed, he threw him in a cold shower where Syd slowly came to life as the fog lifted.

Pockets stuffed Syd into the Suburban and returned to the clinic, where he found the team tapping their fingers. Dragging him inside, Pockets carried Syd to the "Husband's Room" and dropped him on the couch.

Syd laughed. "You gonna watch?"

Pockets stepped outside and stood opposite the door while Syd made obscene noises inside that sounded more like a cackling hyena. A few minutes later, Syd appeared, fumbling with his zipper. He looked at Pockets and pointed toward the car. "Home, James. I need a cigarette."

CHAPTER 36

BEFORE

Over the next six months, two healthy, fertilized eggs were placed in Joe's body. Neither took. When it came time to place the third, she was weary, run-down, and tired of hoping.

It was Pockets who found her. He sat, saying nothing. She sat, pensive. After a moment, she confided, "I don't know if I can do it again." A pause. He knew her well enough to read her body language. She was telling the truth. "It's not the work." A tear trailed down one cheek. "It's the hope."

"No one would blame you. If you—"

She finished his sentence. "Throw in the towel?" She tapped herself on the chest. "I would." She folded her hands and shook her head. "Because what if . . ." Her voice fell to a whisper. "Two of the most powerful and yet painful words ever spoken."

He let her talk.

"Every morning, I eat this dish called *hope*. Crumbs mostly, but without it, I'm not even human." A long pause while her mind spun. "But that's just it. There are no guarantees. Because if you can guarantee it, it's not hope." She made invisible quotation marks with her fingers. "I'm 'hoping' I can carry a baby to term. I'm 'hoping' I can be a good mom. I'm 'hoping' Syd will . . ." She trailed off again. Finally, she looked at Pockets. "I know this has been hard on you as well. You've had to endure all this and all my hormones and panic attacks and hissy fits and—"

"You are not a burden, mum."

The calm in his voice cracked her and she wept. Holding her face in her hands. He placed a handkerchief on the table in front of her, which she accepted, blowing her nose and wiping her eyes. "Thank you, Pockets."

After a quiet minute, he said, "May I say something?"

She nodded.

He adjusted his feet. "I've been in some places where there is no hope, and yet somehow it swims through the cracks. Rises to the surface. I've found hope staring me in the face when reason screamed I had none. No matter what you do—ignore it, shove it in a closet, drown it with drink and pill, or stab it with science, experts, and talking heads— you can't kill hope. Not in all of human history has hope ever been laid to rest. When we breathe in, it's the stuff that expands our lungs. It's the reason we're not just dust."

She tried to laugh. "I thought love did all that."

He sucked through his teeth. "It's tough to tell those two apart, mum. But if you press me, love is what makes us who we are. Hope is how we express us. Hope is love with legs."

She laughed and turned sideways, faced him, and blew her nose into his handkerchief. "Never knew you had such a deep philosophical side."

Pockets looked around, noting the absence of anyone else. "Sometimes another voice can be a comfort."

She stood, wanting to but careful not to cross the line. "Thank you again." Then she folded the handkerchief and offered to return it.

"Maybe you better hold on to that."

She laughed. "Probably a good idea."

Doctors inserted the third egg and put her on active bed rest, during which Pockets was never farther than earshot.

A month passed and life returned to some version of normalcy, though no one whispered the *p* word because it was almost too good to be true. To his credit, Syd sobered up. Delayed a project. Stayed home. And took an interest in what interested Joe. They even read a book together. Out loud. Maybe the prospect of fatherhood shook some things loose. Whatever the case, his friends said he'd turned over a new leaf as evidenced by the fact that he made the morning talk-show circuit speaking openly about his sobriety and his desire to be a good father, and poking fun at his own contribution to the process and admitting how, in fact, Joe had done all the work. Given his honest and self-deprecating conversation, he landed on the cover of a parenting magazine. Inside, the article claimed Syd helped make uncomfortable fathers comfortable in that he gave a voice to a very real struggle and what can be a difficult conversation. In an unexpected twist, Google later highlighted one unintended effect of Syd's efforts. The name "Syd" rose to the top of the list for baby boys that year. While "Joe" took the girls' title three years running.

When producers eventually came calling for their golden boy, looking for the star of their next world-saving blockbuster, Syd declined. The doctors had instructed Joe not to walk farther than the kitchen. To get her outside, Syd bought a rolling chair made for the beach. Something with fat tires and wheels that allowed him to push her along the shore. Even came with a sunshade. He'd wake her before the sun, bring her coffee, and push her along the edge of the shore where the water washed over her feet.

During her forced convalescence, Joe breathed in. Then out.

Followed by another in. Trying to will her body to grow something. Which it was doing.

She spent weeks in bed; she and Syd shared stories, sundown, possible scripts. If ever she and Syd found Camelot, it was here. Alongside the beach. And much of that was to his credit. Syd was becoming who she'd hoped.

After six weeks, Syd could delay a contract no further, so he tucked her in, boarded a jet to Alaska, and returned to the camera.

When the spot appeared, followed by another, she tried him on the satellite, but he didn't answer. Doctors were brought in but there was nothing they could do. Somewhere that night, number three quietly passed out of her life while Pockets sat at the kitchen table, listening to the sound of Joe's soul cracking down the middle.

CHAPTER 37

AFTER

Amber had resumed her vigil by the pool by the time I returned in my borrowed kayak. Hat on, top off, she was attempting to garner the attention of every man at the Ritz across the lake, and judging by the number of sunglasses currently poking up above the infinity pool waterfall, she had accomplished her goal. But while Don's pool deck sat perched on a hill, offering everyone around a great view of his Amber and giving her the attention she craved, it presented me with a problem. Whatever I did would be in plain view unless I waited until dark. And I could only hide under the dock for so long.

Thanks to Julio, I didn't have to wait that long. He returned as promised and began trimming the hedges, though he did so now with no shirt and a Rambo-style bandanna. Julio was late twenties, eight-pack abs, and thick gold chains.

Julio trimmed for the better part of an hour, giving credence to the "perfect" in Perfect Cut. He was good, and I got the feeling he was taking his time this afternoon as his perch on the ladder offered him an unobstructed view of the pool. And Amber. Who, pretending to be oblivious behind the noise-canceling AirPods, feigned indifference despite Julio's gas-powered, two-stroke Stihl.

After little more than an hour, Julio made his move. He worked his way around the hedges toward the lake, then back up toward the pool. This put him in line of sight of Amber and forced her to take notice of him. Which she did. She covered with a towel, then beckoned him to the pool deck. Julio pointed at his dirty boots but she waved him on anyway. I had a feeling I was looking at boyfriend number four.

Looking like a Brazilian jiu-jitsu fighter, Julio approached and the two shared a polite conversation during which Amber made feeble attempts to cover herself. After two or three minutes, she pointed at the fridge and invited Julio to help himself. Which he did. Returning with two beers. When she refused, pointing at her tummy, he opened one and began drinking with a bit of a swagger. He could see where this was going. Husband was away. Leaving the missus all by herself. Not meeting her needs. Julio was the right man at the right place.

Halfway through his beer, Amber patted the chair next to her and Julio took a seat. I couldn't hear what they were saying, but judging by the body language, Amber was making her pitch while Julio opened the second beer, looking serious and concerned. I couldn't begin to guess how she was selling it, but Amber was inviting Julio to join the delivery.

At first, Julio protested. Shaking his head. Waving her off. A true gentleman. But Amber wasn't even warmed up. She smiled, leaned over, and put a hand on his thigh—then, in a show of sudden discomfort, she placed a hand on her chest, then her head, and then her stomach. Her condition worsening, she lay back, eyes closed, breathing, her towel mostly concealing her chest. As the discomfort grew, she asked for water, saying something about the heat and feeling dizzy. Julio never saw it coming. Finally, she extended her hand, at which point he nodded, helped her stand, and began walking her slowly into the house for what she no doubt intended to be the best ten minutes of his life.

Once inside, they made their way up the basement stairs toward the kitchen, giving me time to skirt the pool, trace their footsteps, and let myself in the sliding glass doors. Closing the door, I cut the pull cords on the blinds, crept up the stairs, and found Julio rubbing her feet after having put a wet cloth on her forehead. I was just starting to think about knocking him out when I heard her say something along the lines of, "Be right back."

When she disappeared into the bedroom, sweaty Julio took a seat on what must have been Don's ten-thousand-dollar couch, so I crept up behind him, sank one arm beneath his chin, and locked it in my opposite elbow, placing immediate pressure and squeezing. Julio, having been enticed, having had two beers, and expecting a scantily clad Amber, was not thinking self-defense. The move is called a "rear naked choke" for reasons I don't understand, but the effect was gratifying. Julio went to sleep. I hog-tied him quickly with the cords, shoving the wet washcloth in his mouth and wrapping his own Rambo bandanna around his face and neck.

Staring down at him as he returned to consciousness, I almost felt sorry for him—and sorry I wasn't going to be here when Don returned home.

Amber would not be quite so easy. I had to be gentle while controlling, and I couldn't risk putting her to sleep. Just then, she called from the bathroom. I could hear water running and see steam rising out from above the door. She called a second time, so I moved to the door, cracked it open, and found her sitting on the edge of the tub, eyes closed, candles lit. Her robe spilling off one shoulder.

Watching this play out in real time, I marveled at the lengths she was willing to go to pull this off. The yard man of all people. Was there anything she wouldn't do? But then again, five million dollars was five million dollars.

Hearing the door swing open, she waved, thinking Julio would walk right in. So, I did, knowing I needed a way to both distract and disorient her. I grabbed a towel and, when I reached the edge of the tub, quickly wrapped it around her face, eyes, and mouth. Then I pulled her forcibly from the edge of the tub. This eliminated her ability to see, breathe, and scream, which meant she'd have to contend first with the towel and then me. Being careful not to bruise her torso, I pulled up on the towel, forcing her head back and flipping her on her side. Straddling her to control her legs, I grabbed both hands and quickly tied them in front of her.

When her hands were bound, I moved to her feet about the time she was able to shake the towel loose and start screaming. She emitted two or three long screams, telling me to get out of her house, but we were inside and the doors were closed and Don's yard was huge. No one heard her. When she saw my face, her complexion changed and what before had been a mixture of fear and anger flipped to rage.

"You!"

I tore the towel into long strips, pulled back on her head, forcing her mouth open, shoved one strip into her mouth, then tied another tight around her head, neck, and face while maintaining an open airway through her nose. I wanted to shut her up, not kill her. Then, just to be sure she was sufficiently hobbled, I tied her knees together, further limiting her mobility and proving she wasn't going anywhere without my help.

I stood her up, pointed to the garage, and said, "Keys."

She shook her head and mumbled something that could have been cusswords, so I dragged her out of the bathroom, past Julio's fish-flopping, wide-eyed, terrorized body, and into the back hall where neat-freak Don had hung a pegboard with all the keys for his various toys. I pulled off the key that read "Speed Baby" and was about to drag her to the garage when fire tore through the flesh of my right shoulder.

Twice. The blasts spun me and knocked the air out of me, dropping me to a knee. When I looked up, she was turning the gun toward my face. Aiming at the sound of me. I grabbed the muzzle as she pulled the trigger a third and fourth time, sending a round through my left hand and a round into the refrigerator.

Of all the possibilities and contingencies, I'd not considered being shot by her. Or the fact that she carried Ricardo's Glock 19 in her purse. Which she did. She didn't strike me as a cold-blooded killer. Which was a credit to how well she played her role. In another life, she'd have made an excellent actress. In retrospect, I should have tied her hands behind her back, but given that she was pregnant, I was worried about what that stress might do to the baby.

Working to fend off shock and not bleed to death at the same time, I wrestled her to the car, placed her in the front seat of the Porsche, duct-taped her hands to her legs, and buckled her in. As she cussed my lineage through muted screaming, I returned to the bathroom to survey the damage. The mirror revealed two entry holes into my shoulder but only one exit, and then a complete pass-through of my hand. I was bleeding, but she had not hit an artery, which meant I'd live. Needing to plug the hole, I walked to the kitchen, turned on the gas stove, and heated a meat cleaver until it turned bright red. Julio watched, his eyes growing wider. When the cleaver turned red, he passed out entirely.

Leaving a trail of blood in my wake, I returned to the bathroom and pressed the cleaver to my skin, fore and aft, plugging the exit hole. That would stop the bleeding of hole number one while sealing the remaining slug inside me, which I'd deal with later. My hand, while bleeding, was not an issue, so I wrapped it in one of the towel strips and tied it off. Assessing myself, I concluded I was still breathing and not hemorrhaging blood, which suggested she'd not nicked anything vital, allowing me to live long enough to fly Amber to Montana.

That said, nobody gets shot three times without some level of shock. I knew that if I was not there already, I would be soon, and with three holes poked in me my blood pressure was soon to plummet. So I lifted a case of bottled water off the back steps and dropped it on the floorboard of the Porsche. I also grabbed Amber's purse as we were going to need her wallet. She was about to buy some airplane fuel with her new Bank of America account. On my way out the door, I grabbed a bottle of honey and a saltshaker from the pantry along with the Glock. Three minutes later I'd downed two water bottles along with some salt and honey, then—with Amber screaming her muted head off—we exited the gated community.

I drove back roads, keeping away from stoplights and traffic, reaching the airfield and Joe's plane parked in a far corner. The great thing about small private airports is you can come and go with little interference. People don't care what you do. To make matters better, there was no tower. Only an unmanned desk operated on the honor system. The place was a ghost town.

I pulled the Porsche out on the tarmac, around the side of the plane, and quickly loaded an angry and kicking Amber into the side cargo door. Departing with a full tank, I'd need to make two stops between here and Montana, but given that it was sundown, we'd do that during the night and no one would be the wiser. I cranked the twin engines and began taxiing, acknowledging that my biggest concern wasn't fueling up, being recognized, or getting caught; it was what I would do if her water broke midflight.

We took off, leveling out at five thousand feet as the sun went down through the windshield. Amber lay on her side, her eyes and mouth covered, while I tried to think through any scenario where I didn't go back to prison. An hour into the flight, I could not find one. Autopilot engaged, I climbed into the back, removed the rag from Amber's mouth, and fed her a bottle of water, which she drank. When finished, I replaced the rag and bandanna and returned to my seat.

We stopped in Missouri and Wyoming at small private airports, both manned by a single attendant. On both occasions, the attendant swiped Amber's credit card without issue, and we landed in Montana nine hours after takeoff, where I loaded a half-asleep Amber into Joe's Blazer.

At 5:30 a.m. on Day 30, with the sun coming up over the mountains, we pulled down the last stretch of dirt road to Joe's cabin.

CHAPTER 38

BEFORE

A year passed. One day passed to another, and to numb the pain Joe answered the phone, accepted jobs, and lived in hotels, working from one film to the next. In eighteen months, she filmed five movies. Offering herself. And her quirky smile. Even laughing from time to time. The movies were no *Gone with the Wind*, but they entertained audiences and made money. Lots of money. As did she.

Aside from the obvious, she was a picture of health. No longer concerned with pregnancy, she took to running. Pockets tried to keep up but Joe was a good runner, a gazelle even, and he was not. Better in the short distances. So he bought a beach cruiser and pedaled along behind while she ticked off the miles.

Given her complications, her doctors changed their tune. Pockets was never privy to those conversations but he drove her to and fro, and he'd learned to read her face in the rearview. Each time she left the office, the wrinkle between her eyes grew deeper. After the third visit, she stepped into the SUV and said, "Pockets, don't you feel like some ice cream?"

"Yes mum."

They returned to the shoreline, he bought two cones, and they sat in the shade while she stared out across the Pacific. After a few bites, she set it down, where it melted through the grate. "They want me to"—she crossed her legs, patted her tummy, and then crossed her arms as a shield against the cold—"be done with it. Surgery." Three teenagers rolled by on bikes, so she turned her head and pulled her sunglasses down over her eyes. "Free to live my life. Put it all behind me, they say."

Pockets had barely touched his cone, which melted down over his fingers. She noticed it. "Pockets."

He tried to mop it up, but it was too late. It dripped all the more.

He dropped it in the can and walked behind her as she descended the steps, took off her shoes, and walked the shore. Alone.

After an hour, she sat while the wind tugged at her hair. When she looked cold, Pockets laid his coat over her shoulders, but she didn't seem to notice. After the sun disappeared, she stood and stared into the horizon. When she spoke, her voice was little more than a whisper. "Sometimes hope hurts the most."

Standing behind her, Pockets made no response.

At dark, she wandered back, meandering through the sand, climbing the steep steps along the cliff, pausing for a moment at the railing along the top, then climbing into the back seat. Pockets adjusted her air vent. "Where to, mum?"

His words seemed to wake her. "Home please, Pockets."

Needing a change of scenery, she rented a smaller cliffside home farther north. Better views. Less space. More secluded. It was new construction. Minimalist. Modern. Something about feng shui. Whatever it was, it did not spark her memories. Pockets lived in the basement while Joe and her team rattled about upstairs. He had grown accustomed to the flurry of constant activity that accompanied her. Planning. Creating. Always strategizing. But every morning and evening, he maintained his routine, checked their perimeter, and never let his guard down. His job was to protect her. What happened inside that bubble was up to other people. His job was the bubble.

One afternoon, he found a man set up in the house next door, looking through a camera mounted with a lens that looked two feet long. The man had two cameras. One pointed out across the ocean. Capturing sunsets. The second camera used a remote trigger and was not visible with the naked eye. It had been mounted on the underside of the roof of the balcony and made to blend in. From it, he had a bird's-eye view of Joe's "private" sunbathing deck. And her bathroom.

What the photographer did not know was that Pockets had convinced Joe to rent that house as well. To protect that view. In the interaction that followed, Pockets was not kind to the man or his camera, and as there were no witnesses, there was no evidence of an assault. Just two mangled cameras and one mangled man. When the dust cleared, a bleeding, expletive-shouting man drove off with little more than camera pieces and no media cards. Joe heard the staff whispering, discovered the truth of the Peeping Tom, and found Pockets eating cereal in the basement kitchen.

She sat down at the table, holding a cup of tea. "You were right."

"Sometimes it helps to think like the crazies." He handed her the two media cards. "I'd imagine there's enough on there to sue him if you want."

She crossed to the sink, dropped the SD cards in the disposal, and turned it on. She spoke as it spun. "There'll be another one tomorrow."

He took a bite. "Probably the same guy."

She returned to the table. "Pockets?"

"Yes mum."

"What should I do?"

He set down his spoon and glanced at the ceiling, where the noise of feet shuffled above him. "Mum, you have enough people telling you what to do."

"But I'm asking you."

He looked at her. Waiting until her eyes found his. "Don't ever quit on your hope. No matter the cost." A pause. "Not ever."

She sipped her tea, then stood and walked to the door. Standing in the doorway, she turned and studied him, then nodded. She tried to say something, but it didn't come out.

Pockets stood. "You okay, mum?"

She smiled. "You realize I don't look at you that way."

"What way is that, mum?"

She paused, shaking her head. "The greatest comfort of my life has been this muscled Scot with his taut lip, high-and-tight haircut, and crow's-feet crowding beautiful green eyes, which he masks behind mirrored shades. He irons his own shirts, ties a perfect Windsor knot, and every time I see his beard, I want to run my fingers through it." A pause. An honest admission. "I keep his aftershave in my bathroom because the smell of him makes me feel safe, and I schedule my workouts around his just so I can see the scars he doesn't talk about." A longer pause. She wiped her eyes. "In all my life, only one person has stood between me and the stuff that wants to hurt me." She placed her hand over his heart. "I can walk into a crowd, and you walk out bleeding. You carry the scars meant for me."

"It's the—"

"No." She stopped him. "It's not the job. It's something else. Something else altogether. Something I've never tasted. But I want to."

"Are you okay, mum?"

She turned to him. Crossed her arms. Her tone uncertain. "I want to ask you something."

He waited.

She reached in her pocket and retrieved an envelope. Turning it in her hands. "I've rewritten this thing a hundred times, trying to get it right. To figure out how to say what needs saying." Finally, she shook her head, uncurled his fingers, and placed the letter in his palm. "You can read it later. But . . ." She stared up at him. "If you can . . ." She placed her palm flat on his chest. Over his heart. "Please promise me you will."

He accepted it. "Yes mum."

She watched him slip it into his pocket. When she spoke, tears had appeared. "It's a lot to ask."

He nodded again.

She turned to leave, then turned back. Uncertain, she hesitated. "I didn't expect you. Didn't see you coming." A tear broke loose and trailed along the line of her cheek. "But I'm so glad you did."

With surgery scheduled, she surprised them all, pushed back against the naysayers, and said she'd give it one last try. Hormones. Shots. Bed rest. The Whac-A-Mole cycle continued. On retrieval day, they found two healthy eggs. Two. A miracle. She'd done it. She could breathe again. The doctors were beaming.

Only one piece remained. Syd was summoned to the "Husband's Room" once more and did his part once more, all while filming a G-rated documentary on the process. While the cameras waited outside the sample room, Syd discreetly and quietly aided the process.

For about fifteen minutes, all the world was right. Hope had a chance.

Moments later, sirens sounded and SWAT converged on the hospital. When the dust cleared, Syd was placed on a gurney and rushed to the operating room where surgeons spent eight touch-and-go hours saving his life while five men were required to subdue Pockets, who was arrested and taken downtown.

Joe never saw him again.

CHAPTER 39

BEFORE

By the time paramedics arrived, there was little left of America's leading man. Internal video footage from hospital security cameras showed five police officers were required to pull Pockets off what was left of Syd, who spent the next week in a medically induced coma due to swelling on the brain. In the days and weeks following, he required several surgeries and extensive plastic surgery to reconstruct his face. Medical records, leaked to the press, detailed multiple broken ribs, fractured facial bones, and a cracked skull with bleeding on the brain. Only proximity to the operating room and the quick work of excellent surgeons saved his life.

It didn't take long for pieces of the story to surface. Pockets was jealous of Syd's life, his career, his public acceptance, and, most significantly, his wife. Several staff members corroborated the story. They'd witnessed Pockets's almost zealous protection of Joe and how, at times, his "guarding" felt manipulative and led to further isolation. The tipping point came the day of the retrieval when Pockets, fueled by jealousy and rage, knowingly and methodically conducted a military-style hit on Syd using all of his military training—including his classified work for both MI6 and SAS. Knowing he had failed to end their marriage and having been unsuccessful in his repeated attempts to convince Joe to leave Syd, Pockets unleashed what the networks labeled a "savage beating upon an unsuspecting, vulnerable, and trusting man."

While Pockets rotted in a jail cell and the attorneys jousted, Syd endured the grueling rigors of therapy. Pictures appeared. Slumped in a wheelchair. Mouth wired shut. Drinking through a straw. Joe at his side. The court of public opinion called for Pockets's head on a platter.

After six months, Syd braved the cameras for a primetime sit-down. Joe wheeled him in, and the two sat holding hands. Syd weakened. Atrophied. The once tanned and muscular action hero with veins like rose vines had melted into an average man. The interviewer began by giving a detailed description of the carnage at the crime scene, and then Syd's resulting injuries.

When prompted, Syd cleared his throat and gave his version, as best he remembered it. He backed up to the early days, how he had tried to befriend Pockets, who, while he admired him and agreed he was good at his job, always presented himself as a loner prone to slight bouts of anger. Bouts that scared Joe. He then relayed how Pockets would sequester Joe, isolating her from staff and friends. He stated how he would return from filming, only to discover that Pockets had been conducting forced walks and runs on the beach because he felt Joe was gaining too much weight and losing her marketability in the fickle Hollywood world.

When he confronted Pockets, stating that such a strict regimen of physical exercise could negatively impact her ability to get pregnant and that he was pushing her body too hard when they were doing everything they could to conceive, Pockets blew him off and orchestrated an elaborate "two months of rehab" at a farm where Joe had experienced trauma and rejection as a young girl. During that time, the abuse she had suffered as a foster child was amplified, which further forced her into depression and the need for medication. When asked for further details, Syd mentioned how Pockets had convinced Joe to buy him a seven-million-dollar ocean-side home next door. Even putting it in his name. So that he might be closer. And how she had continued to pay the property taxes despite the fact that he lived there alone.

While Syd reiterated that he admired Pockets for his service, he also admitted that admiration had caused him to overlook what he now saw as glaring deficiencies in his character, and he questioned Pockets's ability to live safely in civilized society when he didn't get what he wanted. Asked if he, based on his experience, found Pockets to be a danger to society, he answered with a question. "We have no idea what he endured in his service, but just based on my experience alone, how can he not be?" Pointing to his own injuries, he said, "I question who's next."

The interview ended with a video of Pockets's vigil in the hotel when he had upended the director and producers who were trying to get into Joe's room. The interviewer asked Syd if he believed Pockets had medicated Joe routinely. With drugs from the duffel, which was clearly seen on camera. Syd responded with tears in his eyes. "God only knows what was happening to Joe behind those closed doors. He's a ticking time bomb."

To the charges of attempted murder and aggravated bodily assault, Pockets pled guilty, robbing the public of a much-anticipated trial.

The same day Syd exchanged his wheelchair for crutches, Pockets began serving a fifteen-year sentence at a California state prison hidden somewhere in the northeast corner of the state. At sentencing, the judge told Pockets the only reason for a lessened sentence was his decorated military service.

Free from the fear of Pockets's retribution, Syd returned home, where he and Joe picked up the pieces. And whereas he had helped nurse her back to health over the last few years, she now switched hats and nursed

Syd, whose rehab took months. Once he was walking on his own again, Hollywood's power couple elected to give pregnancy one last go. For Joe, Syd and the baby were her singular focus.

So, one last time, she endured the shots and the hormonal swings, and when the time was right, fertilized egg number one was unfrozen and medically reinserted into her body.

Two weeks later, blood tests confirmed the impossible had become possible. Amid the trauma and horror of the last few months, and against all odds, Joe was pregnant. She was making something, no, someone, grow.

For four glorious weeks, Syd was the consummate husband. He smiled for the documentary crew and their cameras, fighting hard with crippled fingers to unbox an espresso maker and make his wife a decaf latte. Then, using both an electric chair and a four-legged walker, he limped to her bedside and served the frothy caffeine-free concoction to Joe. Coffee in bed. Where she would remain for the duration. Doctor's orders. Days later, Syd sold the documentary rights for eight figures.

Three months in, surrounded by a mountain of books, eight or ten half-finished knitting projects, and just as many nowhere-near-completed watercolors on canvas, Joe had named her swollen stomach Pooch. All the world was right. She could no longer fit into her jeans, and she could not have been happier.

Then, just as Syd was regaining the dexterity in his hands and could open bottles, doors, and jars and use a spoon without assistance, the pictures populated Instagram. And the videos landed on TikTok.

The collage of pictures detailed not one but four ongoing relationships. All wanting their piece of Syd. The "ice storm" in the tropics with the Swedish model. The Brazilian bombshell who had kept him warm while he saved the world from aliens. The waitress in New York City, waiting tables to pay for acting school, who had helped him practice his lines. And the Silicon Valley exec whom he'd met at a meditation retreat in South America. Turned out, all the stories were true.

Two days later, Joe's body responded to the news with spotting. There would be no baby. Given the development and size of the baby, her medical team admitted her to a neonatal intensive care unit where she walked laps around the room and spent thirty-six hours delivering a stillborn. When she asked if she could hold her baby, they placed her daughter in her hands and she wept.

Given the trauma to her heart, mind, and soul, three different medical teams recommended a partial hysterectomy. She didn't blink. Take it. She was done. So they did. And when she woke, they gave her OxyContin for the pain.

Syd's attorney said he wanted a quiet parting. Joe didn't care. They, whoever they were, could have him. With Syd gone and Pockets in prison, she closed her heart and drifted into the only thing she knew how to do. Her work. Role after role, she pretended to be anyone but herself. The critics would later write it was seven years of her best work. "No one in the history of the silver screen did or could do what she did in that time span. It was pure cinematic and box-office history."

CHAPTER 40

BEFORE

Syd was into his third girlfriend since the divorce, and Pockets was five years into his sentence, when Joe traveled to the Northwest. Filming in Washington and Oregon. Content with the single life and vowing quietly never to fall in love again, Joe agreed to star in a rom-com in which she would play five different characters. When the makeup artist tore an ankle tendon while on vacation prior to shooting, production scrambled to find a fill-in.

Enter Amber Paxton. Amber had dropped out of high school in the tenth grade because she didn't see the purpose. She moved to LA to study makeup and hair, finally interning with a successful artist with Hollywood connections. Having been made promises, she ended up carrying boxes, picking up coffee, driving midnight food runs, and answering email for the better part of a couple of years. The only advantage to her twenty-four-seven busywork was that it immersed her in the costume world. Every aspect. And to her credit, she was a sponge.

Despondent, disillusioned, and recently single, she sat working at the computer one afternoon when an email came in. "HELP. Short notice. Start ASAP." So she put together a résumé, lied about 90 percent of her experience, and clicked Send. Thirty minutes later, her phone rang. Five minutes after that, she bought a ticket to Oregon.

Despite lying on her CV, Amber was good at her job and could make anyone feel comfortable in her chair. She was a natural. Not to mention the fact that she was an artist with other people's faces. She just needed a chance. That afternoon, they brought her in to meet Joe and explained the movie and the multiple roles Joe would play: a twentysomething yoga instructor, a midseventies cigarette-smoking angry divorcée with thinning hair and bad teeth, a middle-aged housekeeper, and a late-fifties secretary who lost the battle with her weight a long time ago. Joe would also play herself. Five roles in total.

She was told that 3D masks and various body accents would be provided as required for each role, but they needed Amber to create a seamless transition from the neck up—and also the sleeve down, including the hands—and do it in a timely fashion. And they needed each change to look identical to the time before. The time crunch was real, and Joe would have to be in and out of costume a lot. Not to mention the makeup artist's chair.

Amber passed with flying colors.

The first week, she worked twenty-two-hour days trying to get it right. Production stayed on time and came off without a hitch. The director said she crushed it. The transformations were nothing short of miraculous. For Joe, the addition of Amber provided something—or someone—she'd not expected. A friend. And not just any friend but an empathetic one to help fill the void. With hours spent every day in the chair, Joe and Amber became confidants. Sisters. Constant companions. Who quickly learned they shared one thing in common.

Relationships with men had been trainwrecks. Total yard sales.

Joe pushed for greater compensation and bought Amber her own custom trailer on par with any LA or New York salon that traveled from set to set. Now solo, Joe included Amber on all flights to and from any filming location, negating Amber's need to fly commercial. Joe exposed Amber to a world she could not have conceived. From dinners with dignitaries to celebrity parties, scuba diving the Great Barrier Reef, skydiving over Iceland, learning to pilot a glider, dogsledding to the North Pole, flying an ultralight over the Grand Canyon, paddleboarding portions of the Amazon, sleeping in treetop tents in the rain forest—Amber's world exploded with possibility and adventure. And Joe's world, the one full of memories and questions, got lost in the shuffle—and in the pills.

When Joe exited rehab for the last time, Amber picked her up. Plane ready. And flew her to Monaco where Joe had been asked to start the Formula 1 race. Those two, along with several staff, stayed a month aboard a rented oligarch's yacht where they took in the sun and watched old movies.

CHAPTER 41

BEFORE

Somewhere on the yacht, in the early morning hours following a celebrity party, under the Monaco moon and buzz of a medicated haze, the conversation occurred. Joe's team knew she trusted Amber, so they tasked Amber with the one question none of them wanted to ask. Because they feared the spiral that undoubtedly would occur when they did. The clinic had called. It'd been five years and, for ethical reasons, they needed to know—what did she want to do with the final fertilized egg?

No one heard the entirety of the conversation, only that the two shared a good, long cry and Joe was heard to say, "I'd give anything, all that I have, to hold my baby." Then, sometime later, they heard the pop of a champagne cork, laughter, and more tears.

The next morning, Joe was happier than she'd been in years. Jubilant even. Walking around with a spring in her step. And if Amber had walked into last night's conversation a makeup artist and friend, she walked out something altogether different. Something far more powerful. With the clock ticking, Joe put a plan in place. They had one shot remaining, and she was going to make it work. With Pockets in prison, never to be seen or heard from again, she would move Amber into the house next door—to make sure she was close. And for safety reasons, she gave her one of her Cadillac SUVs. She then spent the morning on the phone talking with doctors and the medical personnel at the clinic to make sure she had the best care on planet Earth.

Which Amber was going to need.

As her surrogate.

CHAPTER 42

AFTER

Amber winced as she spoke. Her breathing was shallow. "My water broke."

I hurried to the cabin, cracked open the door, and spoke without the computerized voice. "You in there?"

Joe was lying in bed. Covers pulled over her head. I thought maybe the sound of my voice might wake her. It did not.

"Could we talk?"

Still nothing.

I stepped closer. "I know I have a lot of explaining to do, but I need to tell you something."

Still no response.

Another step. "You can be mad at me later, but right now . . ."

I gently pulled back the sheet, revealing pillows lined up like a body. "Uh-oh."

I searched the house, but Joe was gone. She'd flown the coop. And we were at least two hours' drive from the nearest hospital. Minutes later, Amber screamed from the Blazer. When I opened the door, she had reclined the front seat, propped her feet on the dash, and latched a white-knuckled death grip on the armrests. Her eyes were wide and wild, and she was dripping sweat.

She spoke through shallow breaths. "How far to the hospital?"

"Two hours of rough driving."

She shook her head. "Can you deliver a baby?"

I stared at the road. The cabin that had been my home for much of the last month. The mountains that offered freedom. And then Amber. If I left now, I could ditch her and leave her to fend for herself. She deserved little else. Who could blame me? I could ease out of these mountains, find some vet, pay him or her to patch me up, then disappear. Rest up in a motel. A week. Maybe two. Then make my way home on a ship or cargo vessel. But when I closed my eyes, Joe appeared on the back of my eyelids. Right where I'd left her. And I couldn't ditch her.

I pressed the limits of the Blazer down the dirt and gravel road, which did not help Amber's situation. Between her cussing me, clutching my arm, and screaming in pain, not to mention three bullet holes, I struggled to maintain focus. I'd lost enough blood to drop my blood pressure, and the edges of my vision were closing in.

When I momentarily lost consciousness, Amber backhanded me. "Hey, dummy! Wake up! You can't die."

She hit me again, my vision returned, and I straightened the wheel. When I spoke, I wasn't in the best space. "Maybe you should have thought about that before you shot me."

But neither was she. "Maybe you shouldn't have kidnapped me."

"And maybe you shouldn't have kidnapped Joe's baby."

She screamed again as another contraction hit. The dirt road from the cabin to the hard road ordinarily took an hour. I cut that in half. When the tires hit asphalt, I mashed the accelerator to the floor. The big-block Chevy roared to life and pegged the speedometer at a hundred miles per hour. I had no business delivering a baby, so I convinced my-self I could outrun the contractions. But when they began hitting just two minutes apart, Amber's screams convinced me I could not make it. I pulled off the road, flung open the back of the Blazer, rolled the back seat forward, spread a sleeping bag, and then carried Amber to the back while she pounded my shoulders with her fists.

"What are you doing?" she asked.

"Delivering a baby."

"Where?"

I set her down as gently as my shoulder and hand would allow. "Right here."

Her wide eyes grew wider. "Why here?" she said through gritted teeth.

"Hospital's too far. We'll never make it. You want to do this in the front seat while I drive?"

"No." Then, in a rare moment of semitransparency, she asked, "And why do you care if I live or die?"

Things were escalating. I could see the top of the baby's head through the canal. I set my phone on the tailgate, dialed 911, and pressed the Speaker button.

"911. What's your emergency?"

"My name is Kelly MacThomas Pockets." Amber screamed. "We are headed west on Highway 121, mile marker 372. Brown Chevy Blazer. I'm delivering a baby. We need paramedics immediately."

Amber's head popped up and she studied me. I heard fingers clack-ing on a keyboard from the speaker. "Location received. Fire and res-cue dispatched. They're en route." The operator continued. "Is she in a birthing position?"

"Yes."

"Can you see the birth canal?"

"Yes."

"Did her water break?"

"Yes."

"How far apart are the contractions?"

"Less than a minute."

"Sir, can you repeat your name, please?"

I knew my face had just popped up on her screen, alerting her to my identity, but I did not have either the time or the energy to explain. "Kelly MacThomas Pockets. And I've never delivered a baby."

More clacking. "I'll walk you through this."

The walls were closing in. "How far away are they?"

"Fifteen minutes."

"I'm not sure I'm going to make that. I've been shot three times and I've lost a lot of . . ." I woke a minute later to the sound of Amber pleading and pounding the tailgate with her heel. "Pockets, please!"

I pulled myself up on the tailgate, wiped my eyes, and examined Amber. The emergency operator was speaking through the speaker. "Mr. Pockets? Mr. Pockets? Did you say you've been shot?"

I shook off the fog. "The head is more pronounced."

"Is she crowning?"

"Not sure what that means."

"Has the head reached the end of the canal?"

"Yes."

The operator redirected. "How old is the mom?"

"Midtwenties."

"Has she ever had a baby?"

Amber screamed over my shoulder, "No, I have not!"

The operator responded, "Hang in there, baby. I've done it five times myself. And a couple dozen over the phone. We'll get you through it."

Amber winced again. "How about drugs? Got any of those?"

"It's a little late for that, baby, but hold on. Mr. Pockets? Update?"

"Just more of the head."

"Mr. Pockets, I need you to run your fingers around the baby's neck. Make sure the cord is not wrapped."

I did as instructed. "No cord."

"You need to make sure."

I did. "I'm sure."

"Momma, what's your name?"

"Amber."

"Amber, baby, I need you to breathe for me. Focus on that."

Amber responded by taking deep breaths.

I could hear the smile in the operator's voice. "Boy or girl?"

I answered, "Boy."

"Amber, sometimes we have to help the shoulders. They can be wider than the space God gave them to come into the world. So we need to make a little room until your hips figure out what they're doing. It's just part of it. You got any kind of oil?"

Amber pointed. "Purse."

I rifled through her purse, pulled out a bottle, and read the label out loud. "Belly Serum—Vitamin D Stretch Mark Reduction Oil."

"Perfect." The operator continued, "Bathe your fingers and hands and Momma. Then try to work your fingers around the head. When you see the top of his eyebrows, run your finger alongside the back of his head and around one shoulder and help slide the shoulder out. You may have to turn him slightly to one side to get him more vertical. But"—she emphasized—"don't do it when she's pushing." The operator then spoke to Amber. "Amber, after the next contraction, I need you to do your best to relax."

"Relax?!" Amber winced and held her breath.

The operator continued. "And I need you to breathe. Come on, baby, breathe. In. Out. Deep breaths."

Amber exhaled, then began breathing rapidly and pushing forcefully, finally letting go with a loud scream. When the contraction passed, Amber relaxed and I did as instructed.

"There's not enough room. She's tearing."

"How much blood?"

"Some. Not a lot."

"Gushing?"

"No."

"Amber, it's okay. Happens to all of us. Baby, you'll be fine. I just need you to hang in there. Couple more pushes and you're home."

Amber's legs tightened and she sucked in a breath and held it.

The operator again. "Come on, baby girl. Breathe."

After a guttural scream and a few well-earned cusswords, Amber nodded, and I spoke again while trying to free the shoulder. "I don't hear any sirens."

The operator spoke calmly. "Nine minutes out."

"He's stuck."

"Mr. Pockets, I need you to help him out. Slide your fingers around his shoulder, then hook a finger under one shoulder. We can't leave the baby in the canal."

I did as instructed, and Amber let out a bloodcurdling scream as the baby moved slightly. As the contraction hit, Amber pushed again, this time longer and harder. Suddenly, the head cleared the canal, allowing me better access to the shoulder.

"Head's out."

"Cord?"

"I don't see it."

"Beautiful," the operator responded. "Amber, you're doing great. I need one more big push. Can you do that for me?"

Amber nodded and reached for my hand, which I gave. She locked her fingers in mine, squeezed them like a vise, and the contraction hit in force. Amber screamed, threw her head back, and let go of my hand, bracing herself on the roof and side of the Blazer. As she pushed, I slid my fingers around the side of the shoulder, and to my amazement, as if shot out of a waterslide, he slid out and landed in my hands. Just like he was supposed to. Amber felt the release of pressure and heard the gush. Then her body fell limp and she started crying and laughing.

The operator interrupted my silence. "Talk to me, Mr. Pockets."

"He's out."

"Is the cord clear? Not wrapped around his neck?"

"Still clear."

"Is he breathing?"

I placed my ear to his mouth. "No."

"Place your mouth over his nose and mouth and breathe gently."

I did.

"Anything?"

"No."

"Again. This time harder."

I did. A second time.

"Anything?"

"No."

"Third time's always a charm. Let's go, Mr. Pockets."

I filled my chest, exhaled, and filled his.

After the longest second of my life, he responded with the loudest and most beautiful cry I'd ever heard. And somewhere in that beautiful, crazy, chaotic, crystal-clear moment, I realized I may never see him again—but I'd always know his first breath started in my lungs. At least I gave him that.

At the sound of his powerful and loud lungs, both Amber and the operator started crying and laughing.

As she caught her breath, the operator asked, "Mr. Pockets, can you wrap him in something?"

Amber pulled a baby blanket from her bag and I wrapped him in it.

The operator again. "How's the bleeding?"

"Not bad. But the cord is still—"

She interrupted me. "Don't worry. Momma's body will take care of that. Give it a few minutes. Nothing to worry about. Just hang tight. EMT and police are four minutes away."

I sat on the tailgate, mesmerized. Not sure how to hold him while he was still tethered to Amber's body and worried I might hurt him. Next to me, Amber lay drenched in sweat, her eyes closed. Breathing deep and calm. After she caught her breath, she placed a hand on my thigh and spoke without opening her eyes. "Thank you."

I tried to laugh. "Not sure we had much choice, but you're welcome."

Another breath, then she turned her head toward me. Looking up. For the first time since we'd known each other, her tone was not acerbic. "I cannot believe I just gave birth in the back of a Blazer."

I was growing dizzier and didn't want to drop the baby, so I wedged the little burrito between us. Together we held him. She covered in her blood and me covered in hers and mine. She opened one eye and forced a laugh. "You're crazy."

I nodded. "I tend to agree with you."

"Why?"

"Why what?"

"Why're you sitting here? Why don't you take the baby, dump me in that ditch over there, and make a run for it?"

I shook my head.

"Why?"

"For starters, somebody shot me and I don't feel too well. Kind of feel like I want to throw up. And second, I'm just too tired. All I want to do is go to sleep."

She nodded and glanced at the bullet hole in my shoulder. "I suppose they'll put me in prison for that."

"Don't sweat it. I'll be there with you."

She laughed. After a few seconds, she patted my thigh and laughed quietly. "Thank you."

"For?"

"Not dumping my body."

I laughed again. "Don't think I didn't think about it. You're just lucky I can't lift my arm and my hand has a hole in it. Otherwise . . ." I smiled.

"Mr. Pockets," she said.

"Yes mum."

"I think you are a good man."

In the distance, sirens sounded. "You might be alone in that."

"Yeah." She shook her head. "But I'm not wrong."

The police arrived first. Two cars. Followed by a fire truck and an ambulance. The paramedics rushed to the car, lifted the baby out of my arms, and were replaced by two officers staring at me down the barrels of Glock 17s. "Kelly MacThomas Pockets, you have the right to remain silent . . ."

"I had a feeling you were going to say that."

I obeyed their commands, rolled onto my side, and they placed my hands behind me. Cuffing me, they searched me for weapons while the paramedics pulled the afterbirth from Amber and cleaned her up. Finding no weapons on me, they led me to the back of the police car, then noticed I'd been shot in the shoulder and that most of the blood covering me was mine.

One of the paramedics came over, found the holes, plugged me up, and started an IV. Sitting in the back of the ambulance, while some really good drugs dripped into my bloodstream, the paramedic smiled and looked from me to Amber and back to me. "You two will have a great story to tell your kids one day."

Amber raised a hand and began shaking her head. "We're not . . ." Realizing it would take too long, she let it go. "Never mind."

Two minutes later, they secured us in the back of the ambulance and sped to a hospital. Jail would have to wait until after surgery. I don't know how long I was out, but when I came to, Amber's hand was clutching my bicep. "Mr. Pockets? Mr. Pockets?"

Noise returned. Then light. Then the sensation of pain. "You don't have to call me Mister."

Amber forced a laugh. "At this point we're pretty much on a first-name basis. I don't have too many secrets left." She slapped me as a serious tone returned. "We all thought you were gone."

I tried to shake off the fog. I wanted to rub my eyes, but my hands had been cuffed to the bed on which they'd laid me. "Not yet."

The driver slowed as he pulled the ambulance into the emergency unload. When the vehicle came to a stop, I heard the driver roll down the window and speak. "What's going on?"

A voice outside said, "Media trucks have got everything blocked. Police are making a way through now."

"What happened?"

"You haven't heard?"

The driver must have shook his head because the voice spoke unprompted. "Maybe Joe Sue is here. In the hospital. Walked through those doors right there not two hours ago. Been a prisoner in a cabin for the last month. Escaped yesterday and walked something like twenty miles over the mountains, then hitchhiked to the hospital. Kid that gave her a ride is over there surrounded by all the cameras."

"She okay?"

"Tired and hungry but unharmed. Word just came in on the radio that officers arrested the sick pervert who's been holding her. Sounds like she put one in him, too, 'cause he's got a gunshot wound to the chest. They're bringing him here now. Paparazzi are in a feeding frenzy."

The driver must have thumbed over his shoulder because the voice said, "No kidding."

Amber squeezed my arm. "Can I ask you something before those doors open?"

The drugs were working, making me loopy. "Fire away."

She nodded toward the commotion at the window. "Did you do that?"

"Do what?"

"Joe."

"Yes."

"Why?"

"Because I promised her I would."

"Would what?"

"Get her clean."

"Did you?"

A pause. "Yes."

"That's good." A moment passed, then she chuckled as all the pieces began settling in place. "Guess that means I've been texting you all this time?"

I nodded as my lips began feeling thick. "Yep."

Another pause. "Can I ask something else?"

I turned and waited, the expression on my face welcoming the question she'd been wanting to ask me.

"You hate me?"

"No. I don't hate you." I tried to shake my head. "In a weird way, I feel sorry for you."

She paused. "Does Joe?"

"You'll have to ask her. But in my experience, Joe doesn't hate anyone. Not even Syd." The drugs were making me talkative, but I was too tired to try to stop the words. "But I'd bet money she takes you off the Christmas card list."

Just before the doors opened, the paramedic laid the baby boy in Amber's arms.

Amber studied him, pushing the blanket out of his face where the paramedic had wrapped him up like a burrito. She whispered, "Hi there, little guy. Been wondering what you would look like."

Before they slid her out of the ambulance, she turned and reached for me one last time. "Pockets?"

"Yes."

When she spoke, she was looking at the boy. "Why would you go to this much trouble for Syd's baby?"

I lifted my head, then realized it had grown too heavy so I let it fall back down, content to melt into the bed. "He's not Syd's baby."

When the door opened, police stood waiting. Having realized my identity but not yet realizing Amber's, the paramedics soured on me and began fawning over her. Sliding Amber out first, they commented, "He's so handsome."

Amber glanced at me, pressed the boy to her bare chest, and admired him, nodding. Tears streaming. With one hand, she was counting his fingers and toes. Unable to keep my eyes open any longer, I closed them and began drifting away. The last words I heard before I dropped off were Amber's. "Yes, he is . . ." A long pause. "But . . . I'm just the surrogate. The mom is Maybe Joe Sue."

CHAPTER 43

AFTER

The inflating pressure from the cuff on my bicep woke me from the best sleep I'd had in a long time. White walls, an IV, bandages, and the smell of antiseptic suggested I woke in a hospital, or at least a surgical ward. A woman dressed in light blue and wearing squeaky shoes appeared next to my bed, muted the machine above my head, recorded my vitals, and left while an armed guard stood opposite her, staring down at me. I tried to scratch my nose but my hands and feet were shackled.

Just outside my door, nurses scurried up and down the hallway as a television news team echoed. "In late-breaking news, former celebrity bodyguard Kelly MacThomas Pockets was arrested late last night after holding three-time Academy Award–winning actress Maybe Joe Sue. Abducting her one month ago from her Malibu home following her historic third Oscar win, he has been holding her captive in the Montana mountains. After a heroic escape and a walk of some twenty miles through the mountains, Mrs. Joe hitchhiked to the hospital. Surprisingly, Mr. Pockets was arrested on Highway 121 after delivering a baby from a second woman he kidnapped, Ms. Amber Paxton, whom he had abducted the day prior from a home in Georgia. No motive is known. Ms. Paxton is safe and recovering, having given birth to a healthy boy early this morning.

"From her hospital room, Mrs. Joe released a statement saying she had not known that her former bodyguard, Mr. Pockets, had escaped prison or that he was her abductor as he only spoke through a computerized voice, never letting her see his face. When asked how she was feeling, Mrs. Joe responded with, 'Better.' Authorities do not know Mr. Pockets's intentions, but he used stolen security devices at the Montana cabin to set an electronic perimeter and control her movements. Mrs. Joe said when she crossed the invisible boundary, the device around her neck would issue a brachial stun and knock her out. In order to escape, Mrs. Joe braved the third stun, only to find the device either malfunctioned or had been deactivated. She then walked all night down mountain roads to Highway 121, where she flagged down a ride.

"As you can see behind me, I'm standing outside the hospital room where Mr. Pockets is recovering from surgery, treating bullet wounds sustained in his abduction of Ms. Paxton, who bravely attempted to defend herself and her baby. Authorities here tell us that upon recovery, Mr. Pockets will begin serving the remainder of his sentence at Russex State Prison while he awaits trial for these most recent kidnappings."

Somewhere in there I nodded off to sleep. The news was not news to me.

The next time I awoke, the sunlight seemed softer, suggesting I'd slept through most of the day. Outside my room, the nurses still squeaked up and down the hall as a new guard sat staring at me through heavy eyelids. I thought about telling him it was okay to grab some sleep, that I wasn't going anywhere, but then thought better of it. From the nurses' station, I could hear the television.

"In late-breaking news today, Amber Paxton was arrested this morning, just four days after giving birth to a healthy boy in the back of a stolen Chevy Blazer. Turns out the boy wasn't hers. Details are still coming in, but, as if straight from a Hollywood script, Ms. Paxton was serving as surrogate to Mrs. Joe Sue. Initially hired as a makeup artist, she had a front-row seat to Mrs. Joe's difficult pregnancy journey, during which she suffered multiple public miscarriages. Mrs. Joe's medical team later determined she was unable to have children, so Mrs. Joe hired Ms. Paxton, for an undisclosed amount, to serve as her surrogate. Ms. Paxton agreed, took an initial payment, then, six months into the pregnancy, disappeared with the baby.

"But the story doesn't end there. Over the next three months, Ms. Paxton teamed up with three men who, according to phone and computer records collected by the FBI, blackmailed Mrs. Joe to the tune of 1.2 million dollars. Tonight, all three men are in custody, including Mr. Pockets. In an exclusive interview today with *Morning Edition*, Mrs. Joe recounted the strange details of her captivity. When asked what she would do now, she said she intended to disappear from the public eye and focus on her son and learning to be a mom."

I tried to lift my head but could not see the screen as the knowledge sank in that I'd slept through the last four days. The news anchor opposite the reporter asked, "Any word on new charges being filed against her former bodyguard, Mr. Pockets?"

The field reporter nodded. "Several new charges have been filed against Mr. Pockets, but a trial date has not been set. Most legal scholars agree Mr. Pockets will live behind bars for quite some time."

CHAPTER 44

AFTER

"All rise. The Honorable Judge Thelma Dixon of the California Ninth Circuit is now presiding."

We stood as Judge Thelma Dixon entered. Judge Thelma Dixon had been on the Los Angeles bench thirty years, ran a tight courtroom, and, from the looks of things, didn't miss many meals. She was a big woman, maybe *force* is a better word, and didn't put up with any foolishness. This was her domain and she ruled it with an iron gavel. She was said to be sympathetic to women and their needs and was known to throw the book at men who mistreated them in any way. She liked to brag she could "sniff out a fraud" and didn't suffer fools.

The judge entered, studied the room over her glasses, muttered something to herself, then sat. She nodded to the bailiff, who led me to the stand. I shuffled forward, my chains rattling, placed my hand on the Bible, said "I do," and the judge told me to sit. So I did.

Given the high-profile nature of the case, the district attorney had fought hard to allow cameras in the courtroom, stating on nightly news channel after nightly news channel how the public needed to know. I disagreed but nobody really seemed to care, so I lost. My defense team had been assigned to me, but they weren't all that helpful, seldom came to see me, and I didn't have much faith in them. When we first met, I'd offered to tell them my story but they declined. I asked how they could defend me if they didn't know the truth, and they said it would come out in court. This left me flying solo. I knew the outcome. Knew where I was headed. And I didn't really care. I was just hoping to get a chance to say a few things that needed saying.

The courtroom was standing room only. Members of the press crowded every corner. The prosecution team sat opposite. Joe sat behind them. Not looking at me. She had not been present the prior two days, but I'd heard on the news that she wanted to be present during my testimony. In support, several other celebrities sat around, which only added to the circus. The networks were calling her harrowing experience "Thirty Days in Hell," and one outlet reported this morning that several streaming services were bidding for documentary rights.

Never one to miss a chance to ride Joe's coattails, Syd showed his tanning-bed face. He glad-handed the other celebrities, slapping backs and working the camera angles. I overheard him say he wanted to make sure I got what I had coming and he hoped they buried me beneath the prison. A guy like me doesn't need to be loose in safe society.

The prosecuting attorney's name was Carl Munson. Carl was competent, good at his job, and possessed a flair for the dramatic that, honestly, I liked. I found his timing to be rather entertaining, even if at my expense. The courtroom quieted; Mr. Munson paced in front of me, taking his time studying the jury, me, and then the cameras. "Sir, would you please state your name for the record."

"Kelly MacThomas Pockets."

"And you're on the stand of your own volition?"

"I am."

"Do you understand you have the right not to testify?"

"I do."

"And no one is compelling you?"

"I'm here because I want to be."

"And your occupation?"

"Currently, I'm employed at Russex State Prison." Laughter rippled through the courtroom. "I work in the garden. Right now we're growing tomatoes and peas."

More laughter.

"What did you do prior to that?"

"I spent twenty years in the Scottish military in various capacities, then five years in personal protection."

"And by 'personal protection,' you mean . . . ?"

"I was a bodyguard."

"Mr. Pockets, do you know Mrs. Joe Sue?"

"I do."

"Did you work in her employ?"

"I did."

"In what capacity?"

"I was her bodyguard."

"For how long?"

"Five years."

"And would you describe her as a fair employer?"

I looked at Joe. "No, sir."

This seemed to surprise him. Murmurs echoed behind him. "Not fair?"

"She was beyond fair. She's one of the most giving and generous people I've ever met."

He nodded. "I understand. How would you describe your five years working with her?"

"Some of the best, if not the best, of my life."

He nodded. "And what were your duties?"

"I was responsible for everything related to her protection. I vetted everyone who came to see her, or places she visited. She never entered a room, car, plane, building, or restaurant that I didn't enter first."

"What about physical activity?"

"If she went on a run, I rode a bike alongside."

He interrupted me. "Why a bike?"

I shrugged. "I couldn't keep up."

More laughter.

"Continue."

"If she and Mr. Syd went anywhere, I accompanied."

"And by 'Mr. Syd' you mean . . . ?"

"Syd Painter. Her ex-husband." I pointed to Syd, who waved for the cameras.

Munson continued, "Long hours?"

"Yes, sir. Often twenty-hour days."

"Did you resent that?"

"No, sir. It's the job."

"During that time, how would you describe your relationship with Mrs. Joe?"

"Very good, I think."

"You think?"

"I never had reason to believe otherwise."

"Define 'good.'"

"I've seldom known such kindness."

He glanced at Joe and then the crowd. "I've heard that celebrities can be a little high-maintenance. Did she ever mistreat you? Even just a little?"

"Never."

"Come on, Mr. Pockets. Not even just a little? Maybe she was the center of the universe and all the planets rotated around her?"

"No, sir." I shook my head. "Often when she was filming, she'd work the food tent prior to her scenes."

"What do you mean she'd 'work the food tent'?"

"She served the food to all the folks working on the film. And she knew them by name. She was always one of us."

"I see. Were you ever employed as a bodyguard prior to working with Mrs. Joe?"

I considered the ramifications of this answer. Not wanting to answer, I looked at the judge, then Mr. Munson. "I'd rather not say."

Judge Thelma Dixon raised an eyebrow.

Mr. Munson said, "I'd rather you did."

"Sir, I don't talk about my previous employers."

"Why?"

"Well . . ." I lifted my chains. "It would bring them dishonor."

"I'm sure they'd understand. I'm attempting to establish your competency as a bodyguard. So I'll ask you again, Mr. Pockets, did you work as a bodyguard prior to your employment with Mrs. Joe?"

"Yes, sir."

I got the feeling that Munson knew the answer but he wanted the admission to come from me. And given the fact that I didn't want to answer, he wasn't going to let it rest. When he spoke, he was looking at the jury. "For whom did you work?"

He let the word *whom* roll off his tongue a little too long. I paused and looked at Joe, who was looking at me. Her eyes were glassy and she looked tired. "Sir, I can't say."

Munson was enjoying this a little too much. "And why exactly is that?"

"Sir, I don't talk about my previous employers."

Munson looked at the judge, who stared down at me. "Mr. Pockets, answer the question."

"Mum, my presence here brings them dishonor. And I don't want to do that."

Judge Thelma Dixon looked irritated, but Munson was enjoying the theatrics, so he capitalized on the moment. He opened a folder and handed an eight-by-eleven glossy photo to the judge. She studied the picture, then me, then handed it back to Munson, who waved it in front of the courtroom. "The prosecution would like to add photo 1A into evidence." Then he sauntered toward me and leaned on the bench. "Do you see yourself in this picture, Mr. Pockets?"

I didn't need to look at it. "Yes, sir."

"And what are you doing in this picture?"

"Working."

"For whom?" Again, he let the word *whom* roll off his tongue.

"My previous employer."

"Who is?"

"The Queen."

He placed his hand on the wooden bench in front of me. His disbelief was palpable. "The Queen?"

"Yes, sir."

"The queen of what?"

A pause. "England."

The courtroom sucked in a collective breath. And held it.

Mr. Munson paced back and forth before the jury, allowing them to view the picture. If he didn't have their attention before, he had it now. "Mr. Pockets, I want to make certain, and I want to give you a chance to tell the truth. Sometimes we fantasize about things and Lord knows what experts can do with Photoshop. So I need to establish for the jury whether this is imagined or real." He waved the picture. "Are you saying you worked personal protection for the reigning queen of England?"

"Yes, sir, I am."

"So this picture isn't fabricated?"

"No, sir."

"It's real?"

"Yes, sir."

"And that's really you?"

"Yes, sir."

The courtroom exhaled and chatter rippled throughout, forcing the judge to slam her gavel and demand, "Order."

The judge interrupted. "Mr. Munson, I would imagine that employment record is classified."

"Yes, Your Honor. We found the specifics and nature of the work would be classified, while the facts of the record would not be."

"And how have you come to know this?"

Munson faced the rear of the courtroom and pointed to a man in a dark suit. "To verify the validity of the picture, we've flown in a British military attorney with knowledge of Mr. Pockets's employment." Munson turned back to the judge. "We can call him forward at this time if you'd like."

"Will he corroborate your story?"

"Yes, Your Honor."

"Leave it. We'll come back to him if needed."

Munson turned his attention back to me. "Did your employment with the Queen end on a good note?"

"Well, sir, it never really ended. Maybe *suspended* is a better word. I was given leave after I requested it."

"So you requested to leave the employ of the Queen?"

"Yes, sir."

"To work for . . . ?"

I pointed at Joe. "Mrs. Joe."

"Wasn't working for the Queen a pretty good gig?"

"Yes, sir."

"Good perks?"

I figured the less I said the better. "Yes, sir."

"But you left there to work with Mrs. Joe here. Why?"

"I had worked as a consultant on a script she and Syd were filming. A few weeks later, she called and asked if she could hire me on a short-term basis as her bodyguard."

"Given that you had just come from working with the Queen, is it safe to say you understood what was appropriate behavior and what was inappropriate behavior? Things you could do and things you would never do?"

"Yes, sir."

"Would appropriate behavior be a focus in your job?"

"Well, sir, in a sense, it is the job."

"Explain."

"In the trade, it's called 'the line.'"

"The line?"

"Yes, sir."

"Can you define that, please, for the court?"

"It's an invisible line of protocol. Something we work hard to maintain and never cross."

"Give me an example."

"At its root, it's a way of thinking. And remembering. We are the protector and they are the protected. Respecting the line demands we remember we are there to serve them. So we never think more of ourselves than we should, even though we have access to intimate personal moments, and we never pretend to be a confidant even though, at times, we are invited to be one."

"Were you ever a confidant to Mrs. Joe?"

"I'd like to think so."

"So you crossed your own line?"

"Yes, sir."

"Did you ever cross a physical line with Mrs. Joe?"

"No, sir."

My attorney finally woke from his slumber and stood. "Objection, Your Honor. What does this have to do with Mr. Pockets's employment with Mrs. Joe? My client is allowed a personal life."

Munson spoke up. "Judge, it has everything to do with his character. I'm trying to establish the nature and rules of their working relationship."

"I'll allow it." Judge Thelma Dixon seemed to be enjoying this as much as the jury. "Continue."

"Thank you, Your Honor."

Munson wasted no time putting me on my heels. "Did you want to?"

A pause. "Yes, sir."

"Did you make advances that she refused?"

"No, sir."

"Were you frustrated in your position with her?"

"No, sir."

"Did she ever do anything to make you uncomfortable?"

"No, sir."

"Did she ever cross the line and make you uncomfortable?"

"No, sir."

"Not even just a little? Maybe slight flirtation?"

"No, sir."

"Did she ever give you reason to believe that your relationship with her was more than protector and protected?"

"No, sir."

"Fast-forward with me to the end of your employment with her. What happened after five years?"

"I was convicted of aggravated battery and excessive bodily harm to Mr. Syd, sentenced to fifteen years, which was reduced to seven, and I served six and a half before I escaped."

"You don't deny that?"

"No, sir."

"Why did you escape?"

"Well, that's part of a longer story we're skipping over, but . . ." Laughter again. "It started with kidnapping Mrs. Joe."

He laughed. The look on his face made it clear I was doing all the heavy lifting for him. "And you don't deny that either?"

"No."

"Mr. Pockets, three days ago, you pled 'not guilty' to the charges against you. Would you like to change your plea to guilty and save us all a lot of time?"

"No, sir."

"But you just admitted to kidnapping Mrs. Joe."

"Yes, sir. That's because I did."

"Against her will?"

"Yes, sir. At least against her will then."

Munson paused and paced before the jury. "What do you mean?"

I clarified. "Her will at that moment and time."

Munson paced. Chewing on my words. "As if it was or is somehow different than her will at any other time?"

I shrugged. "Sir, I don't know how to joust with you, and if you could just let me—"

Judge Thelma Dixon interrupted me. "Mr. Pockets, answer his question."

"He's skipping over aspects of the story and not allowing me—"

The judge interrupted me again. Her voice loud and stern. "Mr. Pockets, you will—"

"Mum, if you'd please let me tell the whole story from beginning to—"

The judge sat upright and slammed her gavel. "Mr. Pockets. I will not suffer fools in my courtroom. Answer his question."

I looked at Munson. "Yes, sir. When I kidnapped her, that was against her present will at that moment in time. But not against her will at another time."

Munson folded his arms. "I don't follow you."

I craned my neck to stare around him at Joe. "Can I talk to you privately, please?"

Joe's eyes were glassy. A tear in one corner. The judge sat up and slammed the gavel again. "Mr. Pockets! You will not make a mockery of my courtroom. Do you understand me?"

"Yes mum."

She looked like she'd eaten something bitter. "What did you say?"

"Yes mum."

"Are you trying to be funny?"

"No mum."

She collected herself. "You will answer when spoken to and only when spoken to. Do you understand?"

"Yes mum."

"And you can respond to me with 'Yes, Judge' or 'Yes, Your Honor.'"

"Yes, Your Honor."

Syd was smiling. Joe looked uncomfortable.

Munson continued. "Since you brought it up, let's talk about the kidnapping. Would you tell the court the sequence of those events?"

"One of the prison guards was a regular reader of newspapers and tabloids. She often left them in the van that I drove making deliveries and pickups. This allowed me to keep abreast of Joe's situation."

"Did Mrs. Joe allow you to call her 'Joe'?"

I nodded. "Yes."

"Isn't that informality a danger to your occupation?"

"It can be."

"Was it?"

"You could argue that."

"I intend to. Let me back up. You said the tabloids allowed you to keep abreast of Joe's situation. And by 'situation,' you mean . . . ?"

"Her difficulty getting pregnant, along with the betrayal of her surrogate, Amber Paxton."

"Did you possess other sources of information other than the tabloids?"

"Yes. Radio and the prison grapevine."

"What do you mean by 'prison grapevine'?"

"One of Ms. Paxton's boyfriends, whose name is Frank, had a brother who was locked up in my block. He talked a lot. I never knew what to believe, but he liked to talk about what all they were going to do with the money they were getting out of Joe."

Mr. Munson straightened his lapel, buttoned his coat, and smiled at the jury, who seemed to be enjoying my confession. "The prosecution would like to enter into evidence File 107, which details the conviction of Amber Paxton for acting as a surrogate for Mrs. Joe, accepting the money, and then stealing the baby only to blackmail Mrs. Joe for over 1.2 million dollars. Ms. Paxton is currently in Ochoa Women's Prison serving a ten-year sentence."

The judge nodded.

Munson again. "Continue please, Mr. Pockets."

"I knew Joe had hired her former makeup artist as a surrogate, and she was using the baby to blackmail Joe. I also knew Joe was wrestling with an Oxy addiction, which I suspected was worsening, and that she would need to be clean if she wanted to be the kind of mom I knew she wanted to be. I also knew she had trouble getting clean in the past, and with all of the present turmoil in her life, it would be all the more difficult."

"And you knew this why?"

"Because I'd driven her to rehab seven times before I went to prison."

Joe closed her eyes as a single tear trailed her face.

Munson gestured. "Continue please."

"After Amber disappeared with the baby, the clock started ticking. I knew that if Joe was to get clean, I would need to act by a certain date, so I projected the due date from what I could piece together."

"And by 'act,' you mean?"

"Kidnap her."

Munson smiled and shook his head once. "Continue."

"So I backed into how much time I needed, which just so happened to coincide with the Academy Awards. Once I'd set the timeline, I developed a plan to act as her limo driver and take her after the ceremony. On the day of the awards, I stole my work release van, then ditched the van, walked fifteen-plus miles to Joe's hangar where she kept both her plane—which I later borrowed—and a restored '80s Ford Bronco, which she bought following work on a beach film where the car featured, and made my way to the limo business. Aside from the fact that I could not rent a car since I had no credit card, the Bronco was useful to me because it contained no computers and no chips, so it could not be tracked and, as I had guessed, was not missed. Knowing security protocols on the night of the Academy Awards, most of which I had installed during my employment with her, and given that I had attended twice before, I disguised myself, subdued the hired limo driver, and proceeded to drive Joe to and from the ceremony."

"What did you do with the limo driver?"

"Restrained him in his own vehicle, then called the police to let them know where he was—after I had kidnapped Joe."

"Can you prove this?"

"I don't know. I haven't tried, but if you request the recorded call, you'll hear my voice."

Munson lifted a stack of papers from his desk. "The prosecution would like to enter limo driver Sam Ramsey's deposition into record, which corroborates Mr. Pockets's story. We would also like to reserve the right to call Mr. Ramsey as a witness if needed."

The judge nodded and motioned for Pockets to continue.

"After Joe won, I drove her home, waiting long enough for her to pass out from the sleeping medication."

"What made you think she would take sleeping medication?"

"The nature of her addiction. She used one type of drug during the day to stay awake, then she used another type at night to sleep. A vicious cycle. I suspected that between the blackmail and not knowing where her child might be, she'd be using more than normal, which would put her in a deep sleep that would allow me to get her out of town."

"How did you get in her house?"

"I had programmed her security system."

"And they had not changed it?"

"No, sir. I was supposed to be in prison."

"I see." More laughter. "Continue."

"With Joe asleep, I loaded her into her Escalade and exited the property. A few miles away, I switched her to the Bronco and then drove to her hangar where I borrowed the twin-engine Cessna she used to earn her pilot's license. I then flew her to a small private airport in Montana, where she owned another small hangar and kept a Chevy Blazer for personal use. Using the Blazer, I transported her to her cabin in the mountains, securing her in the basement while I readied the upstairs for what

I hoped would only be a monthlong stay. Before she woke, I installed a stun-cuff around her neck, which I stole from the prison detail."

"Explain 'stun-cuff' for the jury."

"The stun-cuff is a wireless prisoner control device that administers eighty thousand volts to the wearer when triggered." I studied the jury. Most of whom seemed to be listening with their mouths open. "It's similar to a shock collar worn by dogs." I turned back to Munson. "When she woke, I explained to her that the cuff would render her unconscious if she broke the electronic perimeter."

"Did you do this in person?"

"No, sir. Through a computerized voice. She never saw my face."

"And did she break the barrier?"

"Yes, sir. Twice."

"So on two occasions, you administered a shock of eighty thousand volts to Mrs. Joe?"

"Yes, sir."

Munson nodded. "And you felt this was necessary?"

"I needed her to know that I was in control and she was restricted to the cabin. That she would spend the next month getting through detox. Getting clean."

"Mr. Pockets, there are fine facilities all around California that do that very thing, and do it quite well, without the trauma of being kidnapped or electrocuted. You felt you were better equipped to accomplish this because . . . ?"

"Because it hadn't worked the first seven times."

"Are you trained as a therapist?"

"No, sir."

"Are you a psychologist?"

"No, sir."

"Psychiatrist?"

"No, sir."

"So you took it upon yourself to play God and do what they could not?"

"No, sir." I pointed at Joe. "She did."

Murmurs rippled throughout the courtroom.

Munson leaned on the bench in front of me. "Can you explain that?"

I looked at Joe one more time. "Can I please speak to you?"

Judge Thelma Dixon slammed the gavel down and spoke to the bailiff. "Bailiff, please install a stun-cuff on Mr. Pockets's ankle."

While the bailiff installed a double cuff on both ankles, the judge spoke to me. "Mr. Pockets, you have traumatized Mrs. Joe enough for one lifetime. I won't tolerate any more outbursts."

"Yes mum. I mean, yes, Your Honor, but I—"

She raised a finger. "Not another word."

"But—"

The judge motioned to the bailiff. "Stun him."

I raised a finger. "If I can just—"

The judge repeated the order. "Stun him."

The bailiff triggered the stun-cuff and sent eighty thousand volts into my legs and spine. Seconds later, I woke on the floor, having lost control of my bladder and soaked my pants. When I climbed back into the chair, the judge was slamming her gavel and calling for order.

Judge Thelma Dixon pointed at me. "No more outbursts, Mr. Pockets. Do you understand?"

I sought to gather my breath. "Yes mum."

Munson pointed to my ankles. "Is that the type of stun-cuff you used on Mrs. Joe?"

"Yes, sir, only—" I looked at the judge. "Mum, may I add to my answer?"

The judge nodded. "You're on a short leash."

I turned to Munson. "I turned down the voltage."

He pointed at me. "Did she urinate on herself?"

"No, sir."

Without prompting, Joe shook her head, as if answering the questions, which was noticed by everyone in the courtroom.

Munson continued, "A moment ago, you pointed at Mrs. Joe and said she told you to play God?"

I hesitated. "No, sir. With all due respect, you said that, but that was her intention."

"Explain."

I opened my hand and began unfolding a worn, tattered, blood-soaked letter. Munson objected to the judge. "Your Honor, this has not been entered into evidence. I've never seen this."

The judge motioned with her hand. "Let me see it."

As the judge read my letter, Joe stood, prompting the judge to look up from the letter. "Mrs. Joe, when it's your time to speak . . ."

Joe spoke while looking at me. "I wrote it."

"You sure?"

"Yes, Your Honor. It might help if I read it."

"You don't have to do that. You're not on trial here."

"I realize that. I'd still like to read it."

The judge sat back. Eyes wide. Looking from Joe to me and back to Joe. "Well, this is unusual." She paused. "Are you sure, Mrs. Joe?"

Joe nodded.

The judge looked at Munson. "Will you allow it?"

Munson, caring less about procedural order and more about his path to the district attorney's desk, nodded. "I will, Your Honor."

The judge pointed to the bailiff and said, "Swear her in."

Joe placed her hand on the Bible and said "I do," and Munson handed her the letter.

The judge interrupted. "Mrs. Joe, you realize you do not have to do this?"

Joe was staring at the letter, wiping her hand across the dried blood. "Yes, Your Honor."

"Proceed."

CHAPTER 45

AFTER

Dear Pockets,

Every time I come back here, I think to myself, "What a strange place." In what kind of world do people like me pay ninety thousand dollars to spend thirty days in a place not my home, with a bunch of people I don't know, to force myself to stop doing something that can kill me? Seems like the thought of certain death ought to be deterrent enough. Seems like stopping would make more sense and cost a lot less money. I did the math. When I get out of here, I will have spent 210 days, more than half a year, and over half a million dollars trying to stop doing something. Which begs the question: How many times will it take? Why not just stop? What's wrong with me? Can this place and these people help me, or am I wasting my time? Maybe seven times is the charm.

I think the answer is somewhere in this letter.

Ever since we met in the deserts of North Africa, you've had that stiff upper lip. Coat. Tie. Beautiful accent. "Yes mum" this and "Yes mum" that. Then I hired you, and you worked tirelessly to protect me. But what I didn't realize was that in order to keep me safe, you erected an invisible wall, or line, between us. A sacred line. One you've never crossed. Where you stand as protector on the outside and I am safe and protected on the inside. At first I didn't understand. Felt alone. Even took it personally that you wouldn't let me in. When you didn't, it became a game. How can I break you down? Slip past your defenses. Nothing worked. I know, I tried. I was shameless. A different bathing suit? Shorter skirts? Different perfume? "Pockets, you mind zipping me up?"

There is a chance that when I get out of here, everything will be up and to the right. All good. Clean forever. No more pills. But what if? What if this doesn't work? It hasn't yet. What makes this time any different? What if I walk out of here no different from when I stumbled in, only better able to fake it? I can read the writing on the wall—the next step in this downward spiral is not a good one. If I get any worse, I'm pretty sure I can't get me back from here.

I had a dream last night. I was in an ambulance, being rushed to the hospital. Lights. Noise. Panic all around. When I arrived, they told me I had a bad heart and needed a transplant. So I scrubbed, walked myself into the OR, stretched out on the table—and here's where it gets weird. I told the nurse, "Scalpel," and began operating on myself. I remember staring into my own chest and thinking, "No wonder. Look at all the scars." So I cut out the dead one and reach for the new. Problem is, I die before I can get it sewn in. I've had the dream several times, and every time, I stitch furiously but the outcome is always the same. I wake to the sound of a flatline.

Any idiot knows the process needs a second set of hands. Someone who can stand alongside me and do what I can't. But where is that person in my dream? Why am I alone?

Pockets, you've spent your life protecting others. Shielding us from the stuff outside that threatens us. But it's the stuff inside me that can kill me. So I need a favor. I'm going to ask you to do something you're not going to want to do. I need you to protect me, from me. To do whatever it takes to rescue me from the mess I've made of me. I know that's weird, but we both know it's honest. What is "whatever it takes"? I don't know, but you do. You know without being told. But whatever "whatever" is or becomes, I need you to realize it and do it, even if I don't like what and how you're doing it. If I argue, if I plead, if I tell you what you're doing is against my will, if I swear or say horrible things to you, don't listen to me. That's not my will. This is. This moment here. This me now. Not that me then. Not that will then. That me will be broken but she won't know it. Seven months in this place, and here's what I know: broken me can't fix broken me. Only not broken you can fix broken me.

Here's the catch: you're the only person in my life who's ever been solely focused on what would be best for me. So if I make it out of here alive, I will need a reason to breathe again. Something I need more than the pills.

I leave that up to you.

Love,
Joe

The courtroom sat unmoving. Quiet. Reverent. Tears streaked Joe's face. Munson looked like he'd been hit by a truck.

Judge Thelma Dixon leaned over her desk. "Mrs. Joe, will you tell me, please, what is stapled to the bottom of the letter?"

Joe stared at it and cracked part of a smile in memory. "It's the get-out-of-jail-free card from a Monopoly game."

"Did you staple it to that letter?"

"I did."

"Why?"

322

"Pockets and I used to play late at night. When I couldn't sleep."

The judge looked at Munson. "Your witness. You may continue."

Munson took the letter. "Thank you, Mrs. Joe. You may be seated." Munson turned to the judge. "If it please the court, the prosecution would like to enter this letter into evidence."

The judge allowed it.

Munson looked at me and continued. "So let's get right to it. You felt like this letter gave you permission to kidnap Mrs. Joe."

I considered my answer. The judge saw my hesitation. "You can answer him, Mr. Pockets."

I nodded. "Yes, sir, I did."

"Did she ever instruct you to do any of this?"

"No, sir, I did it on my own initiative."

Munson looked confused. "Mr. Pockets, I tend to think you're crazy and should be stuck in the loony bin for a long time. We can't have people trolling society and abducting celebrities simply because they don't agree with their diet. That said, I'm going to ask you the one question a good prosecuting attorney should never ask, but . . ." He waved his hand dismissively across the courtroom. "It's the singular question on everybody's mind, including mine." He turned to me. "Why?"

I glanced at the wet stain on my pants and then the judge. "Your Honor, may I back up? I need to tell another part of the story."

She pointed at me. "Short leash."

I waved my hand across the press in the courtroom. "Thanks to many here, it's no secret Joe had a tough time getting pregnant. Multiple miscarriages. Couple rounds of in vitro." I shook my head. "It was taking its toll on her body and—"

Munson interrupted me. "What do you mean?"

"I've never met anyone who wanted to be a mother as badly as Joe. And, having been around her, I knew she'd make a great mom."

"Mr. Pockets, you're a bodyguard. Maternal matters are not your specialty. What gave you reason to suspect that?"

"She reminded me of my own."

Joe seemed to choke, cough, and then collect herself.

"Continue."

"Even though in vitro had been really difficult the first time, she wanted to give it another chance. She also knew the odds were not in her favor, that it would probably fail, and she wasn't sure her heart could take it."

"What did you think?"

"Sir, I'm afraid to say what I thought."

Munson glanced at the judge and the judge looked at me. Both waited.

"I thought it was a shame she was going through it alone."

Munson pointed at Syd. "Mr. Pockets, had you forgotten she was married to a devoted husband?"

"Sir . . ." I paused and looked at the judge. "With all due respect, Mr. Syd was only devoted to himself and his perfectly edited online image. He still is. It's why he's sitting here." I looked at Syd and waited until he looked at me. "He married Joe because he got to ride her coattails. The social media evidence that led to their divorce supports this . . ." I paused. Making sure I had Syd's undivided attention. "As would Syd's personal video collection, which he thought no one knew about."

Following their divorce, as his girlfriends fought over the pieces he promised them, several outlets obtained and posted countless compromising photos of him with other women. Not Syd's best moment. The date stamps proved that while Joe struggled to get pregnant, Syd had sought pleasure in the arms of multiple women over a period of years. Fortunately, Joe starred in none of these films, and because of them, Syd got nothing from her in the divorce.

Joe turned slowly to study Syd as snickers spread throughout the press. Syd grumbled something and attempted to look offended. Munson stepped closer to me and spoke as though we were friends. "So it's safe to say you were jealous of Mr. Syd and his marriage to Joe?"

"Absolutely. He didn't deserve her and he used the wounds of her childhood to manipulate her."

"Explain, Mr. Pockets."

I looked at Joe. "May I answer that?"

She nodded and, in doing so, pushed a single tear out along the contour of her face.

"Throughout her relationship with the press, Joe had been honest about her own father wounds. She aged out of foster care and had what the press has called 'daddy issues,' which resulted in her having trouble trusting men. But she's also kindhearted to a fault, so she feels guilty when she doesn't trust. As if somehow she's responsible for her own wound. It's a result of the trauma of having been passed over for so long. Syd knew this, so he played her and made her feel guilty throughout their marriage for their problems. Specifically, her inability to get pregnant."

"How would he do this?"

"He constantly reminded her that their pregnancy troubles were in fact hers."

"What did he mean by that?"

"He had been to the clinic and been tested."

"And you know this because?"

"I drove him. He tossed the results at me. Bragging about his numbers and how virile he was."

"Did he make you feel insignificant? Or less than?"

"All the time. But that, too, is not new. It can be part of the job."

"Was it part of the job with Syd?"

"Yes, sir. He seemed to enjoy it."

"Did your previous employer also make you feel insignificant?"

"No, sir. Never—"

Munson interrupted me. "Did you take your jealousy out on Syd?"

"No, sir."

"Mr. Pockets, your actions put him in the hospital for months."

"That wasn't jealousy. That was justice."

Munson laughed. "Justice?"

"Yes, sir. He had it coming."

Munson was peacocking for the jury. "Says who?"

"Me."

"Do you always take it upon yourself to be the sole arbiter of justice?"

"No, sir, but in Syd's case I made an exception."

This time, the jury laughed. I tried to continue. "Sir, I don't feel like you're letting me—"

"Wasn't Syd, in fact, the victim of your continued attempts to prey upon his wife?"

"Sir, if I could just—"

"Mr. Pockets, did you want to kill Syd Painter?"

"Sir, anyone who's ever worked with Syd wants to kill him."

More laughter.

Munson strutted before the jury, undeterred. "So he did make you feel insignificant?"

"Syd tries to make everyone feel insignificant, including his wife, but I've never really cared much for what Syd thinks."

"Do you often act so cavalier toward your employers?"

"He wasn't my employer." I pointed. "She was."

"Oh, but we're splitting hairs now, Mr. Pockets."

"No, not rea—"

"Mr. Pockets."

Munson wasn't letting me get a word in edgewise and time was running short. Maybe it was Munson's smug look and the fact that he wasn't listening to me, but I almost made my next mistake when I tried to stand. Halfway out of my seat, the judge raised a finger. "Um, Mr. Pockets, are you sure you want to do that?" She pointed to the bailiff's control panel, which was plugged into the wall. "We have an unlimited supply of electricity."

"No, Your Honor."

"I didn't think so."

She looked to Munson. "You may continue."

Munson knew he had me on the ropes. "Mr. Pockets, are we to understand that violence is how you react when you don't get your way?"

"No, sir, you're to understand it's how I act when warranted."

"And who determines when it's warranted?"

"In this case, I did, but didn't we just cover—"

"Mr. Pockets?"

Risking electrocution, I cut him off. "Sir, I've already been convicted for violence against Mr. Syd." I lifted my hands to expose my chains above the bench. "I did it, and I'd do it again. No problem. He was a pathetic little man then. He's a pathetic little man now. I've made my point. He would very much like for this trial to focus on him, making him out to be the victim. He loves the attention, and if you press him, it's why he's here. To grab the spotlight at Joe's expense. It's the only reason he hung around as long as he did. But if I could bring us back, what's getting lost here is Joe and what she endured."

I must have gotten his attention because he nodded and said, "Continue."

"Joe agreed to in vitro round two. She did all the things. Took all the injections. Followed her doctor's advice, and when you put all that together, it's really difficult on a woman, but she's a fighter so she did it—and then came the day of retrieval, and the doctors extracted two good eggs. Two chances in this lifetime to create a baby with her own body. You all know her as that iconic lady on the screen, bigger than life, and she is. But deep down, all she's ever wanted was to hold her baby and have her baby hold her back. Her whole life comes down to that one minute. All her hope, all her love, all that she is, is held in those two eggs. But she's sedated on the table, helpless to do any-thing about it, so the medical team starts looking for"—I pointed—"Mr. Syd."

Syd began fidgeting in his seat. He even glanced at the door.

"So I—"

The judge interrupted me. "Mr. Pockets, you waived your right to a trial when you pled guilty. You may not use this courtroom to argue conditions of your current sentence."

Joe stood up.

The judge recognized her. "Mrs. Joe, the court thanks you, but—"

"Your Honor, almost seven years ago, Pockets pled guilty to beating Syd and was sentenced. There was no trial. No explanation. And no record of those events. I'd like to hear what he has to say." She gestured to the court. "We all would."

Syd's head rotated on a swivel.

The judge noticed Syd's discomfort and then looked to me. A new expression on her face. "Mr. Pockets, I will not allow you to turn this courtroom into any more of a circus." She pointed to the bailiff without saying a word.

"Yes, Your Honor."

"Continue."

"Joe had done all she could. Her entire world depended upon Syd, who had been filming a documentary about this process. He promised never-before-seen footage and behind-the-scenes access to the most difficult journey of one of Hollywood's most famous couples. Over the previous week, he had jetted to New York, back to LA, and then overnighted to London, making the rounds on the nightly talk shows, calling it *Love Does: A Father's Role.* He spent most of his time talking about"—I made quotation marks in the air with my fingers—"'societal problems' caused by absentee fathers. Then he talked at length about how he hoped this film would be a defining work unapologetically addressing the problems couples face, even celebrity couples who are not immune to these struggles. He said, 'Infertility affects all of us. It is no respecter of persons. Even two people like Joe and me.'

"He then talked about how, given his unique perspective, this film would also focus on the husband's role. That he wouldn't shy away from what few men are willing to talk about. Feelings of embarrassment, inadequacy, and being relegated to little more than a donor. He said he wanted the viewers to know that 'husbands who love their wives do what is required because that's what love does.' Then he clasped a cross hanging around his neck, something he'd taken to lately for its strength, and talked about how 'greater love has no one than this, than to lay down one's life for his friends.' He said they had shown rough-cut versions to several streaming services that were currently in a bidding war for rights.

"When he finished with all that—" I shot a glance at the judge, who was tapping the bench with a pencil.

I turned to her. "Am I saying too much?"

"No."

"Taking too long?"

She quit tapping. "No."

"May I continue?"

"Please."

I turned to face the courtroom. "When he finished with all that, he walked inside the 'Husband's Room' while the guy with the camera filmed the closing of the door. In dramatic fashion, he panned from a close-up on the door handle to a wide angle of the large wall clock. The second hand ticking. After several ticks, he returned to the handle. The clock. Et cetera. Back and forth while we all stood waiting. Us on one side of the door. Syd on the other. The moment of truth. In the quiet, the photographer whispered, 'Life hanging in the balance.'

"A few minutes later, Syd reappeared without the usual bravado. Now the humble expert, just doing his part because that's what love does, he stood in front of the camera and began talking about next steps. He made a point of opening the door and pointing across the room to the sample cup with his name scribbled on it sitting on the discreet window shelf where, at any moment, a technician would lift the separator and take the cup into the lab where the microscopic contents would be mixed with Joe's egg, incubated, and then surgically implanted into Joe in two to five days. The camera panned from Syd to the cup and back while Syd talked emotively about the precarious life it held. What precious mystery it contained, the miracle that was modern medicine and what promise that held for Joe, for him, and for their life together.

"Finally, pausing to collect his emotions, he said his real desire was to offer hope to the hurting. 'If I could just inspire one couple . . .' The cameraman stopped filming only when Syd was unable to control his emotions and waved him off."

I looked from the judge to Munson to Syd and then Joe. "Syd was so convincing, even I was starting to believe him. Maybe I was wrong. Maybe I'd misjudged him. But . . . that's when I got the phone call."

Munson looked dubious. "Phone call?" He was tiring and growing irritated at having to juggle so many pieces.

"Yes, sir."

I'd talked a lot and was moving a lot of pieces around the board, but I also knew it was important for Joe to have all the facts. And while the entire courtroom was listening, I was really only talking to an audience of one. Judging from the look on her face, I had her complete and undivided attention.

When Joe spoke, her voice was soft. As if she were bracing herself against the answer. "Who called?"

I looked at the judge but pointed at Joe. "May I ask her a question?"

"Is it relevant?"

"Yes, Your Honor."

She nodded.

I turned to Joe. "How do you like your coffee?"

Joe looked irritated that I'd not answered her question. "You of all people know the answer to that."

"Yes mum, I do. But—" I waved my hand across the room. "I need them to know it."

She never took her eyes off me. "Black."

"Cream?"

"Never."

"Why?"

"Working the all-night diner, cream cups were twenty-five cents each. And I didn't have it. So I learned to drink it black."

"So never any cream?"

"Never."

"Any exceptions?"

She shrugged. "Just when Syd brought me coffee."

"Why?"

She glanced at Syd then back at me. "Because I didn't have the heart to tell him."

"Why not?"

"It's no secret our marriage was difficult, filled with big people problems over several years. In the grand scheme of things, cream in my coffee didn't really matter. I was just thankful to have someone bring me coffee."

"Just making sure. The only time you ever drank cream in your coffee was when Syd brought it to you?"

Joe nodded once. "Correct. But what does this have to do with me?"

Syd chimed in with a forced laugh. "Now you tell me." He spoke more to the courtroom than Joe. "Always thought you liked it." He played to the audience. "Now I know why we're divorced."

A third of the courtroom laughed, but I heard no humor in it.

A rose stem–sized vein had popped out on Joe's temple. Her lip quivered once. She pressed me. "Who called you?"

Without explanation, Syd stood up and began making his way toward the door. The judge raised a finger. "Mr. Syd, you're already here. You might as well hear this. Please take a seat."

Syd tried to argue but the judge motioned to the police officer standing at the door, who escorted Syd back to his seat.

I knew I was risking another eighty thousand volts, but at this point, I waved my hand toward Syd and began speaking directly to Joe. "Go ahead, Syd. Tell her."

Joe straightened and looked from me to Syd. "Tell me what?"

Syd looked like he wanted to be anywhere but that courtroom.

I raised my voice. "Explain the powdered creamer you put in Joe's coffee. Tell her, Syd."

Every camera in the courtroom was aimed at Syd as he shook his head. "I don't know what you're talking about." He turned to the judge. "Your Honor, I'm not the one on the stand."

"No, but I can change that. Answer his question."

Syd sat back, tilted his head slightly, and refused to say a word.

Joe stepped toward him. "Syd, what's he saying? What'd you put in my coffee?"

"I was trying to heal our marriage."

"Syd."

Looking to Joe, I spoke up. "For a long time I thought nothing about it, until you decided to go ahead with the final retrieval. When you did, I thought through everything you or anyone put into your body. I wanted to know if any outside substance was part of the problem. Something we could eliminate. So I had the water tested. Your cosmetics and hair products. Massage oils. Fingernail polish. I tested the garden soil for any type of toxic substance. I tested every cleaning product, detergents, and the air quality of all your homes. I studied and tested for possible toxic effects of synthetic mattresses and pillows, scented candles, and residue from plastic water bottles. I studied nutrition and hormones and preg-nancy and"—I pointed at Syd—"that's when I remembered you don't like cream in your coffee. Never have. Yet Syd put two scoops of powdered creamer in your cup every morning. Without fail."

She nodded but said nothing. Neither did Syd, who didn't look too comfortable.

"And yet you drank it. Day after day after day."

Joe nodded.

"So I tested it."

Syd jolted upright and Joe's eyes narrowed. "You did what?"

"Tested the creamer."

"Why?" Joe tilted her head slightly.

Syd had turned pale.

"Ask Syd."

Joe looked at Syd, who said nothing.

Joe pressed me. "Tell me about the phone call."

"The creamer was, in fact, creamer. Cheap, store-bought creamer. But the lab found traces of two other substances. Two substances you can only acquire with a very specific prescription."

Joe waited.

"Mifepristone and misoprostol."

Joe's head tilted slightly as the words rattled around inside her head.

I explained. "The first cuts off blood supply and nutrients to your uterus. The second causes the uterus to expel the baby by inducing early labor."

Joe was shaking her head, unable to grasp the totality of what I was telling her.

"They cause a medical abortion."

Joe just stared at me as the meaning of the words sank in. Then she looked at Syd. Her disbelief palpable. "Syd?"

He said nothing.

"Syd . . . did you kill our babies?"

The judge and every member of the jury looked as though someone had inserted a steel rod into their spines.

Joe shook her head. "All this time, I'm thinking it's my fault. That I'm no good. That I'm a horrible woman. That I can't give you children. And then you bring me coffee laced with an abortion pill? And you did it with a smile?" Joe was breaking. When the reality of her life hit her, Joe launched herself at Syd as if shot out of a cannon. She crossed the distance like a spider monkey and began beating him in the face with both fists. Screaming. The sound of her voice more animal than human. Despite his jiu-jitsu training and his size advantage, Joe had pulled Syd onto the floor where her fists rocked his head back and forth like a rag doll.

The courtroom erupted in chaos. Two police officers jumped into action and pulled Joe off Syd, leaving him curled up in a fetal position on the floor. I was about to stand when the bailiff looked at me and placed a finger on the control panel. "Don't even think about it."

A tense minute passed as the judge slammed her gavel and the courtroom settled. When Syd returned to his seat, his face was bleeding, one eye was swelling shut, and he was missing a tooth. All of which was captured on camera.

The judge restored order and everyone took a breath. "Mrs. Joe."

Joe wasn't listening. She was lost in memory.

The judge let it pass. Then she stared at Syd and waited for his response. After a tense moment, Syd shook his head.

The judge pressed him. "I'm sorry, Mr. Painter, are you trying to say something?"

"I don't know what any of you are talking about." He pointed at me. "He's on trial here. Why should anyone believe a word he's saying? He's just another jealous bodyguard." He looked at the judge and held up his tooth. "I'm the vic—"

She wasn't having it. "Mr. Painter, be quiet."

Since our last encounter, I'd wanted to finish the job I started on Syd Painter. Watching Joe remember each miscarriage and come to grips with the fact that their children had been willingly aborted by Syd, that moment came. Electricity or not, I moved fast enough to catch the bailiff off guard because I was able to get over the railing and latch my hands around Syd's neck about the time the bailiff lit me up. The shock coursed through me like lightning. I think I screamed like a girl, and when I woke I found a goose egg on my head and tasted blood where I'd bitten my tongue. Unfortunately for Syd, he got a pretty good jolt, too, as my hands around his neck completed the electrical circuit.

Ninety seconds later, the judge walked around from behind her bench and looked down on me. Somewhat amused. "Mr. Pockets, do you really want to keep playing this game?"

I swallowed, wiped my mouth on my orange jumpsuit, and crawled back across the floor to my chair. I'd learned long ago that no matter how much I trained or prepared, there was always somebody bigger, stronger, faster, more powerful. It just works that way, so I learned to prepare for that too. Right now, the judge was more powerful.

"No, Your Honor. It's just that—"

"Just what?"

I read the writing on the wall and figured I'd better shut up. "Nothing, Your Honor."

"That's what I thought."

The judge declared a short recess while a medic attended to my face and they cleaned me up. This time, they put me in a diaper and returned me to my seat. When they did, the judge was looking at me differently. She looked curious. She said, "I trust you will behave yourself."

I nodded. "Yes, Your Honor."

The judge looked at Munson. "Your witness."

Munson looked like he needed a drink. This had not gone the way he'd planned. He read back through the court reporter's transcription. "You were telling us about the phone call."

I turned back to Joe. "Syd had no intention of ever giving you a child. He had played you throughout your marriage and taken what he wanted. Riding your coattails. So I thanked the caller, hung up, and made my decision."

Munson swallowed, afraid of my response. "Decision?"

I nodded and held up two fingers. "First, that Syd Painter would never make a baby with Joe. And two, that I was going to hurt him."

Munson's voice softened. "And?"

"I trashed Syd's sample, then walked upstairs and found him."

Munson was about to speak when Joe stood. The look on her face suggested she had finished the puzzle and the pieces had not fit together the way she'd been told. Her voice betrayed the crack in her soul. "Then how did Syd and I make a baby?"

I shook my head and never took my eyes off her. "You didn't."

Joe approached the bench and spoke softly to me. "Are you telling me I made a baby with some random donor?"

I shook my head. "No mum."

She asked a second time. This time louder. Her lip quivering. "Then how did Syd and I make a baby?"

A pause. The room was pin-drop quiet.

"You and Syd didn't make a baby."

Joe gripped the railing in front of me. She was shaking but she couldn't let go. Her voice was pleading. Guttural. "Then who made a baby with me?"

Everything in her life had led to this moment. My answer would either crush her or liberate her. I was just sorry that it would be revealed here. Recorded for posterity on every news agency across the country. I also knew the only thing worse than knowing the truth was not knowing it. And she needed to know. Of all people, she had a right to know no matter how heavy it might land on her.

Joe shook her head slightly. Her lip still quivering. "Pockets, what are you saying?"

I shrugged. "Joe . . ."

"Who made a baby with me?" She looked at Syd. Then back at me. "Pockets." Her voice pleading.

"Mum, I'm sorry. I know it's weird. Maybe even gross. Hell, I'm not proud of it." I waved my hand across the courtroom. "You think I want all these people knowing this? But what else could I do? I knew that when you learned the truth of Syd, and you began thinking back through the circumstances of all your miscarriages, all the moments you sat in the bathroom alone, you'd never want to share a child with him. Least of all custody of that child. Syd is the worst kind of man, and I knew he'd use the child as leverage to manipulate and control you. And in that moment, with only a few seconds to consider the ramifications for all of us, myself included, I just knew I couldn't let him father your child. I'm not saying I'm right, and I'm not saying I'm justified, but I knew no matter what, he could never be your child's father. Yet you needed a father. So I did the only thing I could."

Munson looked like he'd been hit by a truck. Every eye in the jury was wide. Even Judge Thelma Dixon leaned forward in her chair. Mouth open.

I tried speaking only to Joe. "What other option did I have? You were soul-weary. Played out. Done fighting. But . . ." I looked at her. Shaking my head. "Please just let me get this out. I need to tell you something. Something I've wanted to tell you for a long time. I've had five years sitting in an eight-by-ten room rehearsing this in my mind, trying to find a right way to say it, but I . . ." I shook my head and waved my hand across all the bodies in the courtroom.

"I wish it were just us, but it's not. So all these people are going to hear it, and all these reporters are going to spread it. And I'm sorry for how they might use that against you in the future, but I'm out of options and if I don't say it now, I might never get another chance." I swallowed. "Joe, I've loved you from the moment we met. From the first second I laid eyes on you. And every day since. That includes that day at the clinic. And it includes today. And I have felt guilty from that first moment because you were married to that idiot and . . ." I stuttered. "I-I stood there in that clinic, knowing your world was about to crumble and land on you, and I doubted your heart could live through it. I'd watched you carry so much for so long that I couldn't stand to watch your soul get crushed. Again. So I decided in that moment, rightly or wrongly, I'd rather spend the rest of my life buried beneath the prison than watch you endure any more of that man's evil."

Joe spoke. Pleading. "Pockets, what'd you do?"

No one made a sound. I studied the courtroom. The jury. Every eye.

"How far would any of you go for someone you love? Really? How far? If someone took your wife, daughter, husband, or son, how far is too far? Where's your limit? Where does love stop you?" I looked at Joe then back at all of them. "Is there anything you wouldn't do?"

My chains rattled. My eyes found Joe's. "As much as I know my own heart, I love you more than I know how to say. And if I love you that much, what other option did I have? You tell me. Because I didn't see one then and I don't see one now. Maybe, at the end of the day, I'm just a bodyguard. Just a man who stands quietly in the corner until it's time to step between you and the arrows aimed at you. If that's the case, then so be it. I'm okay with that. But all of you should know there is a love that doesn't count the cost. The pain. Or the reward. I'm not standing beside you because of what that gets me." I touched my stomach. "This love is wrapped around my soul. It can't be doused. Or appeased. Or talked off the ledge." I tapped my chest. "And it doesn't die because you lock it up. Or grow old." I held out my hand and uncurled my fingers, noticing the scar where the bullet entered. "This kind empties itself. Holds nothing back. Gives you all of me. When your hope hurts, this love stands on a rooftop, or shackled in a courtroom, and screams at the top of its lungs."

I paused, my voice growing soft. "This love stands up and stands between. It says to those who would hurt you or steal from you, 'Not today. Not as long as I have breath.' So that's what I did. I stood up. I gave you me."

The courtroom was silent. All eyes on me. "If that was wrong, if I am guilty of some great crime, then . . ." I glanced at the judge. Then the jury. And finally, Joe. "I'd willingly and without hesitation or regret do it again. A thousand times over."

Joe looked from me to Syd. The bailiff moved to return her to her seat, but Judge Thelma Dixon waved him off. Joe's eyes had narrowed and her hands were shaking and lip trembling. When she spoke, she was focused on me. "Are you telling me"—she pointed at Syd and began shaking her head—"he's not . . ."

The judge leaned forward, studying me. Then Syd. Other than the judge's squeaking chair, there was no sound in the room. Munson had heard enough. He moved to his chair, sat down, and wiped his face with a handkerchief. A gray shade of pale.

The judge's voice was sympathetic. "Mr. Pockets, you're saying you're the . . ." She gestured to me.

"Yes mum."

"And you realize a simple paternity test will confirm the truth of this?"

I nodded. "Yes mum."

"And you're sticking with your story."

"It's the truth, mum."

The courtroom sat unmoving. And unbreathing. Joe stared at me; the puzzle had revealed its picture. Its collective whole. "But you said nothing. Made no claim. Why?"

I shrugged, then whispered, trying to ease the weight of my words. "I thought you'd come see me and I could tell you . . . in private."

She shook her head. "But I didn't. I let you sit in prison, where . . ." She waved her hand across the media. "Instead of selling the lucrative story of Syd's crimes, you sat quietly. Letting them crucify you for what you did to Syd." She paused, shaking her head. "You stood between me and . . ." She cupped her face in her hands. "Oh, Pockets . . ."

I wasn't sure how to respond.

We all watched as the truth settled. She was crying now. "You sat in silence and continued to protect me? From a prison cell."

I shrugged.

"And never told a soul."

In my time working for Joe, I had tried to protect her from the things outside that sought to hurt her. Whether words or press or people. That said, there was one thing I had not protected her from because it's the one thing on planet Earth that sets us free from the stuff that enslaves us and holds our heads under the water. The stuff trying to kill us. We can lie to one another to soften the blow, but lies only strengthen the chains. There's only one thing in this universe or any other that cuts through prison bars and sets us free from the prisons in which we live. And that thing is the truth. Without it, there is no freedom.

"And I never came to see you." Joe closed her eyes as the blast enveloped her. "The worst betrayal."

Standing in the courtroom, before the eyes of the world, Joe was coming to grips with the truth of us. Of me. And while I didn't want to protect her from that, I wanted to hold her while the impact hit her. To be the one she reached for when the aftershocks shook her foundation. I glanced at the letter, then back at Joe. "You wrote me and made me promise to get you clean. No matter the cost. And I did. But you also made me promise to give you a reason to stay clean. And so I did." I paused. "And he has my eyes."

Somewhere in here, the pain that had enveloped Joe's soul cracked down the middle and she shed it like a blanket. It couldn't hold her anymore. Her hope, which she thought was dead, bubbled to the surface, returning the light to her eyes. Joe crossed the distance between us, pulled me to her, and kissed me, pressing her tear-swept and snotty face to mine. I don't know if it was the practice she'd had making films or just an innate talent, but Joe was a good kisser. Her lips were soft and salty and her hands were warm and trembling.

It was the best moment of my life, and I didn't want it to end. I kept waiting for Judge Thelma Dixon to light me up, but she didn't. She just sat there, smiling. For which I was thankful.

When finished, Joe stood back, her face inches from mine, shaking her head. Then she came in a second time and kissed me all over again. The new best moment of my life, making the last best moment now the second best moment. Finally, she looked at me. Studying my face. A smile breaking through the tears. Her expression reflected the question on everybody's mind.

When she spoke, she tilted her head sideways. "You gave me a son?" After a pause, she said it again. This time the tone was different and softer. And she was nodding, answering her own question. "Pockets, you and I have a son. We made a baby. Together."

I hesitated. Unsure how to answer. I knew what I wanted to say, but I wasn't sure that I should say it. Or that I had the right to say it. Finally, I offered, "He'll always be my flesh, but he's only my son if you let him be."

"Oh, Pockets. You and your stupid, stoic, magnificent, beautiful, invisible line."

I swallowed. "It's the job, mum."

She laughed. Cradled my face. "Pockets, I'm not your job anymore." Choking back tears, she shook her head. Her disbelief palpable. "You really did this? All of this? And never said a word?"

My eyes darted to the jury, the judge, and back to her. "Not until this moment."

Joe pulled me to her. Wrapping her arms around me. Smiling. Laughing. Crying. A beautiful mess. She shook her head. "Why?"

Another glance. All eyes on me. Joe had been made for the spotlight. The stage. I was not. I was made for the shadows because I can do my job best from there. I cleared my throat. "I'm your bodyguard, mum. I was trying to protect your heart."

CHAPTER 46

AFTER

Joe broke social media again. All of it. Including Twitter. Although, in truth, I understand none of that. The press ran stories for weeks, digging into the truth and plastering my face on every cover in every grocery store line and on every late-night news show. The more they dug, the more they discovered I was telling the truth. Then Joe walked out front of her Malibu home and announced with a smile that the DNA test confirmed my story.

Things went a little crazy from there.

No one had ever seen Joe happier and more confident.

As more details bubbled up, fans called for Syd's head on a platter, forcing him off his television series and into hiding. Some tabloid hired a European investigator to look into his prescriptions—which they found, sealing his fate. The nightly news interviewed a disgruntled fan saying they should charge him with five counts of premeditated murder. Things spiraled downhill from there. Last I heard, he'd moved his family to Australia to open a cattle operation.

After reading the writing on the wall and coming to grips with the fact that she could not avoid prison, Amber changed her tune, played the victim card, and gave paid tabloid interviews from prison, saying, "If only she had known . . ."

Following a *60 Minutes* exclusive, a petition circulated calling for clemency. Or at minimum a reduction in sentence. They argued she had been a pawn of abusive men and forced to carry a baby she had not wanted. The movement gained traction until a judge asked a forensics expert to dig into her phone and tablet. When he did, and the transcripts were printed, the petition died. Amber's own words built a bulletproof counternarrative proving she was the instigator, mastermind, and abuser. Last I heard, she was serving ten years in a women's prison in Florida where the warden allowed her to open a salon on Tuesday afternoons.

As for me, the general public was divided. Some thought me a sick pervert of a human being. No better than Amber. A jealous and passed-over wannabe lover, driven by dollar signs, who capitalized on a fragile woman in her time of weakness. They painted a rather brutal picture, and if my only source of information had been the tabloids, I could see their point. Others argued mine had been a selfless act fueled by some crazy kind of love. Whatever the case, the court of public opinion raged with haters and debaters, sparking my own Facebook fan club page. For whatever that's worth.

Given the growing conversation, Joe took an afternoon break from filming and sat down for a prime-time exclusive, detailing her experience and squashing the naysayers.

The interviewer asked her, "You've heard the critics—how do you respond?"

Joe turned to the camera. "There's a reason the critics are called 'critics.'"

The interviewer interrupted her. "Your critics will use those very words to diagnose you as suffering from Stockholm syndrome."

Joe smiled. "I've heard that too."

"You disagree?"

She chose her words. "Pockets gave me what no man has ever given me."

The interviewer postured. "Which is?"

Joe never hesitated. "Himself. Without expectation. And without manipulation. A selfless gift with no equal."

"You love him?"

"With every cell in my body."

"Is it true you named your son Thomas Mac?"

"Our son." Another nod. "And yes."

That pretty much doused the fire.

Turns out the governor's wife was a fan of Joe's. Seen all her movies. So she invited her to the mansion for tea, which she timed with the governor's "tough on crime" reelection campaign press conference. He was midsentence, glad-handing for the cameras, when the first lady appeared in the background. Umbrellas. Biscuits. Tea. A guest in sunglasses. Reminiscent of an old Audrey Hepburn movie.

Not wanting to be upstaged, he beckoned both to the podium. Stepping aside, he said, "Honey, would you like to introduce our guest to the great state of California?"

He emphasized the word *our* a little too much, but she let it go. Midge squared to the mic and said, "She needs no introduction," then stepped aside.

A reporter stepped forward. "Joe, there's quite a legal battle brewing in the courts right now over Kelly MacThomas Pockets. The man who kidnapped you."

"Yes." Joe leaned into the mic. "I know who he is."

The reporters laughed.

The man continued, "So you agree he kidnapped you?"

A practiced pause. "What would you call it?"

"So you don't deny it?"

"'Course not. Neither does he. I also don't deny that I pretty much begged him to help me, no matter what."

"So you're saying Pockets was justified?"

"Absolutely." Joe raised a finger. "And if and when I ever break again, he has my permission and invitation to do it all over."

"To kidnap you again?" The reporter was digging and raised his voice when saying "kidnap."

Joe nodded. "I trust him with me. More than I trust me with me."

He raised an eyebrow. "How are you okay with a man making decisions about your body over which you had no control? No say?"

"Frame it however you like, but broken me couldn't fix broken me. It's why I wrote the letter."

The reporter interrupted her. "Yeah, but—"

She wasn't finished. "If I could have, I would, but my track record proved I could not. So Pockets did for me what I could not do for myself."

"Which was?"

"The last exchange."

"The what?"

She spoke slowly. Enunciating. "Last exchange."

He looked confused. "I don't under—"

She cut him off. "It's when you cross paths with someone who's broken, just a mess of pieces, unable to fix anything about anything, and yet for some inexplicable reason, you stoop down, reach out and say . . ." She paused. Collecting herself. "Me for you."

He protested. "But he took you—"

Joe cut him off again. Her voice stronger. "He took my pain from me and gave me what I do not deserve."

"Which is?"

"My next breath." She tapped her chest. "And the reason to take another."

"Yeah, but . . ." He was peacocking now. "What message are you sending to women?"

She studied him. "Brokenness is not weakness." She waved her hand across the crowd. "Look around. We're all broken. Welcome to the human race. Weakness is being broken but too proud to ask for help. Sitting there thinking you got this." She shook her head once. "You don't got this. You don't got this at all. Real strength is knowing that and understanding that you're broken. Only then do you got anything."

He sat back. "We don't normally see such transparency. Especially out of Hollywood. How's that poss—"

Joe's voice was soft yet confident. "Need is not weakness. And knowing that need is the beginning of something strong." A pause. "I needed Pockets then. I need him now."

"You give Pockets a lot of credit. What'd he teach you that Syd did not?"

Joe tried to speak but something stopped her. Maybe the tears. After a few seconds she said, "A life laid down is better than a life picked up."

"Ah." The reporter almost smiled and gestured with his hand. "Me for . . ."

Joe nodded once, not feeling the need to say more.

The reporter gestured to the governor. "With the stroke of a pen, the man to your right has the power to return Pockets to you. What would you say to him?"

Joe never looked at the governor. "I wouldn't. I leave that up to you."

In the days following, the governor was inundated with mail, including one hand-delivered letter from the United Kingdom.

CHAPTER 47

AFTER

Crowds lined the streets. Waving banners. Clamoring for a glimpse. Passing her star on the boulevard, she asked the driver to stop the car and waited while security exited the vehicle behind. With the perimeter secure, she mingled, posed for selfies, and even agreed to a video call with a kid's mom.

Approaching the red carpet, the car parting the crowd thronging the street, she reached for the pill fob around her neck. A constant reminder that now held a lock of Thomas's hair.

The door opened, and she extended one leg and paused. Long enough for the cameras to catch a glimpse. Had she worn "the dress"?

She exited the limo with Thomas. Hand in hand, the two walked—or in his case, crawl-climbed—to the fourth step, where Thomas decided to take a break and run his dump truck back and forth across the now infamous step. Unhurried, Joe sat, and the two played trucks. Somewhere in the media frenzy that followed, a savvy photographer noticed the hem of her dress was still duct-taped.

From that point, the awards ceremony was secondary.

The night closed with a Lifetime Achievement Award. While two decades of photos flashed on the screen, one iconic role after another,

Joe sat in as much wide-eyed wonder as everyone else. They detailed her early career, the diner, never-before-seen footage of her first audition, then sequences of clips from her movies. Comedies. Dramas. Adventure romance. Interspersed with her first and second Academy wins. The boulevard star. Then Seven Pines. Her third win. A montage of news outlets detailing her disappearance and eventual escape and walk out of the wilderness back to civilization. The video ended with a single voice. Her own. Reading what had since become known as "the letter."

While she read, the film slowed to a sequence of pictures of her cabin, the neck cuff, the long walk out. Of prison and concertina wire. My face shone on the screen.

Her voice sounded healthy:

Here's the catch. Even if I make it out of here alive, I need a reason to breathe again.

I leave that up to you.

Love,

Joe

When they called her name, Joe walked up onstage and waited beneath the ovation. The raucous, standing, never-ending applause for her life and which, to her, never made sense. She was just a girl. Passed over at birth and for eighteen years thereafter. Then, in the only job she could get, behind on rent and low on food, she had flipped burgers until someone discovered she was good at pretending to be others. A talent forged in the homes of people who didn't want her. Where she tried, twenty-seven times, to transform herself and become someone anyone would love. But each time they passed her on to another. Girl rejected. Love denied. Staring at the crowd, she knew what they did not. She was just a girl. A mess of a girl.

Maybe it was the moment. Maybe it was freedom. Maybe it was the hope that had reemerged. Maybe it was a soul satisfied. Whatever it was, Joe smiled and then knelt and picked up Thomas, who had crawl-climbed up the steps. All by himself. Dragging his dump truck and tartan baby blanket, his wet diaper having bulged out the sides of his shorts. Standing with Thomas on her hip, a mother in bloom, she nuzzled his nose, at which point he mimicked the crowd and gave them his best version of patty-cake, which only served to send them into a frenzy again. Joe laughed, studying them, her son, her life, the moments that had brought her here.

Maybe it was the knowing. Or the enormity. Or the gratitude. Or the fact that her wound had healed and no longer controlled her. Or maybe it was something else. Whatever the reason, when the tear that had been hanging finally broke loose, trailed down along her nose and around her lips to her chin, Joe stood on that stage and shed her past. No longer identified by her scars.

Now she was identified by mine.

She shook her head, crossed her eyes, stuck out her tongue, bowed slightly, pressed Thomas to her heart, and exited stage left.

Beauty in the mess.

EPILOGUE

The clock on the wall read 10:02 p.m. The prison was quiet save the guard and me. I dipped the mop in the bucket, rinsed it, and continued working my way around the cafeteria.

Sergeant Rob Petersen worked two jobs to put his son through college. The night shift was his second. He slept little but talked often of his boy and the dean's list. He was also the only man I'd ever met who whistled, nonstop, while he worked. As a result, he was the best whistler I'd ever heard in my life. We stared into his phone at the image of Joe standing beneath the spotlight, her iconic shrug and smile, her hugging our son, and their walking off. When the credits rolled, he closed the screen, slid his phone in his pocket, and sat shaking his head.

"Sorry, Pockets. Wish you could've been there."

I stared at the polished concrete floors but said nothing.

He continued, "What'll you do now?"

"Joe has hired some folks. Given new information, they're asking for a retrial."

Rob was a law-and-order guy, and I always liked him for that. He knew my chances were slim. "But that doesn't change the facts."

I shook my head. "Nope. I hurt Syd, and I kidnapped Amber and Joe, carrying both across state lines. The pardon was my best chance."

"The governor denied?"

I nodded. "Yesterday."

"Even with a letter from the Queen?"

"Even with."

"That may not bode well with the voting public come November." He shook his head. "Hard to imagine a guy who used to guard the Queen is stuck down here with me." A pause. Rob glanced down a hallway. "Want me to let you slip out the side door?"

I laughed.

"How much longer?"

"Four years, two hundred twenty-two days, and . . ." I studied the clock. "Forty-five minutes."

"Can you do it?"

I leaned on the mop and thought of Joe and Thomas. Standing on that stage. Alive. Laughing. Hope-filled. And free.

I nodded at the phone in his pocket. "For those two? Yes."

I washed both the bucket and the mop and hung them in the utility closet. Rob patted me down, scanned me with the metal detector, then walked me through a locked door, eighty-seven steps down a hallway where we turned left, through another locked door, and up two flights of stairs and forty-two steps to a cell where he waited while Mary clicked a button in Control and remotely opened my door. Rob nodded. "Night, Pockets. See you tomorrow."

I smiled. "I'll be here."

I stepped inside, Mary clicked the button again, and I listened in the dark as Rob's footsteps, and whistle, faded. As my eyes adjusted to the dim, my ears to the quiet, and my heart to the six-by-ten cell, my mind began replaying the slideshow. Images of Joe. In random order.

The shower floor. Muscadines in the garden. Tea with the Queen. The cabin. The fields where I grew up. The sands of North Africa.

I don't know how long I'd been watching the movie when Joe's voice whispered out of the darkness, "I didn't expect you. Didn't see you coming. But I'm so glad you . . ."

I reached out, across the line, and touched my finger to her lips. "Yes mum."

DISCUSSION QUESTIONS

1. Do you agree with young Joe's philosophy that "if you don't know something about somebody, you fill the gap with trust until you do"? Why or why not? Has that philosophy served Joe well in her life?

2. How did Joe's celebrity fuel her loneliness? How else did fame affect her life, both positively and negatively? What about the lives of those she was close with, like Syd, Amber, and Pockets?

3. Joe's childhood was difficult—living in twenty-seven foster homes—and likely traumatizing. How might her formative years have played a role in her acting ability and her eventual drug dependency?

4. Which character triggered the strongest emotional response (positive or negative) in you? Why?

5. What do you think of Pockets's method of getting Joe sober? Did Joe's letter to Pockets serve as a strong enough justification for his actions? Explain. What did you think of Pockets's pursuit of Amber? Do you think he was "playing God"?

6. How did you feel about Pockets's reveal of the paternity of Joe's baby? Do you think Pockets did the right thing? Why or why not?

7. What are your hopes for Joe's and Pockets's future?

8. Was there a piece of wisdom or philosophical thought that Pockets shared that you emotionally connected with? If so, which one and why?

9. What do you think Pockets meant by "a life laid down is better than one picked up"?

10. Hope is an enduring theme in the book. What do you think of Pockets's explanation of hope: "Love is what makes us who we are. Hope is how we express us. Hope is love with legs"?

11. Does this story strike you as allegorical? If so, in what way(s)?

12. Were you satisfied by the ending? Why or why not?

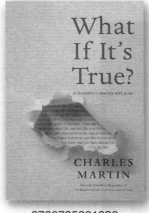
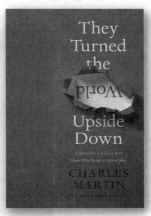

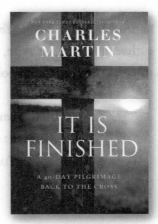